About the Authors

Brenda Jackson is a *New York Times* bestselling author of more than one hundred romance titles. Brenda lives in Jacksonville, Florida, and divides her time between family, writing and travelling. Email Brenda at authorbrendajackson@gmail.com or visit her on her website at brendajackson.net

Ever since **Lisa Childs** read her first romance novel (a Mills & Boon of course) at age eleven, all she ever wanted to be was a romance writer. Now an award winning, best-selling author of nearly fifty novels for Mills & Boon, Lisa is living the dream. Lisa loves to hear from readers who can contact her on Facebook, through her website www.lisachilds.com or snail mail address PO Box 139, Marne, MI 49435.

USA Today bestselling author **Lynn Raye Harris** burst into the scene when she won a writing contest held by Mills & Boon. The prize was an editor for a year – but only six months later, Lynn sold her first novel. A former finalist for the Romance Writers of America's Golden Heart Award, Lynn lives in Alabama with her handsome husband and two crazy cats. Her stories have been called "exceptional and emotional," "intense," and "sizzling."

Hot Heroes

May 2020
Protection Detail

June 2020
Armed and Dangerous

July 2020
The Rules of Her Rescue

August 2020
Surrender Your Heart

September 2020
Undercover Temptation

October 2020
Tough Love

Hot Heroes: Armed and Dangerous

BRENDA JACKSON

LISA CHILDS

LYNN RAYE HARRIS

MIX
Paper from
responsible sources
FSC
FSC C007454

This book is produced from independently certified FSC™ paper
to ensure responsible forest management.

For more information visit www.harpercollins.co.uk/green

Printed and bound in Spain
by CPI, Barcelona.

MILLS & BOON

First Published in Great Britain 2020
By Mills & Boon, an imprint of HarperCollins*Publishers*
1 London Bridge Street, London, SE1 9GF

HOT HEROES: ARMED AND DANGEROUS © 2020 Harlequin Books S.A.

Bane © 2016 Brenda Streater Jackson
Beauty and the Bodyguard © 2016 Lisa Childs
Captive but Forbidden © 2011 Lynn Raye Harris

ISBN: 978-0-263-28159-0

BANE

BRENDA JACKSON

To the man who will always and forever be the love of my life, Gerald Jackson, Sr.

So then, my beloved brethren, let every man be swift to hear, slow to speak, slow to wrath.
—James 1:19

Prologue

"You wanted to see me, Dil?" Brisbane Westmoreland asked, walking into his eldest brother Dillon's home office.

The scenic view out the window was that of Gemma Lake, the main waterway that ran through the rural part of Denver the locals referred to as Westmoreland Country. For Bane, this was home. This wasn't Afghanistan, Iraq or Syria, which meant he didn't have to worry about booby traps, enemies hiding behind trees and bushes or the boat dock being wired with explosives set to go off the second someone stepped on it. Westmoreland Country was a place where he felt safe. All in all, he was glad to be back home.

Thanksgiving dinner had ended hours ago, and keeping with family traditions, everyone had gathered outside for a game of snow volleyball. Now the females in the Westmoreland family had gathered in the sitting room to watch a holiday movie with the kids, and the men had gone upstairs for a card game.

"Yes, come on in, Bane."

Bane stopped in front of Dillon's desk. He knew Dillon was studying him with that sharp eye of his, taking in every detail. And he could imagine what his brother was thinking. Bane was not the same habitual troublemaker who had left Westmoreland Country five years ago to make something of himself.

Bane would be the first to admit that a lot in his life had changed. He was now military through and through, both mentally as well as physically. Since graduating from the naval academy and becoming a navy SEAL, he'd learned a lot, seen a lot and done a lot...all in the name of the United States government.

"I want to know how you're doing," Dillon inquired, interrupting Bane's thoughts.

Bane drew in a deep breath. He wished he could answer truthfully. Under normal circumstances he would say he was in prime fighting condition, but that was not the case. During his team's last covert operation, an enemy's bullet had nearly taken him out, leaving him flat on his back in a hospital bed for nearly two months. But he couldn't tell Dillon that. It was confidential. So he said, "I'm fine, although my last mission took a toll on me. I lost a team member who was also a good friend."

Dillon shook his head sadly. "I'm sorry to hear that."

"Me, too. Laramie Cooper was a good guy. One of the best. We went through the academy together." Bane knew Dillon wouldn't ask for specifics. Bane had explained to his family early on that all his covert ops were classified and linked to national security and couldn't be discussed.

Dillon didn't say anything for a minute and then he

asked, "Is that why you're taking a three-month military leave? Because of your friend's death?"

Bane eased down in the leather armchair across from Dillon's desk. When their parents, aunt and uncle had gotten killed in a plane crash over twenty years ago, Dillon, the eldest of the Denver Westmorelands, had acquired the role of guardian of his six brothers—Micah, Jason, Riley, Stern, Canyon and Bane—and his eight cousins—Ramsey, Zane, Derringer, Megan, Gemma, the twins Adrian and Aidan, and Bailey. As far as Bane was concerned Dillon had done an outstanding job in keeping the family together and making sure they each made something of themselves. All while making Blue Ridge Land Management Corporation, founded by their father and uncle, into a Fortune 500 company.

Since Dillon was the eldest, he had inherited the main house in Westmoreland Country along with the three hundred acres it sat on. Everyone else, upon reaching the age of twenty-five, received one hundred acres to call their own. Thanks to Bailey's creative mind, each of their spreads were given names—Ramsey's Web, Zane's Hideout, Derringer's Dungeon, Megan's Meadows, Gemma's Gem, Jason's Place, Stern's Stronghold, Canyon's Bluff and Bane's Ponderosa. It was beautiful land that encompassed mountains, valleys, lakes, rivers and streams.

Again, Bane thought about how good it was to be home, and safe here talking with his brother.

"No, that's not the reason," Bane said. "All my team members are on leave because our last operation was one from hell. However, I'm using my leave for a specific purpose, and that is to find Crystal."

Bane paused before adding somberly, "If nothing

else, Coop's death showed me how fragile life is. You can be here today and gone tomorrow."

Dillon would never know that Bane wasn't just referring to Coop's life, but also how close he'd come to losing his own more than a few times.

Bane watched as Dillon came around and sat on the edge of his desk to face him, unsure of how his brother had taken what he'd just said about finding Crystal. Especially since she was the main reason Dillon, and the rest of Bane's family, had supported his decision to join the navy. During their teen years, Bane and Crystal had been obsessive about each other in a way that had driven her family, as well as his, out of their wits.

"Like I told you when you came home for Jason's wedding…" Dillon said. "When the Newsomes moved away they didn't leave a forwarding address. I think their main objective was to put as much distance between you and Crystal as they could." He paused, then said, "But after your inquiry, I hired a private investigator to locate their whereabouts, and I'm not sure if you know it but Carl Newsome passed away."

Bane shook his head. Although he definitely hadn't been Mr. Newsome's favorite person, the man had been Crystal's father. She and her dad hadn't always seen eye to eye, but Crystal had loved him nonetheless. "No, I didn't know he had died."

Dillon nodded. "I called and spoke to Emily Newsome, who told me about Carl's death from lung cancer. After offering my condolences, I asked about Crystal. She said Crystal was doing fine, working on her master's degree at Harvard with plans to get a PhD in biochemistry from there, as well."

Bane tipped his head to the side. "That doesn't surprise me. Crystal was pretty smart. If you recall she was two grades ahead and was set to graduate from high school at sixteen."

What he wouldn't bring up was that she would have done just that if she hadn't missed so many days of school playing hooky with him. That was something everyone, especially the Newsomes, blamed him for. Whenever Crystal had attended school steadily she'd made good grades. There was no doubt in his mind she would have graduated at the top of her class. That was one of the reasons he hadn't tried to find her for all these years. He'd wanted her to reach her full potential. He'd owed her that much.

"So you haven't seen or heard from Crystal since that day Carl sent her to live with some aunt?"

"No, I haven't seen her. You were right at the time. I didn't have anything to offer Crystal. I was a hothead and Trouble was my middle name. She deserved better and I was willing to make something of myself to give her better."

Dillon just stared at him for a long moment in silence, as if contemplating whether or not he should tell him something. Bane suddenly felt uneasy. Had something happened to Crystal that he didn't know about?

"Is there something else, Dil?"

"I don't want to hurt or upset you Bane, but I want to give you food for thought. You're planning to find Crystal, but you don't know what her feelings are for you now. The two of you were young. First love doesn't always mean last love. Although you might still care about her, for all you know she might have moved on, gotten on with her life without you. It's been five years. Have you considered that she might be involved with someone else?"

Bane leaned back in his chair, considering Dillon's

words. "I don't believe that. Crystal and I had an understanding. We have an unbreakable bond."

"But that was years ago," Dillon stressed. "You just
said you haven't seen her since that day Carl sent her
away. For all you know she could be married by now."

Bane shook his head. "Crystal wouldn't marry anyone else."

Dillon lifted a brow. "And how can you be so sure
of that?"

Bane held his brother's stare. "Because she's already
married, Dil. Crystal is married to me and I think it's
time to go claim my wife."

Dillon was on his feet in a flash. "Married? You?
Crystal? B-but how? When?"

"When we eloped."

"But you and Crystal never made it to Vegas."

"Weren't trying to," Bane said evenly. "We deliberately gave that impression to send everyone looking
for us in the wrong direction. We got married in Utah."

"Utah? You have to be eighteen to marry without
parental consent and Crystal was seventeen."

Bane shook his head. "She was seventeen the day we
eloped, but turned eighteen the next day."

Dillon stared at him. "Then, why didn't the two of
you say something? Why didn't she tell her parents that
she was your wife or why didn't you tell us? You let
them send her away."

"Yes, because I knew that although she was my wife,
I could still be brought up on kidnapping charges. I violated the restraining order from that judge when I set
foot on her parents' property. If you recall, Judge Foster was pissed about it and wanted to send me to the
prison farm for a year. And knowing Mr. Newsome,

had I mentioned anything about me and Crystal being married, he would have demanded that Judge Foster send me away for even longer. Once I was gone, Newsome would have found a way to have our marriage annulled or forced Crystal into divorcing me. She and I both knew that so we decided not to say anything about our marriage no matter what…even if it meant being apart for a short while."

"A short while? You've been apart for five years."

"I hadn't planned for it to be this long. We figured her old man would keep her under lock and key for a while. We were prepared for that seven-month separation because it would give Crystal a chance to finish high school. We hadn't figured on him sending her away. But then something you said that day stuck with me. At the time I had nothing to offer Crystal. She was smart and deserved more than a dumb ass who enjoyed being the town's troublemaker."

Bane didn't say anything for a minute before adding, "I told you earlier that I hadn't seen Crystal, but what I didn't say is that I managed to talk to her after she left town."

Dillon frowned. "You made contact with Crystal?"

"Only once. A few months after she was sent away."

"But how? Her parents made sure no one knew where she'd gone."

"Bailey found out for me."

Dillon shook his head. "Now, why doesn't that surprise me? And how did Bailey find out where Crystal was?"

Bane held his brother's gaze. "Are you sure you want to know?"

Dillon rubbed his hand down his face. "Does it involve breaking the law?"

Bane shrugged his shoulders. "Sort of."

Bailey was their female cousin who was a couple of years younger than Bane and the baby in the Denver Westmoreland family. While growing up, the two of them, along with the twins, Adrian and Aidan, had been extremely close, thick as thieves, literally. The four used to get into all kinds of trouble with the law. Bane knew that Dillon's close friendship with Sheriff Harper was what had kept them out of jail.

Now the twins were Harvard graduates. Adrian had a PhD in engineering and Aidan was a cardiologist at Johns Hopkins Research Hospital. And both were happily married. Bailey, who had her MBA, was marrying Walker Rafferty, a rancher from Alaska, on Valentine's Day and moving to live on his spread. That announcement had definitely come as a shock to Bane and everyone else since Bailey had always sworn she would never, ever leave Westmoreland Country. Bane had met Rafferty today and immediately liked the ex-marine. Bane had a feeling Rafferty would not only handle Bailey but would make Bane's cousin happy.

"So if you knew where she was, what stopped you from going to her?" Dillon asked, holding Bane's gaze.

"I didn't know where she was and I made Bailey promise not to tell me. I just needed to talk to her and Bailey arranged a call between me and Crystal that lasted about twenty minutes. I told her about my decision to join the navy and I made her a promise that while we were apart I would honor our marriage vows, and for her to always believe that one day I would come back for her. That was the last time we talked to each other."

Bane remembered that phone call as if it had been yesterday. "Another reason I needed to talk to Crystal was to be certain she hadn't gotten pregnant during the time we eloped. A pregnancy would have been a game changer for me. I would not have gone into the navy. Instead, I would have gone to her immediately."

Dillon nodded. "Do you know where she is now?"

"I didn't know up until a few hours ago. Bailey lost contact with Crystal a year and a half ago. Last week I hired someone to find her, and I got a call that she's been found. I'm heading out in the morning."

"To where?"

"Dallas, Texas."

One

Leaving her job at Seton Industries, Crystal Newsome quickly walked to her car, looking over her shoulder when she thought she heard footsteps behind her. She tried ignoring the sparks that moved up her arms, while telling herself she was probably getting all worked up for nothing. And all because of that note someone had left today in her desk drawer.

Someone wants the research you're working on. I suggest you disappear for a while. No matter what, don't trust anyone.

After reading it she had glanced around the lab. Her four colleagues seemed preoccupied, busy working on their individual biochemistry projects. She wondered who'd given her the warning and wished she could dismiss the note as a joke, but she couldn't. Especially not after the incident yesterday.

Someone had gotten inside her locker. How the person had known her combination she wasn't sure, since there hadn't been any signs of forced entry. But whoever it was had taken the time to leave things almost exactly as she'd left them.

And now the anonymous note.

Reaching her car, she unlocked the door and got inside, locking it again behind her. After checking her surroundings and the other cars parked close by, she maneuvered out of the parking lot and onto the street. When she came to a stop at the first traffic light, she pulled the typed note from her purse and reread it.

Disappear? How could she do that, even if she wanted to?

She was currently working on her PhD as a biochemist, and was one of five chosen nationally to participate in a yearlong research program at Seton Industries. Crystal knew others were interested in her research. Case in point: just last month she'd been approached by two government officials who wanted her to continue her PhD research under the protection of Homeland Security. The two men had stressed what could happen if her data got into the wrong hands, namely those with criminal intent. She had assured them that even with the documented advances of her research, her project was still just a theoretical concept. But they had wanted to place her in a highly collaborative environment with two other American chemists working on similar research. Although their offer had been tempting, she had turned it down. She was set to graduate from Harvard with her PhD in the spring and had already received a number of job offers.

But now she wondered if she should have taken the men's warning seriously. Could someone with criminal intent be after the findings she'd already logged?

She glanced in her rearview mirror and her heart pounded. A blue car she'd noticed several traffic lights back was still there. Was she imagining things?

A short while later she knew she wasn't. The car was staying a few car lengths behind her.

Crystal knew she couldn't go home. The driver of that blue car would follow her. So where could she go? Who could she call? The four other biochemists were also PhD students, but she stayed to herself the majority of the time and hadn't formed relationships with any of them.

Except for Darnell Enfield. He'd been the one intent on establishing a relationship with her. She had done nothing to encourage the man and had told him countless times she wasn't interested. When that hadn't deterred him, she'd threatened to file a complaint with the director of the program. In anger, Darnell had accused her of being stuck-up, saying he hoped she had a lonely and miserable life.

Crystal had news for him. She had that already. On most days she tried not to dwell on just how lonely the past five years had been. But as far as she was concerned, Loneliness had been her middle name for further back than five years.

Born the only child to older, overprotective parents, she'd been homeschooled and rarely allowed to leave the house except to attend church or accompany them to the grocery store. For years, her parents wouldn't even allow her to go outside and play. She remembered when one of the neighbor kids had tried befriending her, the most she could do was talk to the little girl through her bedroom window.

It was only after their pastor had encouraged her parents to enroll Crystal in public school to enhance her social skills that they did so. By then she was fifteen and starving for friends. But she'd discovered just how cruel the world was when the other girls had snubbed her and the guys had made fun of her because she'd been advanced in all her studies. They'd called her a genius freak. She had been miserable attending school until she'd met Bane.

Brisbane Westmoreland.

The man she had secretly married five years ago on her eighteenth birthday. And the man she hadn't seen since.

As a teenager, Bane had been her best friend, her sounding board and her reason for existing. He'd understood her like no other and she'd felt she had understood him. Her parents made the four-year difference in their ages a big issue and tried keeping them apart. The more her parents tried, the more she'd defied them to be with him.

Then there was the problem of Bane being a Westmoreland. Years ago, her and Bane's great-grandfathers had ended their friendship because of a dispute regarding land boundaries, and it seemed her father had no problem continuing the feud.

When Crystal came to another traffic light she pulled out a business card from her purse. It was the card those two government officials had left with her. They'd asked her to call if she changed her mind or if she noticed any funny business. At the time she'd thought their words were a scare tactic to make her give their offer more consideration. But could they have been right? Should she contact them? She replaced the card in her purse and looked at the note again.

No matter what, don't trust anyone.

So what should she do? Where could she go? Since

her father's death, her mother was now a missionary in Haiti. Should Crystal escape to Orangeburg, South Carolina, where her aunt Rachel still lived? The last thing Crystal wanted was to bring trouble to her elderly aunt's doorstep.

There was another place she could hide. Her childhood home in Denver. She and her mother had discovered, after going through her father's papers, that he'd never sold their family homestead after her parents moved to Connecticut. And even more shocking to Crystal was that he'd left the ranch to her. Had that been his way of letting her know he'd accepted that one day she would go back there?

She nibbled her bottom lip. Should she go back now? And face all the memories she'd left behind? What if Bane was there? What if he'd hooked up with someone else despite the promises he'd made to her?

She didn't want to believe that. The Bane Westmoreland she had fallen in love with had promised to honor their wedding vows. Before marrying someone else he would seek her out to ask for a divorce.

She thought about the other promise he'd made and wondered if she was the biggest fool on earth. He'd vowed he would come back for her. That had been five years ago and she was still waiting. Was she wasting her life on a man who had forgotten about her? A lot could have happened since he'd made that promise. Feelings and emotions could change. People could change. Why was she refusing to let go of teenage memories with a guy who might have moved on with his life?

Legally she was a married woman, but all she had to show for it was a last name she never used and a husband who'd left her with unfulfilled promises. Her last contact with him after her father had sent her away was when he'd called to let her know he was joining the navy. Did he expect her to wait until he got tired of being a sailor, moving from one port to the next? What if an emergency had come up and she'd needed him?

She knew the answer to that without much thought. Had an emergency arisen, she could have reached him through his family. Although the Westmorelands had no idea where she lived now, she'd always known where they were. She could have picked up the phone and called Dillon, Bane's eldest brother, if she'd ever truly wanted or needed to contact Bane. Several times she'd come close to doing that, but something had always held her back. First of all, she knew the Westmorelands blamed her for a lot of the trouble Bane had gotten into.

As teens, her and Bane's relationship had been obsessive and she didn't want to think about the number of times they'd broken the law to be together. She'd had resorted to cutting school, and regardless of what her parents had assumed, the majority of the time it had been her idea and not his. Nothing her parents or his family said or did had torn them apart. Instead, their bond had gotten stronger.

Because of the difference in their ages, her parents had accused Bane of taking advantage of her, and her father had even put a restraining order in place and threatened Bane with jail time to keep him away from her. But that hadn't stopped her or Bane from being together. When they'd gotten tired of their families' interference, they had eloped.

She reached inside her shirt and pulled out the sterling-silver heart-shaped locket Bane had given her instead of a wedding ring he couldn't afford. When he'd placed the locket around her neck he'd said it had belonged to his deceased mother. He'd wanted her to have it, to always wear it as a reminder of their love. His love. She swallowed a thick lump in her throat. If he loved her so much, then why hadn't he kept his promise and come back for her?

Her mother had mentioned that Bane's eldest brother, Dillon, had called a year ago when he'd heard about her father's death. According to her mother, the conversation had been brief, but Dillon had taken the time to inquire about how she was doing. According to her mother the only thing he'd said about Bane was that he was in the navy. Of course her mother thought her daughter was doing just fine now that Bane was out of her life, and the Westmorelands probably felt the same way since she was out of Bane's. What if her mother was right and Bane *was* doing just fine without her?

Drawing in a deep breath, Crystal forced her thoughts back to the car following her. Should she call the police for help? She quickly dismissed the idea. Hadn't the note warned her not to trust anyone? Suddenly an idea popped into her head. It was the start of the holiday shopping season and shoppers were already out in large numbers. She would drive to the busiest mall in Dallas and get lost in traffic. If that didn't work she would come up with plan B.

The one thing she knew for certain was that she would not let the person tail her home. When she got there, she would quickly pack her things and disappear for a while. She would decide where she was going once she got to the airport. The Bahamas sounded pretty good right about now.

What would Seton Industries think when she didn't show up for work as usual? At present that was the least of her worries. Staying safe was her top priority.

Half an hour later she smiled, satisfied that plan A

had worked. All it took was to scoot her car in and out of all those tenacious shoppers a few times, and the driver of the blue car couldn't keep up. But just to be certain, she drove around for a while to make sure she was no longer being tailed.

She had fallen in love with Dallas but had no choice except to leave town for a while.

Sitting in the SUV he had rented at the airport, Bane tilted his Stetson off his eyes and shifted his long legs into a more comfortable position. He checked his watch again. The private investigator's report indicated Crystal was employed with Seton Industries as a biochemist while working on her PhD, and that she usually got off work around four. It was close to seven and she hadn't gotten home yet. So where was she?

It *was* the holiday season and she could have gone shopping. And she must have girlfriends, so she could very well be spending time with one of them. He just had to wait.

None of his family members had been surprised when he'd announced he was going after Crystal. However, except for Bailey, who knew the whole story, all of them were shocked to learn he'd married Crystal when they had eloped. His brother Riley had claimed he'd suspected as much, but all the others hadn't had a clue.

Bailey had given Bane a huge hug and whispered that it was about time he claimed his wife. Of course others, like Dillon, had warned Bane that things might be different and not to expect Crystal to be the eighteen-year-old he'd last seen. Just like he had changed over the years, so had she.

His cousin Zane, who was reputed to be an expert on women, had gone so far as to advise Bane not to expect

Crystal to readily embrace her role as loving wife or his role as long-lost husband. Zane had cautioned him not to do anything stupid like sweeping her off her feet and carrying her straight to the bedroom. They would have to get to know each other all over again, and he shouldn't be surprised if she tried putting up walls between them for a while.

Zane had reiterated that regardless of the reason, Bane hadn't made contact with his wife in almost five years and doubts would have crossed Crystal's mind regarding Bane's love and faithfulness.

He had appreciated everyone's advice. And while he wished like hell he could sweep Crystal off her feet and head straight for the nearest bedroom when he saw her, he had enough sense to know they would have to take things slow. After all, they had been apart all this time and there would be a lot for them to talk about and sort out. But he felt certain she knew he would come back for her as he'd promised; no matter how long it had taken him to do so.

He was back in her life and didn't intend to go anywhere. Even if it meant he lived with her in Dallas for a while. As a SEAL he could live anywhere as long as he was ready to leave for periodic training sessions or covert operations whenever his commanding officer called. And as long as there was still instability in Iraq, Afghanistan and Syria, his team might be needed.

Thinking of his team made him think about Coop. It was hard to believe his friend was gone. All the team members had taken Coop's death hard and agreed that if it was the last thing they did, they would return to Syria, find Coop's body and bring him home. His parents deserved that and Coop did, too.

For the longest time, Bane had thought he could keep

his marriage a secret from his team. But he found it hard to do when the guys thought it was essential that he got laid every once in a while. Things started getting crazy when they tried fixing him up with some woman or another every chance they got.

He'd finally told them about his marriage to Crystal. Then he wished he hadn't when they'd teased him about all the women they were getting while he wasn't getting any. He took it all in stride because he only wanted one woman. His team members accepted that he intended to adhere to his wedding vows and in the end they all respected and admired him for it.

Now the SEAL in him studied his surroundings, taking notice. The one thing he appreciated was that Crystal's home appeared to be in a safe neighborhood. The streets were well lit and the houses spaced with enough distance for privacy yet with her neighbors in reach if needed.

The brick house where she lived suited her. It looked to be in good condition and the yard was well manicured. One thing he did notice was that unlike all the other houses, she didn't have any Christmas decorations. There weren't any colorful lights around her windows or animated objects adorning her lawn. Did she not celebrate the holidays anymore? He recalled a time when she had. In fact the two most important days to her had been her birthday and Christmas.

He'd made her birthday even more special by marrying her on it. A smile touched his lips when he recalled how, over the years, he had bought her birthday cards and anniversary cards, although he hadn't been able to send them to her. He'd even bought her Valentine's Day cards and Christmas cards every year. He had stored them in a trunk, knowing one day he would give them to her. Well, that day had finally arrived and he had all of them packed in his luggage. He had signed each one and taken the time to write a special message inside. Then there were all those letters he'd written. Letters he'd never mailed because he hadn't a clue where to send them.

He'd made Bailey promise not to tell him because if he'd known how to get to Crystal he would have gone to her and messed up all the effort he'd made in becoming the type of man who could give her what she deserved in life.

Five years was a long time and there had been times he'd thought he would lose his mind from missing her so much. It had taken all he had, every bit of resolve he could muster, to make it through. In the end, he knew the sacrifice would be worth it.

He figured he would give Crystal time to get into the house before he got out of the car and knocked on the door, so as not to spook her. No need to give her neighbors anything to talk about, either, especially if no one knew she was married. And from the private investigator's report, her marital status was a guarded secret. He understood and figured it wouldn't be easy to explain a husband who'd gone AWOL.

His phone rang and a smile tugged at the corner of his mouth when he recognized the ringtone. It was Thurston McRoy, better known to the team as Mac. All Bane's team members' names had been shortened for easy identification during deployment. Cooper was Coop. McRoy was Mac. And because his name was Brisbane, the nickname his family had given him was already a shortened version, so his team members called him Bane like everyone else.

"What's up, Mac?"

"Have you seen her yet?"

He had spoken to Mac on his way to the airport to let him know his whereabouts, just in case the team was needed somewhere. "No, not yet. I'm parked outside her place. She's late getting off work."

"When she gets there, don't ask a lot of questions and please don't go off on her as if you've been there for the past five years. You may think she's late but it might be her usual MO to get delayed every once in a while. Women do have days they like to get prettied up. Get their hair and nails done and stuff."

Bane chuckled. He figured Mac would know since he was one of the married team members. And Mac would tell them that after every extended mission, he would go home to an adjustment period, where he would have to get to know his wife all over again and reclaim his position as head of the house.

When Bane saw car lights headed toward where he was parked, he said, "I think this is her pulling up now."

"Great. Just remember the advice I gave you."

Yours and everybody else's, Bane thought. "Whatever. I know how to handle my business."

"See that you do." Then without saying anything else, Mac clicked off the phone.

As Bane watched the headlights get closer, he couldn't stop the deep pounding of his heart. He wondered what changes to expect. Did Crystal wear her hair down to her shoulders like she had years ago? Did she nibble her bottom lip when she was nervous about something? And did she still have those sexy legs?

It didn't matter. He intended to finally claim her as his. His wife.

Bane watched as she pulled into her yard and got out of the car. The moment his gaze latched on to her all the emotion he hadn't been able to contain over the years washed over him, putting an ache in his gut.

The streetlight shone on her features. Even from the distance, he could see she was beautiful. She'd grown taller and her youthful figure had blossomed into that of a woman. His pulse raced as he studied how well her curves filled out her dark slacks and how her breasts appeared to be shaped perfectly beneath her jacket.

As he watched her, the navy SEAL in him went on alert. Something wasn't right. He had been trained to be vigilant not just to his surroundings but also to people. Recognizing signs of trouble had kept him alive on more than one mission. Maybe it was the quickness of her steps to her front door, the number of times she looked back over her shoulder or the way she kept checking the street as if to make certain she hadn't been followed.

When she went inside and closed the door he released the breath he only realized now that he'd been holding. Who or what had her so antsy? She had no knowledge that he was coming, so it couldn't be him. She seemed more than just rattled. Terrified was more like it. Why? Even if she'd somehow found out he was coming, she had no reason of be afraid of him. Unless...

He scowled. What if she assumed he wasn't coming back for her and she'd taken a lover? What if she was the mother of another man's child? What if...

He cleared his mind. Each of those thoughts was like a quick punch to his gut, and he refused to go there. Besides, the private investigator's report had been clear. She lived alone and was not involved with anyone.

Still, something had her frightened.

After waiting for several minutes to give her time to

get settled after a day at work, he opened the door to the SUV. It was time to find out what the hell was going on.

With her heart thundering hard in her chest, Crystal began throwing items in the suitcase open on her bed. Had she imagined it or had she been watched when she'd entered her home tonight? She had glanced around several times and hadn't noticed anything or anyone. But still...

She took a deep breath, knowing she couldn't lose her cool. She had to keep a level head. She made a decision to leave her car here and a few lights burning inside her house to give the impression she was home. She would call a cab to take her to the airport and would take only the necessities and a few items of clothing. She could buy anything else she needed.

But this, she thought, studying the photo album she held in her hand, went everywhere with her. She had purchased it right after her last phone call with Bane. Her parents had sent Crystal to live with Aunt Rachel to finish out the last year of school. They'd wanted to get her away from Bane, not knowing she and Bane had married.

Before they'd returned home after eloping, Bane had convinced Crystal it was important for her to finish school before telling anyone they'd gotten married. He'd told her that if her parents tried keeping them apart that he would put up with it for a few months, which was the time it would take for her to finish school. They hadn't counted on her parents sending her away. But still, she believed that Bane would come for her once the school year ended, no matter where she was.

But a couple of months after she left Denver, she'd gotten a call from him. She'd assumed he was calling to let her know he couldn't stand the separation and was coming for her. But his real purpose had been twofold. He'd wanted to find out if she had gotten pregnant when they eloped, and he'd told her he'd enlisted in the navy and would be leaving for boot camp in Great Lakes, Illinois, in a few weeks. He'd said he needed to grow up, become responsible and make something out of himself. She deserved a man who could be all that he could be, and after he'd accomplished that goal he would come for her. He'd also promised that while they were apart he would honor their wedding vows and she'd promised him the same. And she had.

She'd figured he would be in the navy for four years. Preparing for the separation, she'd decided to make something of herself, as well. He deserved that, too. So after completing high school she'd enrolled in college. She had taken a placement test, which she'd aced. Instead of being accepted as a freshman, she had entered as a junior.

Sitting on the edge of the bed now, she flipped through the album, which she had dedicated to Bane. She'd even had his name engraved on the front. While they were apart she'd kept this photo journal, chronicling her life without him. There were graduation pictures from high school and college, random pictures she'd taken just for him. She'd figured that by the time she saw him she would have at least two to three years' worth of photos. She hadn't counted on the bulky album containing five years of photographs. The last thing she'd assumed was that they would be apart for this long without any contact.

She thought of him often. Every day. What she tried not to think about was why it was taking him so long to come back for her, or how he might be somewhere enjoying life without her. Forcing those thoughts from her mind, she packed the album in her luggage. Her destination was the Bahamas. She had done an online bank transfer to her "fun" account, which had accumulated a nice amount due to the vacations she'd never gotten around to taking. And in case her home was searched, she'd made sure not to leave any clues about where she was headed.

Was she being impulsive by heeding what the note had said when she didn't even know who'd written it? She could report it, what happened to her locker and that she'd noticed someone following her to those two government officials. If she couldn't trust her own government, then who could she trust? She shook her head, deciding against making that call. Maybe she'd watched too many TV shows where the government had turned out to be the bad guy.

Crystal thought about calling her mother and Aunt Rachel, and then decided against it. Whatever she was involved with, it would be best to leave them out of it. She would contact them later when she felt doing so would be safe. Moments later, she had rolled her luggage out of her bedroom into the living room and was calling for a cab when her doorbell rang.

She went still. Nobody ever visited her. Who would be doing so now? She crept back into the shadows of her hallway, hoping whoever was at the door would think she wasn't home. She held her breath when the doorbell sounded again. Had the person on the other side seen her enter her house and knew she was there?

Moments passed and the doorbell did not sound again. She sighed in relief—and then there was a hard knock. She swallowed. The person hadn't gone away. Either she answered it or continued to pretend she wasn't there. Since the latter hadn't worked so far, she rushed into her bedroom and grabbed her revolver out of the nightstand drawer.

She'd grown up around guns, and thanks to Bane she knew how to use one. This neighborhood was pretty safe, and even though she'd figured she'd never need to use it, she had bought the gun anyway. A woman living alone needed to be cautious.

By the time she'd made it back to the living room, there was a second knock. She moved toward the door, but stopped five feet away. She called out, "Who is it?" and tightened her hands on the revolver.

There was a moment of silence. And then a voice said, "It's me, Crystal. Bane."

Two

The revolver Crystal held almost fell from her hand.

Bane? My Bane? No way, she thought, backing up. It had to be an impostor. It didn't even sound like Bane. This voice was deeper, huskier.

If it was a trick, who knew of her relationship with Brisbane Westmoreland? And if it really was Bane, why had he shown up on her doorstep now? Why tonight of all nights?

It just wasn't logical for her to have been thinking about him only moments ago and for him to be here now. She would go with her first assumption. The person at the door claiming to be Bane wasn't him.

"You aren't Bane. Go away or I'll call the police," she threatened loudly. "I have a gun and will shoot if I have to."

"Crystal Gayle, it *is* me. Honest. It's Bane."

Crystal Gayle? She sucked in a deep breath. Nobody

called her that but her parents...and Bane. When she was young, she had hated being called by her first and middle names, which her father had given her, naming her after his favorite country singer. But Bane had made her like it when he'd called her that on occasion. Could it really be him at the door?

Lowering the gun, she looked out the peephole. Her gaze connected to a gorgeous pair of hazel eyes with a greenish tint. They were eyes she knew. It *was* Bane.

She was about to open the door when she remembered the note. *Trust no one.* But this wasn't just anyone, she reasoned with herself. This was Bane.

She unlocked the door and stepped back. Soft porch light poured into her foyer as Bane eased open the door. He'd always been tall and lanky, but the man entering her house appeared a lot taller than she remembered. And he was no longer slender. He was all muscles and they were in perfect proportion to his height and weight. It was obvious he worked out a lot to stay in shape. His body exemplified endurance and strength. And when her gaze settled on his face, she drew in a deep, sharp breath. He even looked different. Rougher. Tougher.

The eyes were the same but she'd never seen him with facial hair before. He'd always been handsome in a boyish sort of way, but his features now were perfectly masculine. They appeared chiseled, his lips sculpted. She was looking into the most handsome face she'd ever seen.

He not only looked older and more mature, but he also looked military—even while wearing jeans, a chambray shirt, a leather bomber jacket, Western boots and a Stetson. There was something about the way he stood, upright and straight. And all this transformation had come from being in the navy?

He closed the door behind him, staring at her just as she was staring at him. Her heart pounded. A part of her wanted to race over to him, tell him how glad she was to see him, how much she had missed him…but she couldn't. Her legs refused to move and she knew why. This Bane was like a stranger to her.

"Crystal."

She hadn't imagined it. His voice had gotten deeper. Sounded purely sexy to her ears. "Bane."

"You look good."

She blinked at his words and said the first thing that came to her mind. "You look good, too. And different."

He smiled and her breath caught. He still had that Brisbane Westmoreland smile. The one that spread across a full mouth and showed teeth that were perfectly even and sparkling white against mocha-colored skin. The familiarity warmed her inside.

"I am different. I'm not the same Bane. The military has a way of doing that to you," he said, in that husky voice she was trying to get used to hearing.

He was admitting to being different.

Was this his way of saying his transformation had changed his preferences? Like his taste in women? He was older now, five years older, in fact. Had he shown up on her doorstep tonight of all nights to let her know that he wanted a divorce?

Fine, she would deal with it. She had no choice. Besides, she wasn't sure if she would like the new Bane anyway. He was probably doing her a favor.

"Okay," she said, placing her revolver on the coffee table. "If you brought any papers with you that require my signature, then give them to me."

He lifted a brow. "Papers?"

"Yes."

"What kind of papers?"

Instead of answering, she glanced at her watch. She needed to call a cab to the airport. The plane to the Bahamas would take off in three hours.

"Crystal? What kind of papers are you talking about?"

She glanced back over at him. And why did her gaze automatically go to his mouth, the same mouth that had taught her how to kiss and given her so much pleasure? And why was she recalling a lot of those kisses right now? She drew in a deep, shallow breath. "Divorce papers."

"Is that why you think I'm here?"

Was she imagining things or had his voice sounded brisk? She shrugged. Why were they even having this conversation? Why couldn't he just give her the papers and be on his way so she could be on hers? After all, it had been five years. She got that. Did it matter that she had spent all that time waiting for him to show up?

"Crystal? Is that why you think I'm here? To ask for a divorce?" He repeated the question and she noticed his tone still had a brusque edge.

She held his gaze. "What other reason could there be?"

He shoved his hands into the pockets of his jeans and braced his legs apart in a stance that was as daunting as it was sexy. It definitely brought emphasis to his massive shoulders, the solidness of chest and his chiseled good looks.

"Did you consider that maybe I'm here to keep that promise I made about coming back for you?"

She blinked, not sure she'd heard him correctly. "You aren't here to ask for a divorce?"

"No. What makes you think I'd want to divorce you?"

She could give him a number of reasons once her

head stopped spinning. Instead, she said what was in the forefront of her mind. "Well, it has been five years, Bane."

"I told you I'd come back for you."

She placed her hands on her hips. "Yes, but I hadn't counted on it being *five* years. Five years without a single word from you. Besides, you just said you've changed."

The look in his eyes indicated he was having a hard time keeping up with her. "I *have* changed, Crystal. Being a SEAL has a way of changing you, but that has nothing to do—"

"SEAL? You're a navy SEAL?"

"Yes."

Now she was the one having a hard time keeping up. "I knew you'd joined the navy, but I figured you'd been assigned to a ship somewhere."

He nodded. "I would have been if my captain in boot camp hadn't thought I would be a good fit for the SEALs. He cut through a lot of red tape for me to go to the naval academy."

That was another surprise. "You attended the naval academy?"

"Yes."

Jeez. She was realizing just how little she knew about what he'd been doing over the past five years. "I didn't know."

He shifted his stance and her gaze followed the movement, taking in his long, denim-clad, boot-wearing legs.

"Bailey said the two of you lost contact with each other a couple of years ago," he said.

Now was the time to come clean and say losing contact with Bailey had been a deliberate move. The periodic calls from his cousin had become depressing since they'd agreed Crystal wouldn't ask about Bane. Just as he wouldn't ask Bailey any questions about Crystal.

That had been Bane's idea. He'd figured the less they knew about the other's lives, the less chance they had of reneging on their promise not to seek the other out before he could meet his goals.

During one of those conversations Bailey had informed her Bane had set up a bank account for her, in case she ever needed anything. She never had and to this day she'd never withdrawn any funds.

"Even if Bailey and I had kept in touch, she would not have told me *what* you were doing, just *how* you were doing. That was the agreement, remember, Bane?"

"You could have called Dil," he said as he raked his gaze over her.

He was probably taking note of how she'd changed as she'd done with him. He could clearly see she was no longer the eighteen-year-old he'd married, but was now a twenty-three-year-old woman. Her birthday had been two weeks ago. She wondered if he'd remembered.

"No, I couldn't call your brother, or any other member of your family for that matter, and you know why. They blamed me for you getting into trouble."

Crystal glanced at her watch again. He'd said he was here to fulfill his promise. If he was doing it because he felt obligated then she would release him from it. Although asking for a divorce might not have been his original intent, she was certain it was crossing his mind now. Why wouldn't it? They were acting like strangers instead of two people who'd once been so obsessed with each other they'd eloped. Why weren't they all over each other? Why was he over there and she still standing over here? The answer to both questions was so brutally clear she had to force tears from her eyes.

Like he said, he had changed. He was a SEAL. Something other than her was number one in his life now. More than likely it had been his missions that had kept him away all this time. He'd chosen what he really wanted.

"Crystal, I have a question for you."

His words interrupted her thoughts. "What?"

"Why did you come to the door with a gun?"

It had taken every ounce of Bane's control not to cross the room and pull his wife into his arms. How often had he dreamed of this moment, wished for it, yearned for it? But things weren't playing out like he'd hoped.

Although he'd taken heed to Zane's warning and not swept her off her feet and headed for the nearest bedroom, he hadn't counted on not getting at least a kiss, a hug…something. But she stood there as if she wasn't sure what to make of his appearance here tonight. And he still couldn't grasp why she assumed he wanted a divorce just because he'd told her he'd changed. He'd changed for the better, not only for himself but also for her. Now he had something to offer her. He could give her the life she deserved.

Crystal nibbled her bottom lip, which had always been an indication she was nervous about something. Damn, she looked good. Time had only enhanced her beauty, and where in the hell had all those curves come from?

She had changed into a pair of skinny jeans, a pullover sweater and boots. She looked all soft and feminine. So gorgeous. Her hair was not as long as it used to be. Instead of flowing past her shoulders it barely touched them. The new style suited her. How had she managed to keep the guys away? He was certain that with her beauty there had been a number of men who'd come around over the years.

Even now Bane's hands itched to touch her all over like he used to. He would give anything to run his fingers across the curve of her hips and buttocks and cup her breasts.

"The gun?"

Her question pulled his concentration back to their conversation. Probably for the best, since the thought of what he wanted to do with his hands was turning him on big-time. "Yes. I watched you get out of your car to come into the house and you seemed nervous. Is something going on? Is some man harassing you or stalking you?"

She lifted a brow. "A man stalking me? What makes you think that?"

He held her gaze. "I told you. I noticed you were nervous and—"

"Yes, I got that part," she interrupted to say. "But what makes you think any man would stalk me?"

Had she looked in the mirror lately? If she'd asked him *why* he thought she was being stalked, then he could have told her that his SEAL training had taught him how to zero in on certain things. But her question had been what made him think *any man* would want to stalk *her*. That was a different question altogether. He could see a man becoming obsessed with her. Hadn't Bane?

"You're a very beautiful woman. You've always been beautiful, Crystal. You're even more so now."

She shook her head. "Beautiful? You're laying it on thick, aren't you, Bane?"

"No, I don't think so. Level with me. Is there some man stalking you? Is that why you had the gun? And what's with the luggage? You're going someplace?"

She broke eye contact with him to shrug. "The gun is to protect myself."

Bane had a feeling that wasn't all there was to it. When he'd first walked into her house he'd seen the luggage, but his mind had been solely on her, entranced with her beauty. This older version of Crystal sent his heart pounding into overdrive. It had been a long time. Too long.

He turned his concentration back to what she'd just told him. "You have the gun to protect yourself... I can buy that, although this seems to be a pretty safe neighborhood," he said. "But that doesn't explain why you were ready to shoot. Has your home been broken into before?"

"No."

"Then what's going on?"

Even after all this time he still could read her like a book. She had a tendency to lick her lips when she was nervous, and unconsciously shift her body from side to side while standing on the balls of her feet. He could tell she was trying to decide how to answer his question. That didn't sit well with him. In the past, he and Crystal never kept secrets from each other. So why was she doing so now?

"After all this time, you don't have the right to ask me anything, Bane."

You're wrong about that, sweetheart.

Without thinking about what he was doing, he closed the distance separating them to stand directly in front of her. "I believe I do have that right. As long as we're still legally married, Crystal, I have every right."

She lifted her chin and pinched her lips together. "Fine. Then, we can get a divorce."

"Not happening." He rubbed his hand down his face. What the hell was going on here? Not only was this reunion not going the way he'd wanted, it had just taken a bad turn.

He looked at her, somewhat bewildered by her refusal to answer his question. "I'm asking again, Crystal. What's going on with you? Why the gun and the packed luggage?"

When she didn't answer, standing there with a mutinous expression on her face, he then asked the one question he hadn't wanted to ask, but needed to know. And he hoped like hell he was wrong.

"Are you involved with someone who's causing you problems?"

Three

That question set Crystal off. She took the final step to completely close the distance between them. "Involved with someone? Are you accusing me of being unfaithful?"

"Not accusing you of anything," he said in a tone that let her know her outrage had fueled his. "But I find it odd you won't answer my question. Why are you acting so secretive? You've never acted that way with me before."

No, she hadn't. But then the Bane she used to know, the one she'd loved more than life itself, would not have forgotten her for five years. He would have moved heaven, hell and any place in between to have her with him so the two of them could be together.

"You're not the only one who's changed. Just like you're not the same, I'm not the same."

They faced off. She didn't see him move, but suddenly his body brushed against hers and she drew in a sharp breath. The touch had been electric, sending a sizzle through her. Suddenly, her mind was filled with memories of the last time they'd touched. Really touched. All over. Naked. Those memories were enough to ignite a fire in the pit of her stomach.

"You may not be the same," he said, breaking into the silence between them, speaking in a low tone, "but you kept your wedding vows."

He spoke with such absolute certainty, she wondered how he could be so sure. But of course he was right. "Yes, I kept them."

He nodded. "And before doubt starts clouding that pretty little head of yours, let me go on record to say that I might not be the same, but I kept my wedding vows, as well."

There was no way. Not that she didn't think he would have tried, but she knew when it came to sex, some men classified it as a *must have*. She of all people knew how much the old Bane had enjoyed it. There was no reason to think the new and different Bane wouldn't like it just as much. Just look at him. He was more masculine, more virile—so macho. Even if he hadn't targeted women, they would definitely have targeted him.

"Now that we have that cleared up…"

Did they? "Not so fast," she said, trying to ignore it when his body brushed against hers again. Had it been intentional? And why hadn't one of them taken a step back? "What kept you sane?"

"Sane?"

"Yes. You know. From climbing the walls and stuff. I heard men need sex every so often."

He smiled and the force of it sent her senses reeling. "Remind me to give you all the details one day. Now, back to our earlier topic, why did you come to the door with a gun and why the packed bags?"

They were back to that?

But then maybe they should be. She needed to call a cab and get to the airport. And just like she didn't want to involve her mother and Aunt Rachel in whatever was going on, she definitely didn't want to involve Bane. Maybe she should have lied and said she was involved with someone else. Then he would have gotten angry and left, and she would be free to do as the note advised and disappear. Whatever was going on was her issue and not his.

She nibbled her lips as she tried coming up with something that would sound reasonable. Something that wasn't too much of a lie. So she said, "The reason for the packed luggage is because I'm taking a trip."

He looked at her as if to say *duh*. Instead, he held her gaze and asked, "Business or pleasure?"

"Business."

"Where are you headed?"

If she told him the Bahamas, he would question if it really was a business trip, so she said, "Chicago."

"Fine. I'll go with you."

She blinked, suddenly feeling anxiety closing in on her. "Go with me?"

"Yes. I'm on leave so I can do that," he said calmly. "Besides, it's time I got to know you again, and I want you to get to know me."

She drew in a breath, feeling her control deteriorating. Those hazel eyes had always been her weakness.

She knew she was a goner when he asked in a husky voice, "You do want to get to know me all over again, don't you, Crystal Gayle?"

Getting to know Brisbane Westmoreland the first

time around had been like a roller coaster, and she'd definitely enjoyed the ride. There was no doubt that getting to know the new Bane would be even more exhilarating. Now she could enjoy the ride as a woman in control of her own destiny and not as a girl whose life was dictated by her parents. A woman who was older, mature and could appreciate the explosiveness of a relationship with him.

As if he knew what she was thinking and wanted to drive that point home, he caressed the side of her face with the tip of his finger. "I definitely want to get to know you again, Crystal."

Then he brought her body closer to his. She felt his erection pressing hard against her middle and a craving she'd tried to put to rest years ago reared its greedy head, making her force back a moan. When his finger left her face to tug on a section of her hair, sensations she hadn't felt in years ran rampant through her womb.

She stared into his eyes. Hazel eyes that had literally branded her the first time she'd gazed into them. Eyes belonging to Bane. *Her* Bane. And he had admitted just moments ago to keeping their vows all this time. That meant he had five years of need and hunger stored inside him. The thought sent heated blood racing through her veins.

Then he shifted. The movement nudged his knees between hers so she could feel his hard bulge even more. Intentional or not, she wasn't sure. The only thing she was certain about was that if she didn't get her self-control back, she would jump his bones without a second thought. And that wasn't good. She didn't even know him anymore.

He leaned in slowly—too slowly, which let her know this side of Bane wasn't different...at least when it came to this. He'd always let her establish the pace, so as not to take advantage of the difference in their ages and experience levels. She'd always known she hadn't been Bane's first girl, but he'd been her first guy. And he'd always handled her with tenderness.

Bane was letting her take the lead now, and she intended to take it to a whole other level. At that moment, she didn't care that they'd both changed; she wanted his hands on her and his tongue in her mouth. To be totally honest, she needed more but she would settle for those two things now…even if she knew there probably wouldn't be a later.

He bent his head closer, and she refused to consider anything other than what she wanted, needed and had gone five years without. She clutched tight to his shoulders and leaned up on tiptoes to cover his mouth with hers.

Bane wasn't sure what was more dangerous. Storming an extremist stronghold in the middle of the night, or having his way with Crystal's mouth after all these years of going without her taste. But now was not the time to dwell on it. It was time to act.

The way their mouths mated seemed as natural as breathing, and he was glad time had not diminished the desire they'd always shared.

When she slid her tongue inside his mouth, memories of the last time they'd kissed flooded his mind. It had been on their wedding day, during their honeymoon in a small hotel in Utah. He recalled very little about the room itself, only what they'd done within those four walls. And they'd done plenty.

But now, this very minute, they were making new memories. He had dreamed about, thought about and wished for this moment for so long. She took the kiss deeper and he wrapped his arms around her waist and pulled her closer, loving the feel of her body plastered against his.

He loved her taste. Always had and always would. When she sucked on his tongue, his heartbeat thundered in his chest and his erection throbbed mercilessly behind his zipper. He was tempted to devour her and tried like hell to keep his self-control in check. But it became too much. Five years without her had taken its toll.

Suddenly he became the aggressor, taking her mouth with a hunger he felt all the way to the soles of his feet. He wanted her to feel him in every part of her body. And when he finally caught her wriggling tongue, he feasted on it.

The one thing that had consumed his mind on their wedding day was the same thing consuming his mind right now. Crystal was his. Undeniably, unquestionably and indisputably his.

He thrust his tongue even deeper into her mouth. He knew he had to pull back; otherwise he would consume her whole. Especially now, when he was filled with the need to do the one thing he shouldn't do, which was to sweep her off her feet and head for the nearest bedroom. He had wanted this moment for so long… Kissing her filled him with sensations so deliciously intoxicating that he could barely think straight.

Bane knew he was embarking on a mission more dangerous than any he'd gone on as a SEAL. Crystal had always been both his weakness and his strength. She was an ache he'd always had to ease. Some way, somehow, he had to show her, prove to her, that any changes he'd made over the past five years were all good and would benefit both of them. Otherwise, the time they'd spent apart would have been for nothing. He refused to accept that.

Reluctant to do so but knowing he should, Bane ended the kiss. But he wasn't ready to release her yet and his hands moved from her waist to boldly cup her backside. And while she was snuggled so close to him, his hands moved up and down the length of her spine before returning to cup her backside again. Now that she was back in his life, he couldn't imagine her being out of it again.

That thought drove him to reiterate something he'd said earlier. "I'm going to Chicago with you."

Slowly recovering from their kiss, Crystal tilted her head back and gazed up at Bane. Her lips had ground against his. Her tongue had initiated a dance inside his mouth that had been as perfect as anything she'd ever known. And he had reciprocated by kissing her back with equal need. Waves of passion had consumed her, nearly drowning her.

But now she had reclaimed her senses and the words he'd spoken infiltrated her mind. She knew there was no way he could go anywhere with her. She was about to open her mouth to tell him so when her cell phone rang. She tensed. Who could be contacting her? She seldom got calls.

"You plan on getting that?" Bane murmured the question while placing a kiss on the side of her neck.

She swallowed. Should she? It could be the airline calling her for some reason. She had left them her number in case her flight was delayed or canceled. "Yes," she said, quickly moving away from him to grab the phone off the table, right next to where she had laid the gun. Seeing the weapon was a reminder of what she had to do and why she couldn't let Bane sidetrack her.

She clicked on her cell phone. "Hello?"

"Don't try getting away, Ms. Newsome. We will find you." And then she heard a click ending the call.

Crystal's heart thumped painfully in her chest. Who was the caller? How did the person get her private number? How did the person know she was trying to get away? She turned toward Bane. Something in her eyes must have told him the call had troubled her because he quickly crossed the room to her. "Crystal, what's wrong?"

She took a deep breath, not knowing what to do or say. She stared up at him as she nervously bit her lip. Should she level with Bane and tell him everything that was going on? The note had said not to trust anyone, but how could she not trust the one and only person she'd always trusted?

"I don't know what's wrong," she said quietly.

She pulled away to reach for her purse and retrieve the note. "I got this note at work today," she said, handing it to him. "And I don't know who sent it."

She waited while he read it and when he glanced back up at her, she said, "Yesterday someone broke into my locker at work, and I noticed someone following me home today."

"Following you?"

"Yes. I thought maybe I was imagining things at first, but when the driver stayed discreetly behind me, I knew that I wasn't. I deliberately lost the car in all the holiday shoppers at one of the busiest malls."

"What about that phone call just now?" he asked, studying her.

She told him what the caller had said. "I don't know who it was or how they got my number."

Bane didn't say anything for a minute. "Is that the reason for the packed bags? You're doing what the note said and disappearing?"

"Yes. Those guys said craziness might start happening and—"

Bane frowned. "What guys?"

"Last month while I was eating lunch at a restaurant near work, I was approached by two government men. They showed me credentials to prove it. They knew about the project I'm working on at Seton and said Homeland Security was concerned about my research getting into the wrong hands. They offered me a chance to work for the government at some lab in DC, along with two other chemists who're working on similar research."

"And?"

"I turned them down. They accepted my answer, but warned me that there were people out there with criminal intent who would do just about anything to get their hands on my research. They gave me their business card and told me to call them if any craziness happened."

"Have you called them?"

"No. After reading the note I wasn't sure who I could trust. At this point that includes Homeland Security."

"Do you still have the business card those guys gave you?"

"Yes."

"May I see it?"

"Yes." She reached for her purse again. She handed the card to him and watched him study it before snapping several pictures of it with his mobile phone.

"What are you doing?"

He glanced over at her. "Verifying those guys are who they say they are. I'm sending this to someone who can do that for me." He then handed her back the card. "Just what kind of research are you working on?"

She paused a moment before saying. "Obscured Reality, or OR as it's most often called."

"Obscured Reality?"

She nodded. "Yes. It's the ability to make objects invisible."

Four

Bane lifted a brow. "Did you say your research was finding a way to make objects invisible?"

"Yes. Although it hasn't been perfected yet, it won't be long before I perform the first test."

Because he was a SEAL, Bane was aware of advances in technology that most people didn't know about, especially when it came to advanced weapons technology. But he'd never considered that objects could become invisible to the naked eye. He could imagine the chaos it would cause if such a thing fell into the wrong hands.

"And you think this note is legit?" he asked.

"If I doubted it before, that phone call pretty much proved otherwise. That's why I'm leaving."

He nodded. "And that's why I'm going with you."

She shook her head. "You can't go with me, Bane, and I don't have time to argue with you about it. I need to get to the airport."

Argue?

It suddenly dawned on him that in all the years he and Crystal had been together, mostly sneaking around to do so, they'd never argued. They had always been of one accord, always in sync with their thoughts, plans and ideas. The very concept of them not agreeing about something just couldn't compute with him. Of course it would be logical not to be in complete harmony since they were different people now.

Even so, him going with her was not up for discussion.

"How were you planning to get to the airport? Drive?" he asked her.

She shook her head. "No. I was going to call a cab and leave my car here."

"Then, I will take you. We can talk some more on the way."

"Okay, let me close up everything. Won't take but a second."

His gaze followed her movements as she went from room to room turning off lights and unplugging electrical items. Her movements were swift, yet sexy as hell and his body responded to them. She'd always had a cute shape, but this grown-up Crystal was rocking curves like he couldn't believe.

Earlier she had asked how he'd maintained his sanity without sex. He wondered how she'd maintained hers. They had enjoyed each other and he was convinced the only reason she hadn't gotten pregnant was because when it came to her, he'd always been responsible. A teenage pregnancy was something neither of them had needed to deal with.

She leaned down to pick up something off the floor and the way the denim stretched across her shapely backside sent heat rushing through him. He drew in a deep breath. Now was not the time to think about how hot his wife was. What should be consuming his mind was finding out the identity of the person responsible for her fleeing her home. Whoever was messing with her would definitely have to deal with him.

"At least I'm going where there's plenty of sunshine."

His brow furrowed. Did she honestly think there was sunshine in Chicago this time of the year? She met his gaze and he knew from the uh-oh look on her face that she'd unintentionally let that slip.

He was reminded now that although they'd never argued, they had lied quite a few times. But never to each other. Mainly the fibs had been for their families. They'd gotten good at it, although Dillon would catch Bane in his lies more often than not.

Crossing the room, Bane stopped in front of her. "You lied to me about where you're going, didn't you?"

She took a deep breath and he could hear the beats of her heart. They were coming fast and furious. Bane wasn't sure whether her heart was pounding because he was confronting her about the lie or because his nearness unnerved her like hers did him. Even when he should be upset about her lying to him, all he wanted to do was lean in closer and taste her again.

"Yes, I lied. I'm not going to Chicago but to the Bahamas. But when I lied about it, it was for your own good."

"For my own good?" he repeated as if making sure he'd heard her right.

"Yes. In the past I was the reason you got into trouble. Now you're a SEAL and I won't be responsible for you getting into more trouble on my account."

He stared at her. Didn't she know whatever he'd done

in the past had been of his own free will? During those days he would have done anything to be with her. There was no way he could have stayed away as her father had demanded. Her parents hadn't even given them a chance just because Bane's last name was Westmoreland. Although Carl Newsome had claimed Bane's age had been the major factor, Bane often wondered if that was true.

Everyone knew how much he'd loved Crystal. Members of his family had thought he was insane, and in a way he had been. Insanely in love. Hadn't his brother Riley even told him once that no man should love any female that much? Bane wondered if Riley was singing that same tune now that he was married to Alpha. Bane doubted it. All it took was to see his brother and Alpha together to know Riley now understood how deeply a man could love a woman.

"Crystal?" he said, trying to keep his voice on a serious note because he knew she actually believed what she'd said. "Stop thinking you're the reason I was such a badass back in the day. When I met you I was already getting into trouble with the law. After I hooked up with you, I actually got in less trouble."

She rolled her eyes. "That's not the way I remember it."

"You remember it the way your parents wanted you to remember it. Yes, I deliberately defied your father whenever he tried keeping us apart, but it wasn't as if I was a gangster or anything."

A smile curved his lips as he continued, "At least not after meeting you. With you I was on my best behavior. You even nailed the reason I behaved that way. You're the one who pointed out it had everything to do with the loss of my parents and aunt and uncle in that plane crash. The depth of our grief overpowered me, Bailey and the twins, and getting into trouble was our outlet. That just goes to show how smart you were even back then, and your theory made sense. Remember all those long talks we used to have?"

She nodded. "Yes, by the side of the road or in our private place. Our family thought all those times the sheriff found us that we were making out in your truck or something. And all we'd been doing was talking. I tried telling my parents that but they wouldn't listen. You were a Westmoreland and they wanted to think the worst. They believed I was sexually active when I wasn't."

He recalled those times. Yes, they had been caught parking, and cutting school had become almost the norm, but all they'd done was spend time together talking. He'd refused to go all the way with her until she was older. The first time they'd had sex was when she'd turned seventeen. By then they'd been together almost two years.

At least Dillon had believed Bane when he'd told his brother he hadn't touched her. However, given their relationship, it would have been crazy to think they wouldn't get around to making love one day, and Dillon had had the common sense to know that. Instead of giving Bane grief about it, his older brother had lectured him about being responsible and taking precautions.

Bane would never forget the night they'd finally made love. And it hadn't been in the backseat of his truck. He had taken her to the cabin he'd built as a gift for her seventeenth birthday. He'd constructed it on the land he was to inherit, Bane's Ponderosa.

It was a night he would never forget. Waiting had almost done them in, but in the end they'd known they'd done the right thing. That night had been so unbeliev-

ably special and he'd known she would be his forever.
He knew on that night that one day he would make her
his wife.

In fact it had been that night when he'd asked her to
marry him once she finished school, and she'd agreed.
And that had been the plan until her parents made things
even worse for them after she'd turned seventeen.

Crystal had retaliated by refusing to go to school.
And when her parents had threatened to have him put
in jail if he came on their property, he and Crystal had
eloped. He hadn't counted on her parents sending her
away the moment Sheriff Harper found them.

Bane had come close to telling everyone they'd gotten married; no one had the right to separate them. But
something Dillon had said about the future had given
him pause.

Once he'd revealed they were married, he'd known
Crystal would not go back to school. And he of all people had known just how smart she was.

That was when he'd decided to make the sacrifice
and let her go. That had been the hardest decision he'd
ever made. Lucky for him, Bailey had put her pickpock-
eting skills to work and swiped old man Newsome's cell
phone to get Crystal's aunt's phone number.

"I need to go, Bane," Crystal said, intruding into his
memories. "I'll give you my number and we can talk
when I get to where I'm going."

Then in a rush, she added, "I'll call to let you know
when I arrive in the Bahamas so you'll know I'm okay."

He stared at her. Evidently she didn't get it and it was
about time that she did. "Crystal," he said in what he
hoped was a tone that grabbed her absolute attention.
When she stared at him he knew it had. "If you think
I'm going to let you disappear on your own, then you

really don't know me. The old Bane did let you disappear when your father sent you away. But at the time I figured it was for your own good. But those days are over. There's no way in hell you're disappearing on me again."

From her blistering scowl he could tell she didn't appreciate what he'd said. When she opened her mouth to reply, he quickly held up his hand. "I know it's been five years and that we have changed. But there's something with us that hasn't changed."

"What?" she asked in an annoyed tone.

"No matter what happens, we're in this together. That's how things have always been with us, right?"

"Yes, but that was then, Bane."

"And that's how it is now. We're married," he said, touching the locket he'd given her on their wedding day. Just knowing she was still wearing it meant everything to him. "We're in this together, Crystal. Got that?"

For a minute Crystal didn't say anything and then through clenched teeth, she snapped, "Yes, I got it."

There was no way she could *not* get it when he'd spoken so matter-of-factly. She'd never liked being bossed around and he knew that, which was why he'd never done it before. They had understood each other so well. And in the past they'd made decisions together, especially those that defied anyone trying to keep them apart, whether it was her family or his.

But this Bane was difficult to deal with. Didn't he understand it was not in his best interest to go anywhere with her?

Without saying anything else she walked away, leaving him standing in the middle of her living room while she went into the kitchen to check the locks on the back door. She needed time alone. Time away from him. His unexpected arrival had torpedoed her world.

As soon as she was out of his view, she leaned against the kitchen counter and released a sigh as blood pounded through her body. The man she'd loved was back after five years. One moment she'd been rushing around, trying to disappear, and the next she was opening the door for Bane. They had been separated for so long she'd thought… What?

That he wasn't going to come for her. But if she'd really thought that then why hadn't she gotten on with her life?

There were a lot of other whys she needed answered. Why had he decided to become a SEAL? Placing his life at risk with each mission? Better yet, why had he wanted to be involved in something that would keep him from her longer? And why had he shown up today of all days, when her normal life was turned upside down?

On top of everything else, he wanted to take over, as if he'd been here all the time. As if she didn't know what she was doing. As if she hadn't taken care of her own business for the past five years without him.

"Need help in there?" he called out.

Crystal gritted her teeth. "No, I've got this." She crossed the kitchen floor to check the locks on the back door.

What did he expect of her? Of them?

And of all things, within ten minutes of being inside her house they had kissed. A kiss she'd initiated. He might have made the first move by lowering his head, but she had been the one to make the connection. The memory of their mouths locking and tongues tasting had her feeling all hot inside. It had definitely proved they were still attracted to each other. That kiss had snatched all her senses and made her weak in the knees. She was certain she could still taste him on her lips.

She pushed a strand of hair back from her face and walked out of the kitchen and stopped in the living room. Bane's back was to her as he stood in front of her fireplace, staring at the framed photographs on her mantel. Except for one picture of her parents, all the rest were of him or of her and him. Most had been taken when they'd dated and the others when they'd eloped.

He turned around and their gazes met. She almost forgot to breathe. Was that heat in her stomach? And why was her heart beating a mile a minute? She drew in a deep breath wondering what he was thinking. Had he remembered each and every moment in those pictures? Did he remember how in love they'd been? Did he realize, married or not, they were different people now and needed to get to know each other all over again?

Should they?

Could they?

She broke eye contact to look at where her luggage had been. Then she glanced back at him. "You've taken my bags out already?"

"Yes."

"I didn't hear anything. Not even the door open."

A smile tugged at the corner of his lips. "That's the way a SEAL operates."

Oh, God. That smile was turning her insides to mush.

A part of her wanted to race across the room and throw herself in his arms like she used to do. But she couldn't. As far as she was concerned, too much stood in the way, keeping them apart.

Five

"I was sorry to hear about your dad, Crystal," Bane said, after easing the car onto the interstate. "Although the two of us never got along, he was still your father."

He felt her gaze on him, and he wanted to take his eyes off the road and look at her but decided not to. She was gorgeous and every time he gazed at her he felt desire seep into his bones. He needed to keep his self-control so he could convince her that he was coming with her when she left town.

"Thanks. Sending me away to live with Aunt Rachel widened the chasm between us but we made amends before he died…as best we could, considering everything." She was quiet for a moment before continuing, "He even told me he loved me, Bane. And I told him I loved him, as well. Dad leaving me the ranch was a shocker because he said he would be selling it to make sure I never had a reason to return to Denver. But after he died I found out he had left it to me. I wasn't aware he still owned it and assumed he'd sold it like he said he would do."

Bane had assumed Mr. Newsome had sold it, as well. Whenever he came home, Dillon had mentioned that the Newsome place was still deserted, but Bane had assumed the repairs needed around the place hadn't made it an easy sale. But there was something else he'd wanted to tell her. "It's admirable that you're working on your PhD, Crystal. For someone who claimed they hated school, that's quite an accomplishment."

"No big deal. Since I didn't have a life I decided to go to school full-time. All year-round. Nonstop. And when I took a placement test, there were classes I didn't have to take. My parents were happy that I was focusing on my studies again."

And not on him, he thought, and then asked her the question that had nagged at him since he'd first seen her tonight. "How did you do it?"

"Do what?"

"Keep the guys away. You're a very beautiful woman so I'm sure plenty tried hitting on you."

He glanced over and saw the compliment had made her blush. He meant it. She had the kind of beauty he'd never been able to explain with words.

"The guys stayed away because they thought I was gay."

Bane almost swerved into another lane. Placing a tight grip on the steering wheel, he glanced over at her again. "They thought what?"

"That I was gay. I didn't have a boyfriend so what else were they to think? The rumor started in college when I refused all their advances, even the guys on the football team, who were in such high demand on campus. They figured if I wasn't into them, then I must be into females."

"Why didn't you tell them you were a married woman?"

"What good would that have done with a husband who never came around?"

He could imagine how she'd felt knowing a rumor was circulating about her. One that was false.

"I thought about you every day, Crystal."

"Did you?"

He heard the skepticism in her tone. Did she not believe him? He was about to question her when she said, "This isn't the way to the airport, Bane."

"We aren't going to the airport."

"Not going to the airport? And just when did you decide that?"

"When I noticed we were being followed."

They were being followed?

Crystal glanced over at Bane. "How do you know?"

"Because although the driver is trying to be inconspicuous, that blue car has been tailing us for a while."

"Blue car?"

"Yes."

Her muscles trembled. "The car that followed me earlier was blue. But how would he know to follow you when we're not in my car?"

"Evidently someone saw us getting into mine."

The feel of goose bumps moved up her neck. "If the person saw us leave that means he knows where I live."

"Pretty much. But don't worry about it."

His calm unnerved her. How could he tell her not to worry? It was her home they were talking about. Whoever was after her would probably trash her house looking for something that wasn't there.

As if Bane read her mind, he said, "The reason I told you not to worry is because Flip is watching your place for me."

She stared over at him. "Someone you know is watching my house?"

He exited off the interstate. "Yes. David Holloway is one of my team members, who happens to live here in Dallas. His code name is Flipper because he's the best diver on the team. I contacted him when my plane landed to let him know I was in town. I called him again when I took out your luggage. I noticed a strange car in the driveway across the street."

Crystal was trying hard to keep up. He didn't live in her neighborhood, so how could he tell when some car was out of place? "How did you know it was a strange car?"

"I sat in front of your place for two hours waiting for you to come home and it wasn't parked there then," he said, turning another corner.

She noticed they were driving in an area she wasn't familiar with and wondered where in the heck they were going. "That's it? You figured it was out of place because it hadn't been there earlier?"

"That was enough. I'm trained to take stock of my surroundings."

Evidently, she thought. "And this Flipper guy went to my house after we left?"

"He got there just as we were leaving. Flip and his brothers will be keeping an eye on the place while you're gone."

She arched a brow. "Brothers?"

Bane looked over at her when he brought the car to a stop at a traffic light. "Yes, he has four. All SEALs. Your place is in good hands for now."

She was glad to hear that, but she couldn't help wishing the only hands her house was in were hers. Granted, she leased it rather than owned it, but it was the only house she'd lived in since moving to Dallas. When she noticed him glancing in the rearview mirror and grinning she asked, "What's so funny?"

"Ambush. I deliberately had the driver of the blue car follow us here and Flip's brothers were waiting."

"How did they know?"

"When Flip's brothers noticed I was being followed, they followed the blue car. Then one of Flip's brothers passed the blue car and got in the front of us to lead me off the interstate. The others went ahead and were ready to stop the guy at that intersection back there."

Nervousness danced around in her stomach. "So now we can continue to the airport?"

"No," he said, pulling the car into what appeared to be the parking lot of an abandoned warehouse. After parking the car and turning off the lights, he grabbed the mobile phone he'd placed on the dashboard. He glanced down at it for a minute before looking back at her. "There might be others looking for us there."

"Why would you think that?"

He pushed back in the seat to stretch out his legs. "Remember those two men who approached you about coming to work for Homeland Security?"

"Yes, what about them?"

"It seems *they* are the bad guys."

Bane wished he could kiss the shocked look right off Crystal's face, beginning at her eyes and moving slowly downward to her lips.

"That's not possible," she said. "I saw their credentials."

"Whatever credentials they had were faked. The department they claimed to work for under Homeland Security doesn't even exist."

"Are you sure?"

"Positive. I texted a copy of that business card to a friend at Homeland Security and a few minutes ago he verified what I'd suspected."

He watched her nibble her bottom lip and wished seeing her do so didn't have such an arousing effect on him. He had to stay focused. "The mystery of that note bothers me."

"How so?"

"Did the person who wrote it have your best interest at heart, or did he or she advise you to disappear for a reason, hoping when you did it would make it easier for those guys to find you?"

She lifted a brow. "You think someone at Seton Industries, the person who put that note in my desk, is in cahoots with those two guys?"

"You have to admit that's a strong possibility. You said someone broke into your locker. Who would have access to that area other than another employee?"

Bane didn't like this. He and Crystal should be at her place talking about their future and how they would get beyond the five years they'd spent apart.

He started to say something else when his mobile phone rang with Flipper's ringtone. He grabbed it off his dashboard. "What you got, Flip?"

"A bunch of crazies, man. No sooner than you and the blue car pull off, a black sedan pulled up and two goons got out. It was like watching a scene out of *Men in Black* with both of them dressed in black suits and all. Not sure how they planned to break into your wife's place but there's no doubt in my mind that was their intent. Until…"

Bane lifted a brow. "Until what?"

"Until they noticed the infrared beam Mark had leveled in the center of their chests. I guess knowing we could blow their guts out freaked them, especially since we could see them but they couldn't see us. I've never seen two men run back to their car so fast."

Bane shook his head. "You and your brothers are having fun with this, aren't you?"

"Yes, I guess you can say that."

Flip would. Although Bane hadn't met any of Flipper's brothers, he'd heard about them. They had inherited their thirst for excitement and danger from their father, who'd retired as a SEAL. "What about the driver of the blue car?"

"He got out and hauled ass. Left the car running. You said not to shoot anybody so my brothers let him go. Sure you don't want to involve the cops?"

"Not yet." Bane told Flipper about who he figured the men in black were.

"Impersonating government officials isn't good," Flipper said.

Bane had to agree. He glanced over at Crystal and saw she'd been trying to follow his conversation. "You're right. But at least you put the fear of God in them. However, don't be surprised if they come back."

"We'll be ready. Take care of yourself and your lady."

Bane nodded. "I intend to."

He had barely clicked off the phone when Crystal asked, "They broke into my house?"

Her shoulders sagged and he wished he had told Flipper it was okay for his brothers to shoot the bastards after all. He hated that she was going through this. "No, but that had been their intent. Flipper and his brother ran them off." There was no need telling her the method they'd used to do so. "They'll be back if they believe you have information or data stored somewhere in your house."

"I don't."

"I doubt they know that, and the first place they'll look is your computer."

"So what now? Where do we go?"

He checked his watch. It was late. "Find a hotel."

She narrowed her eyes. "Why?"

Not for the reason I want, he thought, again remembering the last time he'd been in a hotel room with her. The memory of her naked on that bed and all they'd been doing before the sheriff had shown up was what had kept him sane during dangerous missions.

"We're going to a hotel to sleep and put a plan of action in place, Crystal. As much as I want to make love to you, I've got a feeling the want isn't mutual."

Which meant it would be a long night.

Six

Crystal broke eye contact with Bane to look out the car window. Of course going to a hotel made sense, but still…

She'd seen the way he'd looked tonight, and she knew that look. Had even fantasized about it a number of times over the years. The memories of what followed that look always made her hot inside. But she wasn't sure she could trust herself alone with him. Her attraction to him was stronger than ever.

"Or we can stay here. Parked," he said, interrupting her thoughts.

She looked over at him. "All night?"

He gave her a smile that had heat swirling in her stomach. "Won't be anything new for us. In fact, it would be just like old times."

Why did he have to go there? Being in a parked car with him would definitely be like old times, but she was no longer a teenager who thought she could never get enough of Bane Westmoreland. She was a woman on the run with a husband she no longer knew. "We're too old for parked cars, Bane."

"I know. That's why I suggested a hotel."

She turned toward him. It was time to burst his bubble. "If we go to a hotel we get separate rooms."

"Why? We're married."

She tried to ignore the sexiness of his voice. And she definitely didn't need to notice the electricity sizzling in the air between them. Yes, they were married, but hadn't it already been established that things had changed? That *they* had changed? For starters, she was no longer a dreamer but a realist. And he was no longer the guy who claimed she would always be his love for life. Apparently the navy had booted her aside.

"Legally yes, we are married, but that's about all. Five years is a long time. We've already established that we're different people now. You may not like the new me, and for all I know I may not like the new you."

"I don't *like* you, Crystal. Never have. I fell in love with you the first time I saw you."

Now, why would he go and say something like that? If he really felt that way, wouldn't he have come back long before now? And why was she now remembering that day when she had been walking home from school, minding her own business, and he'd passed her on his motorcycle. He'd made a U-turn and the moment he'd stopped his bike, taken off his helmet and turned those hazel eyes on her, she'd been lost. So if he wanted to say that he'd fallen in love with her the moment he'd first seen her, she could certainly make that same claim about him.

But there were still those five years apart between them.

"Will it make you feel better if there were two beds in the room?"

Crystal took a breath. *Not really.* Even after being separated for five years she still found him captivating. Even now, tingles of awareness were invading her entire body. She couldn't look at any part of him without getting naughty thoughts. Being in close quarters with him all night would only be asking for trouble. She shook her head. "Doubt that will work, Bane."

He shrugged broad shoulders. "It will have to work, because I don't plan on letting you out of my sight until we get to the bottom of what's going on."

Her gaze narrowed on him. She was about to tell him that when it came to her he didn't make any decisions, when his cell phone went off again. He quickly reached for it. "Yes?"

Crystal studied his face. Whatever the caller was saying was making him angry. She could tell by the fire she saw forming in the depths of his eyes, the tightening of his jaw and the way his fingers gripped the phone. And she couldn't miss the abrasive tone of his voice.

She was certain the call was about her, which was why his gaze flicked to her time and time again. Gone was that hot and steamy I-can't-wait-to-get-some-of-you look in his eyes. It had been replaced with a look that clearly said that if pushed, Brisbane Westmoreland was liable to hurt somebody.

She pushed her hair back from her face and silently tapped her fingers on the car's console. She couldn't wait for the call to end so she could find out what was going on.

As soon as she heard him click off the phone she turned, ready to inquire, but he held up a finger to silence her. Already he had clicked someone else's number. He then quickly barked the words into his phone. "Code purple. Will enlighten everyone in a few."

As soon as he disconnected the call she asked, "What was that about?"

He didn't say anything for a long moment. He just stared at her as if he was trying to make up his mind about something.

She frowned and said, "And don't you dare think about not telling me what's going on, Bane."

Bane had contemplated doing just what she'd accused him of. But he knew he couldn't. Crystal was too intelligent, too quick to figure out things. Besides, she needed to know what they were up against and the caution they would have to take.

But more than anything, he needed her to trust him and to believe that he would never let anyone touch a single hair on her head.

"Bane?"

He took a deep breath. "First, give me your cell phone."

"My cell phone?"

"Yes."

She stared at him for a second, then went into her purse to retrieve her phone. He took it and then got out of the car. Throwing the phone on the pavement and ignoring her shocked gasp, he used his foot to stomp it into pieces.

"Are you crazy? What do you think you're doing?" she asked in outrage after getting out of the car to save her phone. Of course it was too late.

"I'm destroying your phone."

She placed her hands on her hips and glared up at him. "I see that. What I want to know is why."

"There's a chance a tracking device is on it."

"What are you talking about?"

"Things are more serious than I thought or what you might know, Crystal."

She stiffened her spine. "Well, I've got news for you. I don't know anything other than what I received in that note today and that my locker was tampered with and a blue car has been following me."

He glanced around. "Come on, let's get back inside the car. I'll tell you what I know."

She looked down at her smashed phone in disgust before going around the front of the SUV to get back inside. As soon as they had gotten inside the car, she said, "Tell me."

She touched his arm and a surge of desire rushed through him. Evidently it shone in his eyes because she quickly snatched her hand away. "Sorry."

He grabbed her hand, entwined their fingers and met her gaze. "Don't ever apologize for touching me."

Instead of a response, she nervously swiped her tongue across her bottom lip and his own tongue tingled, dying to mate with hers. Since he figured he couldn't kiss her anytime soon, he would tell her what she wanted to know. What she needed to know.

Ignoring the thud in his chest from holding her hand in his, he said, "My contact at Homeland Security did some more digging, even went so far as to tap into classified information. It seems you've been watched for a while."

She lifted a brow. "By who?"

"Mainly the government. They are aware of the research you're working on."

She shrugged. "I figured they were. Seton sent periodic reports to them as part of national security. Besides, the funding for my research was a grant subsidized by the government."

"Well, it seems the report got into the hands of someone it shouldn't have. To make a long story short, a plan was devised to kidnap you and the two other biochemists working on similar projects. They were to take the three of you to a lab underground somewhere and force you to work together and perfect a formula they'd use to their advantage."

Crystal shook her head. "That plan is preposterous."

Bane wished she wouldn't do that. Shake her head and make her hair fan across her face and place more emphasis on her dark eyes. Momentarily he lost his concentration. He couldn't afford any distractions now. There was too much at stake. "Whoever came up with the idea evidently didn't think so. And now you're the missing link."

She leaned back and frowned. "What do you mean I'm the missing link?"

His hand tightened on hers. "The other two chemists were abducted yesterday. One was leaving his home for work and the other chemist was leaving the gym around noon. The plan was to kidnap the three of you within hours of each other. However, their plan to grab you was foiled. But since they are determined to get their hands on the formula, they won't give up."

The spark in her eyes told him she clearly understood what he was saying. She was vital to these guys' plans and they didn't intend to fail. That spark also told him something else. She would like to see them try to grab her. He still had the ability to read her mind sometimes. She still had the spunk he'd always admired in her.

He swallowed hard when she eased her hand from his and broke eye contact to gaze out of the car's windshield. She was thinking, trying to come up with her own plan. One that didn't include him. More for his safety than anything else, he figured. And while she was spending that time thinking, he was spending his time feeling possessive, protective and proactive. If anyone thought they would grab her from him, then they didn't know Bane Westmoreland.

She looked back at him and because he had a feeling he knew what she was about to say, he cut her off before she could start. "I won't leave you unprotected, so forget it."

When she just continued to look at him, he added, "I need you to trust my ability to keep us safe."

A ripple of awareness floated between them and he tried to ignore it. Knowing he had her trust was more important at the moment.

"It's going to be hard, Bane," she said softly. "I've been on my own for a long time."

Five years. And not for the first time he wondered if he'd done the right thing in staying away. She had been his wife, yet he'd left her believing that living apart was the best thing for both of them. That they'd both needed to grow up and mature. Especially him. And he had. But what if he hadn't shown up today? What if she'd gotten kidnapped like those other two chemists? What if—

"I will trust you in this, Bane."

Her words intruded into his thoughts. He nodded. He was more than ready to be the husband she deserved, but he had to show her that she could trust him. Not just to keep her safe, but to build a life with her.

"So…" she said with a heavy sigh. "What now?"

A smile touched his lips. "Now we show them that together we're a force to reckon with."

A force to reckon with.

Crystal couldn't help but smile. That was how Sheriff Harper used to describe them. Nothing, not even the threat of jail time, could keep Bane from her or her from him. They'd been that fixated on each other.

Bane's cell phone signaled a text massage had come through and he grabbed the phone off the dashboard. Out the car window she saw they were parked in an unlit area. The only illumination was from the stars and moon overhead. Bane read the text with his full attention while her full attention was on him. She couldn't help but admire the way his wide shoulders fit his leather jacket and the casual way he sat in his seat. He had pushed the seat back to accommodate his long legs. And speaking of those long legs…

She loved how they looked bare, whenever he went swimming, and when they were covered in jeans, like they were now. Or when he rode his motorcycle or one of the horses from his family ranch. She'd known how to ride when she met him, but with his help, she had perfected the skill. He'd also taught her how to ride a motorcycle, shoot a gun and climb mountains. She had shared his love for the outdoors and they would spend time together outside whenever they could.

She swept her gaze over him from head to toe, thinking he was definitely sheer male perfection, the epitome of every woman's fantasy. It was only when he'd cleared his throat that she realized he had finished reading the text and had caught her ogling him.

"Yes? Did you say something?"

He chuckled. "No. Just wanted you to know that our ride will be here in a few minutes."

She lifted a brow. "Our ride?"

"Yes. We're changing vehicles. Chances are the people looking for you have already ID'd this one, so we need to swap it out."

"So who's bringing us another vehicle?" she asked,

glancing out the window. Other than a huge vacant building, the parking lot was empty.

"Flip's dad."

She frowned. "His dad?"

"Yes. He's an ex-SEAL."

Moments later Crystal heard the sound of another vehicle pull up and noted the driver had turned out the headlights. Bane looked over at her.

"That's our ride."

Seven

Bane gathered their belongings out of the SUV so they could place them in the trunk of the car Mr. Holloway had delivered.

Flip favored his father. Same shade of blue eyes and blond hair, although the older man had streaks of gray. It was easy to tell the man had been a SEAL. A commanding officer. He was still alert and wore an intense look on his face. And it was quite obvious that even at the age of sixty-five, he was in great shape physically. He was ready for anything and could probably still hold his own.

"Don't need to know where you're headed. The less people who know the better. Just be safe," the older man said, handing Bane the keys.

"I will, and thanks for everything, Mr. Holloway. I owe you and your family."

Mr. Holloway waved off his words. "No, you don't.

David told me and his brothers what happened during your last mission when you saved his life. Besides, any friend of my boys is a friend of mine. If you get in a pinch, just give us a call."

Bane didn't plan on getting in a pinch, but figured it was best to accept the offer just the same. "I will, and thanks."

Crystal was already seated inside the new car with her seat belt snapped in place. The older man followed Bane's gaze. "I understand that's your wife who you haven't seen in a while."

Bane nodded as he looked back at the man. "Yes, that's right."

"And she waited for you to come back for all that time?"

Bane nodded, remembering what Crystal had told him. She had kept her promise like he'd kept his. "Yes, she waited."

The older man smiled. "Then, you're a very lucky man. Take care of yourself and your wife."

His wife. He liked the sound of that. He was ready to finally claim her as his wife—but he had to keep her safe first. "I will. Again, thanks for all you and your sons have done. Are still doing." He knew Flip and his brothers would be keeping an eye on Crystal's place for a while.

"Don't mention it." Mr. Holloway gave him a supportive pat on the shoulder before getting into the SUV to drive off.

Bane quickly walked to the car, got inside, closed the door and locked it.

Crystal glanced over at him. "Where to now?"

He could hear the exhaustion in her voice. It was close to eleven. Probably past her bedtime. "A hotel, but not here in Dallas. Get some sleep. We'll be riding for a while."

"Okay."

She didn't ask where they were headed and as he started the ignition, he watched her lower her seat into a reclining position. He couldn't stop his appreciative gaze from sweeping over her, taking in how the denim molded to her hips and thighs. At eighteen she'd had a slender figure. Now she was amazingly curvy with a small waist. Forcing his eyes off her, he adjusted the car's temperature to a comfortable setting. It had gotten pretty cold outside.

As he pulled out of the parking lot he saw her starting to doze off. She looked just as beautiful with her eyes closed as she did when they were open. This was what he had dreamed about, what he had craved. The two of them together again.

Bane had driven a few miles and had made it to their first traffic light when he heard the sound of her chuckle. He glanced over at her and saw that her eyes were closed, yet a smile had formed on her lips. Was she having a dream or something? No sooner had that thought entered his mind than she opened her eyes, saw him looking at her and shifted upright in her seat. "What's wrong?" she asked.

"Nothing is wrong with me. You chuckled in your sleep just now."

A smile touched her lips. "I wasn't asleep. Just resting my eyes. And I got to thinking that this is getting to be the norm for us."

"What?"

"Being on the run. The last time we were together we eloped and were running from Sheriff Harper. Remember?"

"Yes, I remember." How could he forget? They had intentionally led everyone on a wild-goose chase thinking they were headed to Vegas when they'd married in Utah.

"Now we're on the run from heaven knows who."

"Doesn't matter. We're together again," he said.

She didn't say anything, and when the traffic light changed, he moved forward. After a while he figured she'd dozed off…or as she put it, had gone back to resting her eyes, when she asked, "For how long, Bane?"

Grateful for another traffic light, he brought the car to a stop and glanced over at her. "How long?"

"Yes, how long will we be together before you leave? Before I'm all alone again? You're a SEAL. That means you'll be gone a lot, right?"

He hesitated for a moment, giving thought to how he would respond. If she thought he would allow her to use his being a SEAL against him, against them, then she was definitely wrong. "Yes, I might be gone on missions whenever my CO calls."

"Your CO?"

"Commanding officer."

"And what if he calls now? You'll have to go, won't you?"

He tightened his grip on the steering wheel. Was she trying to insinuate that when it came to her he wasn't dependable? "Unless there's a national threat of some kind, it won't happen. I'm on military leave. My entire team is."

"Why?"

Now, this was where things got kind of sticky. He had to let her know that parts of his job weren't up for discussion, but he'd save that heart-to-heart conversation for later. Right now he merely said, "We were due one." That was the truth, although he wasn't telling her everything.

"You take risks. Put your life in danger."

Now it was his turn to chuckle.

"What's so funny?" she asked.

"I was just thinking that right now it's not my life that's in danger. I'd say we both have unusual occupations."

"There's nothing unusual about mine. I just happen to be working on research that's pretty sensitive."

He smiled, figuring that was one way of looking at it. "I guess you can say I work on things that are pretty sensitive, as well."

"There's no comparing what we do so don't even try, Bane."

Okay, so she had a point. But still, like he'd told her, he wasn't the one in danger now. "I'm well trained in what I do. Six months ago I made master sniper." That had been a major accomplishment for someone who was new on the team. But Bane's skills as a sharpshooter were what had caught the eye of his chief in boot camp. When he discovered Bane could hit a bull's-eye target with one eye closed, the man had put the thought of becoming a SEAL in Bane's head. The chief had made the captain aware of Bane's skill and the captain had pulled a lot of strings to get him into the naval academy.

"Master sniper? That doesn't surprise me. You were the one who taught me and Bailey how to shoot. And you always held your own against JoJo."

Yes, he had, he remembered proudly. And the Westmorelands sure knew how to shoot. He hadn't been surprised when he'd gotten home and everyone had told him about that grizzly bear Bailey had taken down in Alaska last month. And Crystal had been just as good a shot as Bailey. Only person better than those two was JoJo, who was now married to his brother Stern.

"And you want me to think your job isn't dangerous, Bane?"

"I admit it's dangerous, but it's also rewarding."

He heard her snort before she said, "I can see you think it's rewarding because it gives you an excuse to kick ass in the name of your country."

He laughed, and considering everything, it felt good to laugh. Especially with her. She always had a knack for bringing humor to any situation, although he was convinced what she'd just said hadn't been meant to be funny.

"You're making a career out of it, though, aren't you?"

Was she seriously asking or did she think she had everything figured out already? "Not sure. It's a decision we will have to make together."

"Oh, no, don't pull me into this, Bane. I won't let you blame me for making your life miserable."

Making his life miserable? What was she talking about? "Define what you mean."

"Gladly. I can see you as a SEAL, and a darn good one. What I don't see is you going into the office at Blue Ridge Management every day. You'd go stark crazy sitting behind a desk. And you'd never forgive me if you saw me as the reason you had to go work there."

She knew him well and was right about his not wanting to work at his family's company. Although his brothers—Dillon, Riley, Canyon and Stern—as well as his cousin Aidan were a perfect fit for Blue Ridge Land Management, he wasn't.

"I could join Jason, Derringer and Zane in their horse-training business," he said. Honestly, he couldn't imagine doing that, either. He didn't have the same love of horses that his brother and two cousins had.

"Bailey told me about their company the last time we talked."

"But she wouldn't tell you anything about me," he said in a gruff tone.

Crystal frowned at him. "That was the rule, Bane, and need I remind you that it was your idea." She broke eye contact with him to glance out the side window.

Yes, it had been. And it was time they talked about it. He suddenly felt the tension flowing in the car between them and didn't like it. "You know why I made my decision, Crystal."

"The decision to desert me?"

He quickly swerved off the road and whipped into the parking lot of what looked like an all-night truck stop. He pulled in between two tractor trailers, which concealed them from the view of anyone driving by. He brought the car to a stop and turned off the ignition.

"Are you trying to kill us, Bane?" she asked, trying to catch her breath.

Instead of answering, he unsnapped his seat belt and turned toward her. "I know you didn't just say that I deserted you."

Crystal could tell Bane was furious. She'd seen him angry before, but his anger had never been directed at her. Now it was. He was glaring at her to the point where the color of his eyes seemed to take on a Saint Patrick's Day green. But she had a feeling it was not her lucky day. Not backing down, she lifted her chin. "And what if I did?"

"Then, we need to talk."

"Too late for that. Nothing you say will make me change the way I feel."

"Then, you need to tell me why you feel that way."

He really didn't know? She would find the whole thing amusing but instead she wanted to cry. She had loved him so much. He had been her world. The yang to her yin. The one person she'd thought would never hurt her or let her down. But he had.

"Crystal?"

Fine, if he wanted to pretend he didn't know why she felt the way she did then she'd tell him. "I understand why you let my father send me away after we eloped but—"

"It was for the best. You were going to drop out of school, Crystal. I couldn't let you do that. I couldn't interfere with your education. It was November. All you had to do was make it to June to graduate."

"I know all that," she snapped. "So I let my father think he was calling the shots when he sent me to live with Aunt Rachel." The memory of that day still scorched her brain whenever she thought about it. "I figured I could put up with it because you would come and get me in June after I finished high school."

She saw the look in his eyes, knew the exact moment he figured out where she was going with this. She took a deep breath and plunged forward. "When you finally called me in January, I thought it was to tell me you couldn't live without me and had decided to come for me early. And that I could finish school back in Denver while we lived together in the cabin you had built for me. As man and wife."

"Dammit, Crystal, I know you. If I had come for you early, you would have come up with all kinds of excuses not to go back to school. Plus, I wouldn't have been able to support you. I wasn't old enough to claim my land or my trust fund. When I finished high school, my income came from working odd jobs. I walked off the job Dillon gave me at Blue Ridge at the end of the first week. I didn't like my supervisor telling me what to do. I was a Westmoreland. My family owned the damn company and I figured that gave me the right to do whatever the hell I wanted."

"I would have gone back to school, Bane. I promised you that I would. And as far as you not having a stable income, we would have made it work."

"You deserved more."

"I thought I deserved you. I was your wife."

"Why can't you understand that I needed to make something of myself?" he asked in an agitated tone. "As your husband, I owed that to you. Why can't you see that you deserved better than what I was at the time? I was an undisciplined man without any goals in life. I enjoyed defying authority."

"Those things didn't matter to me, Bane."

"They should have."

She narrowed her gaze at him. "Your family got to you, didn't they? Convinced you we didn't belong together. So you told no one we were married. No one but Bailey."

She watched him rub his hands down his face in frustration. As far as she was concerned, he had no right to be frustrated. She was the one he'd forgotten about when he'd chosen a career as a SEAL over her.

"You're wrong about my family, Crystal. They knew how much I loved you, but they saw what we refused to see. They knew we couldn't keep going the way we were headed. So I made a decision that I felt was best for us. And I want to believe that it was. Look at you now.

You not only finished high school, but you went on to college and got your master's degree and are working on your PhD. You were always smart and I was holding you back. Had I been selfish enough to claim you as my wife, I would have taken you to that cabin and made a pitiful life for you there. And it would have been just our luck if you'd gotten pregnant. What sort of future would our kid have had?"

She quickly turned her face away so he wouldn't see the tears in her eyes, but she hadn't been quick enough. Bane knew her. He could read her when she didn't want to be read. And she knew he was doing it now when he reached out, used his finger to turn her face back toward him. He studied her features intently.

Moments later he narrowed his gaze. "What's wrong? What aren't you telling me, Crystal?"

She knew she had to tell him. There was no reason to keep her secret any longer. "That day when you called and told me you had decided to go into the navy, you asked me if I was pregnant and I told you no."

He didn't say anything for a minute and a part of her knew he'd already guessed what she was about to say. "But you lied, didn't you? You *were* pregnant, weren't you?" he said in an accusing tone.

She didn't say anything for a long moment and then answered, "I didn't lie. When you asked, I wasn't pregnant…any longer. I had miscarried our baby, Bane. A few days before. The day you called was the day Aunt Rachel brought me home from the hospital."

Eight

Bane literally buckled over as if he'd been kicked in the gut. In a way he had. He drew in a deep breath as if doing so would ease the pain. It took a few moments for him to get himself together, and when he looked over at Crystal, she was sitting up straight in her car seat and the first thing he noticed were the tears streaming down her face.

His breath caught. He'd always been a sucker for tears…especially hers. But a part of him couldn't ignore that she'd been pregnant with their child and hadn't told him. Although he hadn't known where her parents had sent her, other than to live with some aunt, she had known how to reach him. And she hadn't even tried.

He recalled the days he had waited by the phone, figuring she would get around to contacting him somehow to let him know where she was. And when she hadn't, he'd figured her parents had probably talked the same sense into her that Dillon had talked into him. It was then and only then, that he had made the decision to follow Dillon's advice and make something of himself before going to claim her.

Trying to pull himself together and keep the anger out of his voice, he asked, "How could you not tell me?"

She looked over at him. "I didn't tell you because you'd already made up your mind about what you wanted to do."

"Dammit, Crystal, I only went into the navy because—"

"You thought I deserved more. You've said that."

A muscle in his jaw ticked. When had she developed such a damn attitude? He felt anger beginning to roll around in his stomach and he worked hard to control it because he'd never lost his temper with her. "Yes, I said it and I will keep on saying it."

Neither of them spoke for a while and the silence between them was thick, full of the tension he knew they both felt. "When did you know you were pregnant?" he finally asked her.

Tears reappeared in her eyes and she swiped them away. "That's the thing, Bane. I didn't know. I was late but I'd been late before, you know that. So I really didn't think anything about it. I was trying to fit into a new school and was focusing on my studies. It was nearing the end of January and I was looking forward to you coming to get me by June. Silly me, I figured even if you didn't know where I was that you would look for me until you found me.

"Anyway, I got really bad stomach pains one night. When I went to the bathroom I noticed I was bleeding profusely and woke up my aunt. She took me to the emergency room and after checking me over, the doctor told me I'd been pregnant and had lost the baby.

They kept me in the hospital overnight because I'd lost a lot of blood."

She swiped at her eyes again. "How can a woman be pregnant and not know it? How could I have carried your baby—our baby—in my body and not know it? That seemed so unfair, Bane. So unfair. The doctor was a nice woman. She said miscarriages weren't uncommon and usually happen within the early weeks of pregnancy. I figured I'd gotten pregnant on our wedding night so I was less than eight weeks along. She assured me it wasn't because of anything I did, and that my next pregnancy should go smoothly."

A deep pain sliced through Bane. It had been his baby as well, and at that moment he mourned for the loss of a life that would never be. A baby that had been a part of him and a part of her. He wanted to reach out and pull Crystal into his arms. Hold her. Share the pain. He felt he had every right to do that. But then he also felt she'd put an invisible wall between them and he would need to tear it down, piece by piece.

"I'm sorry about our baby," he said, meaning every word. It was true he'd gotten careless on their wedding night. It had been the first time they'd ever spent the entire night together, wrapped in each other's arms, and he had been so overjoyed he'd gotten carried away and hadn't used a condom. "I never deserted you, Crystal. I could no more do that than cut off my arm. Do you have any idea what I went through when we were apart?" he asked softly. "How much I suffered each day not knowing where you were?"

"I called you."

"When?"

"As soon as I could get away from my parents. They kept an eye on me during the entire plane trip to South

Carolina, but when the plane landed I went into the ladies' room and asked some woman to use her cell phone. It was around five hours after we parted."

Bane frowned. He hadn't gotten her call. But then he figured it out. "I know the reason why you couldn't reach me," he said, remembering that day. "I was at the cabin, and there's no phone reception out there."

He paused and then added, "After Sheriff Harper told me you'd left Denver, I stormed out of the police station and got into my truck and went to your parents' place and found it deserted. I drove around awhile, getting angrier by the minute. Somehow I ended up at the cabin and I stayed there for two whole days. On the third day Riley came and convinced me to go home with him."

She nodded. "That's probably why I still couldn't reach you the next night, either. I waited until everyone had gone to bed and sneaked downstairs and used my aunt's phone. I couldn't get you, which was just as well because Dad caught me trying. He got upset all over again, and said he knew I would try calling you and figured it was time for me to know the truth."

Bane frowned. "What truth?"

"That he and your brother Dillon had met when we first went missing and made a deal."

"What kind of a deal?"

"The two of them agreed that when we were found, Dillon would keep you away from me and Dad was to keep me away from you."

"That's a damn lie!" Bane said bluntly, feeling red-hot anger flow through him.

"How can you be so sure?"

Her question only infuriated him more. "First of all, Dil doesn't operate that way. Second, Dillon wasn't even in Denver when we eloped. He was somewhere in Wyoming following up on leads to learn more about my great-grandfather Raphel. Ramsey called Dil but he didn't get home until after we were found."

Bane angrily rubbed his hand over his head. "I can't believe you fell for what your dad said. You knew how much he despised the Westmorelands. Did you honestly think he and Dillon sat down and talked about anything?"

She lifted her chin. "I didn't want to believe it but…"

"But what?"

"I called you twice and you didn't take my calls."

"I didn't take them because I didn't get them," he said.

"Well, I didn't know that."

"You should have."

"Well, I didn't. And when you finally called me… two months later…it was to tell me you were going into the navy and it would be best for us to go our separate ways."

His frown deepened. "The reason it was two months later was because it took me that long to find out where you'd gone. And Bailey had to pickpocket your dad's phone to find out then. And as far as saying it was best for us to go our separate ways, that's *not* what I said."

"Pretty much sounded like it to me."

Had it? Frustrated, he leaned back in his seat, trying to recall what he'd said. Joining the navy had been a hard decision, but he'd made it after talking to his cousin Dare, who'd been in the marines. He'd also talked to Riley's best friend Pete. Pete's brother, Matthew, had joined the navy a few years before, and Pete had told Bane how much money Matthew had saved and how the military had trained him to work on aircrafts. Bane had figured going into the navy would not only teach him a skill but also get him out of Denver for a while. Being there without Crystal had made him miserable.

As he recalled all he'd said to her that day, he could see why she'd assumed it was a break-up call, considering the lie her father had told her. His only saving grace had been the promises he'd made to her that he would keep his wedding vows and would come back for her. That made him wonder…

"You think I deserted you. Did you not believe me when I told you that I would come for you once I made something of myself? And that I would keep my wedding vows?" he asked.

She glanced out the window before looking over at him. "Yes, at the time I believed you, although I sort of resented you for putting me out of your life even for a little while, for whatever the reason."

Her words took him by surprise. How could she think he would do such a thing? And she had said, "at the time I believed you." Did that mean at some point in time she had stopped believing? Now he wondered if he'd made a grave mistake not keeping the lines of communication open between them.

"I never put you out of my life and I had every intention of coming back for you. That never changed, Crystal. I thought about you every day. Sometimes every hour, minute and second. I longed for you. I went to bed every night needing you. There were days when I wasn't sure I could go on without you and wanted to give up. That's why I made sure Bailey didn't tell me where you were. Had I known, I would have given up for sure and come after you. And had you told me about your miscarriage, nothing would have stopped me from coming for you. Navy or no navy."

Unable to stop himself, he released his seat belt and reached out and unfastened hers before pulling her across the console to hold her in his arms.

Crystal buried her face in Bane's chest. She couldn't stop her tears from flowing and was surprised she had any tears left to shed. She'd figured she had gone through all of them when the doctor had broken the news to her that day that she had lost her baby. And then getting Bane's call, the same day she'd come home from the hospital, had been too much.

Her aunt Rachel had been wonderful and understanding, the one to hold Crystal each time she wept. And when she'd begged her aunt not to tell her parents about the baby, her aunt had given Crystal her word that she wouldn't. Whether it had been his intention or not, his phone call that day had made her feel as if he was turning his back on them and their love. Deserting her. It had been her aunt who had persuaded her to pull herself together and make decisions about her life…with or without Bane. So she had made them without him. But each time Bailey had called after that, a part of her had hoped it was Bane instead of his cousin. Then, when it had gotten too much for her to deal with, she'd had her number changed.

After listening to Bane's words just now, she remembered all too well how she had thought about him every day, sometimes every hour, minute and second, as well. He had longed for her, gone to bed needing her, and she had done the same for him. At one point she had been tempted to go to Denver to find him. But then she'd known he wouldn't be there and hadn't a clue where he would be. And at some point, how had he expected her not to doubt he still cared when he hadn't contacted her in five years?

"I'm fine now, Bane," she said, pushing back from him and wiping away her tears.

He looked down at her with an intense scrutiny that sent shivers through her body. "Are you, Crystal? Are you fine? Or will you hold it against me for wanting to give you the best of me?"

"I thought I already had the best of you, Bane. You didn't hear me complaining, did you?"

He didn't say anything and she used that time to scramble out of his lap and back into her seat. She stared out the window and could see from the reflection in the glass that he was staring at her.

Without turning back around to him, she asked, "Have you decided where we're going?"

He started the ignition. "Yes, I know where we're going."

Instead of telling her where, he pulled the car out of the parking spot and headed back to the main road.

Nine

"I'll take the bed closer to the door, Crystal," Bane said, dropping his luggage on the floor by the bed.

Instead of answering him, she merely nodded and rolled her luggage over to the other bed. Figuring that she had missed dinner, he'd stopped at an all-night diner to grab orders of chicken and waffles. Then he had driven four hours before finally settling at this hotel for the night. During that time she hadn't said one word to him, not a one. And her silence bothered the hell out of him. How could she be upset with him for wanting to give her a better life? How could she think he'd deserted her? It now seemed that not keeping in contact with her had been a mistake, but what she failed to understand was that she was his weakness.

She said she would have been satisfied with him just the way he was. Flaws and all. But she deserved more. Deserved better. No matter what she thought, he would always believe that. He would admit he had been separated from her longer than he'd planned, and for that he would take the blame. Five years was a long time to expect her to put her life on hold. But that was just it. He hadn't expected her to put her life on hold. He had expected her to make something worthwhile out of it, like he had been doing with his. And she had. She had finished high school, earned both bachelor and master's degrees and was now working on her PhD. All during the five years he'd been gone. Why couldn't she understand that when he'd decided to go into the navy, he'd believed that he was giving them both the chance to be all that they could be, while knowing in the end they would be together? They would always be together. Although he'd loved her more than life, he had been willing to make the sacrifice. Why hadn't she? Had he been wrong to assume that no matter what, their love would be strong enough to survive anything? Even a long separation?

"I need to take a shower."

His heart nearly missed a beat upon hearing the sound of her voice again. At least she was back to talking to him. "All right. I figure we'll check out after breakfast and head south."

"South?"

"Yes, but that might change depending on any reports I get from people I have checking on a few things."

"Is that what that Code Purple was all about?"

So she had been listening. "Yes. That's a code for my team. It means one of us is in trouble and all hands on deck."

"Oh, I see."

She then opened her luggage and dismissed him again. He placed his own travel bag on the bed and opened it. The first thing he came to was the satchel containing all the cards and letters he'd saved for her over the years. He had looked forward to finally giving them to her. But now...

"You haven't heard anything else about my home, have you?"

He looked over at her. Although she'd taken several naps while he'd been driving, she still looked tired and exhausted. However, fatigued or not, to him she looked beautiful. "No. Flip has everything under control."

She nodded before gathering a few pieces of clothing under her arms and heading for the bathroom, closing the door behind her. Deciding he would really try hard to not let her attitude affect his, he took the satchel and walked over to place it on her bed. It was hers. He had kept it for her and had lived for years just waiting for the day when he could give it to her. He wouldn't let the bitterness she felt keep him from giving it to her.

His phone beeped, letting him know he'd received a text message. He glanced at his watch. It was two in the morning. He pulled his phone from his jacket and read Flip's message. All quiet here.

He texted back. Let's hope things stay that way.

He tried to ignore the sound of running water. He could just imagine Crystal stripping off her clothes for her shower. He would love being in there with her, taking pleasure in stepping beneath the spray of water with her, lathering her body and then making love to her. He would press her against the wall, lift her up so her legs encircled his waist and then he would ease inside her. How many nights had he lain in bed and fantasized of doing that very thing?

To take his mind off his need to make love to his wife, he glanced around the hotel room, checking things out in case they needed to make a quick get-away. This room was definitely a step up from the one they'd shared on their wedding night. He'd taken her to a nice enough hotel in Utah, but tonight's room was more spacious. The beds looked warm and inviting and the decor eye-catching.

Crystal had accompanied him inside when he'd booked the room. He could feel her body tense up beside him when he'd told the hotel clerk he wanted one room. He'd then heard her sigh of relief when he'd added that he wanted a room with two beds.

He lifted a brow when his cell phone went off and he recognized the ringtone. It was a call from home. Dillon. He pulled his phone out of his back pocket again. "Yes, Dil?"

"You didn't call to let us know you'd made it to Dallas. Is everything okay?"

How could he tell his brother that no, everything wasn't okay? "Yes, I made it to Dallas. Sorry, I didn't call but things got kind of crazy."

"Crazy? Were you able to find Crystal?"

"Yes, went straight to her place but…"

"But the warm, cozy, loving reception that you had expected isn't what you got."

He shook his head. His brother could say that again. "I figured we would have to work through some issues, but I didn't expect her to open the door with a loaded gun in her hand, her luggage packed and a bunch of bad guys trying to kidnap her."

There was a pause and then Dillon said, "I think you need to start from the beginning, Bane."

Crystal toweled herself off and tried not to think of the man on the other side of the door. The man she had shared her first kiss with. Her body. The man who had been her best friend. The one who'd defied her father's threat of jail time just to be with her. And the man who was her husband.

She glanced at herself in the mirror. Did Bane see the changes? Did he like what he saw? She couldn't attribute her figure to spending time in the gym or anything. The changes had just happened. One day she was thin and then the next, right after she'd turned twenty, the curves had come. The guys at college had noticed it, too, and tried causing problems. That was when she wished she'd had a wedding ring on her finger that would have deterred their interest. Instead, she had this, she thought, glancing at her locket.

She brought it to her lips and kissed it. It had been what had kept her sane over the past five years. She would look at it and think of Bane and remember the promise. Even on those days she hadn't wanted to remember or thought he'd possibly forgotten.

Her heart began thumping in her chest when she recalled how he had looked at her a few times tonight. The last had been when she'd told him she was going to take a shower. Nobody could turn her on quicker with a mere look than Brisbane Westmoreland. When he had leveled those hazel eyes on her, she could feel her skin get flushed. He was the only one in his family with that eye color, which he'd inherited from his great-grandmother.

She slid into a pair of sweats and then pulled on an oversize T-shirt. Looking into the mirror again, she nervously licked her lips as she thought of Bane. *What a man. What a man.* She even used her hands to fan herself. A number of times on the ride tonight she had pretended to be asleep just so she could study him with-

out him knowing she was doing so. If his eyes weren't
bad enough, he had an adorable set of lashes. Almost
too long to be a man's. He had taken off his jacket
and she couldn't help but appreciate the breadth of his
shoulders. Bane was so well toned that it was obvious
he lifted weights or something. SEALs were known to
stay in shape. If it was required of them, then he was
passing that test with flying colors.

Knowing she had spent more time than she needed
in the bathroom, she gathered up her clothes in her arms
and slowly opened the door. She saw Bane sitting at the
desk staring at a laptop.

A laptop? How many times in the past when she'd
tried showing him how to surf the net had he claimed
he was technology challenged and just couldn't get the
hang of using a computer? She sniffed the air and picked
up the smell of coffee. Evidently he'd made a pot while
she was taking a shower. Coffee was something she'd
never acquired the taste for. She preferred hot chocolate or herbal tea.

Crystal cleared her throat. "I'm finished."

"Okay."

He didn't even turn around, but kept his back to her
as he stared at the computer screen. Shoving the clothes
she'd taken off earlier into the small travel laundry bag,
she turned to put it into her luggage and saw the satchel
on the bed. She picked it up. "You left something on
my bed."

It was then that he looked over his shoulder at her
and at that moment she wished he hadn't. Having those
hazel eyes trained on her was sending spikes of desire
up her spine. "I put it there. It's yours."

She lifted a brow. "Mine?"

"Yes." He turned back to his computer.

She glanced down at the satchel. "What's in it?"

Without turning back around to her he said, "Why don't you look inside and see?"

Bane returned his attention to the computer screen, or at least he pretended to. He'd known the moment Crystal had walked out of the bathroom. Hearing the door open had sent all kinds of arousing sensations through him. The last thing he needed was to glance over at her. His control wasn't all that great. Going without her for five years was playing havoc on his brain cells. Although he kept his eyes glued to the computer, he could hear her ease the leather strap of his satchel open. His wife never could resist her curiosity, and he'd known it.

"There are cards in here. A lot of cards and envelopes," he heard her say. Yet he still refused to turn around.

"Yes. I remembered your birthday, our wedding anniversary, Valentine's Day and Christmas every year. Although I couldn't mail them to you, I bought them anyway and tucked them inside my satchel. I knew one day, when we got back together again, I'd have them for you."

He could hear her shuffling through all those sealed envelopes. "There are letters in here, as well," she said.

"Yes. Most of the other guys had wives or significant others to write home to, but again, I couldn't do the same for you. So I got in the habit of writing you a letter whenever you weighed heavily on my mind." He hoped she could tell from the number of letters he'd written that she'd consumed his mind a lot of the time.

"Thanks, Bane. This is a surprise. I hadn't expected you to do this...for me."

This time he couldn't help but turn around when he said, "I would do just about anything for you, Crystal."

It never ceased to amaze him how easily he could make her blush. At least that hadn't changed. He could actually feel her gaze moving across his face as she held his stare and he wondered if she could feel him doing the same thing. Suddenly, she broke eye contact with him while drawing in a deep breath. He could see the nipples of her breasts pressing against the T-shirt she had on. It was supposed to fit large on her, but she still looked sexy as hell wearing it.

She glanced back down at the satchel. "I can't wait to read the cards and letters."

He nodded and then turned his attention back to his laptop just when the shrill ring of his mobile phone got his attention. He grabbed it off the desk. "This is Bane."

He nodded and his jaw tightened as he listened to what his friend was telling him. Nick Stover, who used to be a member of his SEAL team, had decided to leave the field and go work for Homeland Security when his wife gave birth to triplets. Bane appreciated his friend's inside scoop. But what he was telling him now had his temper rising.

When Nick was done, Bane said, "Okay. Thanks for letting me know so I can get in touch with Flip."

He clicked off the phone and immediately called Flipper. There was no doubt Crystal had stopped whatever she was doing to listen to his conversation. He would have to tell her what was going on. But first, he had a question for her. He turned around and saw her staring at him.

"Is there anything in your home you want saved?"

She frowned. "What?"

"I asked if there's anything in your house that you want to save."

He could tell by the look on Crystal's face that she was trying to figure out why he would ask her such a thing. Before he could explain himself further, he heard Flip pick up the phone. "This is Bane." He knew Nick had already relayed the same information to Flip that he'd just told him.

"Yes, there are some things she wants to save." Since Crystal hadn't answered his question, just continued to look at him like he'd grown a set of horns or something, he said to Flip, "I know for certain she'll want to save all the photographs on her fireplace mantel."

Crystal crossed the room to stand next to him. "Hold it! Why are you telling him that, Bane? What's happening to my house?"

Bane spoke into the phone. "I'll call you back in a sec, Flip." He then clicked off the phone and placed it back on the desk.

He regretted having to answer her question, but knew he had to. "In a couple of hours or so, your house will get burned down to the ground."

Ten

Crystal felt the room spinning and wondered if she was about to fall flat on her face. Bane was obviously wondering the same thing because he was out of his chair in a flash and had grabbed hold of her arm to steady her.

"I think you need to sit down, Crystal," he said, trying to ease her down into the chair he'd just vacated.

"No. I won't sit down," she said, telling herself she'd just imagined what he'd said about her house burning down. There was no way he could have said that. But all it took was to see the concerned look on his face to know she hadn't imagined anything at all.

"Why would anyone want to burn my house down?" She just couldn't fathom such a thing.

"Actually, it's not just anyone. The order came from Homeland Security."

Shock took over her features. "Homeland Security? Why would the government do something like that?"

"I told you about those other two chemists who were kidnapped. And now the kidnappers are trying to get their hands on you. It's a serious situation, Crystal, and you're talking about national security. As long as there's a possibility something is in your house connected to the project you're working on, then—"

"But I told you there wasn't. I never bring work home."

"The Department of Homeland Security can't take any chances. Without you the bad guys will try to piece together what they need, and DHS can't let them do that."

"Fine. Get them on the phone."

"Get who on the phone?"

"Someone at Homeland Security. Evidently you have their number. If they don't believe you, then maybe they will believe me."

"I can't do that."

"Why not?"

There was a moment of silence before he said, "Because right now we can't trust anyone. Not even Homeland Security. At least until they find out what's going on. Evidently, there's a mole within the organization. Otherwise, how else would your project come under such close scrutiny?"

He moved around her to the cabinet that held the coffeepot, poured a cup and took a sip. He leaned back against the cabinet and added, "Homeland Security has no idea where you are. All they know is the bad guys haven't nabbed you yet because they're still trying to find you. Obviously, the person who sent you that note is one of the good guys and figured out what was about to go down, which is why he or she told you to disappear. For all they know, that's what you did."

He took another sip of his coffee. "So beside those framed photographs over your fireplace, is there anything else in your house you want to save?"

Crystal drew in a deep breath. Technically, it wasn't her house since she was leasing it. But it was where she'd made a home for the past year, putting her own signature on it with the decorating she'd done. What she'd liked most about her home was the screened-in patio. She could sit out there for hours and read. That made her realize that all the furniture she did own would probably be destroyed because it was too big to move out without attracting attention. The impact of that made her slide down in the chair. It was still warm from when Bane had sat in it.

"We don't have much time, Crystal."

She sat upright, glad she'd already packed her marriage license and placed it inside the photo album she'd kept for Bane. "My family Bible," she said with resolve. "It's in the nightstand drawer. And there are more pictures in a small trunk under my bed."

"Okay."

He returned to the desk and when he reached for his phone, his arm brushed against hers. The feel of their skin coming into contact made her draw in a sharp breath. He looked at her, holding her gaze for a minute, and she knew he'd felt the sizzle, as well. He continued to hold her gaze, letting her know she had his full attention while he talked on the phone. "Flip, check the nightstand drawer next to her bed and grab her family Bible. And there's a small trunk under her bed."

Moments later he clicked off the phone. "I see you haven't outgrown that."

"What?"

"Blushing."

"Was I supposed to outgrow it?"

He smiled. "I have no complaints. In fact I've always enjoyed watching you blush."

She tried to give him a small smile, but in all honesty, she had very little to smile about right now.

"I didn't ask if you wanted a cup of coffee. Since you didn't order a cup at that diner earlier tonight, I figured you're still not a coffee drinker."

She nodded. "And I see that you still are."

"Yep."

She frowned and broke eye contact with him to look at the cup he held in his hand. "Too much caffeine isn't good for you."

He chuckled. "So you've always said."

"And so I know. Especially now that I've become a biochemist. It's not good for your body."

Why had she said that? And why after saying it did her gaze automatically move up and down his solid frame? Bane Westmoreland was so overwhelmingly sexy. He'd always possessed a magnetism that could draw her in. The man was such a perfect hunk of carved mahogany, it was a crying shame.

She moved her gaze off his body and up to his face, thinking his facial hair gave him a sexier look. He gave her a roguish smile and she could feel her cheeks flush. "Looking at me like that can get you in a lot of trouble, Crystal Gayle," he murmured in a deep husky voice.

He was standing close, so close she could inhale his scent. Manly. Deliciously provocative. "Then, I won't look at you," she said, cutting her eyes elsewhere. Namely to her bed and all the cards and letters she'd pulled out of the satchel. "I don't need any more trouble than I'm already in. It's pretty bad when you have the government burning down your house. I'd like to see how they explain their actions to the insurance company."

"They won't have to. They will handle it in a way that makes it look like an electrical fire or something. It definitely won't appear intentional."

She lifted her chin. "Still, I don't like it." She eased up out of the chair, assuming he would step back and give her space. He didn't, and it brought their bodies within touching distance of each other.

"You look good in your T-shirt and sweats, by the way," he said softly. They were standing so close the heat of his words seemed to fan across her face.

She looked down at herself, thinking he had to be kidding. Both garments were old and ratty looking, but she remembered her manners and glanced up and said, "Thank you."

The moment she looked into his face, she wished she hadn't. The intense desire in the hazel eyes staring back at her was so profoundly sensual she felt a tug in the middle of her stomach.

Setting his coffee cup down, he moved closer. Before she knew what he was doing he reached out and placed his hands at her waist. But he didn't stop there. As he inched his hands upward and gently caressed the curve of her body, he said, "I can't get used to these. Where did all these curves come from?"

She shrugged. "Wish I knew. I just woke up one morning and they were there." Why wasn't she telling him to keep his hands to himself? Why did his touch feel so good?

He chuckled. "Only you would think these curves were an overnight thing."

Although a part of her wished he didn't do that, she kind of liked the way he would subtly remind her that they had a past. And she needed that because at times he seemed like such a stranger to her.

"Well," she said, making a move to scoot around him. But he held tight to her waist and when he began lowering his head, she could just imagine how their tongues would mingle.

The moment he took hold of her mouth, his lips ground against hers and she was powerless to do anything but kiss him back.

Bane loved kissing Crystal. Always had and figured he always would. Their kisses weren't just hot, they were flaming red-hot, and in no time he was shivering with desire. And like in the past, he had to taper his lust; otherwise he would have her spread out on that bed in no time. And he doubted she was ready for that just yet.

So he enjoyed this. The way she was provocatively returning his kiss. The way his mouth seemed to be in sync with hers, feeding off hers with a hunger he felt in every part of his body. As when he'd kissed her earlier tonight, it felt as if he'd finally come home to the woman he loved. He had been hungry for her taste for five years. He'd tried to remember just how delicious it was and knew his memories hadn't come close. The intensity was clouding his mind and he could tell she wasn't holding back, pouring everything into the kiss like he was doing.

She suddenly pulled her mouth away and drew in a deep breath. When she licked her bottom lip, he was tempted to kiss her again, take his own tongue and lick her lips.

"We should not have done that, Bane," she said softly. And the look of distress in her eyes touched him.

"Don't see why not. You're my wife."

"I don't feel like your wife."

"That can be remedied, sweetheart," he said in a provocative drawl.

"I know," she said, looking at him with a serious expression. "But sleeping with you won't make me feel as if I know you any better. I need time, Bane. I don't need you to rush me into anything."

"I won't."

She crossed her arms over her chest and he wished she hadn't done that when he saw her nipples pressed against her T-shirt. "Then, what was that kiss about just now?"

He smiled. "Passion. You can't deny you felt it. I want you so much, Crystal." He saw uneasiness line her pupils. "Relax, baby. You will let me know when you're ready. One day you will realize that no matter how long it's been, I'm still your husband."

She shook her head. "But we haven't seen each other in five years."

He frowned. Was she saying that because she wasn't sure she still loved him after all this time? He refused to believe that. "Trust me, Crystal," he heard himself say softly. "After reading all my cards and letters to you, I have no doubt you'll see what I mean."

His cell phone rang and when he turned to pick it up, she used that time to quickly move away from him and back to the bed.

"This is Bane." He nodded a few times. "Okay, Flip. Thanks and I owe you." He then clicked off the phone.

He looked over at her. "That was Flip. He wanted to let me know he collected all the items you wanted saved. And by the way. Did you know your house was bugged?"

* * *

Crystal was experiencing one shock after another. First Bane returned after five years. Then she was on the run from men who wanted to kidnap her. Then the government wanted to burn her house down. And now she was being told it was bugged?

"That's not possible. Nobody I work with has ever been invited to my home. They consider me a recluse."

Bane nodded. "Where did the stuffed giraffe come from?"

She frowned. "The stuffed giraffe?"

"Yes."

She thought for a minute. "It was a gift from one of my coworkers, who took a trip to South Africa earlier this year. She brought everyone souvenirs back."

"Who was this generous person?"

"A biochemist by the name of Jasmine Ross."

"Well, yours was given to you with a purpose. Flip saw it on your dresser and figured it would be something you'd want to keep, as well. When his sensor went off he knew it contained an audio bugging device. He proved his suspicions true when he gutted it. I guess someone thought they could catch you saying something about your research on the phone or something."

"Well, they were wrong." Things were getting crazier by the minute and she couldn't believe it. "Were there others?"

Bane shook his head. "Flip and his brothers combed the rest of the house and didn't detect anything. Now you see why Homeland Security wants to burn it down to the ground?"

No, she still didn't see it. "They could have found another way."

"Evidently not."

She didn't like Bane's attitude, as if he was perfectly fine with someone torching the place where she lived. Turning her back to him, she angrily began shoving all the cards and envelopes back into the satchel. She was in no mood to read anything now. All she wanted to do was get into bed and rest her brain.

"I'll take my shower now."

"Fine." Crystal was tempted to turn around but refused to do so. She planned to be in bed and dead asleep by the time he came out of the bathroom.

When she heard the bathroom door close she released a deep sigh. How were she and Bane going to share a hotel room without…

She shook her head. The thought of them making love was driving her nuts. All of a sudden the memories of their last time together were taking hold of her. They had been happy. They had just gotten married and thought the future was theirs to grab and keep.

When she heard the water from his shower she couldn't help but recall when they had showered together. All the things he had taught her to do. Bane had been the best teacher, and he'd always been easy and gentle with her.

As she drew the bedcovers back and then slid beneath them, she tried to not think of Bane. Instead, she thought of her house and how at that very minute it could be going up in flames.

Eleven

Twenty minutes later Bane walked out of the bathroom and glanced over at the bed where Crystal lay sleeping. Or was she? He found it amusing that she was pretending to be asleep while checking out his bare chest and the way his sweats rode low on his hips. He had no problem with her ogling him; she could even touch him if she liked. Better yet, he would love for her to invite him to her bed. He would love to slide between the sheets with her.

Intending to give her more to look at, he decided he might as well get on the floor and do his daily exercises. He'd begin with push-ups after a five-minute flex routine that included bending to touch his toes. Maybe a vigorous workout would work out all the desire that was overtaking his senses and at the same time arouse her enough that she would want him to make love to her. It was worth a try.

Less than thirty minutes into his exercises he wondered if she realized her breathing had changed. He most certainly had noticed. Now he was off the floor and running in place. His sweats had ridden even lower on his hips and his bare chest was wet from sweat. Now for a few crunches.

"What you're doing doesn't make sense, Bane."

He forced himself not to smile. "I thought you were asleep," he said, lying, when he knew she'd been peeking through a slightly closed eye at him.

"How could I sleep with all that racket you're making down there on the floor?"

"Sorry if I disturbed you. And what doesn't make sense?"

"For a person to take a shower only to get all sweaty again."

He chuckled. "I'll take another shower. No problem."

She had shifted in bed to lie on her side and look over at him. "You did three hundred push-ups. Who does that?"

"A SEAL who needs to stay in shape." Evidently she'd been counting right along with him but had missed a few. "And I did three hundred and twenty-five." He wondered where her concentration had been when he'd done the other twenty-five.

"Whatever. I just hope that's the last of it."

"For tonight. I do the same thing each morning. But I'll try to be a little quieter so as not to disturb you."

The sound of him exercising wasn't what was disturbing her, Crystal thought, trying not to let her gaze roam all over Bane. Jeez. How could sweat look so good on a man? It was such a turn-on. All that testosterone being worked up like that. Rippling muscles. Bulging

biceps. Firm abs. Mercy! She'd gone without sex for five
years and it had never bothered her before. But now it
did. Only because the man here with her now was Bane.

She had pretended to be asleep when he'd come out
of the bathroom. But seeing him bare chested and wearing sweats was just too much. She had tried closing
her eyes and holding them shut. Tight. But the sounds
of him grunting sent all kinds of fantasies through her
mind and she'd begun peeking. And definitely getting
an eyeful. If she didn't know better she'd think he'd deliberately gone after her attention.

"I've worked up an appetite. Do you want something?"

She had worked up an appetite watching him as well,
but it wasn't for food. She definitely wanted something,
but it was something she'd best do without—it was just
too soon since Bane had come for her, and she needed
to stay focused until she was out of danger. "No thanks.
I'm still full from those waffles and chicken we ate earlier. But you can order room service if you like. The
hotel clerk did say the kitchen was open twenty-four
hours." But who wanted to eat at four in the morning?

He glanced at the clock on the nightstand separating the beds. "I think I'll order something up. Nothing
heavy. If I do it now, it will probably arrive by the time
I get out of the shower. But if they come while I'm in
the shower, don't open the door for anyone. They can
wait a few minutes. If they can't, then they can take it
back to the kitchen."

She wondered if all that was necessary. But then all
she had to remember was her house was probably getting burned to the ground about now. "Fine." She hoped
by the time he got out of the shower for a second time
that night she would be asleep for real. But that hadn't

worked during his first shower—the sound of running water and picturing him naked beneath that water had kept her awake.

She watched as he moved over to the desk and picked up the phone to order a steak dinner with potatoes. At four in the morning? She lifted a brow. Hadn't he said nothing heavy? If that wasn't heavy then what was his definition?

And speaking of heavy...

Why had her breathing suddenly gone that way? Could it be because her gaze had now landed on the perspiration dripping off his hard chest, past those chiseled muscles, and making a path toward the waistband of his sweats? And why did the thought of licking it before the drops of sweat could disappear beneath the waistband actually appeal to her?

He had grabbed more clothes and was about to go into the bathroom when his cell phone rang. "That's Nick," Bane said, turning and heading back toward the desk.

Crystal felt a tightening of her stomach. It seemed that whenever this guy Nick called, he was the bearer of bad news. "Maybe they changed their minds about burning down my house."

The look Bane gave her all but said not to count on it. "Yes, Nick?"

She saw the tightening of Bane's jaw and the dark and stormy look in his eyes. And when he said, "Damn" three times she felt uneasy and suspected the news wasn't good.

"Thanks for letting me know. We're on the road again. Contact Viper. He'll know what to do."

Crystal had eased up on the side of the bed. As soon

as he clicked off the phone she was about to ask what was wrong when he asked, "Where's your jacket?"

She lifted a brow. "My jacket?"

"Yes."

"Hanging up in the closet. Why?"

"It has a tracking device on it."

"What!"

Already Bane had reached the closet and jerked her jacket off the hanger. She watched in horror as he took a pocketknife and ripped through a seam. "Bingo." He pulled out a small item that looked like a gold button.

She drew in a deep breath and met Bane's gaze when he looked over at her. "Does that mean…"

"Yes. Someone has been keeping up with our whereabouts all this time, and chances are they know we're here."

"But how did someone get my jacket?"

"Probably at work. Do you keep it on during the day?"

"No. I always take it off, hang it up and put on my lab coat."

He nodded. "Then, you have your answer. And I suspect the person who put this tracker in your coat is the same person who gave you the stuffed giraffe." He rubbed his hands down his face. "Come on. Let's pack up and get the hell out of here."

"But what about your food? Your shower?"

"I'll stop somewhere later to grab something, but for now we need to put as much distance between us and this place as we can. As for my shower, you'll just have to put up with sharing a car with a musky man."

"I can handle it." She was already on her feet and pulling out her luggage. She considered how Bane hadn't expected all this drama when he'd come looking for her. "I'm sorry, Bane." She glanced over at him and saw he was doing likewise with his luggage.

He paused in tossing items into his duffel bag and looked back at her. "For what?"

"For being the cause of so much trouble. I guess you hadn't figured on all of this."

"No, but it doesn't matter, Crystal. You're my wife, and I will protect you with my life if it came to that."

She shivered at the thought and hoped it didn't. But still, the words he'd just spoken had a profound impact on her. She pushed several locks of hair back from her face to focus on Bane as he continued to pack. Surprisingly, it wasn't Bane's sexiness that was wearing her down, but his ability to still want her in spite of everything.

"Ready?"

She nodded. "Yes."

"We need to be aware of our surroundings more than ever and make sure we aren't being tailed. There's a pretty good chance someone is sitting and waiting for us in the parking lot, which is why I'm putting plan B in place."

"What's plan B?"

"You'll see."

After Bane checked up and down the hallway, they left the hotel room, moving quickly toward the stairwell instead of the elevator. She followed his lead and didn't ask any questions. And when they came to a locked door that led to the courtyard, he used what looked like a knitting needle to pick the lock.

"Still doing that, I see," she said.

He shrugged. "Not as much as I used to."

In no time the lock gave way and she saw they were in the courtyard, which was located on the other side of the building from the parking lot. "How will we get to our car?"

"We won't."

She was about to ask what he meant when suddenly a white SUV pulled up, tailed by a dark sedan. Since Bane didn't seemed alarmed by the two vehicles, she figured he knew the occupants. When the door to the SUV opened and a big bruiser of a man got out, she saw Bane's lips ease into a smile.

When the man came to a stop in front of them, Bane said. "Crystal, I want you to meet Gavin Blake, better known as Viper. Another one of my teammates."

Bane wasn't bothered by the way Viper was checking out Crystal. He was curious, as most of his teammates were. They had wondered what kind of woman could keep a man faithful to a wife he hadn't seen in five years. Bane could tell that Viper, a known ladies' man, was in awe, if his stare was anything to go by.

Moments later, Viper switched his intense gaze from Crystal back to Bane. "She's beautiful, Bane."

"You forgot to check out my teeth," Crystal said, frowning.

Viper let out a deep laugh. "And she has a good sense of humor," he added. "I like that. She's definitely a keeper."

"Yes, she is." Bane had known that the first day he'd met Crystal. "Did you check out the parking lot?"

Viper nodded. "Yes, and it was just like you figured. A car with two men inside is parked beside the one you were driving. I phoned in the description and the license plates to Nick, and according to him, it's the same vehicle an eyewitness saw in the area when one of the other biochemists was kidnapped. So you did the right thing by having Nick call me."

Viper nodded toward the SUV. "Here's your new ride. Chances are those guys don't know you're onto them. They probably planned to snatch your wife the minute you checked out of the hotel tomorrow morning."

"Like hell."

"That's what I said," Viper said, chuckling. "I figured they don't have a clue who they're messing with. I'm going to keep those guys busy while you and your lady get a head start. This ought to be fun."

Bane frowned. "Don't enjoy yourself too much."

"I won't. I brought my marine cousin with me to make sure I stay out of trouble. At least as much as I can," Viper said, handing Bane the keys to the SUV. "Do you have a plan from here?"

Bane nodded. "Yes. My brother is calling in family members with connections to law enforcement."

Viper nodded. "That's good. There's nothing like family backing you when you're in a pinch." He then turned his attention back to Crystal and smiled. "It was nice finally getting to meet you. You have a good man here. And, Bane, if you need my help again, just call." With those words, Viper walked away and got inside the dark sedan before the driver pulled off.

Bane watched him leave before turning his attention to Crystal. "Come on, let's get the hell out of here before those guys sitting in the parking lot figure out we're one up on them." He opened the trunk and placed their luggage inside.

"Do you want me to drive, Bane? You have to be tired."

He smiled when he opened the SUV's door for her to

get in. What he was enduring was nothing compared to missions he and his teammates typically encountered. "No, I'm fine. We're together, and that's all that matters to me."

We're together, and that's all that matters to me.

A half hour later, as Bane took the interstate with a remarkable amount of ease for a man who hadn't gotten much rest, Crystal couldn't help but continue to recall those words. Shouldn't that be all that mattered to her, as well? The one thing she knew for certain was that she was glad he was here with her. No telling what her fate would be if he wasn't. She wouldn't have known where to go or what to do. Her plans had been to head for the Bahamas, not knowing someone would have been there, waiting for her at the airport to grab her before she could get on the plane.

But Bane had known. Through his intricate network of teammates, he'd been able to stay one step ahead of the bad guys. What had gone down at the hotel was too close for comfort. She would never have known a tracker had been sewn inside her jacket.

She was surprised Jasmine Ross was involved. The woman was a few years older than she and seemed perky enough. Jasmine had even tried to befriend her a few times, but Crystal hadn't been ready to become the woman's friend. She hadn't thought anything about the stuffed giraffe, since Jasmine had given everyone working in the lab a gift. And as for her jacket, Crystal hung it on the coatrack like everyone else, so Jasmine had access to it. She could have sneaked off with it and placed a tracker inside without being detected.

Crystal wondered what would entice a person to be on the wrong side of the law. What was in it for the woman? Crystal didn't want to think about what those other two chemists were enduring against their will. They'd been separated from their families and probably didn't know if anyone would find and rescue them. Were they even still in this country?

"You okay over there?"

She glanced at Bane. As far as she was concerned, she should be asking him that. At least she'd gotten a couple hours of sleep earlier tonight. "Yes, I'm fine. What about you?"

He chuckled. "I'm great."

To a degree, she believed him. Bane was definitely in his element. This was a different Bane. More in control. Disciplined. Not impulsive, irresponsible or reckless. The Bane she remembered would have gone out to the parking lot to confront those guys, ready to kick ass. The old Bane had an attitude and detested anyone telling him what to do, especially when it involved her. That was why he'd butted heads with her father countless times and defied the law.

And defied his family. She recalled how often his brother Dillon had sat them down and talked to them, urging her to stay in school. He had lectured them to stop acting impulsively and to start thinking of someone other than themselves.

Deciding to continue the conversation with the goal of keeping him awake, she asked, "So what's going on with your family? Are your brothers and cousins still single?"

His laugh was rich and filled the car's interior. The sound filled her as well, and she wondered how the deep throatiness of his voice could do that to her. "Not hardly. In fact, after Valentine's Day when Bailey ties the knot, that will take care of everyone."

"Bailey is getting married?"

"Yes, and she's moving to Alaska. Her husband-to-be owns a huge spread on an island there."

Crystal was shocked. "Bailey always swore that she would never marry and move away."

"Well, evidently Walker Rafferty was able to change her mind about that. I got a chance to meet him over Thanksgiving. A pretty nice guy. Ex-marine."

The man must really be something if Bane approved of him. As the youngest two Westmorelands, Bane and Bailey had been close growing up. They'd done a lot of things together. Even got into trouble. "I'm happy for her."

"So am I."

She then listened as he brought her up-to-date on his other siblings and cousins and the women and men they had married. His cousins Zane and Derringer, and his brother Riley were also shockers. She remembered they had reputations around Denver as being ladies' men.

She shifted to get comfortable in her seat as Bane continued to fill her in on his family. She loved hearing the sound of his voice and could tell he was proud of everyone in the Westmoreland family. He also told her about more cousins his family had tracked down in Alaska with the last name of Outlaw.

As she continued to listen to him, she didn't think to question where they were headed. Like he'd said earlier, they were together, and that was all that mattered. She felt safe with him, and at the moment she couldn't imagine being anyplace else.

Twelve

"I'm taking the bed closer to the door again."

"All right."

Bane tossed his duffel bag on the bed and glanced around the hotel room. This one was roomier than the last and the bed looked inviting as hell. The first thing he intended to do was take a shower. He had driven for nine hours and he had to hand it to Crystal, she had tried keeping him company by engaging him in conversation about his family and his job as a SEAL. He had explained that due to the highly classified nature of what he did, there was a lot about his missions he couldn't divulge. She understood and seemed fascinated by what he had been able to tell her.

He glanced over at her and could tell she was exhausted, as well. It was daylight outside but he figured as long as they kept the curtains drawn the room would have the effect of nighttime. Right now he doubted his body cared that it was just two in the afternoon. As long as he could get a little sleep, he would be ready for the next phase of his mission to keep his wife safe.

He turned to place his cell phone on the nightstand. He'd received text messages from Flip letting them know Crystal's house had been burned down to the ground, which probably infuriated those thinking she had data stored somewhere inside it. And then Viper had texted to say that before turning those guys in the parking lot over to Homeland Security, he and his cousin had given them something to think about. Bane hadn't asked for details, thinking it was best not to know. But he figured the men wanting Crystal had to be insanely mad when their plans were derailed time and time again. Hopefully, if those guys were the same ones who had kidnapped the other two chemists, it would be just a matter of time before they were found.

"Do you want me to order you something to eat? That way when you get out of the shower your food will be here," Crystal asked.

He glanced back over at her. "That would be nice. Thanks."

"Anything in particular you want?"

It was close to the tip of his tongue to answer and say, *Yes, you. You are what I want*. Instead, he said, "Whatever looks good. I'm game." Grabbing some fresh clothes out of the duffel bag, he went into the bathroom and closed the door behind him. And then he leaned against it and drew in a deep breath.

Needing a shower was just an excuse. What he really needed was breathing space away from Crystal. Sharing a room with her, being in close proximity to her after all this time was playing havoc on every part of his body. Every time he looked at her he was filled with desire so deep, the essence of it seemed to drench his pores. And he couldn't ignore the sensations he felt knowing they were finally together after being apart for so long.

The sound of his phone alerted him to a text message from Nick. Pulling the phone out of his back pocket, he quickly read the lengthy text before placing his phone on the vanity.

Stripping off his clothes, he stepped into the shower. A cold one. And he didn't so much as flinch when the icy cold water bore down on his skin. Instead, he growled, sounding like a male calling out for a mate he wanted but couldn't have.

Deciding to focus on something else to get his mind off Crystal for the time being, he mentally ran through all the information Nick had texted him. Crystal's co-worker, Jasmine Ross, was nowhere to be found. Rumor within Homeland Security indicated she'd had help from inside, and for that reason Nick agreed with Bane's way of thinking to not let anyone, especially Homeland Security, know of his connection to Crystal. Right now everyone was trying to figure out where she'd gone.

The plan was for him and Crystal to stay put at this hotel until tomorrow. Then they would drive overnight to the Alabama and Georgia line and meet with some of his family members. Namely his cousins Dare, Quade, Cole and Clint Westmoreland. Dare, a former FBI agent, was currently sheriff of College Park, a suburb of Atlanta. Clint and Cole were former Texas Rangers and Quade still dabbled from time to time in secretive assignments for a branch of government connected directly to the White House.

Bane stepped out of the shower and began toweling himself off, ready to have something to eat and then finally get some sleep. After slipping into a pair of jeans and a T-shirt, he grabbed his phone and slid it into his back pocket. He then opened the bathroom door and walked out to find Crystal pacing the hotel room. "What's wrong?"

She paused and looked over her shoulder at him. "What makes you think something is wrong?"

"You're pacing."

"So I was." She moved to the desk and sat down in the black leather armchair. "Too much nervous energy, I guess. I don't want to bother you."

"You aren't bothering me," he said, moving to his duffel bag to discard the clothes he'd just taken off. "I just don't want you to wear yourself out."

"You're worried about me wearing myself out? You? Who barely got any sleep or ate a decent meal in the past twenty-four hours?"

"I've survived before on less."

"Well, I prefer not hearing about it."

He wondered if she was ready to hear what Nick had texted him earlier. "Jasmine Ross is missing."

"Missing?"

"Yes. Nick thinks she might have suspected DHS is onto her and went into hiding." At that moment there was a knock on the door, followed by a voice that said, "Room service."

"Great timing," Bane said as he headed for the door. Deciding not to take any chances, he grabbed his gun off the table and then looked through the peephole before opening the door.

After the attendant had rolled in a cart loaded down with a variety of foods, arranged everything and left, Bane smiled over at Crystal. "The food looks good. You're joining me, right?"

She nodded. "Yes, I'm joining you."

* * *

"I doubt if I can eat another bite, Bane," Crystal said, sliding her chair back from the table. Her goal had been to make sure he got something to eat and not the other way around. But he'd had other ideas and had practically fed her off his plate. She recalled how they used to do stuff like that years ago. Until now, she hadn't realized just how intimate it was.

"Mmm, you've got to try this. The piecrust is so flaky it nearly melts in your mouth," he said, reaching over and offering her his fork with a portion of apple pie on it.

It slid easily between her lips and she closed her eyes and moaned. He was right. It was delicious. In fact, everything was. Instead of ordering an entrée, she had chosen a variety of appetizers she thought he might like. And from the way he'd dived in, he had been pretty hungry. She was glad he had enjoyed all her selections.

She watched him finish off the last of the pie and tried ignoring the way her own stomach fluttered. He even looked sexy while he ate. Seriously, how totally ridiculous was that? Sighing, she glanced around the hotel room, deciding she could handle looking at just about anything right now except Bane. More than once she'd noticed him looking at her and had recognized that glint in his eyes. He'd always had that look when he wanted her. And why was she having such a hard time getting past that look?

"It's hard to believe the sun is about to go down already."

She glanced over at him and saw he was looking out the window. She had opened the blinds while he was taking a shower so the room wouldn't look so dark. The light coming through the window had helped, but now they would be losing that daylight soon.

"We'll make the twenty-four-hour mark in a few hours."

She lifted a brow. "Twenty-four-hour mark?"

He smiled and stared at her for what seemed like a minute or two before saying, "We will have spent the past twenty-four hours together. That's a pretty good start, don't you think?"

Pretty good start? Considering everything, he could think that? "I suppose." She glanced at her watch. "Now it's my turn to shower. I plan on getting into bed early."

"So do I."

She glanced at him and saw gorgeous hazel eyes staring back at her across the rim of a coffee cup. She couldn't help but return his stare. Okay, what was going on here and why was she encouraging it? He shouldn't be looking at her like that and she certainly shouldn't be returning the look. She should be saying something… or better yet, shouldn't she be getting up from her chair and heading for the bathroom? Yes, that was exactly what she should be doing.

She cleared her throat before easing to her feet. And because she felt she needed to say something she said, "Umm, I think I'll take a tub bath instead of a shower. I feel the need to soak my body in bubbles for a while." She frowned. Seriously? Wasn't that too much information?

She knew it probably had been when she saw his smile. It wasn't just any old smile but one that was so sexy it had sparks of desire shooting all through her.

"Sounds nice. Mind if I join you?"

Why had he had to ask her that? And why had his gaze just lowered to her chest just now? And why were her nipples stiffening into buds and feeling achy against her T-shirt? "You took a shower earlier. Besides, you'd be bored to tears."

His rich chuckle filled the room. "Bored to tears? In a bathtub with you? I seriously doubt that, sweetheart. In fact, I know for sure that won't be the case."

She raked her eyes over him from head to toe. She had a feeling that wouldn't be the case as well, but would never confess that to him. "But I'm sure such a macho SEAL wouldn't want to smell like vanilla," she said, moving quickly to the bed where she'd laid out a change of clothes.

Grabbing the items off the bed, she dashed into the bathroom and closed the door behind her.

Bane took the last sip of his coffee as he continued to stare at the closed door. Did he have his wife running scared? He grinned, thinking how he'd at least asked about taking a bath with her…even if she'd turned him down. Already he heard the sound of running water and his mind was beginning to work overtime, conjuring up all kinds of fantasy scenarios involving Crystal's naked body and a bathtub full of bubbles.

He had it bad. Yes, he most certainly did. But hell, that could be expected. He was a full-grown man who hadn't shared a woman's bed in five years, and the woman he'd been holding out for was behind that closed door without a stitch of clothes on, playing with bubbles and smelling like vanilla.

He shifted his gaze from the closed door to glance out the window. He might as well get up and close the blinds, since it was getting dark outside. However, instead of moving, he continued to gaze thoughtfully out of the window. He wondered how long it would be before he could officially bring Crystal out of hiding. According to Nick's text messages, two arrests had been made, but so far those guys weren't talking.

Just then, his phone went off. He picked it up when he recognized the ringtone. "Yes, Bay?"

"Just checking on you and Crystal. Dillon told us what's going on."

Bane leaned back in his chair. "So far so good, considering someone had sewn a tracker inside Crystal's jacket. Luckily, we were able to stay ahead of them anyway."

"Dillon said you're headed south. Why not come home to Westmoreland Country?"

"Can't do that. The last thing the family needs is for me to deliver trouble to everyone's doorstep."

"We can handle it, Bane."

"It's not the old days, Bay. My brothers and cousins have wives and kids now. We're dealing with a bunch of crazies and there's no telling what they might do. I can't take the chance."

"Then, come to Kodiak. Walker told me to tell you that you and Crystal are welcome there. We're leaving for home tomorrow and won't be returning to Westmoreland Country until a week before Christmas."

Bane smiled. "Did you hear what you just said?"

"About what?"

"Kodiak, Alaska. You said that you and Walker were leaving for *home* tomorrow. It's strange hearing you think of anywhere other than Denver as home."

Bailey chuckled. "I guess I'm beginning to think of wherever Walker is as home for me."

Bane nodded. "You really love the guy, don't you?"

"Yes. Now I know how you and Crystal felt all those years ago. Especially the obsession. I can't imagine my life without Walker." She paused a moment and then asked, "And how are things going with you and Crystal? You guys still love each other, right?"

"Why wouldn't we?"

"The two of you haven't seen each other in five years, Bane. That's a long time to not have any kind of communication with someone."

Yes, it was, but he'd known the moment he'd seen Crystal that for him nothing had changed. But could he say the same about her feelings for him?

Before his cousin could ask him any more sensitive questions, he said, "I need to make a call, Bay. Thank Walker for the offer and tell him if I decide to take him up on it, I'll let him know."

"Okay. Stay safe and continue to keep Crystal safe."

"I can't handle my business any other way."

He ended the call, then stood and closed the blinds before wheeling the table and dishes out into the hall. Once back inside he reached for his phone, figuring now was a good time to check in with Nick before calling it a night. His friend picked up on the second ring. "What's going on, Nick?"

"Glad you called. I was about to text you. Jasmine Ross has been found."

Crystal drew in a deep breath as she slid into her bathrobe. She felt good and refreshed. Soaking in the tub for almost an hour had definitely relaxed her mind. Hopefully Bane was asleep by now and she would be soon, too. They both needed a good ten hours' worth before heading out again.

Opening the bathroom door she allowed her eyes to adjust to the semidarkness. The first thing she noticed was that Bane was not in bed sleeping as she had hoped but was sitting at the desk with his back to her.

He turned around when he heard her and she could tell from the look on his face that something was wrong.

"Bane? What's going on?"

He stood and stuck his hands into the pockets of his jeans. "I talked to Nick a short while ago."

Nick, who was usually the bearer of bad news, she thought, tightening the belt of her robe around her. "And?"

"They found Jasmine Ross."

"Really?" she said, moving toward Bane with a feeling of excitement flowing through her. "That's good news, right? Hopefully Jasmine will confess her part in all this and work out a plea deal or something. Maybe they'll get her to tell them where those other two chemists are being held."

"Unfortunately, Jasmine won't be telling anyone anything."

Crystal frowned. "Why?"

"Because she's dead. She was shot in the head and dumped in a lake. A couple of fishermen came across her body a few hours ago."

Thirteen

"Here. Drink this."

Crystal's fingers tightened on the glass Bane placed in her hand, and she fought hard to hold it steady. Jasmine was dead? Suddenly everything seemed so unreal. So unbelievable.

She glanced down into the liquid. It was alcohol, and the smell alone was so strong it had her straightening up a little in her chair. "Whoa. What is it?"

"Scotch."

She lifted an arched brow. "Where did Scotch come from?"

"I ordered it from room service after I talked with Nick. I figured you'd need a glass."

"I don't drink, Bane."

"You need to drink this. It will help with the shock of what I told you."

Crystal nodded, took a sip and frowned. Like coffee, liquor was a taste she'd never acquired. She drew in a deep breath as her gaze flickered around the room.

"She brought it on herself, Crystal," she heard Bane say. "Evidently, the woman didn't have any problem setting you up. Don't forget she placed a bugging device in a gift she gave you and a tracker inside your jacket."

"I know, but it's still hard to believe she'd do something like that. She was nice most of the time. At least she pretended to be," Crystal said, leaning forward to place her glass on the desk. One sip had been enough for her. "How could she have gotten mixed up in something so devious?"

Bane shrugged. "Who knows what makes people do what they do? Unfortunately, she got in too far over her head. And the people she thought she could trust saw her as a threat instead of an asset."

Shivers passed through Crystal, and when Bane touched her arm she nearly jumped out of her skin. "You okay?" he asked softly.

She tipped her head all the way back to gaze up at the ceiling before lowering it to look at him. "Not really. It was bad enough to know one of my coworkers was involved in heaven knows what, but then to find out she lost her life because of it is a little too much."

"Are you sure you're okay?"

She glanced at Bane. "Yes, pretty much. But I think I'll go to bed now and try to get some sleep."

Crystal stood up. Without saying anything else and feeling Jasmine's death weighing her down, she moved across the room, threw back the covers and slid into bed. She turned her back to Bane so he wouldn't be able to see her tears.

Bane came awake with a start. First there was a small whimper from the bed next to his. Then he heard a rumbled, emotional plea. "Please don't! Don't shoot him. Please don't."

It took only a second to realize Crystal was thrashing around in her bed having a bad dream. He was out of his bed in a flash and flipped on the small lamp on the nightstand, bathing the room in a soft glow. He sat on the edge of her bed, gently shaking her awake. "Crystal, it's okay. Wake up, baby. You're having a bad dream. Wake up."

He watched as her eyes flew open just seconds before she threw herself into his arms. Automatically he held her tight and used his hands to gently stroke her back. "It's okay, Crystal."

"Bane."

She whispered his name against his neck and the heat from her breath set off a fire in the pit of his stomach. Her arms tightened around him and he refused to let this moment pass. She needed him and he wanted to be needed.

"I'm here, baby."

She pulled back slowly, meeting his gaze and holding it. "It was an awful dream. They came for us, and you wouldn't let them take me. You put yourself in front of me. To protect me. And the man raised his gun to shoot. They were going to shoot you and I felt so helpless."

He slid one hand to the back of her neck and used the other to push several strands of hair back from her face. He saw fear in her eyes, and more than anything he wanted to take that look away. "It was just a dream, Crystal. No one is here but us, and no one is going to shoot me."

"B-but I…"

"Shh, baby. It's okay. I'm okay. We're okay."

He leaned in close to kiss the corners of her lips but

she tipped her head at an angle and his mouth landed over hers. Instinctively, she parted her lips at the moment of impact and he swept his tongue inside her mouth to kiss her fully.

They'd kissed a couple of times over the past twenty-four hours, but nothing like this. There had been a hunger, but tonight this was about taking care of an ache. He deepened the kiss to taste her more fully as desire quickened inside him. She whimpered, and the sound was so unlike the one that had awakened him earlier. This one sent sensations jolting through him, filling him with the awareness of a sexual need that he felt all over.

And when she reached up and wrapped her arms around his neck it became the kind of kiss that curled a man's toes and made his entire body get hard. She tangled her tongue with his in a way that made every cell in his body come alive and he could only moan out loud.

A swirl of heat combined with a heavy dose of want overtook him as he continued to ply her mouth with hungry, languorous strokes of his tongue. There was only so much of her he could take without craving more, and his desire for more was nearly eating him alive, driving him insane.

And he didn't want to just kiss her. He wanted to make love to her the way a husband would want to make love to his wife. He wanted to taste her all over. Feel his hands touching every inch of her. And reacquaint himself with being inside her.

Exploring her mouth this way was making his already aroused body that much more unrestrained. It was hard to remain in his good-guy lane and stay in control. Especially when she was returning his kiss with just as much bone-melting fire as he was putting into it. Explosive chemistry was something they'd always shared. Nothing had changed. The taste of her was incredibly pleasurable as always. To his way of thinking, even more so.

Unable to take any more, he broke off the kiss and pressed his forehead to hers while releasing pent-up breath from deep in his lungs. "Crystal." He wasn't sure why he needed to whisper her name at that particular moment, but he did.

"I'm here, Bane."

Yes, she most certainly was, he thought, breathing hard. He briefly considered giving her another kiss before tucking her under the covers and returning to his bed, but for some reason he couldn't do that. He wanted to continue holding her in his arms, so she would know she was safe here with him.

Bane shifted their bodies so they were stretched out together in the bed, and as they lay there beside each other, he wrapped his arms around her. "Sleep now," he whispered softly, trying to ignore how the angle of her backside was smacked up against his groin. He had a hard-on and there was no way she couldn't feel it.

She began writhing around in the bed trying to get comfortable, and each time she did so he felt his engorged erection get that much harder. Finally, after gritting his teeth a few times, he reached out and cupped a firm hold to her thigh. "I wouldn't do that too often if I were you," he warned.

"Why? Because you want me?"

With a guttural hiss, he positioned her body so that she was lying flat on her back. He loomed over her and looked down into her eyes. "What do you think?"

She broke eye contact with him for a mere second before returning his gaze. "I think I might not be as good with that as I used to be."

"Why would you think that?"

"It's been a while. Five years."

A smile curved his lips. "Are you saying that because you think that I might not be as good as I used to be, as well?"

Surprise leaped into her eyes and she exhaled sharply. "No. That never crossed my mind."

"Good. And just for the record, the thought that you're not as good as you used to be never crossed mine, either."

"Not even once?"

He stared at her in the lamplight. Her features were beautiful, the look in her eyes intense as she waited on his answer. "Not even once," he said, meaning every word. "But I have been wondering about something, though," he added, breathing her scent deep into his nostrils.

She lifted a brow. "What?"

"Can my tongue still make you come?"

Bane's words caused Crystal to squeeze her eyes shut as sensations, namely memories of him doing that very thing, assailed her. She always thought Bane's mouth should be outlawed. And it didn't take much to recall everything he used to do, while licking her from the top of her head to the bottom of her feet, paying close attention to those areas in between.

Especially those areas in between.

"Open your eyes, sweetheart."

She did and her gaze met his. Held it. She felt the sexual tension mounting between them, easing them into a comfortable and mutual existence where memories were surrounding them in ways they couldn't ignore or deny. And at the exact moment his fingers shifted from her thigh to settle between her legs, she knew just what he'd found.

A woman who was hot and ready.

Crystal wasn't exactly sure when the amount of time they'd been apart no longer mattered to her. The only thing that mattered was that he still wanted her after so long. That he hadn't been with another woman just like she hadn't been with another man. It was as if her body was his and his was hers. They had known it, accepted it and endured the loneliness. She hadn't wanted any other man but him, and now her body was demanding to have what it had gone without for quite some time.

"Do you know how many times I lay in bed at night and envisioned touching you this way, Crystal?" Bane whispered.

He shifted his hand and his fingers began moving, sliding inside her, and automatically her thighs eased apart. "No, how many?" she asked, loving how the tip of his fingers stroked up and down her clit.

"Too many. Those were the times I had to take matters into my own hands. Literally. That's how I kept from going insane. But I like this better," he said as he continued working his fingers inside her, causing a deep ache to spread through her. "The real thing. No holds barred."

No holds barred. As he stroked the juncture between her thighs, Crystal couldn't recall the last time she had felt so electrified. For so long, she had mostly ignored her body's demands, except for those rare occasions when she couldn't and had resorted to self-pleasure the way he had.

But Bane's fingers were not toys. They were real, and what they were doing to her was as real as it could get. The sensations being generated inside her were so intense she actually felt air being ripped right out of her lungs with every breath she took. Her heart rate had picked up, and she felt as if she was being driven off the edge, falling headfirst into one powerful wave of pleasure.

"You like this?"

Before she could answer, he reached down, sliding his free hand beneath her shirt and settling it on the center of her stomach. She felt the heat radiating from his touch and began writhing. "Hey, it's okay, baby. It's just me and my touch. I want to put my imprint on you everywhere," he whispered.

Did he think his imprint wasn't already there? She was convinced his fingertips had burned into her skin years ago. And when he pushed her T-shirt up, she felt a whoosh of air touch her skin, especially her breasts. She wasn't wearing a bra and could feel the heat of his gaze as he stared down at the twin globes.

"Hmm, beautiful. Just as I remembered. Do you have any idea how much I used to enjoy sucking these?"

Yes, she had an idea because he used to do so all the time. At one point she'd been convinced his mouth was made just for her nipples. And now, when he used his tongue to lick his lips just moments before lowering his head toward her breasts, she could actually feel a fire ignite inside her. She felt her nipples harden even more. And all it took was one look into his eyes to know he was about to devour her alive.

He buried his face in her chest and took her nipple easily between his lips. Then he began sucking hard. She wasn't sure if it was his fingers working inside her below or his mouth torturing her nipples that would do her in first. When it happened, she had a feeling it was both.

"Bane!"

An orgasm tore through her immediately and she couldn't hold back the scream. But he was there, capturing her mouth with his, smothering her deep moans with his kiss. Still, he didn't let up, his fingers continuing to work her, rebuilding a degree of passion within her that she could not contain. And when he released her mouth, he began licking her skin from the base of her chin, all over her breasts, down past her stomach all the way to where his mouth met his fingers. He pulled his fingers out of her only to lift her hips to bring the essence of her toward his mouth. The moment his tongue slid inside her she shuddered, filled to the rim with flames of erotic desire.

She pushed on his shoulders but he wasn't letting up. It was as if he was a hungry beast who intended to get his fill, and when another orgasm ripped through her, she cried out his name again. For a fraction of a second, she was convinced she had died and gone to heaven.

But she was quickly snatched back to earth when she felt him lower her hips and remove his mouth from her. Then she watched through languid eyes as he stood and began stripping off his clothes before reaching down to practically tear off hers. A raw, primitive need was overtaking him. It stirred the air, and she could see it in the passion-glazed eyes staring down at her. She felt the heat in every part of her body.

"That was just the beginning," he whispered as he slid a condom on his engorged erection. "Just the beginning."

And then he was back, spreading her thighs, looming over her, and when their gazes met, she saw what she'd always seen when he'd made love to her. Love. Pure, unadulterated love. Bane still loved her and she knew at that moment that no matter what they'd gone through and what they were going through now, she still loved him, as well.

She reached out and slid her hands up his back, feeling the deep cords of his muscles and flinching when she came to several scars that hadn't been there before. But before she could even imagine what story those scars told, he was taking her mouth again, pulling her in and consuming her with a need that was demanding her full concentration. On them. On this. Never had she been filled with such overwhelming desire, need and passion. She wanted him. Her husband. The man who had been her first and only best friend. The man who'd always had her back and had defied anyone who'd tried keeping them apart.

He ended the kiss to stare down at her. "You ready?"

She looked up at him, dragging in a deep whoosh of air filled with their heated scents. "Yes, I'm ready."

And then, holding tight to her hips, spreading her thighs even wider, he slid inside her.

Bane pushed into Crystal all the way until he couldn't go any farther, not sure where his body began and hers ended. The only thing he knew was this was home. He was home. He had been gone five years and that was five years too long. But now he was back and intended to remind her just how good they were together. Remind her why she was his and he was hers.

His blood was boiling, and at that moment it seemed as though all of it had rushed to the head of his erection buried deep inside her. He felt compelled to move, to mate, to drown even deeper into her sweet, delicious depths. He felt her inner muscles clamp down on him, begin milking him, and he threw his head back and growled. Then he began moving, pumping into her, thrusting over and over again until her climax hit so hard that he was convinced they would have tumbled to the floor had he not been holding on to her tight.

"Bane!"

"Crystal!"

Never had he wanted any woman more than he wanted her. Nothing had changed. But in a way, things *had* changed. They were older, wiser and in control of who they were and what they wanted. No one could dictate when and where they could love. The sky was now their limit. And as he continued to rock his hips against hers, thrusting in and out of her, working them both into yet another orgasm, he knew that this was just the beginning, just like he'd told her.

He wanted her to feel every hard, solid inch of him; he wanted to rebrand her, reclaim her. And when another climax hit them both, this one more earth-shattering and explosive than the last, he met her gaze just moments before claiming her mouth, kissing her with a hunger he knew she felt. The ecstasy was bone-deep, mind-blowing, erotic.

And when he released the kiss and she screamed his name once again, he knew that no matter what, Crystal Gayle Newsome Westmoreland was his destiny. He knew it with all his heart.

Fourteen

Crystal slowly opened her eyes and squinted against the bright morning sun coming through the open window blinds. She shifted her gaze to Bane, who was down on the floor doing push-ups. She watched and listened to him keeping count. He was up to three hundred and eighty and his entire body was glistening with sweat. She dragged in a deep breath, thinking the man had more energy than anyone she knew.

That was just the beginning...

He had been deadly serious when he'd issued that warning last night. He had proved that yes, he could still make her come with his tongue. Nothing had changed there. And what he was packing between those fine legs of his wasn't so bad, either. She had barely recovered from one orgasm before he'd had her hurling into another. She didn't recall him having the ability to do all that before. At least not in such rapid succession.

She switched her gaze to the clock on the nightstand and saw that it was almost nine. She had slept late and didn't have to wonder why. It had been a late night and early morning with Bane. He had the ability to make her body want him over and over again, to satisfy her each and every time.

This morning she felt sore, but at the same time she felt so gratified and contented she had to force back a purr. She couldn't stop smiling as she shifted in bed to stretch out her limbs, feeling the way her body was still humming with pleasure. If his goal had been to make up for all their lost time, he definitely had succeeded.

"Good morning. It's nice seeing you smile this morning."

She glanced back at Bane. His deep, husky voice sent erotic shivers down her spine. He had finished exercising and was standing across the room with a cup of coffee in his hand. His feet were braced apart, his sweats hung low on his hips and his chest was bare.

"Good morning to you, too, Bane. You gave me a lot to smile about last night," she said honestly.

"Glad you think so."

From his smile she knew he was pleased by her admission. She saw no reason to pretend regret when there wasn't any. And Bane of all people knew there had never been a shy bone in her body. However, seeing him two days ago after all those years had given her pause. She had to take things slow and get to know him all over again. It would be a process and, as far as she was concerned, making love was part of the process.

"I wanted to wait for you to wake up before ordering breakfast," he said, placing the coffee cup aside to come sit on the edge of her bed.

She pulled herself up, being careful to keep the

bedsheet over her naked body. "You didn't have to do that. I'm sure with everything…and especially those exercises…that you must be hungry."

"Starving."

"Then, let's order."

"Okay, but this first."

He leaned down and pulled her into his arms. It didn't bother her one iota that her naked body was revealed in the daylight. She recalled having a problem with Bane seeing her naked before since she'd always thought she didn't have enough curves to show off. Now she did.

He kissed her and she wrapped her arms around his neck and returned the kiss. She could feel every hard inch of him, all solid muscles, and immediately thought back to last night. Her pulse began hammering inside her veins. Only his kisses had the ability to do that to her. If she didn't put a halt to things, she was liable to short-circuit. Like she had last night.

Typically, she wasn't a demonstrative person, not in the least. However, last night had been a different story. She could blame it on the fact that she'd gone a long time without having sex, and once she was getting some, she was like a woman starving for more and more. Bane was a man who had no problem delivering, and she had experienced one orgasm after another. Yes, she could definitely say last night had been off the charts in more ways than one.

She broke off the kiss at the sound of her stomach growling. She chuckled. "I guess that's my tummy's way of letting me know it needs to be fed."

"Then, I'll order breakfast," Bane said, standing and reaching for the phone on the nightstand. "Anything in particular that you want?"

"Pancakes if they have them. Blueberry ones preferably. Maple syrup and bacon. Crisp bacon. A scrambled
egg would be nice and a glass of orange juice."

He looked at her and grinned. "Anything else?"

"Umm, not at the moment. And while I'm waiting,
I'll take a shower and put on some clothes."

"If you want to walk around naked, I wouldn't mind."

After last night she could definitely see where he
wouldn't mind. "I'd rather put on clothes."

"Your choice."

As he placed their order, she slipped out of bed and
looked around for the clothes he'd taken off her last
night. But she didn't see them. When she found his
T-shirt under a pillow she slid it over her head.

"Nice fit."

She looked down at herself. "It will do in a pinch."
She looked back at him. "Any calls this morning?"

"No. I think we got enough excitement yesterday."

She nodded as she began pulling clean clothes from
her luggage. "What are the plans for today?"

"We stay here most of the day and rest up. When it
gets dark then we'll leave."

"And go where?"

"We'll meet up with my cousins Quade, Dare, Clint
and Cole near the Alabama-Georgia border."

She nodded, recalling having met those particular
cousins at a family get-together around the time that the
Denver Westmorelands had discovered they had rela-
tives living in Georgia, Texas and Montana.

Crystal glanced over her shoulder. Bane was back
to doing his exercises, and the woman in her couldn't
help but admire the way his muscular hips rocked while
he ran in place. Drops of perspiration trickled off his

face and rolled down his neck and shoulders toward his bare chest.

She drew in a deep breath as she imagined her tongue licking each drop and the way his skin would taste. But she wouldn't stop there. She would take her hands and run them all over his body, touching places she might have missed out on last night, although she doubted there were any. She had been pretty thorough. But still…

What if there were places she had missed and—

"Anything wrong?"

She blinked and realized she'd been standing there staring. Swallowing deeply she said, "No, nothing is wrong." She wanted to turn and rush off toward the bathroom to take her shower, but for some reason she couldn't get her feet to move. It was if they were glued to the floor.

Now he was the one staring at her. She could actually feel his gaze on every part of her. Any place it landed made her body sizzle. She closed her eyes to fight off the desire that threatened to overwhelm her but when she saw it was no use, she opened them again and let them roam over every single, solid inch of him. He was so muscular, and so big and hard. She glanced down at his middle. Umm, did she say big and hard?

She drew in a deep breath when she saw him moving slowly toward her. She wanted to back up but again her feet wouldn't cooperate. All she could do was stand there and watch all six foot three of him gaining ground on her. She felt herself breathing faster with every step he took and her hands actually began shaking. Her fingertips were even tingling, but what she noticed most of all was how the juncture of her thighs seemed to throb like crazy.

When had her desire for him become so potent? Had making love to him all night suddenly turned her into a lustful woman? A woman whose needs dictated how she behaved with him? She could only imagine. But then she thought, no, she really couldn't. She hadn't been with a man taking up her space and time for so long, she wasn't sure how to deal with Bane now.

"Are you sure nothing is wrong, Crystal?" Bane had come to a stop directly in front of her. He was standing so close it wouldn't take much to reach out and touch him, feel those hard muscles, that solid chest glistening with sweat.

"Nothing's wrong, Bane. I'm fine."

He gave her a knowing grin, which put her on notice that he knew she was lying. She wasn't fine. Thanks to him she had gotten a taste of what she'd been missing for five years, and just how well he could still deliver. But it was more than just sex when it came to him. She'd always known it, ever since they'd held out those two years before even making love.

During that time they had developed a closeness and an understanding she knew very few couples shared. She had thought that maybe it hadn't survived their separation, but it seemed to have. Of course she knew better than to expect everything to go back to the way it had always been between them. They weren't the same people. They still needed to work out a few things, make adjustments and get a greater understanding of who they were now. But it could be done.

"May I offer a suggestion?" he asked her.

She licked her lips. It was either doing that or giving in to temptation and leaning over and licking him. "What?"

"Let's shower together."

Now, why had he suggested that? All kinds of hot and searing visions begin flooding her brain. "Shower together?"

"Yes. I suggested that same thing the night before last but you sort of turned me down."

Yes, she had. "I wasn't ready."

He took a step closer. "What about now, Crystal? Are you ready now? After last night, are you ready to give your husband some more playtime?"

It wasn't his request that caused her mind to shatter. It was his reference to himself as *her* husband. Because at that moment it hit her that he was hers and had been since her eighteenth birthday, probably even before then.

Bane had always told her she was his, regardless of what her parents or his family thought about it. And she had believed him. At no time had she doubted his words. Until that day he'd called to tell her he had decided to go into the navy. But now he was back and was letting her know that although he might have changed in some ways, he was the same in the way that mattered to her. He was still hers.

"That shower isn't very big," she decided to say. "And it might get messy with water sloshing all over the place."

"I'll clean it up," he said.

His smile made her weak in the knees, it was so darn sexy. "Well, if you don't mind doing that, then who am I to argue?" And without saying anything else, she forced her feet to move and walked toward the bathroom. But she didn't close the door behind her. When she turned toward the vanity to look in the mirror, out of the corner of her eye she saw that he was still standing in the same spot staring at her. So she figured that she might as well give him something to look at.

"Down boy," Bane muttered under his breath, trying to get his hard-on under control as he watched Crystal strut off toward the bathroom. As he stood there watching, she proceeded to wash her face and brush her teeth. When had seeing a woman doing basic morning tasks become a turn-on? He could answer that easily. The woman was his wife, and the times he'd seen her do those things had been few and far between.

So he watched her and began getting harder. He couldn't help noticing how his T-shirt clung to her breasts as she leaned toward the sink to rinse out her mouth, how the hem of the shirt had inched up and barely covered her thighs. The same thighs he'd ridden hard last night.

And back to her breasts… He could clearly see how hard the buds were and how well defined the twin globes looked. They were a nice size and nice shape. And he knew for certain they had one hell of a nice taste. As far as he was concerned everything about Crystal was nice. The word *nice* wasn't good enough. He could come up with a number of better ways to describe his wife. *Shapely. Sexy. Mesmerizing. Hot. Tasty.*

Did he need to go on? He doubted it. Instead, as he stood there and watched her take a washcloth to wet her face, he was suddenly turned on in a way he'd never been turned on before. Hell, it was worse than last night, and he hadn't believed that could be possible.

Feeling like a man who needed his wife and needed her now, he moved toward the bathroom. She had to know he was coming, but she didn't turn and look his way. Instead, she began removing his T-shirt and then tossed it aside. By the time he reached her she was naked.

Bane moved behind her and looked into the mirror, holding her gaze in the reflection. He moved closer and took hold of her backside, settling his groin against it. Perfect fit. And when he began grinding, feeling his engorged erection working against her buttocks, the contact nearly sent him over the edge. He broke eye contact with her in the mirror to lean over to lap her shoulder, licking it from one end to the other, taking a few nibbles of her flesh in between. He liked the way her skin tasted this morning. Salty. Womanly.

"I haven't taken a shower yet," she whispered in a voice that let him know the effect his mouth had on her.

"We'll eventually get around to it. No rush."

Then he remembered there was a certain spot on her body, right underneath her left ear, that when licked and sucked could make the raw hunger in her come out. So he licked and sucked there and immediately her body began shivering in a way that sent a violent need slamming through him.

"Bane…"

"I know, baby," he whispered. "Trust me, I know. And I want you just as much. Now. I need to be inside you. Bad. I got five years of want and need stored up just for you."

"And last night?" she asked in that same sexy whisper.

"Just the beginning. One night can't alleviate everything. To be honest, I doubt one hundred nights can."

"Oh, my."

"Oh, yes."

And with that said, he turned her around to face him,

lifted her off her feet and sat her on the vanity. "Spread your legs for me, Crystal."

As if they had a will of their own, her thighs parted. He pulled a condom pack out of the side pocket of his sweats and moved back only far enough to ease the sweats down his legs.

"You don't have to use that unless you want to," she said softly. "After I lost the baby my aunt suggested I go on the pill. More to help keep me regulated than anything else."

He nodded. So in other words she was letting him know that this time or any time they felt like it, they could go skin to skin, flesh to flesh. Just the thought made his entire body feel as if it was on fire. "Then, I won't use one."

With his pants out of the way, he got back into position between her spread legs. His shaft was ready, eager to mate and greedier than he'd ever felt it to be. He cupped himself to lead it home.

"Let me."

He looked up and gazed into her eyes. The thought that she'd asked to guide him inside her almost made him weak in the knees. "All right."

When she reached out and took hold of him, he felt himself harden even more in her hands. And then she led him to her center, and it was as if a thousand watts of electricity jolted through her nerve endings to him. And instinctively he pushed forward, thrusting into her hard and deep, all the way to the hilt. Reaching out, he grabbed hold of her hips, and began moving inside her like crazy.

Needing even more of a connection with her, he leaned forward to capture her lips with his. She had the minty taste of whatever mouthwash she'd used and he intended to lick the taste right from her mouth. She returned the kiss and he deepened it as much as he could while thrusting even more deeply into her body. Setting the same rhythm for both, the same beat. The same drive.

And the beat went on. He could hear her whispering in a choppy breath for him not to stop. So he didn't. He couldn't. It seemed that everything was out of his control. He was out of control. His entire body was ablaze for her.

"Bane!"

She screamed his name and tightened her legs around his waist. He thrust harder in response and before he could catch his next breath, his body exploded. But he wasn't done.

"Hold on, Crystal. I'm coming again."

"Bane!"

He threw his head back and sucked in a deep gulp of air that included a whiff of her scent. He practically lifted her hips off the vanity as he pushed deeper, and he came again with a primal need that made his entire body tremble. Now he knew that this woman who'd gotten under his skin so many years ago, who'd been his world, still was. And would always be so.

Fifteen

There was a knock on their hotel room door. "That should be dinner."

Crystal felt an immediate sense of loss when Bane separated his limbs from hers. Had they gone through breakfast and lunch? A part of her knew they had but the only thing she could recall with clarity was their seemingly nonstop lovemaking sessions. They'd only taken time out to grab something to eat and indulge in a couple of power naps in between.

She watched as he quickly slid into his jeans. When he grabbed his gun off the desk and inserted it into his waistband, it was a stark reminder of the situation they were in. There was a group of people out there who wanted her, and Bane was just as determined that they would not get her.

"Yes?" Bane asked as he looked out the door's peephole.

"Room service."

"Just a minute." He looked over his shoulder at her. "Decent?"

She was pulling his T-shirt over her head. "Now I am." But she still slid beneath the covers and pulled the bedsheet practically up to her chin.

He opened the door to a smiling young woman who couldn't help roaming her gaze all over Bane as she pushed a cart into their hotel room. "Everything you ordered, sir."

"Thanks."

Once the woman left, Crystal slid out of bed and glanced at the food. The cart was set like a table for two. Bane was finally getting his steak and potatoes, and as far as she was concerned, he deserved it. She was certain he'd worked up an appetite over the past few hours.

"I need to wash my hands first."

"So do I."

"But not together. I'll go first," she said, racing off toward the bathroom and closing the door behind her. Every time she and Bane entered the bathroom together they ended up making out all over the place. He had taken her on the vanity and in the shower just before breakfast. And then again in the shower right before lunch.

After washing her hands she quickly dried them off before opening the bathroom door, only to find him standing right there waiting. "My turn now," he said, grinning. "If you want to keep me company, I won't mind."

Yes, she just bet he wouldn't. "No thanks. I'll be okay out here waiting for you. I promise not to start without you."

"I won't be long because I'm sure you're hungry,

too," he said with a grin. He went into the bathroom and closed the door behind him.

Crystal rubbed her hand down her face. Jeez. This new Bane was almost too much for her. He'd always had a pretty hefty sexual appetite, but in the past, due to her lack of experience, he'd always kept that appetite under control. Now it was obvious he wasn't holding anything back. In a way she couldn't help but smile about that because now he was treating her as an equal in the bedroom. He'd taken off the kid gloves and wasn't treating her like a piece of china that could easily break.

"I'm back."

She glanced up and thought that yes, he was back, looking sexy as ever and easily transforming her into one huge bundle of sexual need. "Umm, maybe I should change clothes. Keeping on your T-shirt might not be a good idea."

He moved around her toward the cart. "Don't know why you think so. Besides, we'll both be changing soon enough since we'll be moving out in a few hours."

That was right. He had mentioned that to her. They'd be meeting up with his cousins. When she approached the cart, Bane pulled out a chair for her. She wasn't surprised. One thing about those Westmoreland men, they might have been hell-raisers a time or two, but they always knew how to act proper and show respect.

"Thanks, Bane," she said, taking her seat.

"You're welcome." He leaned down and placed a kiss on her lips. "Eat up."

"Do you know what the plan is after we meet with your cousins?"

He took a sip of coffee and shook his head. "Not sure. Quade has connections with the White House. He may have some insight into the mole at Homeland Security."

Crystal didn't say anything as she began eating, but she couldn't help wondering what could be done to keep her safe. She doubted Bane could continue to protect her on the run. What if he had orders for an assignment? Then where would she be?

"You're frowning. You think the food isn't good or something?"

She glanced over at him. "The food is good," she said of the grilled chicken salad she'd ordered. "I was just wondering about something."

"What?"

"What happens if you get that phone call?"

"What phone call?"

"The one from your commander that you're needed on one of those covert operations."

He shrugged. "Like I told you, my team and I are on military leave for a while. However, if something comes up, I'll let my commander know I can't go. You're my wife and I won't be going anywhere until I know for certain that you're safe."

"Because of your sense of duty and obligation?" she asked, needing to know.

He stared at her as a moment of silence settled between them. Then, he spoke. "I'm not sure what it's going to take for you to realize something, Crystal."

"What?"

"That you're more than an obligation to me. I love you. Always have and always will. That's why I joined the navy five years ago instead of hanging around in Denver and getting into more trouble. In all honesty, I think had I claimed you as my wife back then we might very well be divorced by now."

His words almost snatched the air from her lungs. "Why do you think that?"

"Because there is more to life than what we had back then."

"We had love."

"Yes," he agreed. "And it was our love that would have held things together for a while. But I could see things eventually falling apart. I had a high school education and barely two years of college, and you were determined not to go back to school to get a diploma. All you wanted was to be my wife and the mother of my kids."

"And you saw something wrong with that?" she asked, not sure what he was getting at.

"No, not at the time. But think about it. How far would we have gotten on our own without finally asking your family or mine for help? And eventually I would have resented having to ask anyone for handouts. Granted, I had my land, though legally it didn't belong to me until I turned twenty-five, which meant we would have had to live in the cabin, but only if Dillon agreed to it. But then I doubt the cabin would have been enough. I would have wanted to build a house just as big as my brothers'. One large enough to raise our kids in."

He paused a moment before adding, "And we talked about having a house full of kids without really giving any consideration to how we would take care of them."

She nodded. Although a part of her didn't want to admit it, she knew what he was saying was true. After her miscarriage she had cried for months because she'd lost his baby. After all, they'd talked so often of having a child together one day. But neither had talked about how they would take care of one financially. She'd known the Westmorelands had money, and her young, imma- ture mind had assumed that whatever she and Bane needed his family would eventually take care of. He was right; all she had wanted to do was marry him and have his babies. And she had hated school. Or so she'd thought. The kids had been mean and hateful and resented her ability to ace every test with flying colors. After a while she'd gotten tired of being the class star and having the haters on her back. She'd finally convinced herself that going to school was a waste of her time. Her family had blamed Bane for that decision but it had been hers and hers alone.

She glanced over at him. He had gotten quiet again as he cut into his steak. *Her Bane.* And then a part of her finally got it. He had loved her back then and he loved her now and had told her so several times since he'd walked through her front door. Bane had wanted to give her a better life five years ago because he loved her enough to believe that she and his kids deserved the best of anything. And to give them that, he had made sacrifices. And one of those sacrifices had been her. But she could finally say she understood why he'd made them.

He had wanted to grow up, but he'd also given her a chance to grow up, as well. And she had. She knew how to think for herself, she had two college degrees and was working on her PhD. That had been a lot to accomplish in five years' time and she had done it thanks to him. He had practically forced her to realize her full potential.

"That steak was good."

She glanced over at his plate. It was clean. "You want some of my salad?'

He shook his head and grinned. "No, thanks. I'm good."

Yes, she agreed inwardly. Bane Westmoreland was definitely good. "Bane?"

He pushed his plate aside and glanced over at her. "Yes?"

"I've finally taken my blinders off, and do you know what I see?"

He leaned back in his chair and stared at her. "No. What?"

"A man who loves me. A man who truly loves me even after five years of not seeing me or talking to me. A man who was willing to give me up to give me the best. And for that I want to give you my thanks."

Instead of the smile she'd expected, she watched as a muscle twitched in his jaw. "I really don't want your thanks, Crystal."

No, he wouldn't want her thanks, she thought. He would want her love. Pushing her chair back, she eased from her seat and went to him. Ignoring the look of surprise on his face, she slid down into his lap and turned around to face him. Wrapping her arms around his neck she leaned up and slanted her mouth over his.

He let her kiss him but didn't participate. That was fine with her because she needed him to understand something with this kiss. She'd know the moment he got it, the moment he understood. So she kissed him, putting everything she had into it, and when she heard his breathless moan, she knew he'd almost gotten it. He then returned her kiss with as much passion as she was giving and she felt his hand slide down to her thighs before moving underneath the T-shirt to caress her naked skin.

She knew things could turn sexual between them real quick if she didn't take control. If she didn't let him know what was on her mind…and in her heart. So she pulled back, breaking off the kiss. But that didn't slow up his hands, which were still moving. One was still underneath her T-shirt and the other was sliding up and down her back, stroking the length of her spine.

"I love you, too, Bane," she whispered against his

lips. "I guess you can say I never knew how much until now. And you never stopped loving me like I never stopped loving you. I get that now."

"No, baby. I never stopped loving you," he whispered back against her lips. Then he tightened his arms around her as he stood with her and headed toward the bed.

After placing her there, without saying a word he tucked his fingers into the hem of the T-shirt she was wearing and took it off her.

She watched him step back and ease his jeans down his thighs and legs. Her gaze roamed up and down his naked form. Good thing she wasn't wearing any panties or they would be drenched. She wanted him just that much. And she could tell from the look in his eyes that he wanted her with all the passion he'd stored up for five years. He'd told her as much a number of times, had proved it last night and all day today. She saw it now while looking at his engorged erection and could hear it in his breathing.

He came back toward the bed, and before he could make another move, she reached out and wrapped her fingers around his swollen sex. It fit perfectly in her hand. "Nice," she said, licking her lips.

She heard Bane groan deep in his throat before saying, "Glad you think so."

"I do. Always have thought so."

When she began stroking him with her fingers, even using her fingernail to gently scrape along the sensitive skin, he threw his head back and released a growl that seemed to come from deep within his gut. And when she leaned down and swirled her tongue over him, she felt his fingers dig through her hair to her scalp. That drove her to widen her mouth and draw the full length of him between her lips.

* * *

Pleasure ripped through Bane to all parts of his body. Crystal was using her mouth to build a roaring fire inside him. A fire that was burning him from the inside out. And when she used her fingers to stroke the thatch of curly hair covering his groin, he could feel his erection expanding in her mouth. That pushed her to suck on him harder and he fought hard not to explode right then and there. Instead, he reached down and entwined his fingers in the silky strands of her hair before wrapping a lock around his fist. And then he began moving his hips, pumping inside her mouth. The more he did so the more she stroked him before using those same fingers to gently squeeze his testicles.

Was she trying to kill him? Did she have any idea what she was doing to him? Did she know how hard it was to hold back and not come in her mouth? He knew if he allowed her to continue at this rate, she was liable to soon find out.

"Crystal," he whispered, barely able to get her name past his lips as his heart raced and blood pulsed through his veins. "Stop, baby. You need to stop now."

She was ignoring him, probably because he hadn't said it with much conviction. And honestly, there was no way he could with all the pleasurable sensations tearing through him. Her desire to please him this way meant more than anything because even with her inexperience she was doing one hell of a job making him moan.

When he could no longer hold back, he shouted her name and tried pushing her away, but she held tight to his thighs until the last sensation had swept through his body. He should have felt drained but instead he felt even more needy. Desperate to get inside her body, he jerked himself out of her mouth and eased her back on the bed.

He felt her body shudder the moment he entered her. She was wet, drenched to the core, which made it easy to thrust deep, all the way to her womb. Then he positioned them so that her legs were wrapped around his waist and back.

He stared down into her face. "I love you. I love your scent. I love your taste. I loved making love to you. I love coming inside you. And I love being buried inside you so deep it's unreal. Heaven. Over-the-top wonderful."

"Oh, Bane."

He was certain she would have said more, but when he began moving, she began moaning. He lifted her hips and began thrusting in and out of her with rapid strokes, taking her over and over again, and intentionally driving her over the edge the way she'd done earlier to him.

He couldn't get enough of her, and when she screamed his name and he felt the heels of her feet dig deep into his back, he knew she was coming. However, he refused to go there yet. But it was the feel of her inner muscles clamping down on him, trying to pull everything out of him that was the last straw, and he couldn't hold back his explosion any longer.

"Crystal!"

He was a goner as he emptied himself completely inside her, filling her in a way that had his entire body shuddering uncontrollably. He could feel her arms wrapped around him and could hear her softly calling his name. Moments later when the earth stopped shaking and his world stopped spinning, he managed to lift his head to stare down at her before crashing his mouth down on hers.

And the words that filled his mind as he kissed her
with a hunger he couldn't contain were the same ones
he'd said a number of times recently.

This is just the beginning.

Sixteen

"Wake up, sleepyhead."

Crystal slowly opened her eyes and looked out the car's windshield. They were parked at what appeared to be a truck stop decorated with a zillion Christmas lights that were blinking all over the place, although she could see the sun trying to peek out over the mountains.

They had checked out of the hotel around six the night before, which meant that they'd been on the road for twelve hours or so. They'd only stopped twice for bathroom breaks. Otherwise, most of the time she'd been sleeping and he'd been driving. She had offered to share the driving time, but he had told her he could handle things and he had.

He probably figured she needed her rest and she was grateful for that. Before getting dressed, the two of them had taken a third shower. The third in a single day, but all that physical activity had called for it. Besides, she enjoyed taking showers with Bane. He could be so creative when they were naked together under a spray of water. The memories of all they'd done had her body tingling.

Pulling herself up in her seat, she glanced over at him. "We're here already?"

"Yes, but plans changed. Instead of meeting up at the Alabama-Georgia line, we're meeting here."

She glanced around and lifted a curious brow. "And where is here exactly?"

"North Carolina."

North Carolina? No wonder they were surrounded by mountains so huge they reminded her of Denver. "Why the change?"

"They preferred meeting at Delaney's cabin but didn't say why. My guess is because it's secluded, and the way Jamal has things set up, you can spot someone coming for miles around."

"I see." And honestly she did. She had met his cousin Delaney once and recalled hearing how she'd met this prince from the Middle East at a cabin in the North Carolina mountains. To make a long story short, the two had fallen in love and married. "I read an article about her in *Essence* a couple of years back."

"Did you?"

"Yes. And she and her prince are still together."

"Yes, they are. Only thing is that now Jamal is king. He gave the cabin where they met to Delaney as a wedding gift. Since she lives outside the country most of the time, she's given us permission to use it whenever we like."

Bane's phone went off and he quickly pulled it out of the pocket of his jacket and answered it. "This is Bane." After a few seconds he said, "We're here." Then several moments later he said, "Yes, I recall how to get there. I'll see you guys in a little while."

After he hung up the phone he glanced over at her. "I know this has to be both taxing and tiring for you, Crystal, but hopefully the guys and I will come up with some sort of plan."

She nodded. "Still no word on the whereabouts of those other two chemists?"

"No. None. I spoke to Nick while you were sleeping and he's not sure what the hell is going on now. It seems that with the revelation of a mole in the agency, everyone is keeping their lips sealed."

Crystal figured that didn't bode well for her, since Nick had been Bane's source of information from the inside. She bit back an exasperated sigh and leaned back against the headrest.

"Everything is going to be all right," Bane said, reaching over and taking her hand in his. Not waiting for her to respond he asked, "Did you enjoy yourself yesterday and last night?"

That brought a smile to her lips as the pleasant memories washed over her. Hot and spicy memories that made her nipples suddenly become hard and sensitive against her blouse. "Yes, I did. What about you?"

"Yes, I thought it was nice. Best time I've had in a long time."

She was glad he thought so because she definitely felt the same way. The chemistry they'd always shared had been alive and kicking. It didn't even take a touch between them. A look sufficed. At one point he'd lain across his bed and she'd lain across hers with the television going. She had been trying to take a power nap and had felt his gaze on her. When she'd looked over at him and their eyes connected, she couldn't recall who had moved first. All she knew was that the glance had sparked a reaction between them. A reaction that had them tearing off their clothes again.

He brought her hand to his lips and kissed her fingers. "I can't wait to get you back home."

"Home?" She thought of her house that had been set on fire.

"Yes, back in Denver."

She nodded. Although she realized there was nothing back in Dallas for her now, it had been a long time since she'd thought of Denver as home. "What's the hurry?"

"I can't wait for everyone to see you, and to finally introduce you to them as my wife. And we'll have a house to design and build."

Instead of saying anything, she met his gaze and couldn't ignore the flutter that passed through her stomach or the way her pulse quickened at that precise moment. She watched his gaze roam over her, and noticed how his eyes were drawn to her chest. Specifically, the hardened buds pressing against her blouse.

Releasing her hand he turned on the car's ignition. "Come on. We better find Delaney's cabin, and if I figure right, it's about a half hour drive from here. If it was left up to me we'd check into another hotel and have another play day."

Crystal glanced over at him. His eyes were on the road and he was concentrating on their surroundings. She should be, too, but at the moment she couldn't help but concentrate on him.

Brisbane Westmoreland had always seemed bigger than life to her. The past five years hadn't been easy for either of them, but they were back together and that was all that mattered. Now, if they could only stop the men who were trying to kidnap her, everything would be great.

When he brought the car to a stop at a traffic light he glanced over at her and smiled. "You okay, baby?"

She nodded, smiling back at him. Releasing her seat belt, she leaned toward him and placed a quick kiss on his lips. "You're here with me, and as far as I'm concerned that's all that matters now."

She rebuckled her seat belt and sat back. Satisfied.

"What the hell?" Bane muttered through clenched teeth.

Crystal looked over at him and then sat up straight in her seat and glanced out the SUV's window. "What's wrong, Bane?"

He shook his head and stared out at all the cars, trucks and motorcycles that were parked in front of the cabin they'd pulled up to. "I should have known."

"Should have known what?"

"That it would be more than just Quade, Dare, Clint and Cole meeting us today. Some Westmorelands will find just about any excuse to get together."

Chuckling, he brought the car to a stop and turned off the ignition before unbuckling his seat belt. He then reached over and unbuckled hers. "Before going inside, there's something I need to give you."

"What?"

"This," he said, pulling a small black velvet box from his jacket. When he flipped open the lid, he heard her breath catch at the sight of the diamond solitaire ring with a matching gold wedding band.

"Oh, Bane, it's beautiful."

"A beautiful ring for a beautiful woman," he said,

taking the ring out of the box and sliding it on her finger. "It looks good on you, as if it's where it belongs."

She held up her hand and the diamond sparkled in
the sunlight. "But when did you get it? How?"

He smiled. "I got it in New York. I had a layover
there for a couple of days due to bad weather, and to kill
time I checked out some of the jewelry stores. When
we got married I couldn't afford to give you anything
but this," he said, reaching out and touching the locket
she still wore. "I figured it was time I get you something better. It was time I put my ring on your finger."

He got quiet for a moment and then said, "You don't
know how much it bothered me knowing you were out
there not wearing a ring. I wondered how you were
keeping the men away."

"I told you what they thought."

Yes, she had, which he still found hard to believe,
but at least it had kept the men at bay.

He lifted her hand and brought it to his lips and
kissed it. He then leaned over and lowered his head to
kiss her. And he needed this kiss. He hadn't made love
to her in over twelve hours, and it was too long.

How had he gone without her for five years? That
showed he had willpower he hadn't known he had.

And the one thing he liked most about kissing her
was the way she would kiss him back, just like he'd
taught her all those years ago to do. Some women's
mouths were made for kissing, and he thought hers
was one of them. She tasted just as good as she looked
and smelled. And that was another thing about her: her
scent. His breath would quicken each and every time
he took a sniff of her.

His cousin Zane swore that a woman's natural scent
was a total turn-on for most men. It had something to

do with pheromones. Bane wasn't sure about all that, but the one thing he did know was that Crystal's scent could literally drive him over the edge. And her scent was a dead giveaway that she wanted him regardless of whether she admitted it or not.

There was a loud knock on the truck's window, and he broke off the kiss to glare at the intruder, who said, "Knock it off, Bane."

Rolling his eyes, Bane returned his gaze to Crystal, mainly to focus on her wet lips. "Go away, Thorn."

"Not until I check you over to make sure you're all in one piece. I'm on my way to a benefit bike race in Daytona and in a hurry, so get out of the car."

Bane shook his head as he eased his car seat back. But then in a surprise move he reached across and pulled Crystal over the console and into his arms. He opened the door with her in his arms and got out.

"Bane! Put me down," Crystal said, trying to wriggle free in his arms.

"In a minute," he said, holding her a little longer before sliding her down his body so her feet could touch the ground.

He then turned to Thorn. "Good seeing you, Thorn."

"Good seeing you, too," Thorn said, giving Bane a bear hug. Thorn then reached out to Crystal and pulled her to him, as well. "You too, Crystal. It's been a while."

Bane watched the exchange and knew Thorn's comment had surprised her. Thorn Westmoreland was the celebrity in the family, a well-known, award-winning motorcycle racer who as far as Bane was concerned also built the baddest bikes on earth. He had several movie stars and sports figures as clients.

Crystal and Thorn had only met once at a Westmoreland family reunion, but Bane knew that when it came to his family, Crystal had assumed they saw her as the reason he'd gotten into trouble all those times.

"Thanks, Thorn. It's good seeing you again, as well," Crystal said, as Bane pulled her closer to his side. "How is your family?"

"Fine. Tara's inside along with all the others."

"And just who are *all* the others?" Bane asked.

No sooner than he'd asked that question, the door to the cabin opened and his family members began filing out. The one person Bane hadn't expected to see was Dillon. His older brother stepped out onto the porch along with their cousin Dare. Bane shook his head, not for the first time, at how much Dillon and Dare favored each other.

Bane smiled as his family kept coming out of the cabin. There was Dare and Thorn's brother Stone, and Quade's brother Jared. And besides Dillon, Bane saw his brothers Riley and Canyon, as well as his twin cousins, Aidan and Adrian. He'd just seen the latter four in Denver for Thanksgiving.

"Hey, what's going on?" he asked chuckling. "Last time I looked, Crystal and I were on the run and not dropping by to socialize."

"Doesn't matter," his cousin Dare said, grinning. "We all wanted to see for ourselves that the two of you were okay."

"And we're ready to take anyone on who thinks they can snatch Crystal away from us," Riley said.

"From *us*?" Bane asked, looking at his brother. He knew that of all his siblings and cousins, Riley had been bothered the most by Bane's relationship with Crystal. Riley was afraid that Bane's quest to find her might prove painful if she hadn't waited for him those five years the way Bane had waited for her.

"Yes. *Us*. She's a Westmoreland and we take care of what's ours" was Riley's response.

Bane looked over at Crystal and pulled her closer to his side. "Yes, she is a Westmoreland."

Quade came forward. "Most of the men arrived yesterday. Figured we would get some fishing in while we waited for you to get here. The women showed up this morning and are out back on the porch frying the fish. First we eat breakfast, then we talk about putting a plan together. There're a couple of others we're waiting on."

Bane wondered who the others were but didn't ask. Instead, he said, "Fried fish in the morning? Hey, lead the way."

Crystal had never felt as much a part of the Westmoreland family as she did now. And she knew she had the women to thank for that. They had oohed and aahed over her ring, telling her how much they liked it and how good it looked on her finger. And they had congratulated her on her marriage to Bane and officially welcomed her to the family.

This was her first time meeting Dillon's wife, Pam. In fact, the last time she'd seen Dillon, he was a single man on a quest to find out more about his great-grandfather Raphel. It seemed that pursuit had landed him right on Pam's doorstep, and it had meant nothing to Dillon that Pam was engaged to marry another man at the time.

And then there was Tara, Thorn's wife, whose sister, Trinity, was married to Bane's cousin Adrian. Crystal thought it was pretty neat that two sisters were married to two cousins. And the same thing went for Pam and her sister, Jillian. Jillian was married to Bane's cousin Aidan. Crystal also enjoyed getting to know

Dare's wife, Shelly, Stone's wife, Madison, Jared's wife, Dana, and Canyon's wife, Keisha.

Quade's wife, Cheyenne, was back home in Charlotte with their triplets—a son and two daughters. The girls had dance class today; otherwise, he said his wife would have come with him.

All the women were friendly and the men were, as well. Crystal fought back tears when they welcomed her to the family in a toast. And when Bane's brother Dillon pulled her aside and said that as far as he was concerned, she'd always been part of the family, and that he was glad she and Bane were back together again, she had to excuse herself for a minute to compose herself. Coming from Dillon, that had meant everything.

After going inside for a quick second to get a beer out of the refrigerator, Bane found her sitting on the dock by the lake. Without saying anything, he pulled her up into his arms. "You okay, baby?"

She looked up at him and nodded. "Yes. Everyone is so nice to me."

He smiled and reached out and caressed her cheek. "And why wouldn't they be nice to you? You're a nice person."

"B-but you and I used to cause your family so many headaches. We did some crazy stuff and got into a lot of trouble."

"Yes." He nodded. "We did. But look at us now, Crystal. I finished the naval academy and I'm a SEAL, and you're just a few months shy of getting your PhD. I think Dr. Crystal Westmoreland will sound damn good, don't you?"

Swiping tears away from her eyes, she said, "Yes. I think so, as well."

"All I'm saying is that you and I have changed, Crystal. We aren't the same people we were back then. We're older, better and more mature, although I'll admit we still have a lot of growing to do. But above all, what didn't change was our love for each other. That's the one thing that remained constant."

Crystal knew Bane was right. Their love *had* been the one thing to remain constant. "I love you, Bane," she whispered.

"And I love you back, baby."

Standing on tiptoe, she slanted her mouth over his, doubting that she could or would ever tire of kissing him. And when he wrapped his arms around her and returned her kiss, she knew she could stay in his arms like that forever. Or maybe not, she thought, when she began feeling weak in the knees.

It was the sound of a car door slamming that made them pull their mouths apart. They both turned to look toward the clearing at the people getting out of the cars that had just pulled up. There were three men and a woman. The only person Crystal recognized was the woman. It was Bane's cousin Bailey.

"I'll be damned," Bane said. "That guy… The one in the black leather jacket sure does look like—"

"Riley," she finished for him. "Riley doesn't have a twin, so who is he?" she asked staring.

"That has to be Garth Outlaw. I never met him but I'd heard how he and his five siblings look just like the Westmorelands. And they *are* Westmorelands. I told you we found out that my great-grandfather Raphel had a son he hadn't known about who was adopted by the Outlaws as a baby."

"Well, if anyone doubts Garth Outlaw is related to your family all they have to do is put him and Riley side by side."

"That's true," Bane agreed. "And the man with Bailey is her fiancé, Walker Rafferty. I wonder why they decided to come here instead of flying back to Alaska. When I talked to her the other day that's where they were headed. And I have no idea who the third guy is. The one in the dark suit."

Bane took Crystal's hand in his. "Come on. Quade is beckoning us to join them."

A few moments later when they reached Quade, introductions were made. Just as Bane said, Riley's lookalike was one of their newfound cousins from Alaska, the Outlaws, and the man with Bailey was her fiancé, Walker. However, the third man, the one in the dark suit, was just what Crystal had figured him to be—a government man. She wasn't surprised when Quade said, "Bane and Crystal, this here is Hugh Oakwood. He was recently appointed by the president to head a special agency under the Department of Defense."

Bane raised a brow. "Department of Defense? I don't understand why this would involve the DOD. Their primary concern is with military actions abroad. The Department of Homeland Security's role is to handle things domestically."

Hugh Oakwood nodded as he glanced from Bane to Crystal. "Typically that would be true, but what's going on here isn't typical. We think we're dealing with an international group. And it's highly likely that some of our own people at Homeland Security are involved. That's why the president has authorized my agency to handle things."

The man glanced around and saw he had an audience. Clearing his throat, he asked, "Is there someplace where we can talk privately?"

Quade spoke up and said, "Yes, come this way, Hugh. I got just the place."

Seventeen

Bane had heard that after Jamal had purchased the cabin for Delaney, he'd hired a builder to quadruple the size of it to expand the kitchen, add three additional bedrooms, three more bathrooms, a huge family room and a study. The spacious study was where they were now.

He couldn't imagine anyone getting any studying done in here. Not with the gorgeous view of the mountains and the lake. And if those two things didn't grab you then there was the room itself, with its oak walls and beautiful rustic decor. A floor-to-ceiling bookshelf took up one wall and another wall consisted entirely of a large plate-glass window.

Bane sat beside Crystal on a sofa facing the huge fireplace. Dillon, Quade, Clint, Cole and Dare grabbed chairs around the room. It seemed that Hugh Oakwood preferred standing, which made perfect sense since he had the floor. It was obvious that everyone was interested in what he had to say.

The man turned to Crystal. "I read the report and you, Dr. Westmoreland, have a brilliant mind."

Bane noticed that everyone's gaze had settled on Crystal and she seemed uncomfortable with all the attention she was getting. They were realizing what he'd always known. His wife was a very smart woman.

Crystal blushed. "I wouldn't say that. And officially I'm not a doctor yet."

"I *would* say that. And it's only a matter of months before you get your PhD. After going over all your research, at least what I have access to, there's no doubt that you'll get it," Oakwood said. "And if you don't mind, although I noted you've never used the Westmoreland name, I prefer using it now."

"No, I don't mind," she said. "Bane and I decided years ago to keep our marriage a secret."

Oakwood nodded. "That in itself might be a blessing in disguise. Because no one knows of your marriage, the group that's looking for you has no leads as to where you might be right now."

He paused a moment, then said, "In your research you've basically come up with a formula to make items invisible. Similar testing and research have been done by others, but it seems you might have perfected it to the degree where it's almost ready to use."

"So what does all this mean?" Bane asked.

"It means that in the wrong hands it can be a threat to national security. Right now one particular terrorist group, PFBW, which stands for People for a Better World, sees it as a way to smuggle things in and out of countries undetected."

"Things like what?"

"Drugs, bombs, weapons, you name it. Right, Dr. Westmoreland?"

Crystal nodded. "Yes. Although there's quite a bit of research that still needs to be done before that can happen."

Oakwood nodded. "PFBW have already nabbed the other two chemists, as you all know, and would have grabbed you if your husband hadn't intervened."

"I got that note from someone as a warning," Crystal said.

"Yes, you did. PFBW started recruiting members a few years ago. But we managed to infiltrate the group. That's the only way we know what's going on. When you join, you join for life and the only way to get out is death. We're lucky that our informant hasn't been identified so far."

He paused a minute and then added, "The best we can figure is that although Jasmine Ross started out as part of the group, somewhere along the way she had a change of heart and is the one who slipped you that note. It seems that she tried to disappear as well but wasn't as lucky as you. They found her."

And Bane was sure everyone in the room was aware of the outcome of that. "My wife can't continue to hide out and be on the run forever."

"I agree," Oakwood said. "The problem we're facing is not knowing who we can trust in Homeland Security. The one thing we do know is that PFBW still wants you, Dr. Westmoreland. You're the missing link. The other chemists' work can only go so far. You have researched a key component they lack, and it's your work that's needed to put their scheme in place."

"Sorry, but they won't be getting her," Bane said through clenched teeth as he wrapped his arms around Crystal's shoulders.

"That's why we have a plan," Oakwood said, finally taking a chair.

"What's the plan?" Bane asked, removing his arm from around Crystal to lean forward.

From the looks exchanged between Quade and Oakwood, Bane had a feeling whatever plan Oakwood had come up with, he wasn't going to like it.

Bane was off the sofa in a flash. "No! Hell no! No one is using my wife as bait!"

Crystal reached out and touched Bane's arm. "Calm down, Bane. It doesn't sound too bad."

Bane stared down at her. "They want to set you up someplace and then tell PFBW where you are so they can grab you and—"

"When they do come for me, it sounds as if Oakwood and his men will be ready to arrest them."

Bane rolled his eyes. As a SEAL, he of all people knew things didn't always go as planned. "But what if something goes wrong? What if they fail to protect you? What if—"

"Their mission is successful?" Crystal asked, still trying to calm her husband down. "I have to take the chance their plan will work. Like you said, I can't be on the run for the rest of my life."

Bane pulled her up into his arms. "I know, baby, but I can't take a chance with your life. I can't have you back just to lose you."

Crystal heard the agony in his voice, but she needed to make him understand. "And I can't have you back just to lose you, either, but every time you'll leave to go on covert operations as a SEAL I'll face that possibility."

"It's not the same. I'm trained to go into risky places. You aren't."

He was right; she wasn't. "But I'll be well guarded from a distance. Right, Mr. Oakwood?"

The man nodded. "Right. And we do have an informant on the inside."

A muscle twitched in Bane's jaw. "Not good enough," he said, bracing his legs apart and crossing his arms over his chest. "She won't be alone. I will be with her."

Oakwood shook his head. "That won't work. The people looking for her expect her to be alone."

Bane frowned. "Damn their expectations. I refuse to let my wife go anywhere alone. At some point they'll suspect she had help. They probably already do from the way we've successfully eluded them up to now. I don't like your plan, Oakwood, and the only way I'll even consider it is if I'm the one protecting my wife."

"May I make a suggestion?" Everyone in the room glanced over at Quade.

"What's your suggestion, Quade?" Crystal asked when it was obvious neither Bane nor Oakwood was going to. Tension was so thick in the room you could cut it with a knife.

"Oakwood ran his idea by me earlier and knowing Bane like I do, I figured he wouldn't go along with it, so I came up with a plan B, which I'm hoping everyone will accept. It still requires using Crystal as bait, but at least Bane will get to stay with her."

Oakwood stared at Quade for a moment and then said, "Okay, what's your plan?"

Quade stood. "Before I explain things, I need to get two other people in here who will be instrumental to the success of this plan. The three of us discussed it last night and feel it will work."

He then went to the door, opened it and beckoned for someone. Moments later, Bailey's fiancé, Walker Rafferty, and the Westmorelands' newfound cousin Garth Outlaw entered the room.

Crystal studied Walker and could see how Bailey had fallen for him. He was a looker, but so was Bane. In Crystal's mind, no man looked better. And Garth Outlaw looked so much like Riley it was uncanny. And she found out that like Walker, Garth was an ex-Marine.

Garth began talking. "Quade brought me up-to-date as to what's going on. If you want to set a trap by using Crystal as bait then I suggest you do it in Alaska."

"Alaska?" Bane asked, frowning. "Why Alaska?"

"Because the Outlaws happen to own a cabin on Kodiak Island and it's in a very secluded area. But it's also secured and the cabin has an underground tunnel," Garth said.

Quade moved forward. "If word intentionally leaks out as to where Crystal is, then the people wanting her won't lose any time going after her."

"In Alaska?" Now it was Crystal's turn to ask doubtfully.

"Yes, in Alaska," Oakwood said, rubbing his chin, as if giving plan B serious thought. "They will check things out to make sure it's not a trap, though. Why would Dr. Westmoreland escape to Alaska? The dots will have to connect."

"They will," Garth spoke up and said. "I understand Crystal attended Harvard. Coincidentally, my brother Cash went there at the same time. He was working on his master's degree. Who says their paths didn't cross?"

"I'm following you," Oakwood said thoughtfully. "The people looking for Dr. Westmoreland will assume that their paths *did* cross, and that in desperation, Dr. Westmoreland, you reached out to Outlaw and he offered you safe haven at a cabin he owns in Alaska."

"Exactly," Quade said. "And from what Garth says, this cabin will be perfect. It's in a secluded location on Outlaw property, and the underground tunnel will provide an escape route if needed."

"And in addition to all of that," Garth said, smiling, "thanks to those strong Westmoreland genes, Bane and Cash look alike. Probably just as much as me and Riley resemble each other. That will work in our favor if someone knows Crystal had help and has gotten a glimpse of the guy she's been seen with. They would expect that same guy to be there with her, still protecting her. They will think it's Cash when it will be Bane."

Dillon spoke up. "That plan will work if no one knows that Crystal is married to Bane. Are you guys absolutely certain no one knows?"

"So far that's a guarded secret," Oakwood said. "I checked and Dr. Westmoreland never indicated Brisbane Westmoreland as her husband on any official school records or other documentation. I wasn't even aware of the marriage until Quade brought it to my attention. However, on the other hand," he said, shifting in his chair, "Brisbane Westmoreland has always indicated on any of his official paperwork that he was married and Crystal Newsome Westmoreland is listed as his wife."

Bane shrugged. "I needed to make sure Crystal was taken care of if anything ever happened to me," he said, pulling her closer to him and placing a kiss on her forehead. "I also have medical coverage on her as well, just in case she ever needed it, and I established a bank account in her name."

"All traceable if someone really started to dig," Dare said. It was obvious his former FBI agent's mind was at work.

"Let's hope no one feels the need to dig that far,"

Clint Westmoreland said. He then looked over at Oakwood. "Can't that information be blocked?"

"Yes, but because I don't know who's the mole at
Homeland Security and how high up in the department
he or she is, blocking it might raise a red flag," Oakwood said. "Our main goal is to try to flush out the
mole. Right now he is a danger to our national security. To know he might be someone in authority is even
more of a reason for concern."

Neither Bane nor Crystal said anything as everyone
looked over at them. The decision was theirs.

"It's a big decision. You might want to sleep on it,"
Cole suggested.

Crystal stood. "Thanks, but there's no need to sleep
on it. And I appreciate everyone wanting to help me.
However, what concerns me more than anything is that
those people want me alive, but they won't think twice
about taking out Bane if he gets in their way. For that
reason, I prefer that Bane not be with me."

"Like hell!"

When Bane stood up to object further, Crystal
reached out and placed a finger over his lips. "I figured that would be your reaction, Bane." She shook her
head. "There's no way you'll let me put my life at risk
without trying to protect me, is there?"

He removed her finger from his lips and stared down
at her with an unwavering expression on his face. "No."

She released a deep breath. "Then, I guess that
means we'll be together in Alaska."

A gusty winter's breeze caused Bane to pull his
jacket tighter as he wrapped his arms around Crystal
and they walked inside the hotel. It was late. Close to
midnight. After making the decision that they would be

traveling to Alaska, they'd needed to put in place concrete plans. Crystal had trusted him to handle things and asked to be excused to join the ladies who'd been outside sitting on the patio.

In a way he was glad she'd left when she had, because more than once he'd ripped into Oakwood. Too often it appeared that the man was so determined to find out the identity of the mole at Homeland Security that he was willing to overlook Crystal's safety. And Bane wasn't having that.

It had taken Dillon, Quade and Dare to soothe his ruffled feathers and remove the boiling tension in the room by assuring him that Crystal's safety was the most important thing. Only after that could they finally agree on anything.

He still didn't like it, but more than anything he wanted to bring those responsible to justice so that he and Crystal could have normal lives…something they hadn't had since the day they married.

"You've been quiet, Bane," Crystal said a short while later after they'd checked into the hotel and gone to their room.

"Been thinking," he said, glancing around at the furnishings. They were staying at the Saxon Hotel, and it was as if they'd walked right into paradise.

Dare had offered them the use of one of the bedrooms at Delaney's cabin, but since some of his kin also planned to stay there for the night, he had opted out. He preferred having Crystal to himself, and was not up to sharing space with anyone, not even his family. After he said that he and Crystal would spend the night at a hotel in town, Quade had offered him his room at the Saxon Hotel. The penthouse suite.

It just so happened Quade's brother-in-law was Dominic Saxon, the owner of the luxurious five-star Saxon Hotels and the Saxon Cruise Line. Quade had a standing reservation at any Saxon Hotel, but since his wife, Cheyenne, hadn't accompanied him on this trip, he preferred hanging out with his cousins and brother at the cabin, figuring a card game would be taking place later.

"Wow! This place is simply gorgeous," Crystal said.

Bane leaned back against the door as she walked past him to stand in the middle of the hotel room and glance around.

"Yes, it is that," he said, thinking the room wasn't the only gorgeous thing he was looking at. Before leaving the cabin she had showered and changed clothes. Now she was wearing a pair of dark slacks and a pullover sweater. Whether she was wearing jeans and a T-shirt or dressed as she was now, as far as he was concerned, she was the epitome of sexy.

Since her original destination had been the Bahamas, most of the items she'd packed were summer wear. Luckily she and Bailey were similar in size and height, so Bailey had loaned Crystal several outfits that would be perfect for the harsh Alaska weather.

"Come on, let's explore," she said, coming back to him, grabbing his hand and pulling him along.

He wished this could have been the kind of hotel he'd taken her to on their wedding night. As far as he was concerned, it was fit for a king and queen. There was a state-of-the-art kitchen, and according to the woman at the check-in desk, the suite came with its own chef who was on call twenty-four hours a day.

Then there was the spacious living room with a beautiful view of the Smokey Mountains. He figured the furnishings alone in the place cost in the millions. There was a private bar area that came with your own personal bartender if you so desired, and a connecting theater room that had box-office movies at the press of a button.

But what really had his pulse racing was the bedroom, which you entered through a set of double doors. The room was huge and included a sitting area and game nook. He was convinced the bed was created just for lovemaking. Evidently Crystal thought so, as well. He watched as she crossed the room to sit on the edge of the bed and bounced a few times as if to test the mattress.

"It will work."

He lifted a brow, pretending he didn't know what she was referring to. "Work for what?"

"For us. I think that last hotel probably had to replace the mattresses on the beds after we left."

He chuckled, thinking he wouldn't be surprised if they had. He and Crystal had definitely given both beds major workouts. He continued to stare across the room at her. There was just something about seeing Crystal sitting on the bed that was causing a delicious thrill to flow through him. When their gazes met and held, he decided there was something missing from the picture of her sitting on the bed.

Him.

Eighteen

Crystal leaned back on her arms and gazed through watchful eyes as Bane moved from the doorway and headed in the direction of the bed. Straight toward her.

As much as she tried, she couldn't dismiss the flutter in her tummy or the way her pulse was beating out of control. All she could do was watch him, knowing what he had in mind, because it was what she had in mind, as well. He was taking slow, sexy and seductive steps with an intensity that filled the room with his sexual aura. There seemed to be some kind of primitive force surrounding him and she could only sit there, stare and feel her panties get wet.

As if he knew what she was thinking, what she wanted, without breaking his stride he eased his leather jacket from his shoulders and tossed it aside. Next came his shirt, which he ripped from his body, sending buttons flying everywhere. And without losing steam he jerked his belt through the loops and tossed it in the air to land on the other side of the room.

Without a belt his jeans shifted low on his hips, and she couldn't keep her eyes from moving from his face to his chest to trace the trail of hair that tapered from his chest down his abdomen to disappear beneath the waistband of his jeans.

And then there was what he was packing between those muscular thighs of his. She had seen it, touched it and tasted it. And what made her body tingle all over was knowing it was hers.

She studied Bane's face and saw the intensity etched in his features. A few more steps and he would have made it to the bed. And to her. It seemed the room was quiet; nothing was moving but him and he was a man with a purpose.

By the time he reached her she was a ball of desire, and his intoxicating scent—a mixture of aftershave and male—wasn't helping matters. Her head began spinning and she could actually feel her nipples tighten hard against her sweater, and the area between her legs throbbed mercilessly.

"Do you know what I love most about you?" he asked her in a low, husky voice.

"No, what?" She was barely able to get the words out.

"Every single thing. I can't just name one," he said, gazing down at her. "And do you know what I was thinking while standing there watching you sit on this bed?"

"No, what were you thinking?" He was asking a lot of questions and she was providing answers as best she could. Her mind was struggling to keep up and not get distracted by the masculine physique standing directly in front of her. Shirtless, muscular and sexy as sin.

"I was thinking that I should be on this bed with you."

"No problem. That can be arranged. Join me."

She watched his eyes darken. "If I do, you know what's going to happen."

"Yes, but we're making up for lost time, right?"

"Right."

"In that case." She slowly scooted back on the bed. "Join me," she invited again.

In an instant he was bending over to remove his shoes and socks. Straightening, his hands moved to the snap of his jeans and she watched as he pulled his jeans and briefs down his legs.

When he stood stark naked looking at her, he said, "You got too many clothes on, Crystal."

A smile touched her lips. "Do I?"

"Yes."

She chuckled. "And what, Bane Westmoreland, are you going to do about it?"

Hours later Crystal opened her eyes and adjusted to the darkness. The only light she could see was the one streaming in through the bedroom door from the living room. The bed was huge but she and Bane were almost on the edge, chest to chest, limb to limb. She didn't want to wake him but she needed to go to the bathroom.

He wasn't on top of her but he might as well have been. With his thigh and leg thrown over hers, he was definitely holding her hostage. When she tried untwining their limbs to ease away from him, his eyes flew open.

"Sorry, didn't mean to wake you."

He stared down into her eyes and she stared back into his. They were sleepy, drowsy, satisfied. He tightened his hold on her. "And where do you think you're going?"

"The bathroom."

"Oh."

He released his tight hold on her and rolled to the side. "Don't be gone too long. I'll miss you."

She smiled when he closed his eyes again. She quickly searched for her clothes but didn't see them anywhere and didn't want to turn the lamp on to look for them further. So she decided to cross the room in the nude, something he'd done plenty of times.

Moments later after coming out of the bathroom, she decided to go through her luggage to find something to put on. Their bags were just where they'd left them, not far from the door. She was able to see in the light coming from the sitting room, so it didn't take her long to open her luggage and pull out one of her nightgowns. After slipping it on she noticed the satchel Bane had given her.

Not feeling sleepy, she decided now would be a perfect time to read. Opening the satchel, she saw Bane had placed the letters and cards in stacks so she could read them in order. He had also banded them together and labeled them. She grabbed the ones marked My First Year.

She decided to sit on the sofa in front of the fireplace. Using the remote, she turned it on and the bright glow and the heat gave her a warm cozy feeling.

Settling on the sofa with her legs tucked beneath her, she opened the first letter and began reading...

Crystal,

I made it to the navy training facility in Indiana. The other recruits here are friendly enough but I miss my brothers and cousins back home. But more than anything, I miss you. A part of me knows I need to do this and make something of myself for you, as well as for myself, but I'm not sure I can handle our separation. We've never been apart before, and more than once I wanted to walk out and keep walking and return to Denver and confront your parents to find out where they sent you. I want to let them and everyone know you are my wife and that I have every right to know where you are.

But on those days I feel that way, I know why I am enduring the loneliness. It's for you to reach the full potential that I know you can reach. You are smart. Bright. And you're also pretty. I want you to make something of yourself and I promise to make something of myself, as well.

Not sure if you will ever read this letter but I am hoping that one day you will. Just know that you will always have my heart and I love you more than life itself and I'm giving you space to come into your own. And the day I return we will know the sacrifice would have been for the best.

Love you always,
Your Bane

Crystal drew in a deep breath and wiped a tear from her eye. *Her Bane*. Putting the letter back in the envelope, she placed it aside and picked up a Valentine's Day card. She smiled after reading the poem and when she saw how he'd signed the card, "Your Bane" once again, she felt her heart flutter in her chest.

She kept reading all the cards and letters in the stack. In them he told her how his chief had noted how well he could handle a gun, and how he could hit a target with one eye closed or while looking over his shoulder. "Show-off," she said, grinning as she kept reading. His extraordinary skill with a weapon was what had made him stand out so much that his chief had brought it to the attention of the captain who had recommended him for the SEAL program.

She also noted that although her birthday and their wedding anniversary were the same day, he'd bought her separate cards for each. By the time she had finished the first stack she felt she knew how that first year had gone. His first year without her. He had been suffering just as much as she had. He had missed her. Yearned for her. Longed for her. She felt it in the words he'd written to her, and she could just imagine him lying down at night in his bunk and writing her. He'd told her about the guys he'd met and how some of them had become friends for life.

Crystal was halfway through reading the second stack of cards and letters when she heard a sound. She glanced up and saw Bane standing in the doorway.

"You didn't come back. And I missed you."

At that moment all she could think about was that the man standing there was *her Bane*. Putting the stack of cards and letters aside, she eased to her feet and crossed the room to him. They had been through a lot, were still going through a lot, but through it all, they were together.

When she reached him she wrapped her arms around his waist and said the words that filled her heart. "I love you, Bane."

"And I love you." He then swept her off her feet and into his arms. "I'm taking you back to bed."

"To sleep?" she asked.

"No."

She smiled as he carried her back into the bedroom. Once there he eased her gown off her and tossed it aside before placing her back in bed. "I began reading your letters and cards," she said when he joined her there. "Thank you for sharing that period of time with me. And I kept something for you, as well. A picture journal. I'll give it to you when we get to Alaska."

He stroked a hand down her thigh. "You're welcome, and thanks for keeping the journal for me."

And then he leaned down and kissed her and she knew that like all the other times before, this was just the beginning.

Nineteen

"**I** can't believe this place," Crystal said, after entering the cabin and glancing around.

Bane knew what she meant because he could barely believe it, either. The cabin was huge, but it wasn't just the size. It was also the location and the surroundings, as well as how the cabin has been built with survival in mind.

They had arrived in Kodiak, Alaska, a few hours ago after spending another full day in North Carolina. They had been Garth's guests on his private jet owned by Outlaw Freight Lines. Garth's three brothers—Cash, Sloan and Maverick—had met them at the tiny airport. Their brother Jess, who was running for senator of Alaska, was currently on the campaign trail and their sister, Charm, had accompanied their father to Seattle on a business trip. Garth had joked that it was business for their father and a shopping expedition for their sister.

As far as Bane was concerned, Garth hadn't been lying when he'd said that there was a strong resemblance between him and Cash. The similarity was uncanny in a way. And the similarities between the Westmorelands and the Outlaws didn't end there. In fact, Sloan closely resembled Derringer, and Maverick favored Aidan and Adrian. The Outlaws had easily accepted their biological connection to the Westmorelands, but according to Garth, their father had not. He was still in denial and they didn't understand why.

After making a pit stop at Walker's ranch to drop off Bailey and Walker, Garth and his brothers had driven them on to the Outlaw cabin, which was deep in the mountains and backed up against the Shelikof Strait, a beautiful waterway that stretched from the southwestern coast of Alaska to the east of Kodiak.

"Let us show you around before we leave," Garth said. He and his brothers led them from room to room, and each left Bane and Crystal more in awe than the last. And then the Outlaw brothers showed them the movable wall that led to an underground tunnel. It was better than what Bane had expected. It was basically a man cave with living quarters that included a flat-screen television on one of the walls. The sofa, Bane noted, turned into a bed. The pantry was filled with canned goods. Then there was the gun case that probably had every type of weapon ever manufactured.

"Our grandfather was a gun collector," Sloan Outlaw explained. "Our father didn't share his passion so he gave them to us to get rid of. He has no idea we kept them. As far as we were concerned, they were too priceless to give away."

"Of course, over the years we've added our own favorites," Maverick said, grinning, pointing to a .458 caliber Winchester Magnum, a very powerful rifle. "That one is mine. Use it if you have to."

A short while later, after the tour of the cabin ended, they had returned to the front room. Bane looked over at Cash, the cousin whose identity he would assume for a while. "Hope I'm not putting you out, man."

Cash smiled. "No problem. I need a few days away from Alaska anyway. A couple of friends and I are headed for Bermuda for a few days. Hate how I'll miss all the action."

The plan was to lead the group looking for Crystal to assume that she was in the cabin with Cash, an old college friend. But in order for that plan to work, in case someone went digging, the real Cash Outlaw needed to go missing for a while.

Oakwood would be calling in the morning to give Bane the final plans and let him know when word of Crystal's whereabouts would be leaked so they could be on guard and get prepared. The DOD already had men in place around the cabin. They had been there when Bane and the group arrived. Other than Garth, no one had noticed their presence, since they blended in so well with the terrain.

A short while later Bane and Crystal were saying goodbye to everyone. After Bane closed the door behind him, he looked across the room at Crystal. He thought she was holding up pretty damn well for a woman who in the next twenty-four hours would be the bait in an elaborate trap to catch her would-be kidnappers. As soon as the DOD purposely leaked her whereabouts, it would set things in motion.

"I like them."

He saw her smile. "Who?"

"Your cousins."

"And what do you like about them?" he asked, moving away from the door toward her.

"For starters, how quick they pitched in to help. They didn't have to offer us the use of this place."

"No, they didn't. Garth and his brothers paid a visit to Colorado the week before Thanksgiving to meet the Denver Westmorelands and from there they headed south to visit with the Atlanta Westmorelands. Dillon told me I would like them when I met them and I do."

He drew her into his arms. "If we pull this off we'll owe them a world of thanks. This place is perfect, and not just because of the underground tunnel. There's also the location, the seclusion. I can see someone hiding out here, and I'm sure the people looking for you will see it, too."

"I wonder when Oakwood will send his men," she said thoughtfully, looking up at him.

Bane chuckled. "They're already here."

Surprise appeared on her face. "What? Are you sure?"

"Pretty much. I haven't seen them but I can feel their presence. I noticed it the minute we pulled up in the yard. And because Garth is an ex-Marine, he did, too."

"He said something to you about it?"

Bane shook his head. "He didn't have to. He knew what to look for." Bane didn't say anything for a minute and then he said, "Nothing can happen to you, Crystal. I won't allow it. Do you know what you mean to me?"

She nodded and reached up to place her arms around his neck. "Yes, I know." And she really did. Reading those cards and letters had left her in awe at the magnitude of his love for her.

"Good." And then he leaned down and captured her mouth with his.

* * *

Later that night, just as before, Crystal untangled herself from Bane and slid out of bed. At least she tried. But Bane's arms tightened around her. "Where are you going?"

"To read. I'm on stack three now."

He rolled over in bed so they could lie side by side. "Interesting reading?"

"I think so," she said. "It means a lot knowing you were thinking about me." Reading those cards and letters, especially the letters, had helped her to understand that he loved being a navy SEAL and that his teammates were his family, as well.

"I always thought about you," he said huskily. He rubbed her cheek. "Sleepy?" he asked her.

"No. I plan to read, remember? So let me go."

"Okay, just as long as you're where I can see you."

"I'll just be in the living room."

He shook his head. "Not good enough. I want you in here with me."

She was about to argue with him, remind him the cabin was surrounded by the good guys, but instead she said, "Okay, I'll read in bed if you're sure I won't disturb you."

"I'm sure. I'm wide-awake, as well."

He released her. After slipping back into the gown that he'd taken off her earlier, Crystal padded across the room to pull the third stack out of the satchel.

While getting the cards and letters, she pulled out the photo album she had packed. Going back to the bed, she handed it to him. "Here. This is my gift to you."

Bane took it. "Thanks, baby." He then got into a sitting position and began flipping through the photo album. He came across their marriage license and smiled. When she saw his smile, she said, "We were so young then."

"Yes," he agreed. "But so much in love."

"We still are," she said, settling into position beside him. In amiable silence, he turned the pages of the photo album while she read his cards and letters. "This is your high school graduation picture?" he asked.

She glanced up from reading the letter to look over at the photograph he was asking about. "Yes. And all I could think about that day was that because of you, I had done it. I had gotten the very thing I thought I hadn't wanted and was actually pretty happy about it."

He looked at several more pictures, and when he came to her college graduation picture he said, "Isn't it weird that Cash was there on campus at the same time you were?"

"Yes. I can't imagine what my reaction would have been had I ran into a guy on campus who reminded me of you. So personally, I'm glad our paths didn't cross."

She was about to go back to reading her cards and letters when Bane's cell phone went off. He reached for it. "This is Bane."

Crystal tried reading his expression while he talked with the caller but she couldn't. The only clue she had that he was angry was the way his chin had tightened. And then when he asked the caller in an angry tone, "How the hell did that happen?" she knew something had made him furious. A few moments later he ended the call and immediately sent several text messages.

"What's wrong, Bane?"

He looked over at her and paused before saying anything, and she figured he was trying hard to get his anger in check. "That was Oakwood. Someone in his department screwed up."

He threw his head back as if to get his wrath under control and said, "Your location has already been leaked. The only good thing is that whoever they suspected as the mole took the bait, and he and his men are headed here believing that you're hiding with Cash."

"And the bad thing?" she asked, knowing there was one.

Bane drew in a deep fuming breath. "Whoever this guy is, he's evidently pretty high up there at Homeland Security. He contacted the person in charge of Oakwood's men and gave an order to pull out because a special task force was coming in to take over."

Crystal frowned. "Are you saying Oakwood's men are no longer outside protecting us?"

"That's exactly what I'm saying. But I don't want you to worry about anything. I got this," Bane said, getting out of bed and slipping on his jeans. "What I need for you to do is to go and get in the tunnel below."

"Is that where you'll be?"

"No," he said, picking up his Glock and checking his aim. "I might need to hold things down for a while. Oakwood ordered the men to return and hopefully they'll be back soon."

Crystal didn't want to think about what could happen if they didn't. Bane expected her to be hiding out below, where she would be safe, while he single-handedly fought off the bad guys until help arrived. "I prefer staying up here with you. I may not be as good a shot as you, but thanks to you I'm not bad."

He frowned. "There's no way I can let you stay here with me."

"I don't see why not," she said, sliding out of bed to begin dressing, as well. "To be honest with you, I feel pretty safe."

He shook his head. "And why are you feeling so safe?"

She looked over at him and a smile spread across her lips. "Because I'm not here with just anyone protecting my back. I'm here with Badass Bane."

Twenty

A short while later, Crystal studied the arsenal of Bane's personal weapons spread out on the table and glanced over at him. "I thought a person couldn't travel on a plane with one weapon, much less a whole suitcase full of them."

He met her gaze. "They can't."

She lifted a curious brow. "Then, how did you get through the security checkpoint when you flew to Dallas?"

"I didn't. Bailey figured I might need them and brought them with her to the cabin. I'm glad she did. And there was no problem bringing them with me on Garth's private plane."

Crystal watched how he checked each one out, making sure there was enough ammunition for each. It was close to one in the morning. "You have some awesome teammates, Bane. I enjoyed reading about them, and they have been here for you. For us. Throughout this ordeal. I can't wait to meet Coop. You mentioned him a lot in your letters."

She noticed Bane's hands go still, and when she glanced into his face she saw pain etched in his features. "Bane? What is it? What's wrong?"

He looked at her. "You won't get a chance to meet Coop, Crystal. We lost him during one of our covert operations."

"Oh, no!" She fought back tears for a man she'd never met. But in a way she had met him through Bane's letters and knew from what he'd written that he and Coop shared a special bond. "What happened?"

"I can't give you the details but it was a setup. I'm not sure how it was done but he was taken alive. Then a few days later they sent our CO Coop's bloody clothes and military tag to let us know what they did to him."

She wrapped her arms around Bane's waist. "I am so sorry for your loss. After reading your letters I know what a special friendship the two of you shared."

Bane nodded. "Yes, he was a good friend. Like a brother. I'm sorry you didn't get to meet him."

Hearing the sadness in his words, Crystal leaned up on tiptoe and pressed her lips to his. It was a quick kiss, because they didn't have much time and the situation wouldn't allow anything else. She released him, took a step back and glanced at the clock on the wall. "That's strange."

"What is?"

"I'm surprised no one has called. I would think Oakwood would be keeping tabs on us, letting us know what's going on or how close those people are to here." When Bane didn't say anything she studied his features. "You noticed it, too. Didn't you?"

"Yes, I noticed it and I think I know the reason."

"Why?"

"Someone blocked any calls coming in or out of here. Whoever did it assumes they have us cornered, but I was able to text Walker and the Outlaws right after talking with Oakwood to apprise them of what's going on. I have every reason to believe they are on their way if they aren't here already." He looked down at her. "I'm asking you again to go down below, Crystal."

"Only if we're down there together."

She heard his deep breath of frustration before Bane said, "Then take this," and passed her one of the smaller handguns off the table. "Not that you should need to use it," he added. She inserted it into the pocket of her jacket.

At that moment the light in the room flickered a few times before going completely out, throwing the entire house into darkness. "Bane?"

"I'm here," he said, wrapping an arm around her.

She jumped when suddenly there was a hard knock at the door.

"Seriously? Do they think we plan on answering it?" Bane said in an annoyed tone.

"But what if it's Walker or the Outlaws? Or even Oakwood?"

"It's not," he said. "Too soon to be Oakwood. And as far as Walker and the Outlaws, we agreed to communicate by a signal."

"What kind of signal?"

"The sound of a mourning dove's coo. I didn't hear the signal so you know what that means."

She nodded. Yes, she knew what that meant.

Bane wished like hell that Crystal had done what he'd said and gone down below. He needed to concentrate and wasn't sure he could do that for worrying about her.

Suddenly a loud voice that sounded as if it came through a megaphone blared from outside. "Mr. Outlaw. Miss Newsome. We are members of the Department of Homeland Security. We're here to take Miss Newsome to safety."

"Like hell," Bane whispered in a growl. "Those bastards expect us to just open the door and invite them inside in total darkness. They figure we're stupid enough to fall for that?"

"If you don't respond to our request," the voice continued, "we will assume the two of you are in danger and will force our way in."

Your decision, Bane thought. *Bring it on.*

"You think they really will force their way in?" Crystal asked softly.

"That's evidently their plan, so let's get prepared," he said, lowering her to the floor with him. At that moment his cell phone vibrated in his pocket. Someone had gotten past the block. He quickly pulled the phone out and read the text message from Walker. 5 of them.

"Somehow Walker got through the block to let me know there are five men surrounding the cabin. At least that's all they see. There might be others."

"At least Walker and the Outlaws are here."

"Yes, and they know to stay low and not let their presence be known unless something serious goes down. We need to get the ringleader."

"So for now it's five against two."

He frowned. "I want you to stay down, Crystal. They won't do anything that will harm you since you're valuable to them. That means they'll try to get inside to grab you."

Suddenly there was a huge crash. It sounded like the front door caving in. "Shh," Bane whispered. "Someone just got inside."

* * *

Male voices could be heard from another room. "Miss Newsome, let us know where you are. We know you think you're safe here with Cash Outlaw, but we have reason to believe he can't be trusted. We need to get you out of here and get you to safety."

Multiple footsteps could be heard going from room to room, which meant more than one man had gotten inside. Suddenly the lights came back on. "Stay down," Bane ordered her as he moved to get up from the floor.

"Not on your life." The moment she eased up with Bane, who had his gun drawn, two men entered the room with their guns drawn, as well. Bane shoved her behind him.

"Miss Newsome? Are you okay?" one of the men asked. Both were dressed in camouflage. One appeared to be well over six feet and the other was five-nine or so.

"I'm fine," she said, poking her head from around Bane to size up the two men. Both looked to be in their forties, with guns aimed right at Bane. He in turn had his gun aimed right at them.

"Then, tell your friend to put his gun down," the shorter of the two men said.

"Why can't the two of you put yours down?" Crystal retorted. She tried to block from her mind the sudden thought that this was how things had played out in the dream she'd had a few nights ago.

"We can't. Like we told you, Homeland Security has reason to believe he's dangerous."

As far as Crystal was concerned, that wasn't an understatement. She could feel the anger radiating off Bane. "Who are you?" she asked the one doing all the talking.

"We're with Homeland Security," the taller man said.

"I want names."

She could tell from his expression that he was getting annoyed with her. "I'm Gene Sharrod, head of the CLT division, and this is Ron Blackmon, head of DMP."

"You're both heads of your divisions. I'm impressed. Why would the top brass personally come for me?"

"The people after you want you for insalubrious reasons. Reasons that could be a threat to our national security."

"I got the note."

"Yes, and we believe you did the right thing by disappearing like it told you to. But now we're here to handle things and keep you safe."

Crystal lifted her chin. "How did you know what the note said?" She could tell from the look on the man's face that he realized he'd just made a slip.

"Let's cut the BS." Bane spoke up in an angry voice. "Bottom line is she isn't going anywhere."

"You aren't in any position to say anything about it, Mr. Outlaw," the shorter of the two men said with a sneer. "In case you haven't noticed, there are two guns aimed at you so I suggest you drop yours."

"And I suggest the two of you drop yours," Bane responded tersely, looking from one man to the other.

The taller man had the audacity to snicker. "Do you honestly think you can take the both of us down, Outlaw?"

A cocky smile touched Bane's lips. "I know I can. And the name isn't Outlaw. Cash Outlaw is my cousin. I'm Brisbane Westmoreland. Navy SEAL. SE348907. And just so you know, I'm a master sniper. So be forewarned. I can blow both your heads off without splattering any blood on that sofa."

The shorter man seemed taken aback by what Bane

had said, but Crystal could tell by the look that appeared in the taller man's eyes that he thought Bane was bluffing.

"Trust me," she said. "He's telling the truth."

The taller man's eyes darkened in anger. "We're not leaving here without you."

"Wanna bet?" Bane snarled. "My wife isn't going anywhere with either of you."

"Wife?" Sharrod asked, shocked.

"Yes, his wife," Crystal confirmed, holding up the finger of her left hand, where her diamond ring shone brilliantly.

"I'm tired of talking," Bane said. "Put your damn guns down now."

Blackmon narrowed his gaze at Bane. "Like Sharrod said. You're in no position to give orders."

Suddenly shots rang out and before Crystal could blink, Bane had shot the guns right out of both men's hands. "I am now," Bane said easily.

The two men bowed over, howling in pain. One of them, Crystal wasn't sure which one, claimed one of his fingers had gotten shot off. Then they heard the mourning dove coo just seconds before Walker, Bailey and Garth stormed into the room with their own guns drawn.

"You guys okay?" Bailey asked, rushing over to them, while Walker and Garth went over to the two men, who were wailing at the top of their lungs, sounding worse than babies. "Sloan and Maverick are outside taking care of the men who came with these two."

"You're going to regret this, Outlaw...Westmoreland, or whatever your name is," Blackmon snarled. "Homeland Security is going to nail your ass. This is treason. You are betraying your country."

"No, I think the two of you are betraying yours," Oakwood said, charging in. "Gene Sharrod and Ron Blackmon, you are both under arrest. Get them out of here," he told his men as they rushed forward.

"We need medical treatment," Blackmon screamed, holding his bloodied hand when agents came to grab him.

Bane frowned. "Better be glad it was just your hands and not your damn heads like I threatened to blow off. So stop whining."

After Oakwood and his agents had taken both men out the door, Bane turned to Crystal and frowned. "I told you to stay down."

She reached up to caress the angry lines around his jaw. "I know, but you forgot what you also said."

"What?"

"That we were in this together."

And then she leaned up to place a chaste kiss on his lips, but he evidently had other ideas and pulled her into his arms and deepened the kiss. She wrapped her arms around him and returned the kiss, not caring that they had an audience.

When one of the men cleared his throat, they broke off the kiss and Bane whispered against her moist lips, "Come on, Mrs. Westmoreland. Let's go home."

Twenty-One

A week later

Crystal hadn't meant to awaken Bane. But when he shifted in bed and slowly opened sleepy eyes that were filled with a heavy dose of desire, she saw he was now wide-awake.

She knew of no other man who could wake up ready to make love after going to bed the night before the same way. But then, hadn't he warned her that as far as the intensity of their lovemaking was concerned, this was just the beginning?

"Good morning," he said in that deep, husky voice that she loved hearing.

She smiled. "And good morning to you, too, Bane."

And as far as she was concerned, it was a good morning, especially after that phone call they had received yesterday. According to Oakwood, Sharrod had caved in under pressure and told them everything, including the location where those other two chemists were being held. By now the two men had been reunited with their families.

She glanced around the cabin. Their cabin. Bane had built it years ago for her as their secret lovers' hideaway. Now it was her home. Originally it had just one large room with a bathroom, but last year Bane had instructed Riley to hire someone to add a kitchen nook and a sitting area and to enlarge the bathroom. His sister Gemma, who was an interior decorator, had put her signature on it both before and after the renovations. There was an iron bed in the bedroom with colorful curtains that matched the bedspread.

The sitting room was the perfect size, just large enough for a sofa, a chair and a table. And she loved the fireplace that provided such great heat on those really cold days and nights. There was also a flat-screen television on the wall. Bane told her that he had begun spending his days and nights here whenever he came home. For that reason, he had installed internet services and didn't have to worry about missing calls due to his phone being out of range. Now he could send and receive phone calls just fine.

Already plans had been made to build the house that would become their permanent home. It wouldn't be far from here on Bane's Ponderosa, the name of the spread he had inherited. They would start looking at house plans next week. The one thing they did know was that whatever house they built would have to be large enough for all the kids they planned to have one day.

She had gotten around to reading all his cards and letters, and if she could have loved him even more than she already did, she would have. He had poured out his heart, his soul and his agony of a life without her in it. She needed no further proof that she was loved deeply by the man who was meant to be hers always, just as she was meant to be his.

Yesterday she and Bane had visited her parents' property. Property that was now hers. The place was deserted and badly in need of repairs. However, they'd decided not to make any decisions about what they would do with it for now.

In a way the five years of separation had done what it was meant to do. It had helped them grow into better people. She definitely saw a change in Bane. He could still be a badass when he needed to be, but there was a calmness about him, a discipline, self-control and purpose that hadn't always been there before. He'd always loved her and his family. And now he loved his country with just as much passion.

And his family was wonderful. She was enjoying getting to know the ladies his brothers and cousins had married. She had always been a loner, and for the first time in her life she was feeling part of the family.

Because Crystal had lost a lot of her things in the fire, Pam had organized a welcome-home party for her and Bane where she had received a lot of gift cards. It just so happened they were all from the ladies' favorite places to shop.

And then there was the Westmoreland family tradition. Every other Friday night, the Westmorelands got together at Dillon's place. The women would do the cooking and the men would arrive hungry. Afterward, the men took part in a poker game and the women did whatever they pleased. Usually they planned a shopping expedition. Tonight would be Crystal's first

Westmoreland Family Chow Down, and she was looking forward to it.

Bane shifted his position in bed and Crystal was instantly aware of the erection poking against her backside. Instinctively, she scooted back to bring her body closer to his. All that desire bottled up inside him was beginning to affect her, as well. "What happens when you get tired of me?"

"I won't. You're in my blood, baby. And in my soul. And especially here," he said, taking her hand and placing it on his chest, right against his heart.

His words touched her deeply. And it didn't help matters that he was staring down at her, seducing her with those gorgeous hazel eyes. "Oh, Bane." At that moment she wanted him. "Make love to me."

"It will be my pleasure."

Later that evening Crystal sat beside Bane at the dinner table at Dillon's home, surrounded by Bane's brothers, cousins and their spouses. And then there were the children. A lot of children. Beautiful children who were the joy of their parents' lives. Seeing them, spending time with them, made her anxious to have a child of her own. A baby. Bane's baby.

Dillon had made a toast earlier to her and Bane, officially welcoming her to the family and telling them how proud he and the family were of them, and their strong and unwavering commitment to each other. He also gave them his blessings, just as he'd known his parents would have done, for a long and happy marriage. His words had almost brought tears to her eyes because she felt she was truly a part of this family. The Westmoreland family.

A short while later, when dinner was over and the

women were clearing off the table as the men geared up for a card game, Bane's cell phone rang. "It's my CO," he said, quickly pulling his phone out of his jeans pocket. "Excuse me while I take this."

She felt a hard lump in her throat. She knew Bane was on military leave until March. Had something come up where his CO was calling the team together for an assignment? It was three weeks before Christmas. Besides that, it was their first week together without all the drama. Crystal wasn't sure how she would handle it if he had to suddenly leave.

You will handle it the same way any SEAL wife would, an inner voice said. *You will love him, support him and be there with open arms when he returns.* She was suddenly filled with an inner peace, prepared for whatever came next.

"What is it, Bane?" Dillon asked.

Crystal, like everyone else, turned to gaze at Bane when he returned to the dining room. There was a shocked look on his face. Although it had been Dillon who asked the question, Bane met Crystal's gaze and held it.

"That was my CO. He wanted to let me know he got a call from the Pentagon tonight that Coop is alive and is being held prisoner somewhere in Syria."

"Your friend Coop?" Crystal asked, getting up out of her seat and crossing the room to Bane.

"Yes. And the CO is getting our team together to go in and get Coop, and any other hostages they're holding, out of there."

She nodded. "When will you be leaving?" she asked softly.

He placed a hand on her shoulder. "I'm not. The CO just wanted me to know. He's aware of our situation and what we went through last week. He's letting me know he's exempting me from this mission if that's what I want."

Crystal studied Bane's features. And not caring if they had an audience listening to their every word, she said, "But that's not what you really want, is it?"

He rubbed his hand down his face. "Doesn't matter. It's three weeks before Christmas. There's no telling when I might return. I might not make it back until after the holidays, and I wanted to spend every single day with you."

"And I with you. But you *must* go," she said, not believing she was actually encouraging him to do so. "Coop is your best friend."

"And you are my wife."

A smile touched her lips. "I'm also the wife of a SEAL. So things like this are to be expected. I know it and I accept it. I will be fine until you get home, and if you don't make it back by Christmas, I won't be alone. For the first time, Bane, thanks to you I have a family," she said, glancing around the room. "I have a big family."

"Yes, you do," Dillon said, joining the conversation. "And whenever Bane has to go out on covert operations we will be here for you."

"Thanks, Dillon." Crystal returned her gaze to Bane. "So go, Bane, and be the dedicated and fierce SEAL that you are. The one you were trained to be. Be careful and do everything in your power to bring Coop home."

Bane stared at her for a long moment before he reached out and pulled her to him and held her close. And then he leaned down and kissed her with all the love she actually felt. The love she knew was there and had always been there between them. Suddenly she was swept off her feet and into big, strong arms.

"Bane!"

Holding her tight, he headed for the door. "We're going home," Bane said over his shoulder as his whole family watched them. "Crystal and I bid you all a good night."

Twenty-Two

Christmas Eve

"**A**nd you're sure you don't want to spend the night at our place, Crystal? You're more than welcome."

Crystal smiled at her brother-in-law when he brought the car to a stop in front of the cabin. "Thanks, Dillon, but I'll be okay."

"I promised Bane I would look out for you."

"And you have. I really do appreciate the invitation, but I'm fine."

She knew she would be a lot better if Bane called, but neither she nor his brothers and cousins had heard from him since he'd left three weeks ago. He had told them that no one knew how long this operation would take. She just hoped he was safe and all was going well.

In the meantime she had tried staying busy. Bane had wanted her to look at house plans while he was gone, and she had helped Pam at her acting school in town. Jason's wife, Bella, had invited her for tea several times, and there had been a number of shopping trips with the Westmoreland ladies. There had been the annual Westmoreland charity ball. It was her first time attending one and she wished Bane could have been there with her. But it had been good seeing the Outlaws again.

And she had been summoned to the nation's capital last week. Dillon, Canyon and their wives had gone with her. She'd had to give a statement about Sharrod and Blackmon. No one had asked about Bane's whereabouts and she figured they knew it was classified information.

The director of Homeland Security had told her of the value of her research and that someone would be contacting her soon. They wanted her, along with the other two biochemists, to come work for the government to perfect their research while she completed her PhD. She promised she would give it some thought but refused to make any decisions until Bane returned.

"I used to worry about Bane whenever I figured he was out on one of those operations," Dillon said softly to her as he unbuckled his seat belt. "But then I figured it didn't pay to worry. Besides, we're talking about Bane, the one person who can take care of himself. If we should be worried about anyone, it's those who have to come up against him."

Crystal smiled, knowing that was true. She had seen how Bane had handled Sharrod and Blackmon. He had been confident, cool and effective, even when it had seemed the odds had been stacked against him.

"Bane will be okay, Crystal," Dillon said when she didn't respond to what he'd said.

She nodded and absently touched the locket she still wore around her neck. "I hope so, Dillon."

"Don't just hope. Believe."

Her smile spread. "Okay, I believe."

"Good."

He got out of the car and came around to open the door for her. "You will be joining us for Christmas breakfast in the morning and then later a special Westmoreland Holiday Chow Down tomorrow night, right?"

"Yes, I'm looking forward to it."

"The Outlaws will be arriving about noon along with Bailey and Walker and some of the Atlanta Westmorelands."

She had gotten the chance to meet Charm Outlaw before she and Bane had left Alaska. Charm and her father had been returning from their business trip. The woman was as beautiful as she was nice. However, Crystal thought the father of the Outlaws had been reserved, as if he'd rather them not be there. Bane had explained that the old man was having a hard time accepting the fact that his father had been adopted.

"You know the drill," Dillon said, grinning when they reached the door of the cabin.

"Yes, I know it." Because she was living in a secluded area, the men in the family refused to let her drive home alone. They either drove her back home or followed behind her in their car to make sure she got there safely. And then before they would leave, she'd have to give a signal that everything was okay by flashing the window blinds.

"Good night, Dillon."

"Good night. Do you need a ride to my place in the morning?"

"No, thanks. I'll drive."

She opened the door to go inside the house and was glad she'd left the fireplace burning. The cabin felt

warm and cozy. She was about to turn and head for
the window to flash the blinds when she saw a movement out the corner of her eye. She jerked around.

"Bane!"

She raced across the room and was gobbled up in
big, strong arms and kissed by firm and demanding
lips. It seemed as though the kiss lasted forever as their
tongues tangled and mingled, and they devoured each
other's mouths. Finally, he broke off the kiss. "I missed
you, baby."

"And I missed you," she said, running her arms all
over him to make sure he was all in one piece. His skin
was damp, he smelled of aftershave and he was wearing his jeans low on his hips. It was obvious he'd just
gotten out of the shower.

"Why didn't you let me know you were coming home
tonight?"

A smile touched his lips. "I wanted to surprise you.
The mission was a success, although it was damn risky
at times. They were keeping Coop and two other American prisoners secluded up in the mountains. Getting
up there was one thing and getting them out alive was
another. It wasn't easy but we did it, and all returned
home safely. No injuries or casualties."

He paused a moment and said, "Coop was glad to
see us and they didn't break his spirit, although they
tried. He said what kept him going was believing that
one day we would come rescue him. And we did. He
and the others were taken to Bethesda Hospital in Mary-
land to get checked out."

Crystal was about to open her mouth to say something when there was a loud pounding at the front door.
"Oops. That's Dillon. He brought me home and I for-

got to flash the blinds to let him know I was okay," she said, racing across the room to open the door.

"Crystal, are you okay? When you didn't flash the blinds I—" Dillon stopped talking when he glanced over her shoulder and saw his brother. "Bane!"

The two men exchanged bear hugs. "Glad to see you back in one piece," Dillon said, grinning as he looked his baby brother up and down.

Bane pulled Crystal to his side and planted a kiss on her forehead. "And I'm glad to be back, too."

"I'll let the family know you're home. And I guess we won't be seeing you bright and early tomorrow morning for breakfast as planned, Crystal," Dillon said, his grin getting wider.

"No, you won't," Bane answered for her. "My wife and I are sleeping in late. We will try to make it for dinner, however."

Dillon chuckled. "Okay." He then looked at his watch. "It just turned midnight on the East Coast. Merry Christmas, you two."

"And Merry Christmas to you, Dillon," Crystal said, cuddling closer in her husband's strong arms. And in that moment she knew that for her this would be the merriest because she had her Bane. It would be their first Christmas spent together as man and wife.

As soon as the door closed behind Dillon, Bane tightened his embrace and looked down at her. "I like the tree and all the decorations."

She glanced over at the Christmas tree she'd put up a couple of weeks ago. What was special about it was that it had come right off Bane's Ponderosa. Riley had chopped it down for her. She'd had fun decorating the tree and had even trailed Christmas lights and ornaments along the fireplace mantel. "Thanks."

And then Bane pulled her even closer into his arms. "I've already placed your gift under the tree, baby."

She glanced over her shoulder and saw the huge red box with a silver bow. She looked back at him, feeling like a kid on Christmas morning. "Thanks. What's in it?"

He chuckled. "You get to open it in the morning." He leaned down and placed a kiss on her lips. "Merry Christmas, sweetheart."

She reached up and wrapped her arms around his neck. "And merry Christmas to you, Bane."

And then their mouths connected, and she knew this was still just the beginning. They had the rest of their lives.

Epilogue

Valentine's Day

"I would like to propose a toast to the newlyweds," Ramsey Westmoreland said, getting everyone's attention and holding up his champagne glass. "First of all, we didn't ever think you would leave us, Bay, but we know you'll be in good hands living in Alaska with Walker. We're still going to miss you showing up unannounced, letting yourself into our homes and eating our food."

"And getting all into our business," Derringer hollered out.

Ramsey chuckled. "Yes, she did have a knack for getting all in our business. But I think we can safely say we wouldn't have wanted it any other way. I know Mom and Dad are smiling down on us today, happy for their baby girl."

He paused as if to compose himself before he continued, "And, Walker, she's yours now and I'm going to tell you the same thing I told Callum when he married Gemma, and Rico when he married Megan. You can't give her back. You asked for her, flaws and all, so deal with it."

Everyone laughed at that. Ramsey then raised his champagne glass higher. "To Walker and Bailey. May you have a long and wonderful marriage, and watch out for the bears." The attendees laughed again as they clicked their glasses before drinking their champagne.

Dillon then stepped up to stand beside Ramsey. The wedding had been held inside the beautiful garden club in downtown Denver. Riley's wife, Alpha, who was an event planner, had done her magic. The wedding theme had been From This Day Forward, and since it was Valentine's Day the colors had been red and white.

"No, I'm not giving Walker and Bailey another toast," Dillon said, grinning. "With so many members of the family gathered here together, I want to take this time to welcome our cousins, the Outlaws of Alaska. Your last names might be Outlaw but you proved just how much Westmoreland blood ran through your veins when you gave Bane and Crystal your protection when they needed it the most. And all of us thank you for it. Our great-grandfather Raphel would be proud. And that deserves another toast."

Crystal felt Bane's arms tighten around her waist. What Dillon had said was true. The Outlaws had come through for them during a very critical time. Their last names might be Outlaw, but they looked and carried themselves just like Westmorelands.

Later, she saw Dillon and Ramsey talking to Garth and Sloan and couldn't help but notice how the single women at the wedding were checking them out. With all the Denver Westmoreland males marked off the bachelor list, it seemed that the single ladies were considering the Outlaws as hopefuls. Evidently the thought of moving to Alaska didn't dissuade them one bit.

"What's this I hear about the two of you moving to Washington?" Senator Reggie Westmoreland approached to ask. He had his beautiful wife, Olivia, by his side.

Bane smiled. "It will be just for a little while, after Crystal graduates in May with her PhD. She will be working at that lab in DC for six months and I was offered a position teaching SEAL recruits how to master a firearm."

"That's great! Libby and I will have to invite the two of you over once you get settled."

Jess Outlaw walked up to join them. Because he had been out on the campaign trail when they were in Alaska, the first time Bane and Crystal had met him had been when the Outlaws had joined the Westmorelands for Christmas.

"And I hope to see you soon in Washington, as well," Reggie said to Jess.

Jess smiled. "I hope so. The race is close and has begun getting ugly."

"Been there before," Reggie said. "Hang in there and stick to your principles."

Jess nodded. "Thanks for your advice, and thanks so much for your endorsement."

A smile spread across Reggie's lips. "No thanks needed. We are family. Besides, I reviewed your platform, and it's a good one that could benefit the people of your state. I think in the end they will see that."

"Let's hope so," Jess said.

A few moments later Crystal found herself alone with Bane. Coop was doing fine and had visited them in Westmoreland Country a few times. So had Nick, Flipper and Viper. Flipper had personally delivered to her the items that he and his brother had removed from her house before the fire.

She had gotten to know all of Bane's team members and thought they were swell guys. And she had met their wives, as well. But Flipper, Viper and Coop were single and swearing to stay that way. Since the three were extremely handsome men, she couldn't wait to see just for how long.

"Did I tell you today how much I love you?" Bane leaned down to ask her, whispering close to her ear.

"Yes," she said, smiling up at him. "But you can tell me again."

"Gladly. Crystal Gayle Westmoreland, I love you very much. With all my heart."

She reached up and caressed his cheek as she thought about all they'd endured over the years. A lot had changed, but the one thing that had remained constant had been their love. "And I love you, too, Bane. With all my heart."

And then they kissed, sealing their words and their love. Forever.

* * * * *

BEAUTY AND THE BODYGUARD

LISA CHILDS

For Kimberly Duffy – with great appreciation for all your years of friendship. Without your support and your wonderful sense of humour, I don't know how I would have survived all the ups and downs in my career and in my life. Thank you!

Prologue

How the hell had he survived? It wasn't possible. It just wasn't possible…

But the proof was in the photo. Sure, he looked different. Then again, who wouldn't, after what he'd been through? He'd been tortured to death. At least Derek had thought he'd killed the man…

Cockroaches were like that, though; they could survive the most extreme extermination attempts. The only thing they couldn't survive was getting crushed.

The picture crumpled in a big fist. He better be enjoying his last moments of life—because he wasn't going to stay alive. And this time when he died, he would damn well stay dead.

Derek Nielsen hurled the wadded-up photo against the bars of his cell. An alarm rang out. He hadn't set it off—directly. But indirectly he had. The alarm was sounding because of him, according to his carefully orchestrated plan.

This was it—his escape.

With a buzz and a clank, the cell door slid open. He slipped through it like other prisoners stepped through theirs. They were confused, though, standing in the hall outside their cells. Derek hurried past them. He knew where he needed to be: the laundry room. He had only minutes to get to the vent leading out from one of the commercial dryers. After his efforts, it was big enough now for him to crawl through and escape.

Derek would be out soon to the vehicle that waited outside for him. The one that would slip through the gates and bring him to freedom.

Derek wouldn't be returning to prison, although he fully intended to commit another crime. He was going to kill the man responsible for sending him to jail.

Chapter 1

Gage Huxton had survived six months in hell for this? Since becoming a bodyguard on his return from Afghanistan, his assignments had been a mixed bag. His first job with the Payne Protection Agency had been to protect an elderly lady with Alzheimer's, who had only been in danger from her disease and not her imagined threats.

But then he had also been assigned to follow the man who was now his brother-in-law. That job had nearly gotten Gage killed. But he had survived being shot at and nearly run down.

He wasn't sure he would survive this: wedding duty. He slid a finger between the bow tie and his skin, trying to loosen the stranglehold it had on him. An image flashed through his mind, of a noose tightening around his neck, squeezing off his oxygen until oblivion claimed him. But, unfortunately, oblivion had never lasted. He grimaced as he remembered other horrors.

"Are you okay?" a soft voice asked him.

He blinked away those horrific images and focused on Penny Payne. She sprang up from her chair and walked around her desk in the office in the basement of her white wedding chapel. It was in River City, Michigan—where his friend Nick had moved and where Gage now lived.

Not wanting to worry her, he jerked his chin up and down in a quick nod.

Her brown eyes warm with affection and concern, she stared up at him. "You look very handsome in the tuxedo."

He probably should have shaved the scruff from his jaw so he'd fit in more with the wedding guests when they arrived. But he hadn't had the time or the inclination. "I must be crazy," he said.

"Why's that?" she asked, and now there was a twinkle of amusement in her eyes.

"To let you talk me into playing a bouncer for your wedding business." Penny was his boss's mother, so he probably hadn't had much choice. But it hadn't been any easier for him to tell her no than it probably would have been for her son.

She reached up, and he reacted as he did whenever someone moved to touch him. He flinched. Sympathy dimmed the usual brightness of her smile. "Gage…"

Instead of pulling back as so many other people did, she gently laid her palm against his cheek. "I'm sorry," she murmured.

He shook his head and dislodged her hand. "I don't want pity," he said. "I just want to do my job."

"That's not what—"

He forced a smile. "It's okay." Nobody had known how

to react to him since he'd been back. So maybe it was good that not many people knew he'd survived.

"Where do you need me?" he asked. "Do I need to make sure the bride and groom's mothers don't get into a catfight?"

Penny's smile dimmed more, and she replied, "The bride's mother passed away years ago."

"That's too bad." He didn't see his mother often since she and his dad had moved to Alaska, but he could call her anytime. He rarely called, though; he didn't want to worry her. "So no catfights between the mothers. What about the bridesmaids?"

Penny's lips curved into a bigger smile. "Why do you sound almost hopeful?"

He chuckled. "Just looking for the upside in this assignment."

"Cake," she told him, and she patted his cheek again as if he was a little boy she was promising a treat if he behaved. Her kids were grown now, but she had raised three boys and a tomboy pretty much on her own. So she knew how to handle kids.

He wasn't a kid, though. He hadn't been one for a long time—not since he'd joined the Marines at eighteen a decade ago. Then there had been that stint with the FBI. But he didn't like to think about those days, because then he inevitably thought about *her*.

The hell he'd endured the past six months was nothing compared to what she had put him through. No. He would rather think about the horrors of his six months in captivity than about Megan Lynch.

He exhaled a ragged breath and shook off all the memories. He had to leave the past in the past—all of it, but most of all Megan.

"So," he said as he focused again on the present. "You want me to guard the cake?"

Dessert was probably all anyone considered him capable of protecting yet. Why else had he been assigned wedding chapel duty?

Penny shook her head. "Of course not. You have the most important job here."

He narrowed his eyes and studied her, wondering if she was patronizing him. "And what's that?"

"Guarding the bride, of course."

"Guarding her?" He couldn't imagine what danger she might be in, but then he had no idea who she was. "Or do you mean making sure she doesn't run?"

He wouldn't blame her if she did. He would never risk his heart on love again. But then he no longer had a heart to lose. Megan had destroyed it.

Penny sighed. "I almost wish she would…"

"The groom's a tool?"

She shook her head. "He seems nice."

So maybe the bride was a bridezilla. "Why does she need protecting?"

"Her father is a very important man," Penny said, and as she said it, her face flushed.

"Who's her father?" he asked. And more importantly, why had the fifty-something-year-old widow reacted with a blush at the very thought of him?

"He's a man who's made some enemies over the course of his career."

Gage should have picked up one of the programs from the basket outside the chapel. He'd passed it on his way downstairs to Penny's office. Then he would know the names of everyone in the wedding party. But he'd wanted to get his assignment before any of the guests arrived.

Now he had it: bridal protection.

"So he thinks some of these adversaries might go after his daughter during her wedding?" The guy had made some seriously ruthless enemies if that was the case.

Penny nodded. "He's the kind of man who wouldn't care what someone did to *him*." Her face flushed a deeper shade of red.

Who was this guy to her? Apparently, someone she knew well. How well? Just how closely did Penny work with widowed fathers of the brides?

She continued, "But if someone hurt his daughter..."

Gage understood. His best friend, Nicholas Rus, had thought that someone was going after Gage's sister for vengeance against him—because Nick loved Annalise and she had always loved him. But that hadn't been about revenge, at least not against Nick or Annalise.

"If this guy has so many enemies," Gage said, "why am I the only one from the Payne Protection Agency here?" Especially when he knew his boss didn't trust that he was at a hundred percent yet. But Logan Payne wasn't the only one who thought that; Gage didn't entirely trust himself.

He was getting better, but it was still a struggle to sleep, to suppress the flashbacks, to forget the pain...

Penny tilted her head and stared up at him. "You're the bodyguard the bride needs."

Gage's stomach lurched as realization suddenly dawned on him. And even without reading the program, he knew who the bride was. Penny had given him enough clues. He should have figured it out earlier. Hell, he should have figured it out when Penny asked him to help out at the chapel. He'd known she was planning a wedding for someone he'd known. Or at least, he'd thought he'd known her.

He guessed the wedding wasn't all Penny Payne had been planning. Nick had warned him that she was a meddler. Her kids might not mind that she meddled in their lives, but he damn well minded.

He shook his head. "No..."

"Gage," she beseeched him.

But he just shook his head again, refusing the assignment. He didn't care if Mrs. Payne went to his boss and got him fired. He couldn't protect this bride—not when he was the one against whom she most needed protecting.

"He's gone," Penny said.

Woodrow Lynch released a ragged breath and closed her office door behind him. "That's probably for the best."

"How can you say that?" Penny asked, her usually soft voice sharp with indignation. "She's miserable."

"She's miserable because of *him*." Anger coursed through him as he thought of the pain Gage Huxton had put his daughter through. Some of it had been inadvertent, like getting captured.

But the rest...

Quitting the Bureau.

Reenlisting.

Those had been Gage's choices.

"Yes." Penny stalked around her desk to stand in front of him. She was so petite despite the heels she wore with a silky bronze-colored dress. Her eyes were nearly that same color bronze. Her hair, chin length and curly, was a deeper shade of brown with red and bronze highlights.

She was beautiful. She was also infuriating as hell. The woman always thought she was right.

And even more infuriating was the fact that she usually was.

"So, it's for the best that she move on," Woodrow said.

It had to be for the best, because the wedding was due to start in less than an hour. And he would rather walk his daughter down the aisle to a man who would not make her miserable.

Penny shook her head and tumbled several locks of hair into her eyes. The curls tangled in her long lashes. Instinctively, he reached out to extract them, but her hand collided with his. Her skin was as silky as her hair. Her fingers trembled beneath his, and she pulled away from his touch and stepped back until his hand fell away from her face.

He'd known her long enough—had attended enough weddings in her chapel—that he'd seen how warm and affectionate she was. With everyone else...

With him she was guarded and skittish. Usually. Right now she was also annoyed.

"Megan can't move on," Penny said, "unless she has closure."

"Are you speaking from experience?" He hadn't meant to ask the question. It had just slipped out, probably because he'd wondered for a while why she had never remarried after her husband died sixteen years before.

Her big eyes narrowed. "We are not talking about me."

She never did. He'd noticed that, too. She only talked about other people: her kids, his agents and now his daughter.

"Our concern should be only about Megan," Penny continued. "I've never worked with a more miserable bride."

Now he narrowed his eyes with indignation and pride. "Are you saying that she's difficult?"

"Of course not," Penny said. She reached out, almost as if she couldn't help herself, and touched his arm. She probably only meant to reassure him about his daughter. But then she added, "She's sad. So sad…"

He shouldn't have been able to feel Penny's touch, not through his tuxedo jacket and shirt, but his skin tingled as if he'd felt the heat and silkiness of her skin against his. What the hell was wrong with him?

Maybe he'd been single too long. Like her, he'd lost his spouse. She had died, more than twenty years ago, when their girls were little. But he didn't need closure— or anything else—but his daughters' happiness. Ellen was older and settled with a good husband and three beautiful little girls.

But Megan…

He'd always worried the most about Megan and never more than when she got involved with Gage Huxton. She'd fallen so hard for him that it was inevitable she would get hurt.

"She's marrying a good man," Woodrow insisted. He wasn't too proud to admit that he'd used Bureau resources to check out the kid. He was a computer nerd— as introverted and shy as she was. "They're perfect for each other."

They'd met in college, in a computer class. They'd been friends for years before they'd started dating. They hadn't been going out very long before Gage had swept her off her feet.

Damn Gage…

Penny shook her head.

"They are perfect for each other," he insisted.

"It doesn't matter how compatible you are," she said, "if you're not in love."

"Love is what made her miserable," Woodrow said. He could relate to that. Love had made him miserable as well. "Compatibility is more important in a marriage—wanting and expecting the same things. That's what will sustain a relationship." And not send one outside the marriage looking for something else.

"Are you speaking from experience now?" she asked.

He wished. He shook his head. "We're not talking about me."

"No," she agreed. "Megan, and her happiness, is our only priority. You need to tell her that Gage is alive."

"Why?" he asked.

Nothing good would come of her knowing the truth; it wouldn't change anything. She and Gage had broken up nearly a year ago—before he'd quit the Bureau, before he'd reenlisted, before he'd gone missing in action.

Penny's grasp on his arm tightened. Her hand was small but strong. He felt her grip and the heat of her touch. "She deserves to know before she marries another man that the man she really loves is alive."

He hadn't seen Gage yet. But Woodrow's former agent and Gage's best friend, Nicholas Rus, had warned him. Gage had come back alive, but he hadn't come back the same.

Woodrow shook his head. "No, the man she loves is gone." And maybe it was better that she never learned the truth.

Megan Lynch stared into the oval mirror, studying the woman reflected back at her. Wasn't she supposed to look beautiful? Weren't all brides?

The gown, while not her style, was certainly eye-catching. With twinkling rhinestones sewn onto the heavy brocade, it sparkled. The lacy veil was beautiful and softened the sharp angles of Megan's face and hid some of the severity of the dark hair she'd pulled into a tight knot to tame. But she didn't look beautiful. She shouldn't have expected that she would; she had never looked beautiful before. Why should her wedding day be any different?

No matter how much makeup the beautician had applied, the dark circles were still visible beneath her dark eyes. Tears brimmed in them, but she blinked them away. She wouldn't feel sorry for herself anymore. She had done enough of that the past several months. She'd nearly drowned in self-pity and guilt.

The knob rattled as someone turned it and began to open the door to the bride's dressing room. She hurriedly tugged the veil over her face to hide the hint of tears she couldn't quite clear from her eyes. They kept rushing back—every time she thought of him.

She had to stop thinking about *him*. He was gone. But even if he wasn't, he wouldn't have ever come back to her, not after what she'd done. She had to stop thinking about the past and focus on the future, not that she deserved one.

Because he didn't have one...

Marrying Richard was the right thing to do. He'd always been there for her. Even after she'd broken up with him, Richard had remained her friend. And when her heart had been broken, he'd tried to piece it back together. Eventually, he had even accepted that there was no patching a heart as shattered as hers. He'd insisted that their friendship was a stronger and safer foundation for a marriage than love.

Safe had sounded good to her. And there was no one safer than Richard. He was quiet and shy and nervous and cautious. He wouldn't put himself or her in any danger for any reason. He would always be there for her—like he'd always been.

Not like Gage…

The door opened fully, but she didn't turn toward it. She suspected it was her matron of honor, who was supposed to have arrived with the beautician an hour earlier. Her sister, Ellen, was always late. She also had three little girls she'd needed to get ready besides herself, though.

Megan's heart swelled with love for her nieces. They and the kids she worked with every day made her yearn to have children of her own. She wanted to be a mom like her sister—loving and fun.

She didn't remember her own mom. Dad had been both a father and mother to her.

Since whoever had entered was quiet—it couldn't be her sister and nieces. It had to be her dad.

"So what do you think?" Megan asked as she focused on the mirror again. The lace distorted her vision, so she nearly saw it: the beauty of being a bride.

But then a shadow stepped behind her. It was tall and dark in a black tuxedo. The mirror showed only his long legs and his chest. He was too thin to be her father. Too tall to be Richard. She had no idea who he was until he stepped closer yet. Then she saw his head—the short golden hair, the bright green eyes, the darker blond stubble on his jaw…

Just how badly had the veil distorted her vision? Who was she mistaking for a dead man?

Her hands trembling, she fumbled with her veil, pulling it back so she could focus on the apparition. She whirled around to face him.

It couldn't be…

Gage was dead. He had died months ago, his body lost in some foreign country. But that hadn't stopped her from seeing him everywhere, every time she'd closed her eyes and tried to sleep.

She shouldn't be seeing him here—not on her wedding day to another man.

"No…" she murmured. Her knees trembled and weakened, threatening to fold beneath her. "No…"

Chapter 2

"So what do I think?" Gage repeated her question. He thought he'd been punched in the gut. The minute he'd opened the door and seen her—sparkling like a vision in white—all his breath had left his lungs. His chest burned, his ribs ached. He felt like he was getting the life pounded out of him all over again.

Her usually honey-toned skin was pale except for the dark circles beneath her enormous eyes. With her sharp cheekbones, small pointed chin and wide dark eyes, she appeared fragile—vulnerable. He knew she was tougher than she looked, though. She'd been tough on him when she'd broken up with him. Then she swayed on her feet, as if she were about to faint.

Instinctively, he reached out to catch her, closing his hands around her waist. She was thinner than she'd been when he'd seen her last. Maybe she was one of those brides who'd been starving herself to fit into her gown, to look good for her wedding photos and her groom. Maybe that was why she trembled in his grasp.

From starvation...

He preferred the sexy curves she'd had over her new svelte figure. She'd been perfect as she was.

Her breath escaped in a gasp. "You're real..." she murmured. "You're alive..."

As he realized what she'd thought, he chuckled. "You're not seeing a ghost."

"I thought—*everyone* thought—that you died in Afghanistan."

"I was presumed dead," he said, "but I was just missing." Missing everyone back home, but most especially her. She had obviously not been missing him at all, though. She'd been dating, getting engaged.

Anger coursed through him, making him shake like she was. His hands tightened around her tiny waist. "So what do I think," he mused again. "I think you make a beautiful bride, Megan Lynch."

He had once planned on asking her to be his; he'd even bought the ring. But he had never gotten the chance to give it to her before she'd broken up with him, before she'd broken him.

She flinched as if he'd insulted her. But she'd never been able to accept a compliment as anything but a lie. She'd actually accused him of lying to her, of using her.

His blood heated. This was why he couldn't protect her—because he wanted to hurt her—like she had hurt him, like her marrying another man was hurting him all over again. "So let me be the first to kiss the bride..."

He gripped her small waist and dragged her up so her feet dangled above the floor. She gasped in shock, her breath whispering across his lips as he lowered his mouth to hers. Her lips were as soft as he remembered, her taste as sweet. He had missed this so much. He'd missed her. He deepened the kiss. Pressing his lips tightly against hers, he slid his tongue into her mouth.

A moan rumbled in her throat. And her hands clasped the back of his head, her fingers sliding over his short hair. She stilled as she touched one of the scars. Those wounds hadn't hurt, though, at least not in comparison to what she'd done to him.

Remembering the pain she'd caused him, he dragged his mouth from hers. Then he lowered her until her feet touched the floor again. When he released her, she swayed and her palm pressed against his chest. His heart leaped beneath her touch, and she must have felt it because she jerked her hand away.

"Gage," she murmured, and she stared up at him as if she still couldn't believe he wasn't an apparition. Then her gaze scanned him, over the tuxedo he was wearing, the damn bow tie choking off his breath.

"*Why* are you here?" She looked both fearful and hopeful, and he realized what she thought.

A chuckle of bitterness slipped through his lips. "Don't worry," he assured her, "I'm not here to stop the wedding."

"Then why are you here?" she asked.

"I work for a security firm now," he said. "The Payne Protection Agency. Penny hired me to make sure nothing stops this wedding from happening." Actually, he suspected just the opposite—that she had imagined some romantic reunion between him and Megan. Since she was a wedding planner, she probably believed in romance and happy endings and all that stuff Gage had given up on nearly a year ago.

There would be no happy ending for him.

Like she had so many times before, Penny tugged the dress over Nikki's head and zipped her into it. "Thank you, honey, for helping me out."

Nikki grimaced. Like she had a choice…

Like anyone could say no to Penny Payne. Even Gage Huxton hadn't been able to, and he could have come up with more excuses than Nikki had.

Her small hands gripping Nikki's shoulders, Penny spun her around to face her. "You look beautiful."

After having three boys, Penny must have been very happy to finally have a girl so she could dress her up like a doll. But having three brothers, Nikki hadn't wanted anything to do with dresses or dolls. She'd wanted to play the sports her brothers had played. She'd wanted to wrestle and fight. She couldn't do that in the dresses Mom had constantly tried to zip her into then—or now.

"Mom…"

Penny's palm cupped her cheek. "I know you don't want to be, but you are beautiful."

Her face flushed, but she couldn't deny that she was beautiful—not without insulting her mother. She looked exactly like Penny.

"I want to be taken seriously," she said. And that was hard when she looked like the doll her mother treated her like she was. She was petite and delicate looking with big heavily lashed eyes. And now her mother had zipped her into a blue satin dress so she looked like a curly auburn–haired Barbie doll.

"I want you to be happy," Penny said.

"I am," Nikki insisted.

But her mother just gave her a pitying smile. Penny didn't think it was possible for Nikki to be happy unless she was all in love like her brothers were. Her brothers had been lucky to find their perfect mates. Nikki didn't think there was anyone out there who would be perfect for her.

She'd once thought another man had been perfect—her father. Of course she only had a child's memories of him, since he'd died when she was nine, so she'd idealized him. When she'd learned that he had cheated on her mother, Nikki had been more upset than Penny had been. Her mother had been able to forgive him. Nikki couldn't.

Nor could she trust any other man.

"Well," Nikki amended her statement, "I'm not happy to be here."

"I appreciate your helping out," Penny said.

"What happened?" Nikki asked. "Why did a bridesmaid get tossed out of the wedding party? Did she sleep with the groom?" And the stupid bride had forgiven him but disowned her friend?

Penny shook her head. "The matron of honor. She's sick. Either food poisoning or…"

"Or? Regular poisoning?"

Penny laughed. "You're hopeless. You'd rather think of the worst than the obvious."

To Nikki, the worst was the most obvious. "What is the obvious?"

"She's pregnant."

Nikki groaned. Fortunately, she wasn't as fertile as the women she knew, like her sisters-in-law and apparently the sick matron of honor. Of course she'd have to actually be involved with someone to have the possibility of becoming pregnant. And she wasn't going to risk that again. She'd had boyfriends, even a fun fling or two. But despite what her mother thought, she didn't need a husband or a family.

"And no one else could fill in for the sick matron of honor?" Nikki asked.

Penny shrugged. "I didn't bother to find out."

That wasn't like the wedding planner who always went the extra mile to make sure the bride's special day was extra special.

But then Penny always enlisted Nikki before any of her other kids to help out at the chapel. She'd probably expected her only daughter to go into the wedding planning business with her instead of into the bodyguard business with her brothers. Even before she'd learned of her father's betrayal, Nikki had never had any interest in weddings.

"Is there any particular reason you want *me* to step in as maid of honor?"

"It's because of the bride," Penny said. "She's Woodrow Lynch's daughter."

Woodrow? The first name basis caught Nikki by surprise. "Do you mean Chief Special Agent Lynch? Nick's old boss?" Her half brother had been an FBI agent before he'd recently quit to join the Payne Protection Agency.

Her mother's face flushed slightly, and she nodded.

How did that make this bride special? And she obviously was to Penny. Nikki had never seen her mother so worried about a wedding, not even the one she'd planned as a ruse to flush out a sadistic serial killer.

"Do you think she's in danger?" Nikki asked. Had her mother enlisted her not as a dress-up doll to play wedding party but as a bodyguard?

Penny's teeth nipped her bottom lip, and she nodded. "I have a *feeling...*"

Nikki's blood tingled with excitement and nerves. Her mother's feelings were legendary, because they were rarely wrong. If Penny Payne thought the bride was in danger, then Ms. Lynch was definitely in danger.

Megan was scared. Even though she lived a relatively boring life as a school librarian, she knew fear well. She had been very frightened when she'd broken up with Gage. She'd had a horrible feeling then that she was making a mistake. And when he'd reenlisted and been immediately deployed...

She'd been scared out of her mind that something would happen to him. Even worse, he'd gone missing and had been presumed dead...

She had nearly lost her mind. She wasn't that scared now, because she knew what she had to do. She was going to thwart Gage's assignment. There was no way she was going through with this wedding.

Minutes ticked away on the clock hanging on the yellow wall of the bride's dressing room. She was still alone inside—although she didn't feel alone anymore. While Gage had been gone for long moments, his presence was palpable in the room, which was another reason she needed to leave it. She needed to find the groom's dressing room and tell him that she couldn't do this. She couldn't marry him.

She shouldn't have accepted Richard's proposal in the first place. While he was okay that she wasn't in love with him, she wasn't. As he had convinced her, it was safer to marry someone you didn't love. There was no chance of getting your heart broken. But then there was no chance of passion, either. She'd had that passion with Gage.

While she'd had boyfriends before—Richard and a couple of high school boys before him—she'd never felt the passion she had with Gage. Only with Gage...

The first moment she'd met him—during a Super Bowl party at her father's house—she'd been overwhelmed by attraction.

He was tall, with broad shoulders and heavily developed muscles. He had looked like a gym rat—then. But not now...

While he'd looked good—damn good—in the black tuxedo, he'd also looked thinner than Megan had ever seen him. What had he endured throughout those long months he'd been missing?

She wanted to know. Most of all she wanted him every bit as much as she'd wanted him that day they'd first met. When she'd closed the refrigerator door to find him leaning against the side of it, she'd thought he was big then, towering over her.

But he wasn't just big physically.

It was his personality that was so big. His voice carried to the point where she'd been able to hear him above the other men gathered in the family room around her father's enormous TV. She and Ellen had bought him that TV for Mother's Day because he'd been both mother and father to them. She'd been invited to sit around that TV, too, but she'd been too shy to join the group of rowdy guys to whom her father had introduced her when she'd come home from a short and boring date with Richard.

Gage Huxton was the rowdiest with his booming voice and his even louder laugh. Or maybe he was the one she heard because he was the one she'd thought the most handsome with his golden-blond hair and smoky green eyes.

She'd never seen a more beautiful man. And, thanks to her father being bureau chief, she'd met some good-looking guys over the years. But they had never noticed her; they'd never sought her out like Gage had in the kitchen.

"Do you need something?" she'd asked him. "More beer?" Her father had a bar in the family room, but the fridge was small. With that many guys, they had probably already emptied it.

He'd shaken his head. "No."

"Food?" she'd asked.

Her father was an excellent cook. He'd had to be, or they would have starved. But maybe he hadn't made enough for the number of guys who'd showed up at their house.

Gage had shaken his head again. And there'd been something in his eyes, a wicked glint that had had her pulse racing.

"Then what do you need?" she'd asked.

He'd stepped closer then, so close that he'd towered over her, until he'd leaned down. His mouth tantalizing close to hers, he'd murmured, "You..."

She'd laughed at him then because she'd thought he was just trying to be funny. Because men like him, men that beautiful, were never interested in girls like her. Chubby girls with unmanageable hair.

"I'm not kidding," he'd told her.

She'd laughed harder then, though it had sounded high-pitched and a little hysterical. "I have a boyfriend."

"Dump him."

"Why would I do that?" she'd asked.

"Because of this..." And then he'd kissed her. For the

very first time in her life she'd experienced real passion. Her flesh had heated. Her heart had pounded so hard and so fast. Other parts of her had reacted, too—like her nipples tightening. Like the pulse that beat in her core, throbbing as pressure built inside her.

She'd never felt anything like it before. She'd felt it every time he'd kissed her or even looked at her. She'd felt it just moments ago when he'd kissed her.

She had never had that passion with Richard, and she never would. No. She couldn't marry him. This wedding was not going to happen.

She had to tell him. Now. Before the wedding began…

She lifted her arms and tried to reach the buttons behind her back. They were too small, though. Penny Payne had buttoned her up before the beautician had arrived. And even she had had to use some kind of tool, which she'd taken with her. Megan couldn't get out of her dress alone. Of course Ellen still wasn't there.

Her sister was beyond late now. Maybe she didn't intend to show up at all. She hadn't agreed with Megan marrying Richard. A loving and biased older sister, Ellen was convinced that Megan could do better. She wasn't a Richard fan. She had been a Gage fan.

But they had thought Gage was dead…

She cursed and gave up the struggle with her dress. It wasn't as if seeing her in it would give her and Richard bad luck in their marriage. They weren't getting married. She'd hoped to slip out of the room and across the church unnoticed. If she wasn't wearing the huge dress Richard had designed and made for her, she wouldn't have been noticed at all. People rarely looked at her. And no man had ever looked at her like Gage had.

Her fingers trembled slightly as she reached for the

knob and pulled open the door. And fear washed over her all over again.

She wasn't afraid of telling Richard she wasn't going to marry him. She was afraid of the gun pointed at her—afraid that it might go off and bore a hole right through that wedding dress and through her.

Of course she'd already had a hole inside her—where she'd lost her heart to Gage.

Now she was about to lose her life…

Chapter 3

Once Gage had realized who the bride was, he hadn't thought about the rest of what Penny Payne had said. He hadn't believed then that the bride could be in any danger aside from making a mistake.

She'd made her biggest mistake nearly a year ago. Or maybe it had been before that, when she'd let him kiss her that first time.

Maybe that had been the mistake she'd made.

Gage had nearly made one himself. He'd started to leave the church. Again.

He'd started leaving once after he'd refused Penny's assignment. But he hadn't been able to walk past the bride's dressing room without looking inside to see Megan. That had been a mistake, seeing her in that sparkling white gown.

Now he couldn't get the image out of his mind. He'd

thought stepping outside would help him clear his head. But he'd been seeking not just fresh air but also an escape. Six months of captivity had made that his first instinct. He'd had no intention of going back inside, either. He'd endured enough torture. Watching Megan marry another man would have been him torturing himself.

He couldn't do it.

But he couldn't leave, either.

Not when he noticed the guns.

They were discreet with them. A man dressed like a waiter carried one in his duffel bag. Another man, dressed like a guest, carried one beneath the trench coat he wore over his suit. There was a woman, too, with a purse that was big and—from the bulge inside it—heavy.

Heavily armed...

After Gage had realized who the bride was, he'd thought Penny's claim about her being in danger had just been a ploy, a manipulation, to enlist him as the bridal bodyguard. But Penny hadn't been lying about Chief Woodrow Lynch. He had a lot of enemies, maybe even more than Gage.

And if those enemies wanted to hurt him, they would go after his daughter. Megan was the one with whom Woodrow had always had the most special bond, and he was so protective of her. So if his enemies really wanted to get to him, they'd go after Megan.

She wasn't his only family at the church, though. A minivan pulled up front and parked between the catering van from which the armed waiter had stepped out, and the long black car from which the armed wedding guests had exited. The side door slid open, and three little blond girls tumbled out. They were dressed in miniature versions of Megan's lacy white dress. The sunlight sparkled off the rhinestones, but they didn't seem to shine quite as brightly as Megan's.

Megan sparkled. But it wasn't just the dress. It was her eyes—those fathomless dark eyes—and her heart-shaped face.

God, she was beautiful.

She couldn't see it herself, though. She had no idea what she actually looked like. Whenever she looked in the mirror, she still saw the chubby girl from her adolescent years with the bad complexion and glasses. Gage had only seen that girl in old photos. There was nothing of her left in Megan the woman.

One of the little girls looked like Megan must have when she was chubby—with rosy, round cheeks. The little girl was cute. She was also heading toward the church, her sisters running after her. Gage didn't want them any closer to the danger. He rushed down the stairs to head them off.

"Wait, girls," he said. "Wait for your parents."

"My aunt Meggie's getting married," one of the girls told him.

No, she wasn't. Now Gage had a reason to stop the wedding. He just hoped he had time. No way could he let Megan's nieces get inside the church. "You have to wait out here," he told them.

The chubby one shook her head. "We're late. Mommy made us late."

The man who stepped from the driver's side hurried after his daughters. "Don't let them inside," Gage warned him. "Get them down here."

While he'd dated Megan, he'd met her brother-in-law. With a headstrong wife like Ellen, Peter was used to doing as he was told. He corralled his kids while his wife came around the front of the van. Her eyes widened when she saw Gage, and a little scream slipped out between her lips.

He hurried toward her. "Ellen, shh…"

He didn't want her drawing the attention of the armed arrivals. He also didn't want her falling on her face, since she looked like death. Ellen was usually so vivacious, with rosy cheeks and bright blue eyes. Now she was paler than her light blond hair, and her eyes were dull. She swayed, and he caught her.

"You look as bad as I do," she murmured.

"You should've seen me a few weeks ago," he replied. He'd finally started to gain back some weight and muscle. And he'd managed to get some sleep.

"We should've seen you the minute you got back," she said. "You're not dead."

"No."

"Does Megan know?"

He nodded.

"So I didn't have to drag myself out of bed to attend a wedding that's not going to happen…" She leaned heavily on the front of the van.

"What's wrong with you?" he asked.

"I thought it was the idea of my baby sister marrying that dweeb Richard that was nauseating me," she replied. "Now I think it's another pregnancy." She shot a glare at her husband.

Gage had no time for congratulations or diplomacy. "You need to leave," he said.

She sighed and admitted, "I would have liked to stay home. I fully intended to bail on my matron of honor duties. But Megan's my only sister."

Ellen had always treated her more like her oldest child than her sibling, though.

"She's not getting married," Gage assured her. "You can go back home. And take your family."

She shook her head. "They want cake. Even if there's no wedding, there is already food here." She gestured toward that catering van.

Gage wasn't so sure that they had brought anything other than weapons. He needed to find out. He also needed to call for backup bodyguards and police. But when he pulled his phone from the pocket, he found no signal. It would've been like Mrs. Payne to have some cell signal jammer so no ceremony would be interrupted in her church.

"And if there is no wedding," Ellen continued, "there will be explanations to make." She narrowed her blue eyes and stared up at him. "What's the reason the wedding is canceled, Gage?"

He had no time for explanations, either. He just leaned closer and whispered, "Something's going on, and you don't want your family in the line of fire."

Her eyes widened now, and her face paled even more. "My family is already in the line of fire," she said. "My dad and baby sister are already in the church."

Gage's stomach lurched. He had to get them out—alive—before the gunmen made their move.

If they hadn't already...

He had no time to drive far enough away that he could get a call out for backup. And he certainly had no time to wait for them to arrive. He had to get back into the church and make sure Megan wasn't in danger.

Megan's heart slammed against her ribs, and she backed up into the dressing room, trying to put distance between herself and the barrel of that gun. She raised her hands. "What do you want?"

The woman holding the gun was dressed in a navy blue bridesmaid's dress. But she wasn't one of Megan's bridesmaids. She had never seen the woman before, although with her curly auburn hair and brown eyes, she looked familiar.

The gunwoman stepped inside the room and shut the door. As she did, she pointed her weapon toward that closed door.

Megan didn't breathe a sigh of relief that it was no longer directed at her. Her breath was stuck yet in her lungs, burning.

"What do you want?" she asked the woman again. And why was she dressed like a bridesmaid? Megan didn't have any besides her sister. She'd wanted to keep the wedding small, probably because she really hadn't wanted one at all.

"I want to protect you," the young woman replied.

"What are you?" Megan asked. "A bridesmaid or a bodyguard?"

"Bodyguard," she replied quickly and emphatically.

"I already have one of those." According to Gage, it was the only reason he was at the church. "And I don't need that one."

The young woman shook her head and tumbled those auburn curls around her delicately featured face. "Yes, you do."

She did. But she wouldn't admit it. She didn't need Gage for protection, though. "I'm not in any danger."

"There are guys coming into the chapel concealing weapons."

Megan snorted. "My father is an FBI bureau chief. All

of his agents were invited to the wedding. They don't go anywhere without their guns."

They had all come armed to that Super Bowl party nearly two years ago.

"I know your dad's agents," the woman replied. "These people aren't them."

Megan's blood chilled. "Then who are they?"

The woman shrugged. "I don't know. Maybe people with a beef with your dad."

Megan bristled. "Why would anyone have a beef with my dad?" He was an honorable man—a fair man.

The only person she could think who'd had a problem with him had been Gage when he'd quit the Bureau. But that hadn't really been because of her father; that had been because of her.

"He's put away a lot of criminals," the woman replied. "Any of them could want revenge."

"Of course…" Megan murmured, embarrassed that she'd been so naive. Of course there were criminals who wouldn't appreciate how good her father was at his job. "But why here? Why now?"

"Your wedding announcement was in the paper," the pseudobridesmaid reminded her. "It provides a great opportunity for anyone looking for vengeance."

"But…"

"Don't worry," the woman assured her. "I'll protect you."

She was armed, but it sounded like the other people might have more weapons.

"How are you going to do that?" Megan questioned her.

The woman's dark eyes narrowed, as if she thought Megan was questioning her abilities.

"If none of those gunmen are my dad's friends, then you're outnumbered." Even if Gage hadn't left…

"I have a plan," the woman replied. "You need to take off that dress."

Megan couldn't agree more.

"No one can know that you're the bride."

She wasn't the bride, because she had no intention of getting married. "You'll need to help me," Megan said. "I can't undo all the buttons."

The woman lifted the skirt of her own dress and slid her gun into a holster strapped to her thigh. "Turn around." But she only fumbled for a few moments before cursing. "Damn it, I should have paid more attention when I've helped Mom out with weddings."

That was why she'd looked familiar. She was the spitting image of her mother. "You're Penny Payne's daughter." Mrs. Payne had said that her sons were bodyguards. She hadn't mentioned that her daughter was as well.

"Nikki," the young woman replied.

"I'm Megan," she said.

"I know," Nikki replied.

She sounded like her mother—like a woman who knew everything except how to get Megan out of the heavy, constrictive wedding gown. She continued to fumble with the tiny buttons, but she only managed to undo a couple of them.

"Cut it off me," Megan urged her. She grabbed a pair of scissors that had been left on the vanity table.

"That won't work."

"Of course it will." She didn't even care if she got cut in the process. She just wanted it off. Now. And it had nothing to do with fear of any suspiciously armed men. It had to do with fear of making a horrible mistake.

Again.

"I won't be able to put it on if it's ruined," Nikki replied.

"Why would you want to wear it?" She turned to face the woman.

Nikki shuddered. "Not because I want to get married. I want to act as a decoy."

"For me?" Megan asked. "You won't pass for me." The other woman was beautiful.

Nikki wrinkled her forehead. "Why not?" she asked. "We have the same coloring and build."

Megan shook her head. Her hair was darker, her body heavier. There was no way she looked like the beautiful bodyguard.

"You're a little curvier," Nikki admitted. "But with how heavy this dress is, no one will notice."

Megan suspected plenty of people would notice. But she didn't care as long as she wasn't the one walking down the aisle. "No one will notice if you snip a few of those buttons off," she said.

"You really want out of this dress," Nikki observed.

"When you came in, I was just getting ready to cancel the wedding," Megan said. "I can't go through with it."

"Gage?"

Nikki Payne might have been like her mother. Penny had pried out of Megan how much she'd loved another man—and how she'd lost that man when he'd gone missing in action and been presumed dead. But she'd lost Gage long before he'd been deployed again.

"Where is he?" Megan wondered.

He'd vowed to make sure no one would stop the wedding from taking place. If he'd noticed the men Nikki had noticed, he might have taken them on—alone. He might have put himself in danger—again.

Nikki sighed. "I don't know. But I could use his help. I left my phone in my mom's office when she enlisted me as your maid of honor."

"Ellen canceled." She wasn't surprised. Her sister hadn't wanted her to marry Richard.

She had no other bridesmaids. She hadn't wanted a big wedding; it was her father who'd convinced her to get married at Mrs. Payne's little white wedding chapel.

Nikki continued as if she hadn't spoken. "So I couldn't call for backup before I hurried in here to make sure you were safe. Do you have a phone?"

Megan shook her head. "Your mom took it from me when I got here," she said. "She wanted to take all my calls to make sure nobody would bother me."

But then she'd enlisted Gage Huxton—who bothered her more than anyone else ever could—as her bodyguard.

Why?

What had the older woman hoped would happen? A happy reunion?

Gage hadn't been happy to see her at all. He was still mad at her. Earlier, that had upset her. But it gave her some comfort now. With as mad as he was, maybe he wouldn't risk his life to protect her. Maybe he wouldn't put himself in any danger.

Nikki cursed. "I need to call for backup."

"Then forget about the dress and let's get out of here," Megan suggested.

Nikki shook her head. "You can't leave this room—not in that wedding gown."

"You can leave," Megan said. "Go—call for help."

Nikki shook her head again. "I can't leave you in here alone," she said, "and unprotected."

Her pride stinging, Megan lifted her chin and said, "I'm not helpless. I can take care of myself." She was Woodrow Lynch's daughter. When she and Ellen had barely been able to walk, their father had taught his daughters self-defense maneuvers as well as other ways to protect themselves.

"Do you have a gun?" Nikki asked.

"No," she admitted. She would have had to carry it in her purse, and she spent too much time at her sister's— with her young nieces—to risk that. They went in her purse all the time looking for gum. But she gripped the scissors. "I have these. I'll be fine. You go call for help."

"A good bodyguard never leaves her subject unprotected," Nikki said.

A good bodyguard would have made certain the door was locked, too. But they both tensed as the knob rattled and began to turn.

Nikki fumbled with her holster, but she didn't have time to draw her gun before the door opened. She cursed and stepped between Megan and whatever danger might be coming through the door.

But Megan doubted the petite bodyguard would be able to protect her from a real threat. Was there a real threat?

Blood had been shed in her wedding chapel before. A groom had been assaulted and abducted. Another man had died.

Brides had been threatened.

Penny's notorious instincts were telling her that there was another threat. Just as she'd told Gage, Megan Lynch was in danger. When she'd told him that, Penny had thought the only real threat had been of Megan making a mistake—of marrying a man she didn't love.

Penny's chapel was so successful because she ran it well. She knew every waiter on the catering staff, so she immediately recognized the one who didn't belong. She also recognized the guests who hadn't been invited. It was obvious none of the other early-arriving guests knew them. If they had ever worked for Woodrow, someone else would have recognized them. And they were armed—just like the unfamiliar waiter.

So who were they? And why had they brought guns into the chapel?

She couldn't tell if any of the other guests who'd arrived early were armed. Most of them were older, though. Probably great-aunts or -uncles of the bride or groom. If any were Woodrow's agents, they probably hadn't thought they needed to bring their weapons. Penny wished they would have.

Because the only person she knew for certain was armed was Nikki. She'd seen the holster when she'd helped her into the bridesmaid dress.

And Gage...

But where was Gage? Had he left like he'd threatened he would? He'd claimed he wanted no contact with Megan again. But if he was that angry and bitter yet, his emotions were still involved. Megan still affected him, hopefully too much for him to have just walked away.

Woodrow hoped he had. But he was an overprotective father. Too overprotective for him to not have noticed the people sneaking weapons into the wedding.

So where was Woodrow?

She scanned the foyer of the church, looking for him

and for Gage. But before she could find either, a strong hand gripped her arm and a deep voice murmured in her ear, "You're in danger."

Chapter 4

Feeling like he'd been sucker punched, Gage gasped for breath. He shouldn't have been surprised. He'd already seen Megan in that damn dress. But it was still a shock—more of a shock than Nikki Payne pulling a gun on him. Everyone knew that Nikki was trigger-happy.

He was damn lucky she hadn't shot him.

"Just your usual amount of jumpy?" he asked. "Or did you notice the armed arrivals, too?"

Her hand shaking slightly, Nikki holstered her weapon beneath the skirt of her bridesmaid dress. He'd had no idea that she and Megan were even friends. But then he'd been gone a long time.

"I'm glad you noticed them, too," she remarked. "So you called for help?"

He shook his head. "Did you?"

"When she asked me to step in for a sick bridesmaid,

I left my phone in Mom's office," she replied. "Where's yours?"

He held up the useless cell. "No signal. Your mom must have a jammer so her ceremonies don't get interrupted because someone forgot to shut off their phone."

Nikki sighed. "What doesn't she think of?"

"Armed gunmen," Gage replied.

"No, she has a plan for those, too."

Gage drew in a deep breath. "That's good," he said. "We need a plan."

"We need backup," Nikki said as she opened the door a crack and peered out into the foyer. "How many did you spot?"

"I made three," he said. "But there could be more." If they were seeking revenge against Woodrow, there would be more. They would know that they'd need an army to take down Chief Special Agent Lynch. "I told Megan's sister to call Nick."

Maybe she'd been frozen with fear. Maybe she'd just been confused by the exchange between Gage and Nikki. But Megan finally spoke, her voice raspy as she asked, "Ellen is here?"

"Not anymore," he assured her. "I told her and her husband and the girls to leave."

"The girls…" Her soft voice cracked with fear, and she trembled.

He found himself reaching for her, his hands lightly grasping her shoulders so she didn't fall. "They're gone," he said. "They're safe."

She peered up at him, skepticism in her dark eyes. "Ellen listened?"

He hoped like hell she had. He'd warned her that if

she didn't follow his instructions, she would put her sister and dad in more danger.

Ellen wouldn't have wanted that. Gage didn't want Megan in any danger. Hell, he just wanted her. His palms heated and tingled from the contact with her shoulders. Only thin lace sleeves separated her skin from his. He stepped back and dropped his hands back to his sides.

"She wouldn't put the girls in danger," he reminded her. She had definitely left with her husband and kids. But he didn't know if she'd listened to him, if she'd called only Nick.

If she had called 911 like she'd mentioned, she risked getting them all killed. When the gunmen heard sirens wailing, they might just open fire. Hopefully, she would do as he had directed: call Nick and tell him to do nothing until Gage contacted him.

Nikki's face had paled, too. "I hope Nick doesn't call Logan. If they all rush in…"

Gage shook his head. "I told her to have him sit tight until I—or someone else from inside the church—make contact with him. So we need your mom to shut off that damn cell jammer."

Nikki nodded. "Yes. You need to find her."

Gage's heart constricted as fear squeezed it. "No. You need to." He wasn't leaving Megan, not when he was certain that she was in danger now.

"I have to stay here," Nikki said. "I have to get her out of that dress."

"Why?" he asked.

"Because nobody can know she's the bride," Nikki said, as if he was an idiot. And maybe he was, because getting her out of the dress was pretty obviously the easiest way to protect her. They had to disguise her.

"I would be out of it," Megan said, "if you would have used the scissors."

Nikki shook her head. "Then I won't be able to put it on and switch places with you."

Gage already knew Nikki was smart. She'd helped Nick figure out why someone was really after him and Annalise. He was impressed as hell that she'd already come up with a plan to protect Megan. His only instinct had been to get to Megan and get her out.

But just like police couldn't come in with sirens wailing, he couldn't sneak Megan out in that damn sparkling gown without drawing attention, either. And if, as he suspected, the armed people were here for her, they wouldn't let him just walk out with her without one hell of a fight.

"You get word to Nick," he said. "I'll get Megan out of the gown."

Nikki nodded in agreement before opening the door and slipping out into the foyer. She disappeared before Gage fully realized what he'd agreed to do: he was going to undress Megan.

"Wait," Megan called out, her voice a faint croak in her suddenly dry throat. But Nikki Payne was already gone, leaving her alone with Gage.

She would rather have taken her chances with the armed gunmen. After all, there were only three of them. That wasn't nearly as dangerous as one Gage Huxton.

"She'll be okay," Gage assured her.

She flinched from a pang of guilt. Of course she should have been concerned about Nikki's safety. "She seems pretty tough," she said. Despite her petite size.

"She has three older brothers," Gage said. "Four, actually, with Nick."

"I know," Megan said. "Mrs. Payne—" The wedding planner was insistent that Megan use her first name. "Penny has told me all about her sons. And she counts Nick among them."

Even though she hadn't given birth to him. While Megan knew someone else who'd loved a child that wasn't really his, she still considered Penny Payne to be very special. Megan had realized that the first time they'd met. Penny was intuitive and empathetic. She'd understood Megan's pain—her grief over thinking Gage was dead—because Penny had lost her husband. But Gage wasn't Megan's husband, and she doubted that he would ever be.

"Penny's great." Gage's mouth curved into a faint grin. "And her sons, they're good guys. They'll come with Nick for backup. It's going to be okay."

Megan released a breath she hadn't realized she'd been holding. Of course everything was going to be okay. She wasn't even convinced that they were really in danger. Nikki and Gage could have been overreacting.

But she somehow doubted that.

"You'll still be able to get married today," Gage continued.

Maybe she would be able to, but she had no intention of exchanging vows. She couldn't promise to love any man but Gage. He didn't want her love, though. He apparently didn't even want to touch her.

But then his hands were on her shoulders again. He didn't hold her, though. He only turned her so that her back was to him. Then his fingers skimmed down the line of buttons on her back. "Nikki didn't undo many of these," he mused.

Just enough that she could feel the brush of his fingertips across an inch of her spine. She suppressed a shiver of reaction. She had always reacted to his touch.

"They're tiny," she said. Every fitting with the seamstress had taken so long, just getting her in and out of the dress.

"They're also slippery as hell," he said with a grunt.

They were clear, either crystal or glass, like the sparkling rhinestones on the bodice of the gown.

"And it's like the holes are too small for them," he mused. "I can't get them through."

Her hand shaking, she held up the scissors again. "I think you just need to cut it off."

He stepped around her, his brow furrowing as he stared down at her. "Why would you want to destroy your wedding gown?"

Because it wasn't really her gown...

She never would have chosen anything so ostentatious for herself. She'd wanted simple and elegant, like the gown her mother had worn. Her father had even taken it out of storage for her. Megan hadn't wanted lace. And certainly no rhinestones. In the elaborate, sparkly gown, she felt more like a beauty contestant than a bride.

"I just want it off," she murmured as panic began to overwhelm her. She didn't care about the possibility of armed gunmen in the church. She just didn't want to get married. Now or ever...

It wasn't as if she needed a husband to have children. She could be a single parent. Like her father had been. Like Penny Payne.

"Don't worry," Gage assured her. "Nikki and I won't let anything happen to you. She has a good plan, switching places with you."

She wasn't as convinced as they were. "Putting her in danger in my place—that's not a good idea."

"Nikki's tough," he reminded her.

"We don't need to go to all that trouble," she said. "We can just cancel the wedding."

He shook his head. "I told you that I'd make sure the wedding happened."

She shivered now, but it wasn't in reaction to his touch; it was because of the coldness in his eyes and his voice. He hadn't changed his mind. He wanted her to marry another man, probably any man but him.

"But if those people brought guns in here to stop the wedding…"

His brow furrowed more. "We don't know why they brought guns in here."

"Nikki thinks they want revenge on my father and that they intend to use me to do it," she said.

Her stomach clenched with dread at the thought. She never wanted to cause her father any pain. He'd already been through too much when he'd lost her mother so many years ago.

"We don't know that for certain," he said.

Maybe they didn't intend to hurt her. Maybe they intended to hurt her father when they figured his guard would be down—when he'd be distracted with his daughter's happiness. But he already knew his daughter wasn't happy. He'd been so worried about her.

Now she was worried about him. Where was her father? Was he okay?

"You need to find my dad," she urged him.

Gage shook his head. "I'm not leaving you."

She would have been touched had she thought he actually cared. But he was only doing his job. She tried to remind herself of that when he turned her around and attacked the buttons of her gown again. She tried to remind herself that he wasn't undressing her for the reason he'd undressed her so many times before.

He didn't want her naked. He didn't want her at all.

"Why would you say I'm in danger?" Penny Payne asked as she closed her office door behind Woodrow.

"You saw the gunmen." He'd been watching her when she'd noticed them. That was why he'd pulled her aside before she could confront them. He wouldn't have put it past her. She was that protective of her chapel and her brides.

But this particular bride was his responsibility. He would keep Megan safe. The only other person he would trust to protect her was Gage Huxton. While his quitting the Bureau and reenlisting had hurt Megan, Gage would never consciously cause her harm.

When Woodrow had seen Gage slip into the bride's dressing room a little while ago, he had breathed a sigh of relief. Then he had guided Penny down the stairwell to the basement and the safety of her office. While Gage protected Megan, he would protect Penny—from herself.

"You don't know them?" she asked. "You didn't plant the waiter among my catering staff?"

"Why would I?"

"For additional security."

"I didn't think I'd need security for my daughter's wedding." And maybe that had been naive of him. There'd been an announcement in the paper, which had probably been like an advertisement for anyone harboring a grudge against him. *Want revenge against Woodrow Lynch? Hurt his daughter on her special day.*

"We need it now," Penny said. "There's only Nikki."

"And Gage."

Her thin shoulders slumped, and the corners of her mouth dipped down in a frown. "He left, remember?"

"He's back."

Despite the situation, she smiled that all-knowing smile that both infuriated and fascinated him. "I knew he wouldn't be able to let her marry another man."

Woodrow sighed. Now he understood what a hopeless romantic was. There was no hope of changing Penny's mind about who she thought belonged with whom. "I think it's more likely that he spotted the weapons, too."

Penny was undeterred and smiled even brighter. "And he came back to protect her."

"It's not personal," he insisted. "Gage was a soldier and an agent and now a bodyguard. It's not in his nature to walk away from danger."

For once Penny didn't argue with him. Her mouth curved down again. "And that nature nearly got him killed. You need to call for more backup," she said.

He held up his blank cell phone. Trying to get a signal had drained its battery. "I couldn't get any reception. Now it's dead."

Penny stared at its black screen. "Why not?"

"You tell me," he said. "I assume you have a cell signal blocker so no calls will interrupt weddings in your chapel."

Color streaked across each of her delicate cheekbones. "I have one," she acknowledged. "But I didn't turn it on today."

"You wanted Megan's wedding to be interrupted." He narrowed his eyes and studied her flushed face. "Is that armed waiter yours?"

"Of course not," she said. "I didn't want to disrupt Megan's wedding. I would have turned on the signal jammer if she decided to go through with the ceremony."

"But you were hoping that she would decide not to."

"I don't want her to make a mistake she'll regret the rest of her life."

"Have you?" he wondered.

"Have I what?"

"Made any mistakes you still regret?" He didn't expect her to answer him since she never talked about herself.

But instead of changing the subject as she always had whenever he'd asked her something personal, she stared up at him, her usually warm brown eyes cool and guarded. And she replied, "Not yet."

Was he a mistake she was considering making? He wanted to ask, but he couldn't risk making a mistake of his own. Not now…

Not with his daughter and other innocent bystanders—and Penny—in danger. He had to act and quickly before more guests arrived at the church. There had only been a few early arrivals, besides those armed people. Unfortunately, they'd been aunts and uncles and cousins of his late wife, unarmed civilians who wouldn't be able to help him protect the others.

If only some of his agents or Penny's sons had arrived already…

"Where do you keep your signal jammer?" he asked.

"Nobody's been in my office," she said.

"Where do you keep it?" he persisted. God, the woman was stubborn. It was good that he'd decided not to ask her out—despite all the times he'd thought about it since meeting her. He'd picked up his phone a million times to call her. But something had held him back.

Fear. He was not good husband material. His late wife had told him that often enough. He had been consumed with his career, had spent so much time away. Of course that had ended when she'd gotten sick. His job was still just as important to him, though.

Like Penny's job was to her…

She pulled a charm from the bracelet on her wrist— a tiny key—and slid it into a lock on a drawer built into the wall perpendicular to her desk. Instead of the drawer opening, the wall slid forward revealing a space behind it large enough for a glass case full of guns and the signal jammer. The industrial-style box jammer was closed and inactive.

"What the hell?" he murmured, in awe of the hiding place and the equipment and guns she'd stowed inside it.

"This church has a lot of history," she said.

He suspected not all of it had been good. She'd been married there. He wasn't sure if that had been a good or bad union.

"There are other hiding places," she said. "And a secret passageway that leads to the little courtyard out back."

"That's good," he said. "You can leave that way." But were there other armed gunmen outside? Would they see her if she escaped that way?

She shook her head. "I'm not leaving."

"We need backup," he reminded her. "And since you're not the one jamming the signals, someone else is." Someone who'd planned to cut off communication to the church.

She turned back toward her desk and opened a bottom drawer. "I have a landline, too," she told him.

He was surprised. Smartphones were more useful, especially for businesses.

She had an old-school kind, the console with the cord attaching the receiver to it. No wonder she put it in a drawer, so it didn't take up too much of the surface of her whitewashed oak desk. When she put the receiver to her ear, her brow furrowed. "There's no dial tone."

That didn't surprise him. If the gunmen had gone to the trouble of jamming the cell signals, they would have made certain to cut the landline, too. And they probably had reinforcements stationed outside. He couldn't send her out alone to the courtyard.

He needed reinforcements of his own.

Penny's eyes widened—looking even bigger and darker—as her face paled. And the woman who usually had all the answers asked, "What are we going to do?"

Something shifted in Woodrow's chest, squeezing his heart. He reached for her—intending to offer her only comfort from the fear gripping her. But her lips parted on a soft gasp, and he had the sudden urge to taste them.

To taste her...

Before he could lower his head to hers, the doorknob rattled. Someone had found them. Would he have time to draw his weapon and protect them?

Chapter 5

Frustration knotted Gage's stomach muscles. The damn little buttons were driving him crazy. His fingers were too big to grasp them, let alone push them through the little loops wrapped tightly around them. The edge of the glass or crystal was sharp, scraping his fingertips. He glanced at the scissors she'd set on the vanity table.

"I should cut it off," he said.

"You should," she eagerly agreed.

But he liked Nikki's plan to change places with the bride. Hell, maybe he just liked it because Megan would no longer be the bride. He shouldn't care that she was going to marry another man. While he'd once considered asking her to marry him, he never would again. She'd said she hadn't loved the man he'd been. She certainly wouldn't love the one he had become. "We can't."

He'd been at it for long moments and had only undone

one button. They were spaced so closely together that even with the couple that Nikki had undone, only a little more than an inch of Megan's skin was visible through the slight opening.

Megan was never comfortable showing much skin. She always dressed in layers. Skirts with tights beneath and tall boots. Blouses buttoned to her throat with sweaters over them. She dressed like the librarian she was. For some reason Gage had found that super sexy. Just like he'd always taken his time unwrapping presents, to draw out the anticipation and excitement, he'd taken his time getting Megan out of her clothes.

He'd toyed with the zippers on her boots before lowering them and pulling them off her curvy calves. He'd taken his time with the buttons on her cardigan sweaters and on her blouses beneath them. Even with the layers, she'd never had as many buttons as this, though.

And at least then his efforts had been rewarded. He'd been able to stroke and taste all that honey-colored skin he'd exposed. He'd been able to elicit soft moans and cries from her as she'd pressed her hot, naked body against his.

Remembering the sensations—the heat, the tension, the pleasure—had a groan slipping from his throat.

"Use the scissors," she told him.

But his frustration wasn't with the buttons. It was with the fact that even if he managed to undo all those buttons, he wouldn't be able to kiss and touch the skin he exposed. She wasn't his anymore.

She'd never really been his, because she'd never trusted him. She'd never trusted what they'd had. Or she wouldn't have accused of him using her.

"I can't..." he said.

She tilted her head and peered over her shoulder at him. "Can't cut it off?"

He couldn't keep thinking about what they'd had, what they'd done to each other. How he hadn't ever been able to get enough of her.

Heat rushed through him, making his blood warm, his skin tingle. He'd bared less than an inch of her silky skin, but he wanted her as obsessively as he'd always wanted her.

Maybe it was her shyness that had appealed to him the first time they'd met. When her father had introduced them, she hadn't met his gaze, and she'd ignored his out-stretched hand, hers shoved deep into the pockets of her skirt. Used to women seeking his attention, flirting with him, he'd been intrigued by the novelty of Megan Lynch. She'd challenged him.

And Gage had never been able to walk away from a challenge…until the end. Until he'd realized there was no way he would ever win her trust or her heart.

He just shook his head.

And her face paled. "You're giving up again?"

"Again?" he asked. "When did I give up before?"

Unless she was talking about them. But she'd given him no choice then.

Now color flushed her face. "You quit the Bureau."

After they'd broken up, he hadn't been able to work for her father. Not only would it have been awkward but it would have killed his pride. He'd learned what everyone thought of him—that he was doing the boss's daughter in order to get ahead. Megan had believed those vicious rumors. So maybe that was another reason he'd quit, to prove her wrong.

"I had my reasons," he reminded her.

She jerked her chin up and down in a nervous nod. "I thought it was my fault. The reason you quit, the reason you reenlisted, the reason you..." Her voice cracked, cutting off whatever she'd been about to add.

"The reason I what?"

"Got killed," she said. "I thought you were dead."

And she'd blamed herself. He shouldn't have been surprised, though. He'd blamed her, too. Getting mad at her had eased some of his pain.

"I didn't die there," he said. He wasn't so certain that he wouldn't here, though. He glanced to the door, wondering if those armed people were out there yet, waiting to force their way inside.

"Do you think it's that dangerous?" she asked.

He didn't have Penny Payne and Nick Rus's notorious instincts or he wouldn't have fallen for Megan in the first place. Nor would he have spent six months in captivity in Afghanistan. But maybe those six months had helped him develop some kind of sixth sense as well.

Because he knew Megan Lynch's wedding day wasn't going to end well—for anyone.

She expelled a shaky breath. "You do..."

"Nikki has a good plan to switch places," he said. But Nikki had been gone a long time. Had one of those gunmen taken her out?

He pulled his cell from his pocket and glanced at his blank screen. She hadn't gotten the jammer turned off yet. They still had no backup. No way of knowing if Ellen had even been able to reach Nick.

Gage flashed back to those six months that he'd spent wondering if anyone was going to come to his rescue, if they knew where he was or even that he was alive.

They hadn't. There had been no help coming. So he'd had to rely on himself. Then. And now.

"We need to get you out of here," he said. Maybe it was time to cut off the wedding dress. He reached for the scissors.

But she caught his hand, her fingers sliding over his. "No."

"It was your idea," he reminded her.

Her face flushed. "I know. But now I don't think it's a good idea…"

He thought he understood, even though it knotted his stomach, this time with dread. It was still her wedding gown. She must have been having second thoughts about destroying it.

"You want to wear it again," he said. "For Richard."

"Richard." His name slipped through her lips on a gasp. "Richard—what if he's in danger?"

Gage didn't give a damn. But then guilt flashed through him. Richard Boersman had never done anything to him. It had been the other way around. Gage was the one who'd stolen Megan from Richard. But he hadn't been able to keep her.

"You really think anyone has a beef with Richard?" he asked with disbelief. "I'm sure he's perfectly safe." There was no doubt why she'd agreed to marry him. Richard was safe and boring and dull, and she didn't have to worry about him breaking her heart like she'd constantly worried Gage would.

The irony was that she'd broken his instead.

She squeezed Gage's hand around the scissors. "Please make sure he's okay."

"I'm not leaving you," he said. If he walked away and

left her alone and unprotected, he might never see her again. And he couldn't risk that.

Couldn't risk never seeing her beautiful face again, never touching her soft skin…

His free hand moved up to cup her cheek. He skimmed his thumb along her chin and tipped up her face. Then he began to lower his head…just as the doorknob rattled. Someone was trying to get inside.

Déjà vu. Nikki wasn't like her mother or half brother with all their premonitions and instincts. She hadn't ever experienced any psychic phenomena until now. Now she had that weird sense of déjà vu. Walking inside the bride's dressing room gave Nikki the exact same feeling she'd had walking inside her mom's office just moments ago. And she murmured, "I keep interrupting."

Gage tensed, and his hand tightened around the weapon he'd drawn from beneath his tuxedo jacket before opening the door for her. "What did you interrupt? Are they making a move?"

She suspected that Woodrow Lynch had been thinking about making one on Penny before Nikki had burst into the basement office. But Penny hadn't been very happy with the man for drawing a gun on her only daughter. She'd been even unhappier with him when he'd agreed with Nikki's plan to switch places with his daughter.

If something happened to her, she doubted her mother would ever forgive the FBI chief. So she had to make sure nothing happened to her.

She shook her head. "Not yet."

"What do they want?" Megan asked.

Nikki exchanged a glance with Gage. They were both

pretty sure they wanted the bride. Even Woodrow and Penny had agreed about that.

"It doesn't matter what they want," Gage said. "We're not going to let them get it." He held up his cell. "It's completely dead now. Didn't you find your mom's jammer?"

"It's not hers."

He sucked in a breath.

"Her landline was cut, too."

Still standing guard at the door, he opened it a crack and peeked out. "Where are all guests?"

"The wedding isn't supposed to start until noon," Megan said. "We have a half hour yet."

"People usually arrive a half hour early," replied the daughter of the wedding planner. Nikki had grown up knowing about weddings—and never planning to have one herself.

Even before she'd learned about her dad's betrayal, she'd never wanted a husband of her own. She'd had enough males in her life with her overprotective brothers. Occasionally, she got lonely, though...

Occasionally, she missed that kind of tension she'd felt in her mother's office and when she'd walked into the bride's dressing room. Then again, she wasn't certain she'd ever felt *that* kind of tension herself.

"Do you think they have someone posted outside the doors?" Gage asked. "Turning guests away?"

"They've planned this out," Nikki said. "So yeah, probably."

"Wouldn't that draw suspicion?" Megan asked.

"They're probably telling everyone the wedding was canceled," Nikki said. "And the guests who know about your past—" she jerked her thumb at Gage "—and his return from the dead probably wouldn't question it."

"But how would those gunmen know about that—" her face reddened as Megan asked "—about us?"

Unless…

Maybe this siege on the church wasn't about revenge on the bride's father. Maybe it was about revenge on the bride's ex-lover.

Because it was clear that hurting Megan would hurt Gage. Nikki narrowed her eyes and studied Gage's face. He was even tenser now than when he'd opened the door to her, his handsome features so tight his face looked like a granite mask—hard and sharp—like his green eyes.

He'd obviously considered the same thing she had. And he didn't like it.

"It doesn't matter," Nikki told them both. "What matters is everyone getting out of here alive."

Gage looked at her then, his glance one of pity for her naïveté. She wasn't so stupid that she hadn't considered the other alternatives. She already knew there was a strong possibility that they wouldn't survive.

Then she would never experience that tension she'd felt in her mom's office and in this room. But you couldn't miss what you'd never had.

She held up the one useful item she had retrieved from her mother's office.

Gage stared at the small tool. "What the hell is that?"

"Crochet hook," she replied. "This'll get those buttons undone."

"That's what your mom used to do it up," Megan said. And she released a ragged breath, as if the dress was constricting her lungs. Maybe it was. It looked tight and heavy and uncomfortable as hell.

Nikki couldn't wait to get it on and put her plan into motion, even though it could quite possibly be the last thing she would ever do.

Megan jerked away as Nikki reached for her. Sure, she wanted out of that dress—so badly that she hadn't even cared if Gage was the one to cut it off her. But it was different now, different since he'd nearly kissed her again.

Wasn't that what he'd been about to do before Nikki had started turning the doorknob? He'd been lowering his head, and his eyes had gone dark, the pupils dilating as he'd stared down at her. He'd looked like he'd wanted to kiss her, just like he'd looked that first day in her father's kitchen.

Now that all the old memories and feelings and longings washed over her, she couldn't bear it, couldn't stand to have him watch her get undressed and know that he wouldn't touch her—wouldn't kiss her.

Not that she wanted him to.

She didn't want to put herself through all that pain again, no matter how much she probably deserved it. She'd hurt Gage. And now she was about to hurt another man, if he hadn't already been harmed.

"You said you'd check on Richard," she reminded Gage.

"I said that I couldn't," he corrected her.

"Because you couldn't leave me alone," she said. "But I'm not alone." Nikki had a gun. And Megan had the scissors. Gage had pressed them back into her hand before he'd drawn his gun and opened the door.

Nikki nodded. "I'll protect her and get her out of the dress," she said. "You should check on the groom. We don't know what the hell could have happened to him."

Megan's stomach lurched, and a gasp slipped through her lips.

And Gage's jaw tightened. He thought she loved Richard. And she did—as a friend. Nothing more. But he was a friend and had been one for a long time. So she was worried about him.

His blond head jerked in a sharp nod. "Sure, I'll check on him."

"Gage…" She wanted to call him back, wanted to explain that she didn't love her groom. She didn't love anyone but Gage. She never had.

But the door slammed behind him.

Nikki jumped. "So much for not drawing any attention to himself."

It wouldn't have mattered if he'd slammed the door or quietly slipped out. Gage Huxton was the kind of man who drew attention with his height and his handsomeness. He wasn't like Megan, whom people rarely noticed.

Why had he ever been interested in her? It was no wonder she'd doubted his feelings. She couldn't believe even now that he'd ever really wanted her.

Richard claimed he did, that he wanted to be her husband, wanted to build a life with her. He'd anticipated that this day would be the first of the rest of their life together. And now the man who'd stolen her once from him was about to take her away again…

Only for her own protection.

But she wasn't sure he would tell Richard that. She wasn't sure what Gage would say to the other man. She only knew that she was the one who should tell Richard that she couldn't marry him. "I need to get out of this dress," she told Nikki.

"I know," the other woman replied. But even with the tool, the buttons weren't opening easily.

During the long moments Nikki struggled with the dress, Megan imagined Gage walking toward the groom's dressing room. Now she didn't worry about what he would say to Richard. She worried about what could happen to him before he got there. She worried that he would take on those gunmen alone.

"No," she said, as she jerked away from the other woman. "We're wasting too much time."

"We still have a half hour before the wedding is supposed to start," Nikki said.

But Gage had already been gone too long, long enough for Megan to worry that he would never come back. She'd lived through that nightmare once. She didn't want to live through it again.

Panic filling her, constricting her lungs even more than the heavy dress, she rushed toward the door and pulled it open. And just like the last time she'd tried to leave, the barrel of a gun stopped her.

Unlike last time, this barrel pushed into her abdomen. And she had no doubt that this woman, who stared at her with cold blue eyes, would pull the trigger and bore that hole right through her.

Chapter 6

Just as Nikki had remarked, the church was too empty for a wedding that was less than an hour away from beginning. Gage didn't know much about weddings, but he knew that people usually liked to get to them early so they could get the good seats. As he passed through the vestibule, he noticed that some of those front pews were occupied by little gray-haired people.

Older people were always early. It was the younger ones that weren't on time. Like the Paynes. Where was Logan or Parker or Cooper? Or had any of them even been invited?

They were Penny's kids. Not Woodrow's agents. Of all the Payne Protection bodyguards, only he and Nick had worked for the Bureau.

What about the agents, though? Where were they? Woodrow would have invited them for certain. Sure, Dalton Reyes hated weddings. But Gage had heard that after finding a bride in a car trunk, the agent had gotten married himself, so he must have changed his mind.

And what about Agents Campbell or Stryker or Bell? They were all close with Woodrow. They wouldn't have missed his daughter's wedding.

But the only one Gage saw from the Bureau was the ass kisser. The young guy had been even more of a rookie than Gage. But he'd been desperate to get ahead and jealous that Gage had. He was the one who'd spread the lies that Gage was only dating Megan for a promotion.

Because it didn't matter how much ass Tucker Allison kissed, he would never make special agent. There was nothing special about him. He didn't have the guts for the job. Or to help Gage and Woodrow take down the armed suspects.

Where the hell were they? He hadn't noticed any of them as he'd crossed the vestibule. But as he stepped through the doors at the back of the church, a man straightened away from the wall. He wore a suit that didn't fit him well. Even as big as it was, it couldn't conceal the bulge of a weapon.

Acting oblivious, Gage forced a smile. "Hi. Bride's side or groom's side?"

He'd like to know who the hell the guy was here for. But he had a sick feeling that he already knew. It had to be for the bride.

But why? Because of Woodrow?

Or because of him?

Keeping the grin plastered on his face, he studied the stranger. The guy's hair was nearly shaved, just stubble showing on his skull. He could have been military. But what army? And more importantly, what side?

"Are you an usher?" the guy asked. His thin lips curved into a faint, mocking grin. "I thought you were the *best* man."

Did he know Gage? And how? Had they met on opposite sides of the law or a battlefield?

He could have been a supporter of the group that had taken him. He and the other gunmen could have been determined to carry out what the others had begun. For some reason his captors had thought he'd had information they'd wanted. But no matter how badly they'd tortured him, he hadn't been able to tell them what they'd wanted to learn.

That didn't mean they'd given up, though. He resisted the urge to reach for his weapon and drop the guy. For one, he didn't know if he would be fast enough, and for two, he didn't know where the other armed people were.

"It's a small wedding," Gage replied. "We're all pulling double duty."

The guy nodded as if he believed him. But he doubted he'd taken him at his word any more than his captors had.

"So which side?" he asked again. "Bride or groom?"

He shrugged. "I'm the plus one, just waiting for my wife. She went to the restroom."

With her big purse with her heavy gun inside? Gage hoped like hell that was really where she was. The guy had answered easily, as if he were speaking the truth.

Some people believed their own lies. Like the little FBI agent who nervously glanced back at him…

Tucker had believed the lies he'd spread. Maybe that was why Megan had believed them so easily as well.

But if she'd trusted Gage, if she'd loved him like she'd once claimed she had, she never would have doubted him. Like Gage doubted this guy.

"Well, I hope your wife returns quickly," Gage said. "The wedding will be starting soon."

The guy arched a brow as if skeptical of Gage's claim. "Really?" he mused. "I've never known a wedding to start on time. Usually brides take longer to get ready than they plan for, especially if they're nervous."

How did this guy know that Megan was nervous? Because he was giving her every reason to be?

"You must have never attended a wedding here," Gage said. "Mrs. Payne's events always start on time. She has a way of quelling every fear of even the most nervous bride." Or at least that was what he'd been told. But knowing Penny, he didn't doubt it.

It was clear she had her doubts, though. She and Woodrow stepped into the vestibule from the basement stairwell. His arm was around her waist, as if he'd had to help her up the steps. But her body was stiff—not trembling—and she pulled away from him. Penny was proud and tough. She had raised her kids alone and had survived her fears over all their brushes with death.

And he knew they'd had many just since he'd met them.

"Well, if you won't let me usher you to a seat, I better assume my best man duties and check on the groom," Gage said.

"That's who should be nervous," the man remarked beneath his breath.

Gage turned back. "What? Why would you say that?"

The guy shrugged again, and a small, mocking grin curved his thin lips. Gage didn't recognize the man but he recognized the look: condescension. Like he thought Gage was an idiot because he didn't know what he knew.

What the hell did he know?

The guy shrugged again. "In my experience the guy always has more reason to be nervous when he's getting married, especially when the *best* man keeps going into the bride's dressing room."

Innuendo joined the condescension now. The man's dark eyes gleamed.

Anger coursed through Gage, making him tense. He didn't give a damn that the guy was armed and had armed friends. He stepped closer to him.

But then a small hand gripped his forearm. "Gage, you need to make sure Richard is ready. The ceremony will be starting soon."

His stomach lurched at the thought of that actually happening, of Megan actually marrying her old boyfriend. But Richard wasn't her old boyfriend anymore.

Gage was.

He stepped back and turned to Penny, who was smiling at him. But unlike all the times she had before, the smile didn't warm her brown eyes, didn't dispel the fear widening them.

"Hurry up," she urged him.

But then his stomach lurched for another reason, at the thought of leaving her alone with an obviously dangerous man.

"Go," she said and her tone brooked no argument. She was stubborn.

And he knew better than to argue with a stubborn woman. Annalise—his sister—had taught him that. So he turned and headed down the aisle toward the front of the church. The groom's dressing room was behind the altar. Sun shone through the stained glass windows, sending a kaleidoscope of colors dancing around the room with its sparkling marble floor and whitewashed oak pews.

It really was a beautiful chapel—a beautiful venue for a wedding. Too bad there would be no wedding today. He only hoped there would be no funeral, either.

Penny lifted her chin and stared into the stranger's cold eyes. She was good at pretending to be brave when she was actually quavering with fear. When her husband had died in the line of duty, she'd had to pretend to her kids that she was fine, that she wasn't scared of raising them alone. That she had everything under control when she'd actually had no idea how she was going to manage.

"Well, you're obviously the one running the show," the man replied.

She wished that were true—then her daughter wouldn't be intent on using herself as a decoy. And her bride would be marrying the man she really loved, the one who was so stubborn he was probably going to get himself killed. That was why she'd intervened. She'd seen the anger course through Gage. She'd worried that he was about to lose more than his temper.

She tilted her head. "Show?"

He gestured around the chapel. "The wedding. This is your place, right? You're Penny Payne."

She held out her hand, proud when it didn't tremble. "Nice to meet you…?"

"D," he said. "Everyone just calls me D."

"The initial?"

He nodded.

It could have been for his last name. Or his first…

"Are you here for the groom or the bride?" she asked.

His mouth curved. "Everyone keeps asking me that."

And he obviously had yet to give an answer.

"And what is your response?" she asked.

His grin widened. "I'm here for my wife."

She glanced around. "Where is she?"

"Powder room," he said. "She wanted to touch up her makeup. Hope she doesn't outshine the bride."

Penny doubted that was the threat this man and his wife posed to the bride. But they definitely posed a threat—to everyone in Penny's chapel. No, she had never been more afraid than she was now.

But she smiled. "Well, it was nice meeting you, D. I have quite a few details to see to before the ceremony begins. I hope you and your wife enjoy it."

He smiled back at her. "I certainly plan on it. Now as for my wife… I can't imagine what could be keeping her…"

"What do you want?" Megan asked. She doubted it was to protect her, as Nikki had professed when she had walked into the bride's dressing room with a gun in her hand.

Nikki obviously didn't know her. She didn't greet her at all, but just quietly studied her.

The woman tossed her long black hair over her shoulder and smiled. "Just wanted to give the bride my best regards."

What was that? A euphemism for a bullet? The way she pointed the gun at Megan certainly implied as much. She swallowed down a lump of fear as the woman stepped even closer and pulled the door closed behind her, trapping Megan and Nikki inside with her.

Nikki was armed, too, though she hadn't drawn her gun. She'd had no time to react because Megan had been the stupid one—the one who'd opened the door without checking to see what danger might be lurking on the other side.

"I don't know you," Megan said. "And I don't know why you have that gun. Who are you?"

The woman uttered a pitying sigh. "That is a problem when you have a big wedding. You have no way of knowing all your guests. You don't know who the groom has invited."

"Richard invited you?" she asked. She doubted that. Richard had invited very few people to the wedding. An only child of only children who were now deceased, he had no family. And because he worked so much at his IT job, he had few friends, either.

The woman continued as if Megan hadn't spoken. "You probably have no way of knowing who all your own family invited. Friends or acquaintances of your parents."

Fear clutched Megan's stomach. This was about her father. He was out there in the chapel somewhere. Hopefully, Gage was with him, protecting him.

"It's much better to marry like I did," the woman said. "It was just me and my husband. The only two people who really matter in a marriage."

Megan nodded in agreement. "That's true. You're right. I didn't want this wedding."

She didn't want this marriage.

"The chapel is beautiful," the woman said, almost wistfully. She had claimed her wedding was better, but she wasn't as convinced as she'd tried to make Megan. "The flowers." She jabbed the gun into Megan's bodice. "Your dress." Her dark eyes narrowed as she studied it. "Your dress..."

That damn dress. Megan wanted it off. Despite the

few buttons Nikki had freed, it was still too tight—too constricting, too heavy...

"It's a mistake," Megan said.

"The dress?"

"The wedding," she said. "You didn't need to come in here with the gun to stop it. I have no intention of getting married."

The woman's face paled, and she emitted a nervous laugh. "Oh, no, stopping the wedding is not my intention at all."

"Then why the gun?" Nikki finally spoke, repeating Megan's earlier question that the woman had already ignored.

The woman glanced down at the barrel as if she hadn't realized she held it. "This isn't to stop the wedding," she said. "This is to make certain that the wedding goes exactly as planned."

Megan shook her head. "No."

"That doesn't make sense," Nikki said. "You and your gun are disrupting the wedding, not making it come off smoothly at all."

The woman snorted. "She just admitted she has no intention of going through with it."

Megan silently cursed her admission. She'd just assumed the woman intended to stop the wedding. That was why she'd admitted she had no intention of getting married.

"You couldn't have known that," Nikki prodded her. "Unless..." She glanced around the room as if looking for cameras.

When they'd hidden the cell jammer, they might have planted a camera, as well. It made sense, or as much sense as any of this did.

"The man who keeps traipsing in and out of this room," the woman said, "is not the groom."

"Do you know Richard?" Megan persisted. Or was it Gage she knew?

"I know you are to marry your groom today," the woman said. "And you're not going to let any other man dissuade you from doing that."

Megan's brow furrowed. "Gage isn't trying to dissuade me."

Disbelieving, the woman snorted again. "A man like that…" She emitted a lustful sigh. "He doesn't have to *do* anything to distract a woman."

"He's not distracting me," Megan said. But for the first time she lied to the woman. She realized now it was what she should have done in the first place. Honesty had only put her in more danger.

She'd only really lied once in her life, and that had had horrible consequences. Gage had quit his job and reenlisted because of it.

So Megan had vowed she wouldn't lie anymore. She saw now that had been a mistake, though.

"Then why were you chasing after him?" the woman asked.

Sticking with the lying, Megan protested, "I wasn't!"

The woman struck her—thankfully not with the gun—but with the palm of her hand. Megan's cheek stung, and her eyes teared at the pain.

"Don't lie to me!" the woman said. "That's what you were doing when you opened the door."

And that must have been why she'd drawn the gun. She hadn't wanted Megan to leave the bride's dressing room unless she was heading down the aisle.

"You really want this wedding to take place," she

mused in confusion. What the hell could this stranger hope to gain from Megan's marriage?

"It will," the woman replied, her dark eyes wild with a determination so fierce it almost appeared to be madness. "Or you will die right here."

And Megan realized that maybe she would rather die than marry a man she didn't love, whom she would never be able to love because another man had already claimed her heart.

Chapter 7

Gage glanced to the back of the church to reassure himself that Penny Payne wasn't in any danger. She'd slipped away from the gunman. And he had let her leave.

The man stared back at Gage, then slowly, mockingly nodded his head. Who the hell was he?

Gage should have taken him down. But it was too great a risk when he didn't know where the other armed people had gone. Where was the guy's date, really?

Gage's blood chilled and pumped heavily through his quickly beating heart.

If Megan was in danger...

Even though Nikki was with her, he shouldn't have left her. But she'd wanted him to check on Richard. After the cryptic remark the guy in the back had made—and the mocking nod he'd just given him—Gage realized he needed to check in with the groom. He lifted his fist and pounded hard on the door behind the altar.

"About time my best man got here," a male voice remarked as the door opened. "What the hell…"

Richard Boersman's mouth fell open, and his already pale face paled with shock. "You came back from the dead?"

Stepping forward, Gage shoved Richard back into the room and closed the door behind them. He grunted in reply. When he'd finally escaped captivity, he had felt as if he'd returned from the dead.

Richard uttered a shaky sigh and murmured, "I did that once myself."

"What?" Gage narrowed his eyes and studied the shorter man. Like Gage, he wore a tuxedo, but his hung even more off his skinny frame. His thick-framed glasses had slid down his long, narrow nose. His whole face was thin and unremarkable, like his bowl-cut brown hair and pale complexion. He looked like he had probably spent most of his childhood being bullied. But maybe he wasn't the harmless geek Gage had always thought he was. "What the hell does that mean?"

He shrugged his thin shoulders. "Nothing…just had a close call myself a few years ago."

Megan had said something about it before, about Richard surviving a house or apartment fire. If Gage looked close enough, he could see a few thin scars along the man's hairline. But those scars were nothing compared to the ones Gage had now.

He remarked, "I think you're about to have another close call."

Richard stepped back, and his Adam's apple bobbed as he swallowed nervously. "What are you doing here? Dressed in a tux? You're not my best man."

"I am now," Gage said. "Not that this wedding's gonna happen anyway."

"You son of a bitch," Richard said, and now his face flushed a mottled red. "How dare you come back from the dead to stop my wedding?"

A laugh slipped out of Gage. He couldn't help it. Richard was that damn ridiculous. "I had no intention of stopping your wedding."

Spit dribbled out of Richard's mouth when he sputtered, "But—but you said it's not going to happen…"

"That isn't because of me," Gage said. "It's because the church is under siege."

Richard laughed now. "That's crazy. Under siege— what the hell are you talking about?"

"Guys—and a woman—with guns," Gage said, "have infiltrated the church."

"Megan's father is the Chicago FBI bureau chief," he patronizingly said, as if Gage wasn't already aware. "Of course there will be men and women with guns at his daughter's wedding."

"These people are not Woodrow's agents," Gage said. "They're strangers. And they're dangerous."

Richard's skin paled again. "What—what are you saying?"

"This isn't random," Gage said. "They've planned this out. Someone has a cell signal jammer. We can't call out, and only a few guests were able to get into the church. They have us surrounded."

"Why?" Richard asked. "What did you do?"

Gage laughed again. "This doesn't have anything to do with me." At least he hoped like hell that it didn't.

Richard snorted. "You've been nothing but trouble

for Megan since the day you met her. This has to be your fault."

Gage laughed again. "I've been nothing but trouble for her?"

She was the one who'd destroyed his life. She'd broken his heart and made it impossible for him to work for her father, the man he'd respected more than any other.

"Why couldn't you have just left her alone?" Richard asked.

"I don't want her," he said. But it was a lie.

And Richard knew it. "That's bull! You're behind this. You've put some sick plan into action to stop our wedding!" Despite the guy's smaller size, he launched himself at Gage.

Gage easily held him off with his hands on Richard's thin shoulders. "I wouldn't have had to go to this much trouble," he said. He was angry, too, so angry that he taunted the groom. "All I would have to do is kiss her, just like I did the last time I stole her from you."

Richard lost it, cursing and swinging. He wasn't able to get in a good punch. But his arms were long enough that he reached for Gage's holstered weapon.

Hearing the tussle from outside the door, Woodrow burst into the room with his gun drawn. He'd expected to find one of the armed strangers inside. Unfortunately, he knew the two men inside, but maybe he didn't know them as well as he'd thought. He had never thought Richard would have had either the courage or the stupidity to take on Gage Huxton.

He'd nearly grabbed Gage's gun—until Gage had shoved him back against the wall, his arm pushing against Richard's throat until the guy struggled for breath.

"Let him go, Gage," Woodrow said. He spoke softly and calmly.

He knew what Gage had been through. After Nicholas Rus had told him that Gage had survived all those months he'd been missing in action, Woodrow had reached out to guys he knew from his own days in the corps. And he'd found out the hell Gage had endured, the kind of hell few other men could have survived. The kind of hell from which nobody ever fully recovered.

That was why Woodrow hadn't told Megan that Gage was alive. He knew his daughter loved the man, so much that she would want to be with Gage again. But with the PTSD that Gage had to have, he wasn't safe for anyone to be around, as evidenced by how tightly he held Richard.

Maybe Woodrow had spoken too softly, because it didn't look as though Gage had heard him. Instead of loosening, his arm momentarily pressed harder. Behind his huge glasses, Richard's eyes began to roll back into his skull.

"Gage!" Woodrow spoke sharply now, making the younger man's name sound like a command.

And like the soldier he was, Gage obeyed. He stepped back.

And Richard slid down the wall, gasping for the breath Gage had momentarily denied him.

"You're crazy," Richard murmured, his voice raspy. Then he turned toward Woodrow. "He nearly killed me."

"You're damn lucky he didn't," Woodrow replied. And with no sympathy for the fool, he added, "You *never* reach for a man's gun." Not unless you were certain you could take it from him without getting killed.

Or Woodrow would have already taken on the armed wedding guests.

"But he's threatening to stop the wedding," Richard said.

Woodrow shook his head. "He's not the threat."

Impatience flashed in Richard's pale eyes. "Of course he is. He put this whole sick plan in motion."

"What the hell are you talking about?" Gage asked, his voice very deep and raspy despite not having had anyone strangling him as he had nearly strangled Richard. Not only did he not look the same, he didn't sound the same, either. The boy Woodrow had known was gone.

His heart ached for the loss. Gage Huxton could have been the best agent he'd ever had.

Through his thick lenses, Richard glared at Gage. "I'm saying you staged this whole scenario just to stop the wedding."

"And I told you I wouldn't have had to go to any of that trouble *if* I wanted to stop it," Gage said.

Richard's face flushed again. And now Woodrow understood why he'd gone for Gage's gun. Huxton could be damn infuriating. As his former boss, Woodrow knew that too well. Maybe there was more left of the boy he'd once known than he'd imagined.

"There is no time for fighting between ourselves," he told them. "We need to work together."

In unison, they snorted.

"We have to," Woodrow said. "We don't know how many of them we're dealing with."

"Ask him," Richard petulantly said.

This wasn't the first time Woodrow had noticed the man's petulance. Maybe it was because Richard Boersman was an only child that he was used to getting his own way all the time. Like that damn dress. Megan had wanted to wear her mother's dress. But Richard had pouted until she'd agreed to wear the gown he'd had designed for her.

Realizing now that Richard had manipulated her—the way Megan's mother used to manipulate him—made Woodrow feel a little better about the wedding being canceled. Maybe Penny Payne was right again—damn her—and Richard wasn't the right man for Megan.

But Penny was wrong about Gage. Woodrow didn't believe he was the right man for Megan, either, at least not anymore. It was doubtful he could ever recover fully, physically and mentally, from what he had endured.

Gage seemed focused now, though. Ignoring Richard, he said, "I only saw the one guy in the back of the church."

"The one Penny stopped you from killing." Letting her be the one to intervene in their tense exchange had nearly killed Woodrow. But Penny had pointed out—rightfully—that two men approaching the wedding crasher might have forced his hand and the hands of whoever else was working with him.

Richard snorted again. "There's only one guy?"

Gage continued to ignore him. "I didn't see the woman or the man who's dressed like a waiter."

"Me neither," Woodrow said, and his stomach muscles knotted tighter than they'd already been.

"We need to make sure Megan's safe," Gage said. He wasn't as muscular as he'd once been, but he easily moved Woodrow away from the door so he could rush out of it.

"Gage…" Woodrow hurried after the younger man as he started down the church aisle. But before he could catch up to him, someone grasped his arm and jerked him to a halt.

While it was something Penny would have done, she

wasn't the one who stopped him. His skin would have tingled, his pulse would have quickened—with attraction. He felt only irritation now.

The man who held his arm was also armed, a gun bulging beneath his jacket. But unlike the others he knew this man. Although with his smooth face, wide eyes and slight build, Tucker Allison looked more like a child than a man. "I don't have time—"

"I see you've thrown out Gage Huxton, sir," the young man said, his voice high with excitement. "I was going to do it earlier myself—"

Woodrow nearly laughed. Him and what army? Because apparently even another army hadn't been able to permanently take out Gage Huxton.

"Gage isn't leaving," he said. Even when he'd said he was, he hadn't been able to walk away from Megan, not when he'd realized she was in danger.

"Do you want me to help you get rid of him again?"

Woodrow narrowed his eyes. "Again? What are you talking about?"

The young man's face flushed. "I—I—uh…"

"Spread some vicious rumors," Woodrow finished for him as he shook off his hand. He hadn't had the time or the patience for the agent's nonsense and gossip then, and he had less time now.

"I—I didn't say anything that wasn't true," the kid nervously insisted.

"You had no idea what was the truth." Then or now. The problem was that neither did Woodrow.

What the hell was going on at his daughter's wedding? Could Gage have staged everything to disrupt the ceremony just as Richard suspected? Or were the gunmen here for revenge against Woodrow?

If that were truly the case, then no one was in more danger than Megan. He had to get to her—before it was too late.

Megan stared at the gun clasped so tightly in the woman's hands. "Are you going to walk me down the aisle with that shoved in my back?" she asked.

The woman chuckled, but her ivory complexion flushed slightly. "That might be noticeable."

"It would be," Megan agreed. "You can't force me to go through with this wedding."

"Maybe not," the woman admitted. "But if you don't, you'll be sending all your guests home in body bags. Is that what you want?"

"Of course not," Megan said. All she'd really wanted was Gage. Even when she thought he was dead, she shouldn't have accepted Richard's proposal, shouldn't have agreed to a loveless marriage. Sure, she wanted children, and she'd thought she could raise them with a man she liked and respected. But it was very clear to her that she'd made a mistake. Another mistake. The last had nearly cost Gage his life. This one would probably cost hers.

"You only have one gun," Nikki said. "How can you kill us all?"

The woman laughed again. "You think I'm here alone?"

No. They all knew better. But Nikki sounded clueless and young and scared as she asked, "You're not? You have a partner?"

"I have more than *a partner*," the woman replied. "So unless you want everyone inside the chapel to die, you will walk down that aisle. You will pretend everything is perfect. And you'll marry your groom."

Megan had already decided she had no intention of doing any such thing. But she didn't want to put innocent lives in any more danger than they already were. But if she were going to be forced into doing something she didn't want to, she had to know. "Why?"

The woman's smooth brow furrowed slightly. She was young—probably only Megan's age or maybe a little older. "Why what?" she asked.

"Why do you care about my wedding?" Megan asked. "Why would you be willing to kill in order to make sure I go through with it?"

"And how do we know you won't kill everyone even if she does?" Nikki asked. She stepped closer to Megan, almost as if using her as a shield.

What kind of bodyguard was Nikki Payne?

Then Megan realized, when she heard the whispering rustle of silk, why Nikki was using her as a shield. She was drawing her gun from the holster on her thigh. Megan reached behind her back, but instead of the gun, Nikki pressed the scissors into her hand. As a weapon, she would have preferred the gun. But she tightened her fingers around the scissors.

"Nobody will get hurt," the woman assured them, "as long as nobody interferes with the plan."

"Plan?" Megan repeated. She hoped like hell Nikki had one, too, for their immediate situation. But she asked the woman instead, "What plan?"

The gunwoman chuckled again. "Your wedding…"

"My wedding is part of some plan? A plan for what?" Revenge?

Against whom? Megan's father? Or Gage? Or had Megan done something that had made someone angry enough to want vengeance against her?

The only person she knew for certain whom she'd really hurt and who didn't seem able to forgive her was Gage. But he wouldn't go to such extremes to hurt her. He hadn't cared enough to fight for her—for them—a year ago. Why would he care enough now?

The woman's face flushed. "I've said too much. You don't need to concern yourself with anything but walking down that aisle and saying 'I do.'"

Megan shook her head. "No. I can't."

"You will," the woman insisted. "Unless you want to get hurt."

Megan was counting on the woman not wanting to hurt her because if Megan couldn't walk down the aisle, she would mess up their plan—whatever the hell it was. So she drew in a deep breath of air and courage, tightened her grip on the scissors, and lunged at the woman.

She didn't hear the gunshot, but she suspected there had been a silencer on the barrel of the gun. It had looked funny when the woman had pressed it into her stomach earlier. And now she felt the blood, thick and sticky, as it oozed from the wound.

Chapter 8

What the hell kind of bodyguard was she?

Nikki had frozen in place with the gun grasped in her hand. She hadn't even disarmed the safety. She stared down at the women lying on the floor in front of her. One minute Megan had been standing—strong and defiant—before her. The next she'd been gone.

Was she gone?

Knowing the other woman who lay on the floor with Megan might still be armed Nikki thumbed off the safety and put her finger near the trigger. She would kill her if she needed to. She had killed before. Or so she thought. Her brothers had never confirmed it.

But even if she pulled the trigger now, she would only be saving herself. She worried that she might be too late to save Megan.

Her veil had fallen off, and some of her dark hair had

slipped free of the knot on the back of her head. It was tangled over her face, covering it and the woman who lay beneath Megan.

"Are you okay?" Nikki asked as she knelt beside her.

A gasp slipped free of Megan's lips. Either she'd had the breath knocked out of her or she'd been holding it. Then she rolled over and held up a hand covered in blood.

Nikki cursed. No, she wasn't all right. "Where are you hurt?"

Megan glanced down at herself. There was a smear of blood on the gown, too. But just a smear. Surely if she'd been shot, blood would have saturated the heavy fabric.

And Nikki hadn't heard a gun go off. Then there had been a silencer on the woman's weapon. She could have fired it. But Nikki smelled no telltale scent of gunpowder.

Megan released another unsteady breath. "I don't think I am."

They both turned to the other woman. She lay on the floor, her face pale again, her eyes closed. She might have struck her head on the edge of the vanity table behind her. Or she might have been dead, as blood oozed beneath her.

"D-did I kill her?" Megan stammered. She was more afraid now than when the woman had been threatening their lives and the lives of everyone in the church.

Woodrow Lynch's daughter had guts. Nikki had been impressed. She moved forward and felt the woman's neck. A pulse pumped steadily beneath her fingers. "No."

She examined the woman. "Looks like you stabbed her shoulder with the scissors." The wound appeared to be the source of the blood.

"Did I hit an artery?" Megan anxiously asked.

Nikki inspected what appeared to be a shallow wound.

The scissors weren't sharp enough to have gone very deeply into the woman's flesh. "No. It's not a bad injury. The blood is already clotting and drying up."

"But she's unconscious," Megan said.

Nikki felt the woman's head. A knot swelled on the back of it. "She hit the table when you knocked her down."

Megan released a shuddery sigh now. "I'm such an idiot."

"No, you're not," Nikki said. She'd acted faster than she had. And Nikki was a trained bodyguard. Megan Lynch had great instincts.

"I could have gotten us both killed."

"You did everything right," Nikki assured her. "You disarmed her without anyone hearing anything. You're awesome."

A giggle, albeit a little hysterical, slipped from Megan's lips. "I just really don't want to go through with this wedding."

Nikki laughed, too. She'd loved growing up with all brothers, and always wanting to be one of the guys, she hadn't ever yearned for a sister. Now she had sisters-in-law and some great female friends. For the first time, she wondered what she might have missed if she'd had a sister, one as kick-ass cool as herself or Megan Lynch.

"I thought you just wanted out of that damn dress," she teased. "But now I see how desperate you are to cancel this wedding." She shuddered at the thought of being a bride herself. "Not that I blame you."

The woman murmured and shifted on the floor as she began to regain consciousness. Megan hadn't knocked her out nearly hard enough. She still posed a threat. But she wasn't the only one. The dressing room door began to open. Nikki grabbed for the woman's gun and turned toward that opening door with the barrels of that gun and hers pointing at the intruder.

Gage cursed. "What the hell!" He'd known he might have been walking into a dangerous situation when he entered the dressing room. He hadn't thought the women he'd left there earlier would pose the threat, though. "Don't shoot me."

"You keep surprising me," Nikki said, as if it was all his fault. But then that was what Richard thought, that Gage had orchestrated the whole scenario. Nikki shook her head. "You're just like your best friend."

"Best friend?" Megan asked from where she lay on the floor. Half of her thick dark hair had tumbled down around her thin shoulders.

"My brother—Nicholas Rus," Nikki replied.

Gage swallowed a gasp, still surprised that Nikki had finally accepted her illegitimate half brother.

She smiled. "I've almost shot him more times than I can remember."

"I'm not entirely sure that was by accident, though," Gage said. "What the hell happened here?"

He doubted it was an accident, either. His heart beating fast with the fear he'd felt that Megan might be in danger, he stepped closer to her. That was when he saw the blood—on her hand and smeared on her dress. He dropped to his knees beside her. "Are you all right?"

She nodded. But her usually tan complexion had paled, making her dark eyes look even bigger and more vulnerable. He'd been so furious with her for so long. His anger now dissipated, leaving only concern and something he refused to acknowledge.

"She's great," Nikki said. "She took down this bitch who had a gun pointed at us."

Gage felt all the blood drain from his face.

"You wouldn't let me use the scissors on the dress," Megan said. And there was that little teasing lilt in her voice—the one she used to use when she'd flirted with him.

The blood rushed lower in his body. Then he realized what they were saying. "You two overpowered her?"

"No," Nikki said. "It was all Megan. She's a badass."

Megan smiled with a pride Gage had never seen in her before. Then the smile dimmed as the woman moaned and shifted on the floor again. "I didn't want to hurt her, though…"

Seeing that Nikki had her hands full with the two guns, Gage grabbed the measuring tape that either Mrs. Payne or a seamstress must have left in the room. He bound the woman's hands and ankles. Then he reached for something to use as a gag. Her eyes were beginning to flutter. She would be fully conscious soon and probably screaming.

But Megan tugged the gauzy fabric from his hands. "You can't use that," she said. "That's my veil." Then she gasped as she glanced down at the blood she'd smeared on it.

"Why do you care?" he asked. It wasn't like she was going to be able to wear it.

"Use this," Nikki said. She'd put down one of the guns on the vanity table and had found a roll of duct tape. "I think Mom keeps a roll in every room, here and at home."

Gage ripped off a piece of tape and fastened it over the woman's mouth just as her eyes opened fully. Her eyes widened as she stared up at him in shock.

"What the hell did she want?" he asked. "To stop the wedding?"

"Just the opposite," Nikki replied. "She wanted to make sure it happened as if nothing was wrong."

"Why?" Maybe he shouldn't have put the tape over her mouth. But he doubted she would willingly give up her reason, especially with her cohorts free and able to carry out whatever their plan was.

"There's only one way to find out," Megan said while trying to wipe the blood from the veil and her hand.

Gage's blood chilled as he noticed the expression on her beautiful face. Her chin was pointed, the skin taut over her cheekbones. It was her stubborn look. And he knew from experience that there was no changing her mind when she was that determined.

He hated to know but he had to ask, "What?"

"I get married exactly as planned."

His stomach lurched. "No, no. It's too dangerous…"

"She's right," Nikki said. "I have to tell my mom and Woodrow that we have no time to waste. The wedding's supposed to start soon." She pulled the door open a crack, peeked out—then opened it fully and stepped out, closing it behind her.

"You really want to do this?" he asked Megan. "You really want to marry Richard?"

She glanced down at the woman who struggled against the measuring tape binding her wrists and ankles. "She's still bleeding," she said with concern and guilt.

Gage pulled the torn edges of her jacket away from her wound. "It's shallow," he said. He ripped off another piece of tape, squeezed her skin together and pressed the tape over it. And as he did it, the woman thrashed around in pain. "That'll stop it from bleeding."

For extra reinforcement, Gage wound a length of duct tape over the measuring tape bindings—to make sure she couldn't get free—because from the way she was glaring at him, with such hatred, he knew he wouldn't be safe from her wrath.

But she was the least of his concerns.

He reminded Megan, "You didn't answer my question. You really want to do this?" Marry another man?

"I *have* to do this," she said. "Please go get my dad for me."

"So he can give you away?" He shook his head. "It's not going to happen." There was no way that Woodrow Lynch would willingly put either of his daughters in any danger.

Megan reached for him, her small hand clasping his forearm. "It has to happen."

"I don't understand why you're so determined." Did she love Richard? Just because she hadn't really loved Gage didn't mean that she wasn't capable of love. She and Richard had much more in common than Gage and she had ever had.

Her hand slipped from his arm, and she pointed at the woman. "She is. She threatened that if the wedding didn't take place as planned, that nobody would get out of the church alive."

Gage uttered a ragged sigh. He'd thought the gunmen were there to stop the wedding, not make sure that it took place without a hitch. Apparently, he was the only one who didn't want Megan to marry Richard.

"She's hardly in a position to carry out that threat anymore," Gage pointed out. He had made certain that she wasn't able to get free.

Megan shivered. "You already know and she admitted that she's not here alone."

He glanced down at the woman again. She glared back at him. It might help things if he questioned her. He reached for the tape over her mouth, but Megan caught his hand.

"Please, get my father," she urged.

"And leave you alone?" He shook his head. "Look what happened the last time I left you alone." He pointed at the woman now.

"And like Nikki told you, I took care of her." She reached for the gun Nikki had left on the vanity table. "And with this, I can take care of myself."

She could shoot. Woodrow had bragged about how good a shot his youngest daughter was. Or maybe he'd only done that because he'd been warning Gage to stay away from her.

It was a warning Gage should have heeded.

"Please," she implored him. "Get my father for me."

Was it Woodrow she wanted? Or Richard? After her close brush with death, had she realized she couldn't live without her groom?

"We already told Richard that the wedding is canceled."

She gasped. "You shouldn't have done that."

"You told me to," he reminded her.

"I told you to check on him," she said.

And Gage had to know. "Does he mean that much to you?"

She glanced at the woman who stared hatefully at them. "I don't want anyone to get hurt," Megan said.

He snorted in derision. She'd hurt him—like hell. But apparently she'd forgotten all about that. "You're right," he said. "You can take care of yourself." He headed toward the door.

But she reached for him again. Her hand grasping his arm, she swung him back around to her.

"What do you want, Megan?" he asked her.

"Gage…"

"You don't want *me*," he said. "You made that clear months ago. And you've made it very clear today. I'll go get your father for you so you can marry the man you really want." But before he could turn back to the door, she stepped forward and closed the distance between them.

With her free hand, she tugged his head down, and after rising up on tiptoe, she pressed her mouth against his. She kissed him deeply, sliding her lips back and forth across his. He wanted to grab her and jerk her body up tightly against his. But he resisted the urge and kept his arms at his sides. Finally she stepped back, her breasts pushing against the bodice of that sparkling dress as she panted for breath.

He'd stopped breathing entirely. He wasn't even sure his heart was still beating.

She said nothing.

Was that kiss supposed to be a message for him? Was he supposed to think that he was the man she wanted? He knew better. She only wanted him to do as she'd asked: bring her father to her so Woodrow could give away the bride.

Derek "D" Nielsen felt sweat trickle down the back of his neck to run between his shoulder blades and soak into the waistband of his dress pants. The suit was hot. But that wasn't why he was sweating.

Andrea had been gone too long. Since his escape a

few days ago, she had rarely left his side. So she would have been back…if she was able.

Had something happened to her?

Of course she could have just been checking in with the other members of the crew she had put together. She was determined that nothing go wrong with the plan. She wanted this wedding to take place probably more than the bride did.

Derek understood how important it was for every element of a plan to come off precisely. The prison break had been his plan—plotted from the inside—but Andrea had made certain that plan had been carried out exactly as he'd ordered. If it hadn't been, he would still be behind bars.

More sweat trickled down his back. He didn't want to go back to prison. Ever.

But it wasn't like anyone would expect an escaped convict to show up here. Except maybe one person.

If he'd heard about the escape…

But Derek suspected he'd been a little preoccupied lately. Right now he was preoccupied himself.

"Andrea," he murmured. "Where the hell are you?"

He needed to check in with the others to find out if they'd seen her or if she'd used her walkie-talkie to contact any of them. But before he did that, maybe he needed to check first where he'd seen her last, heading through the vestibule to the back of the church.

The guy with the military haircut, scars and attitude had just been back there again. He also had a gun. Derek had seen the bulge of it beneath his tuxedo jacket. That guy wasn't the only one armed in the wedding party. The gray-haired guy had a gun, too, and at least one of the guests.

More and more people had permits to carry concealed weapons. But Derek suspected something else was at stake, that these guys weren't just carrying because it was their constitutional right to bear arms. They weren't civilians who'd taken a weekend firearms class. These guys were trained. And they wouldn't be easy to take down.

Andrea had hired all those reinforcements for them. Derek felt he would need every one of them. Most of all, he needed Andrea. If anything had happened to her, the plan be damned. He would finish this now, and he didn't care who died in the cross fire when he went down shooting.

Chapter 9

Nerves fluttered in Penny's stomach. It wasn't just because of the people with guns who'd crashed the wedding. It wasn't just because of the danger they were all in. It was because of Woodrow Lynch.

He had looked like he was in such a hurry when he'd started down the church aisle a short time ago. After speaking with one of the guests, he'd joined her in the vestibule where she was checking the basket for programs and making sure the flowers weren't wilting yet. Then he'd guided her through the door leading into the coatroom off the vestibule. It had a stained glass window dividing it from the church. But she doubted anyone could see them through the colored glass.

"Where were you going?" she asked, keeping her voice low in case the stranger with the gun was hovering nearby yet. "I saw you following Gage from the groom's dressing room." Maybe the better question was: "Where was he going?"

"Like you need to ask," he said.

And she smiled. "To Megan." Gage hadn't been able to stay away from her since finding out this was her wedding. Maybe the gunmen and the danger were just an excuse. "I'm proud of you for letting him talk to her alone."

"I doubt he's talking," Woodrow said then shook his head when her smile widened. "That's not what I meant. I'm not matchmaking. He thought she might be in danger and wanted to make sure she was safe. And there was no way to stop him."

"We didn't need his help," Nikki said as she joined them inside the coatroom. She must have seen Woodrow guiding her mother through the door. Hopefully, she hadn't overheard them because then someone else—like one of the gunmen—could have as well. "Megan and I overpowered the woman."

The color drained from Woodrow's handsome face, and he sputtered, "Wh-what? Overpowered what woman?"

"The one who forced her way into the bride's dressing room with a gun."

Penny reached out and clasped Woodrow's arm for support, since he looked like he was about to keel over with shock and fear. "She's all right." She turned toward her daughter and scanned her. Not even a curl was out of place, which was unusual for Nikki when she hadn't been in a fight. "You're both all right?"

"Yes," Nikki said. "Thanks to Megan. She's amazing. She took the bitch out with the scissors before I even had a chance to pull the trigger of my gun."

Penny had hoped Nikki and Megan might bond. But she hadn't wanted it to be over an encounter with a dangerous woman with a gun. She wasn't even sure why she'd wanted them to become friends. It wasn't like they would see each other again. Nikki lived here in River City and Megan lived in Chicago. She had only decided to get married in Penny's chapel because her dad had suggested it.

Why had he?

Sure, Penny had done a few weddings for his agents. But this was his daughter whose special day he'd entrusted to her. And she was failing him.

Why hadn't Penny realized she would need more security? Woodrow had been a lawman for so long that he must have made enemies—criminals who wanted revenge for their incarcerations.

"Is Megan really all right?" her father anxiously asked.

"She's fine," Nikki assured him. "She's very smart and strong. She's also determined to go through with this wedding."

"That's out of the question," Woodrow said. "I won't allow it."

And Penny couldn't help but think that was what he should have done from the beginning instead of bringing Megan to her to plan this wedding. He should have told his daughter that marrying someone she didn't love was out of the question. She must have let out a soft snort or something, because Woodrow looked at her as if he knew exactly what she was thinking. From the way his dark brows lowered, he wasn't pleased.

"If you won't allow it," Nikki said in a tone her mother knew too well, a mixture of stubbornness and defiance, "then you'll be getting everyone killed."

"Nikki!" Penny admonished her daughter.

"Hey," her daughter replied. "That's what the woman swore would happen if Megan canceled the wedding."

Woodrow looked at Penny again, his blue eyes wide with alarm. Penny's heart began to pound quickly and heavily, too. "No. There has to be another way."

"There isn't," Gage said as he stepped into the coatroom doorway.

Woodrow glanced around Gage, and his voice sharpened with concern when he asked, "You left Megan alone?"

"She's not alone," Nikki said. "The woman's with her."

"She's tied up," Gage said. "And Megan has her gun."

Obviously unappeased, Woodrow shook his head. "You still shouldn't have left her."

Penny silently agreed. How could Gage and Megan realize that they still loved each other if they kept running from each other?

"She won't be alone long," Gage said. Maybe he intended to return to her immediately. Then he added, "She wants to see you."

Woodrow's face paled. "Of course after what she's been through…" A girl would want her father.

Penny glanced at Nikki. She'd been so young when she'd lost her dad that she'd never looked for him to comfort or rescue her. She'd never looked to anyone for comfort or rescue. Not her three big brothers or even her mother.

"Megan wants to see you," Gage reiterated, "because she wants you to walk her down the aisle. Just like Nikki said, she's determined to get married today."

But Penny suspected it wasn't for the reasons Gage obviously thought. His face was grim, his green eyes dark, his mouth drawn into a grimace. He was hurt thinking that she wanted to marry someone else.

Woodrow shook his head again. "It's not going to happen."

Nikki shushed him as she glanced nervously around. "It has to... That woman isn't here alone. They are determined that this wedding takes place. I don't think her threat that everyone would die was an idle one."

Gage nodded grimly in agreement.

Penny's stomach lurched. She felt sick. Maybe she'd been wrong. Maybe Gage didn't love Megan anymore if he could let her marry another man.

Megan's lips tingled yet from the contact with Gage's. She wasn't sure what she'd been thinking to kiss him like she had. But he'd looked so upset with her, like he'd looked that day she'd broken up with him. Just like that day, he'd looked betrayed.

She hadn't cared back then, because she'd thought she was the one who'd been betrayed, who'd been used. But when Gage had quit the Bureau and reenlisted with the Marines, she'd been afraid that she might have been wrong. Now she was all but certain.

"Gage," she murmured, hoping he would come back.

She doubted that he would. He didn't understand why she wanted to go through with the wedding. He thought it was because of Richard, but it was because of him. She didn't want anyone else getting hurt but most especially not Gage. He had already been through too much.

Was that her fault? Had he reenlisted because of her? She would never forgive herself if she'd caused him that much pain. And the way he'd snorted when she'd said that she didn't want anyone getting hurt...

She must have hurt him. She couldn't go back. She couldn't change the past. But she could make certain no one else got hurt because of her.

Over the tape covering her mouth, the woman narrowed her eyes and glared at Megan. She struggled against the tape binding her wrists and ankles, flinching as she aggravated her wound.

Guilt flashed through Megan. But she'd needed to disarm the woman before she'd shot someone. If she managed to get loose, someone was certain to get hurt. But she wouldn't get loose, Megan assured herself.

She wouldn't…

A knock at the door startled Megan, and a gasp slipped through her lips. She'd locked the door behind Gage. So it was probably her father. Hopefully, he would understand why she had to go through with the wedding. She had no choice.

Before she could unlock the door, a deep voice called out, "Andrea?"

That wasn't her father's voice. It wasn't her father at the door, rattling the knob as he tried to force it open. Megan's heart rate quickened as fear gripped her. She tightened her grasp on the woman's weapon.

"Andrea, are you in there?" the man asked.

The woman struggled harder and murmured against the tape over her mouth. Megan pressed her free hand over the tape, making certain that no sounds could escape it.

"Sweetheart," Megan said, pretending that she knew the man, that she thought he was her groom. "I know you're anxious but you'll have to wait until our wedding night. It won't be long now." Like never. While the wedding had to happen, there would be no wedding night—no honeymoon—no real marriage.

She held her breath, waiting to see if she'd fooled the would-be intruder. But the door rattled as the guy twisted the knob again. It was locked, but it wasn't a dead bolt. It wasn't going to hold out someone who really wanted to get inside.

Megan gripped the gun more tightly and made certain the safety was off. She knew how to shoot—at targets. She'd never pointed a gun at someone and fired. She wasn't certain that she would be able to do it, to take another life.

Megan had only been able to overpower Andrea with Nikki's help. On her own, she had no hope of protecting herself from Andrea's very determined male friend, unless she found the courage to pull the trigger. And then she wasn't certain she would actually hit him. Targets didn't move, didn't fire back. She suspected that this man, being a friend of Andrea's, would. And he probably wouldn't miss...

Woodrow tightened his grasp on his gun handle before releasing it—reluctantly. The guy wasn't alone in the chapel. If Woodrow took him out, he would force the others to react. So he called out instead, "Hey, that's not the restroom."

His hand under his jacket, the guy tensed. But like Woodrow, he didn't pull his weapon. He turned to Woodrow, his lips curved into a forced smile.

His hair was buzzed so short that Woodrow couldn't tell what color it was. His eyes were dark and cold. He seemed vaguely familiar. But that was probably because he looked like a thousand other perps Woodrow had either personally arrested or had arrested.

Was he here because of that—for revenge?

The guy betrayed nothing. No recognition. No flicker of emotion, of anger or of fear.

Woodrow gestured down the hall. "The men's room is down there. But you better hurry. The wedding is about to start soon."

The guy narrowed his dark eyes and skeptically asked, "Really?"

Woodrow nodded. "Of course. Everything is right on schedule."

The guy nodded. "Yeah, I heard Mrs. Payne puts on the perfect wedding."

Woodrow hoped that was true this time, too, that the wedding ran perfectly according to the plan they had quickly concocted just a short while ago in the coatroom.

"So you better use the restroom and take your seat in the church," Woodrow urged the man.

The guy hesitated and glanced back at the door to the bride's dressing room. "I was actually looking for my plus one," he replied. "I thought my wife went into that room."

Woodrow forced a laugh. "Not likely. My daughter has been obsessive about no one seeing her in her dress yet. She wouldn't have let anyone in there."

The guy chuckled. "The best man has been in and out of there since I arrived."

"Best man?"

"The grim-looking blond guy."

He'd described Gage perfectly, but he didn't reveal whether or not he knew him. He hadn't mentioned his name. If he wasn't here for revenge against Woodrow, he could have been seeking revenge against Gage.

But if not…what the hell did he want? Why were he

and his female friend—or wife or whatever she was—
determined that the wedding take place?

The guy's mouth curved into a smirk as he continued,
"The bride has let *him* inside that room."

Woodrow narrowed his eyes now. "Any reason you've
been watching that room?"

The guy glanced around then stepped back. "No. Just
anxious for the wedding to start."

"It will," Woodrow said. "So you better…"

The guy chuckled. "I know, take my seat." And finally
he moved back toward the chapel.

Woodrow knocked on the bride's room door.

"Go away," she said, her voice pitched low. "Please,
go away…"

"Megan, it's Dad."

The lock clicked, the knob turned and the door
opened. As soon as he'd stepped inside and closed the
door again, she threw her arms around him and held on
tightly, trembling against him. "I thought I was going to
have to shoot him."

He doubted his softhearted little girl would have actually been able to pull the trigger. Like Nikki had claimed,
she had obviously overpowered the woman who lay tied
up on the carpet. But taking a life… He didn't think she
could have. He hoped she was never put in the situation
where she had to or risk losing her own life.

He would make certain she was never put in that situation. "It's okay," he told her as he held her like he had
when she was a little girl frightened after a nightmare.
"It's okay, my beauty."

While he had made certain to teach her and Ellen
how to protect themselves, he had also tried to shield his

daughters from the ugliness of his job, of his life. Now he'd brought that ugliness to her.

Or maybe Gage had. Again.

She pulled back and stared up at him, her eyes glistening with unshed tears and irritation. "Don't lie to me, Daddy," she said.

He didn't know if she was talking about his assurance that everything was okay or that she was beautiful. She'd always argued his nickname for her. She had no idea how beautiful she was.

"We have a plan," he said. "It's going to be okay." He hoped.

Megan shook her head. Her hair had fallen down around her shoulders, the curls springing free for once. She looked even more beautiful than when she wound it into a tight knot on the back of her head. She also looked scared.

"They're the ones with a plan," Megan said, gesturing at the woman.

If there was time, Woodrow would have tried to get the plan out of the woman. He'd once been a master interrogator. But now he only supervised and left the interrogations and fieldwork to younger agents. There wasn't time for him to try, though.

The music began. "That's our cue," he told her.

If everything didn't go according to plan, there was a good chance that none of them would make it out of the wedding chapel alive.

Chapter 10

Gage stood uneasily at the front of the nearly empty chapel. He had never been anyone's best man before, not even for his best friend, Nicholas Rus. Nick had chosen his half sister, Nikki Payne, to stand by his side while Gage had walked his sister, Annalise, down the aisle to the man she had loved almost her entire life. At least Gage hadn't had to give Megan away. But he hadn't imagined—even in his worst nightmares—that he would be the best man at *her* wedding.

Richard wasn't thrilled, either. He probably would have refused had it not been for Mrs. Payne.

Nobody told Penny no, not even Woodrow. But the bureau chief had won one argument with the stubborn wedding planner. Gage would have wondered what the hell was going on with the two of them if he wasn't more concerned about what the hell was going on at the church.

Why would gunmen crash a wedding, not to stop it but to make certain it happened?

None of it made any sense.

The only one who had anything to gain by making sure the wedding took place was Richard. He gained Megan as his bride, as his wife. But that was good for Gage, too. He'd wanted the wedding to happen, too. He'd wanted Megan off-limits, so he wouldn't be tempted to forget the pain she'd caused him. But her kisses tempted him. And her beauty. And her strength.

She was much stronger than he'd ever realized. He'd once been furious with her for not trusting him. But then maybe she hadn't known him any better than he'd known her.

Even if he could forget the pain, he couldn't forget what he'd been through the past six months. He couldn't forget how it had changed him. Megan was stronger than he'd known, but she wasn't strong enough to deal with what he couldn't even manage himself.

The music began, an organ playing from the balcony above the pews. Everyone stood and turned toward the back of the church, where the veiled bride appeared on the arm of the debonair-looking father of the bride.

Gage and Richard were already standing next to the minister in the front. Richard was ahead of him but so much shorter that he didn't block Gage's view. He could see the back, but he studied Richard instead. Sweat trickled down the guy's neck to wick against the collar of his tuxedo. His face was flushed, his skin red and blotchy.

Having never been a best man before, Gage wasn't certain if Richard's nervousness was normal. Or was it the knowledge of the gunmen and the plan that had freaked out the groom?

Richard had been opposed to more than Gage being his best man. He'd been opposed to the entire plan, almost violently opposed. But Woodrow had cut off his argument. If Richard really loved Megan, wouldn't he be willing to do anything to protect her?

Gage was willing to do anything to protect her, even pose as Richard's best man. He'd never liked the guy before, but now suspicion joined his dislike. The comment he'd made earlier, about coming back from the dead, and his reaction to their plan…

What the hell was the real story about Richard Boersman? He certainly wasn't the harmless computer nerd everyone thought he was.

As Woodrow and the bride started down the aisle toward them, Richard began to shake. He wasn't just nervous, though. He was scared.

If he had anything to do with the gunmen being in the church, he should be scared—not of the gunmen but of Gage.

Her mom had forced Nikki into a lot of different dresses over the course of her twenty-five years. But this was a dress Nikki had promised herself that she would never wear. If only there'd been time to get Megan out of hers.

But they had been too busy overpowering a crazy woman with a gun to use the tool Mom had given her. Nikki suspected there would have been time after they'd all agreed to the plan, though. Her mom could have helped Megan out of her gown and Nikki into it. Penny had insisted it would be easier for Nikki to wear this one.

Her gown…

It was beautiful, with its intricate lace and beading,

but it was also a joke. A farce. This dress hadn't brought good luck to Penny and Nicholas Payne's marriage. It hadn't stopped him from betraying his bride or from dying in the line of duty.

Nikki just hoped it didn't cause her to die, too. Her fingers trembled slightly as she clutched Woodrow Lynch's arm. Her knees trembled, too, as they started down the aisle. Not only had she vowed to never wear this damn dress, she'd vowed to never do this—have a man walk her down the aisle to some guy who would make empty promises. Like her father had made empty promises to his bride.

She wasn't being forced to do any of this. In fact she'd had to argue for the right to switch places with Megan. Eventually, she had convinced everyone else that this was a good plan, such a good plan that it would work.

She had only been able to convince them because Logan wasn't in the church. Her oldest brother would have nixed her plan for certain. Maybe she was so used to his doing that, though, that she hadn't considered all the consequences of what she had plotted to do. Like her either getting married or killed...

Megan's stomach churned with nerves and guilt. She should have been upstairs, walking down that church aisle on her father's arm. Instead she'd slipped out of the bride's dressing room and down the back stairs with Penny Payne.

The wedding planner hadn't taken the time to help Megan out of that damn dress. Instead she'd thrown Woodrow's trench coat around Megan's shoulders to cover up her and the gown. Then she'd hustled her down the stairs to the hallway leading to her office. But they'd passed the door to it.

They were heading to a hidden door to a secret underground tunnel to the courtyard outside the church.

Penny held Megan's hand to lead her down the dimly lit corridor. The reception area, with its stone walls, rafter ceiling and twinkle lights, was at the other end of the basement. This area looked even older. It was also eerily quiet except for the faint echo of the organ music drifting down from the chapel above them. The traditional wedding march…

Megan's nerves and guilt increased. She squeezed Penny's hand. "I'm sorry," she murmured. "I shouldn't have let Nikki take my place."

Penny stopped walking and turned back toward Megan. With her free hand, she gently patted her cheek. "Don't feel bad," she said. "You had no choice."

That was what she'd thought—that she'd had no choice, that she would have to go through with the wedding. But then they had all come up with another plan, one to protect Megan. She and Mrs. Payne were the only ones who would be safe. Everyone else was in danger.

"But I shouldn't have let her risk her life for mine," Megan insisted.

Penny sighed. "I know my daughter. There is no one more stubborn than she is."

"Gage." The name almost unconsciously slipped out of Megan's lips. He was always on her mind, though. He had been since that day she'd met him in her father's house. "He's more stubborn than Nikki."

Too stubborn to ever forgive her.

Penny squeezed her hand now. "That may be true. He

is an obstinate man. But in Gage's case, that's a good thing."

Megan gasped in surprise that the older woman would say such a thing.

"Being stubborn is probably what kept Gage alive those six months he was missing," Penny explained. "But Nikki..." She was clearly worried that her daughter's stubbornness would get her killed instead. "Gage wouldn't be here, he wouldn't have come back to you if he wasn't stubborn."

"Gage hasn't come back to me," Megan said. "He would much prefer that I was the one getting married right now." Earlier he'd promised her that he would make certain nothing disrupted her wedding. But he'd broken that promise. He'd agreed to Nikki's dangerous plan.

Penny chuckled. "I think Gage would only prefer that if you were marrying him."

That wasn't likely to happen. But being a hopeless romantic must have been an occupational hazard of being a wedding planner, like being in danger was an occupational hazard of being a bodyguard.

A librarian really had no occupational hazards, except maybe reading all those books had made Megan a bit of a dreamer. She found herself wistfully asking, "Do you really think..."

But she couldn't even complete the thought. It was too ridiculous, not after their horrific breakup.

Penny finished the thought for her. "That Gage loves you?"

"No." Her face flushed with embarrassment. She'd broken up with Gage because she hadn't been able to believe he'd loved her then. He had even less of a reason to love her now. "No. I know that isn't a possibility."

She listened to the music drifting faintly down from the chapel. "Do you really think the plan will work?"

Mrs. Payne didn't need to answer. The reply to Megan's question stood at the end of the hallway ahead of them. A man, dressed as a waiter, blocked their way out with his burly body. He also held a gun, pointed at them.

Megan raised the weapon she held, the one she'd knocked out of the woman's hands. She hadn't been certain before that she could fire it to protect herself. But now she wasn't protecting just herself.

She had to protect Mrs. Payne, too.

Before she could fire, she heard another trigger cock as a cold barrel pressed hard against the side of her head.

No, their plan was *not* going to work.

Chapter 11

As the music wound down, fear clutched Gage's heart. The plan wasn't going to work. They'd known that once Woodrow pulled back Nikki's veil, the gig was up. So the plan had actually been just to buy enough time for Megan and Penny to get to safety and call Nick and the rest of Payne Protection to rush to the rescue.

But as Gage scanned the chapel, he realized they hadn't bought themselves any time. They hadn't fooled anyone. The armed man he'd spoken to, the one Woodrow had caught outside the bride's dressing room, wasn't present, but he had representation. There was a guy in the back and another near the front who were fidgety, their hands sliding too frequently beneath their jackets as if to assure themselves that their weapons were ready. Gage hadn't noticed them earlier, so they must have recently sneaked into the chapel.

Something had definitely been planned to go down

during the ceremony. So why would the smug guy, who'd looked like the ringleader, be missing? Unless he'd already figured out the bait and switch, which meant Megan and Penny were in danger.

Gage began to cough, as if he was choking. Everyone turned toward him, but he waved off the attention and rasped, "Water." Then he headed quickly for the back of the church.

His ruse must have worked because no one followed him. Of course they were all focused on the bride whom the father had yet to give away. Her veil hadn't been lifted; the gig wasn't up yet.

Once it was, Nikki and Woodrow would be in danger. But Gage knew Nikki could take care of herself. He was more worried about Megan.

And Penny, too, of course.

He hurried toward the stairwell leading to the basement. He had to get to Megan and Penny before the smug gunman found them. He just hoped like hell he wasn't too late to save them.

Megan held her breath, afraid to move even a fraction of an inch with the cocked gun pressed to her temple. The weapon she held was snapped from her hand.

"This is Andrea's gun," the man said. "How the hell did you get this?"

Still holding her breath, Megan had no air to answer him.

The barrel moved from her head as the guy jerked her around to face him, pulling her father's jacket from her shoulders. It dropped onto the concrete floor. "Did you kill her?"

With the barrel gone, Megan shook her head. "N-no…"

"That's crap," the waiter said. "The only way someone would get Andrea's gun away from her is if she's dead."

"I knocked her out," Megan explained.

The guy narrowed his eyes and looked her up and down as if he doubted her claim. "What the hell really happened?"

"I knocked her into a table—" she swallowed the nerves choking her in order to continue "—when I stabbed her with a pair of scissors."

The guy sucked in a breath.

"She hit her head. Hard," Megan said.

And then the man hit her hard, so hard that Megan's head snapped back and she tasted blood inside her mouth. She must have bitten her tongue or the inside of her cheek.

"Don't!" Mrs. Payne exclaimed as she tried to step between the man and Megan. She wasn't a bodyguard like her children, but she had the tendencies.

Nobody could protect Megan from being too honest, though. How had she managed to lie so easily to Gage that once? Because she'd been trying to protect herself. She needed to do that again.

"You bitch!" the man yelled at her. "You stabbed her? You really stabbed her?"

"Yes," she admitted. Now she had a reason for being so forthcoming.

The man reached for her again, but Penny caught his arm. He lifted his other hand—with the gun—to swing toward the older woman.

"No!" Megan yelled. "Your friend needs your help. She's wounded, but she's alive. For now."

He drew back his arm. "Where is she?"

"In the bride's dressing room," Megan replied. "You

need to get her medical attention." Gage had taped her wound to stop the bleeding. But she was probably in pain, especially if she'd continued her struggles to free herself.

The guy glanced at the waiter. "Shoot them if they move." Then he turned to leave.

But Megan called out to him. "No!"

He turned back, his eyes narrowed again and hard with anger. "What?"

"Unless you're going to call 911, you're not going to be able to get her the help she needs alone."

"Now you want to help her?" the man scoffed. "You've left her bleeding while you're playing a runaway bride." He peered around the hallway. "Where the hell were you running?"

She shook her head. "Not running. Hiding."

"If she's not alive," he began, his voice cracking.

"She won't be if you keep wasting time," she warned him, surprised that she'd finally managed to refrain from being honest. "But if you want to help her, you're going to need your friend. One of you will need to carry her, the other drive..." Or hold a gun.

The guy smirked. "So the two of us should just leave you alone?"

"No," Megan said. "Have him tie us up, so we can't get away."

The smirk widened. "You're pretty sure that'll buy you time for someone to rush to your rescue, huh? The big blond guy with the chip on his shoulder? The gray-haired guy who looks like a retired Marine?" He chuckled. "They won't get out of that chapel alive. No one will."

Panic clutched Megan's heart. Thinking Gage was dead had been like living a nightmare, but this was worse.

She was going to lose him all over again and her dad, too. Probably her own life as well.

"Your friend certainly won't," Megan said. "With every minute you waste here threatening us, she loses more blood. And she's in more pain."

He flinched as if she'd struck him. Then he gestured at his friend. "Tie them up and stash them in a closet or office where no one will find them. Then meet me upstairs." He pointed one gun at Penny and the other at Megan. "Don't make me regret letting you live."

As soon as he disappeared down the hall, the waiter expelled a shaky breath. He was nearly as afraid as they had been.

"He's not going to let us live, is he?" Penny asked, her voice tremulous, as if she were overcome with fear.

Maybe she was. Megan wouldn't blame her. She was scared, too. But she wasn't ready to give up yet.

The guy's face flushed. "D's a dangerous dude. I heard he tortured and killed his best friend."

"Why would you work with him, then?" Penny asked. "Why would you trust that he won't do the same to you?"

The guy shuddered. "I don't trust him. But I don't work for him," he said. "I work for Andrea. She controls him."

And apparently everyone one else, as well.

Penny sighed. "But if Andrea dies…"

"You better go," Megan urged him. "You need to make sure he gets her help."

The guy shook his head. "I have to tie you up."

Megan glanced around the hall. It had widened after passing the office and now doubled as storage space. Boxes lined one stone wall. Ribbon dangled from one of them.

"Let me tie us up," she offered. "That way you won't have to juggle the gun."

The guy studied her face, his skeptical as if he worried that she was tricking him. But he was probably more worried about how D would react if they got away.

"You'll check," she said. "You'll make sure we're tied tightly."

"You can't tie up each other," he said.

"Of course not," she agreed. "I'll tie up Mrs. Payne." She unwound some of the ribbon and tied Penny's delicate wrists and ankles together as she'd been taught. Then she handed the ribbon to him.

"Now you tie me up," she said. When the ribbon cut into her wrists and ankles, she almost regretted the offer. But the discomfort would be worth it—if her ploy worked.

He glanced around for a hiding place. "I need to put you out of sight."

Megan tried to move, but with her ankles bound, she stumbled forward and fell to her knees. The thick gown should have cushioned her fall, but one of the sparkling rhinestones ground through the fabric, scratching her skin. She cursed. God, she hated this damn dress.

"We can't walk," she needlessly pointed out.

"This is just a storage area, for things I probably should have thrown out years ago, at the end of this hall," Penny said. "Nobody will come back here."

The waiter snorted. "Unless you yell for help…"

"We won't," Megan said.

The guy glanced around the space again. Then he walked around them to inspect the boxes.

Penny sucked in a breath as if afraid that he might find

something—probably the opening to that secret passage. If he knew it was there…

He would never leave them.

He pulled a few cloth napkins from one of the boxes. "Now you won't," he said as he shoved one of the cloths in Penny's mouth and then another in Megan's.

"Don't screw me over," he threatened. "Or you won't need to worry about D. I'll kill you myself."

Megan knew then that there was no use appealing to the better nature of any of the gunmen. None of them had a conscience. None of them would hesitate to take a life—any life.

Penny's throat dried of any moisture, and she struggled not to gag on the cloth shoved so deeply in her mouth it nearly choked her. She had only to wait until the fake waiter disappeared down the hallway before the cloth was gone.

After spitting out her cloth, Megan had twisted around and used her teeth to pull out Penny's. "You can untie yourself now," the younger woman told her.

Penny lifted her hands, which Megan had tied in front of her, unlike how the man had tied Megan's behind her back. "How?"

"Pull on the end of your ribbon with your teeth," Megan directed her.

Following instructions, Penny leaned forward, and with one tug, the ribbon easily unwound from around her wrists. Using her newly freed hands, she tugged loose the ribbon around her ankles. "How did you do that?"

"My dad taught me and my sister when we were little," Megan replied as if it was a perfectly normal part of childhood to learn how to tie slipknots.

"Didn't that scare you?" Penny asked, worried about how that single dad had raised his little girls. Not only had he been a single parent, but he was also a lawman.

"He made a game of it," Megan said nostalgically. She smiled then added, "Kind of like hide-and-seek on steroids."

Penny laughed. "Nikki would have loved that."

"Yes, she would have," Megan agreed.

So Penny hadn't been the only one who'd raised her kids in fear that something horrible could happen to them. Woodrow had been out there, fighting criminals despite knowing his work could make his family a target for revenge. So he'd obviously done his best to provide them with the skills to protect themselves.

"Unfortunately, the waiter didn't tie me up the same way I tied you," Megan said.

Penny inspected the ribbon binding Megan's wrists and ankles. The fake waiter had bound her so tightly that the edges of the ribbon were cutting through her skin. Penny sucked in a breath, unable to bear the thought of a bride—but especially this bride—being in pain.

While Penny didn't carry a weapon like her children, she did always have a small knife on her person. She pulled it from the pocket of the silk jacket that matched her dress. The blade was narrow but sharp. Being careful of Megan's skin, she sliced through the ribbon.

Megan expelled a shaky little sigh and rubbed her wrists. "Thank you."

"Thank you," Penny said as she hugged the young woman. "You were brilliant, the way you manipulated those men."

This Megan was nothing like the miserable bride Penny had worked with on her wedding plans. But then the young woman had been grieving the love of her life. Now, knowing Gage was alive, Megan Lynch was once again the woman she must have always been, the one her father had raised her to be: strong and savvy.

Megan pulled back and humbly replied, "I just bought us some time. We need to get out of here before either or both of them return. Or worse yet, Andrea comes back with them." She shuddered with fear.

Penny shuddered, too. When she'd gone back to the bride's dressing room to help Megan downstairs to the secret passage, she'd seen the other woman lying on the floor. Andrea had radiated hatred and resentment. Penny had no doubt that she was probably the most dangerous of all the wedding crashers.

"Yes," she heartily agreed. "We need to get out of here and get help."

She was actually surprised that Nicholas hadn't arrived yet. Even if Woodrow's daughter Ellen hadn't been able to reach him, he would have been on his way to the church anyway. He had been invited. And if the men outside the church had tried turning him away, he would have known something was wrong. He knew all Penny's staff and Woodrow's agents. He wouldn't have been fooled.

Her stomach pitched as fear unsettled her. If Nick had been here, he wouldn't have left without making sure they were all right. He would have put himself in danger for them. She hoped that he hadn't. He had a baby due soon. Annalise and their unborn son needed him.

Annalise had loved the boy who'd grown up next door to her too long to lose him now, when he'd just finally admitted he'd always loved her, too.

But they needed Nick here, too. Hopefully, he had left without incident and called his brothers, her sons. Logan,

Parker and Cooper would help them. But she had to make certain they knew what was going on, that they were all in danger but no one more than Nikki.

Penny headed toward the stack of boxes. They were only being stored at the end of the hallway in order to hide the door to the secret passage to the courtyard. When the fake waiter had rummaged through them earlier, Penny had been afraid that he might see the door.

There was no way he would have left them here if he had. But he'd been worried about Andrea. When they found her and discovered that her injury wasn't serious, they would be back.

The same thing must have been on Megan's mind, because she said, "We need to hurry."

Before Penny could reach for the first box, a dark shadow dimmed the already faint light at the end of the hallway, making the glint off the metal object he held even more noticeable.

They hadn't moved fast enough. One of the gunmen had found them.

Chapter 12

The minister spoke softly and slowly. "Who gives this woman in marriage?"

Just as slowly and softly, the father of the bride replied, "I do."

Nikki hoped like hell she wouldn't have to say those words herself. She had no intention of marrying anyone. Ever. Most especially not this guy. FBI bureau chief Woodrow Lynch pulled back her veil, leaned down and kissed her cheek. Something twisted inside Nikki, making her heart twinge. Her father would never be able to do that, never be able to give her away. She drew in a shaky breath. It wasn't a big deal since she never intended to marry anyone.

And knowing now what she knew about her father, about his cheating, Nikki wasn't sure she would have wanted him to give her away even if he had been alive. He'd been dead for nearly sixteen years, though. When she'd found out about his betrayal, it had been like losing him all over again.

Woodrow stared down at her, his eyes dark with concern. For her. He had wanted to protect his daughter, but he'd made it clear, maybe more for her mother's sake than Nikki's, that he hadn't wanted to sacrifice her in order to do that. She knew that. She'd convinced him and everyone else that this was the only way to buy enough time for Megan and her mom to get out of the church.

They must have had enough time to make it to safety now. They had to be out in the courtyard where they could get help for everyone else. She nodded at Woodrow and whispered, "Go."

He had to make certain that they were safe. For some reason Gage must have thought they weren't. Or he wouldn't have staged that coughing spasm in order to slip out before she and Woodrow had even made it down the aisle to the front.

With a wink she turned away from Woodrow to focus on the front and her groom. It was the first time she had seen Richard Boersman, and disappointment washed over Nikki. But her disappointment was more with the woman she'd begun to consider a friend than with the man. How had a feisty woman like Megan ever considered marrying such a dweeb?

His face was pale, and he visibly trembled as he stood alone next to the minister. She doubted his best man would return from his coughing spasm. And now the father of the bride was slipping toward the back of the church, as well. That left her alone at the front.

Or relatively alone. The minister was secretly armed. He'd performed enough weddings at Penny's chapel to understand the value of protection. But the groom was more likely to be a hindrance than a help.

"Act like I'm Megan," she whispered to him.

But he didn't look capable of acting anything except confused and scared. Not that anyone probably would have been fooled, even if he'd been capable of an award-winning performance. Murmurs were already moving through the pews as the guests realized Nikki was merely a substitute for the real bride.

She didn't see any of the gunmen she'd spotted earlier, and yet there were replacements. A guy near the front reached beneath his jacket where she'd already noticed he had a bulge.

No, Nikki wasn't worried about having to say "I do." She was worried about not making it out of the chapel alive. If that happened, at least she wouldn't have to listen to Logan tell her *I told you so.*

Her oldest brother had never believed she had what it took to be a bodyguard. So maybe she had concocted this plan to subconsciously prove him wrong. Even if she didn't make it out alive herself, she could still prove him wrong—if Megan and Penny had made it to safety.

They had to have gotten out of the chapel unharmed. Then even if Nikki lost her life, it would have been worth it. She would have done her job.

"Gage!" Penny exclaimed as she pressed a hand over her heart. "You scared me. I thought you were one of the gunmen returning."

Gage had nearly run right into the armed waiter after he had quickly descended the stairs and rushed down the basement hallway. Luckily, he'd been able to duck into the shadows of Penny's office before the guy had noticed him. As soon as the guy was gone, Gage had retraced his steps, his heart beating fast, his hand not quite steady on his weapon. He'd dreaded what he might find: injured women or, worse yet, dead bodies.

He didn't know how he would have handled finding Megan like he'd found so many other people over the years: lifeless, staring helplessly up at him as if berating him for not making it in time, for not being able to save her…

His breath shuddered out with relief that instead he had found them untying each other and getting ready to escape. And he'd thought about just letting them go. He probably would have just let them go if Penny hadn't noticed him.

"He might be back soon," Gage warned. "So you need to leave now."

But instead of moving the boxes away from what must have been the doorway to the underground tunnel, she paused and turned to him. Her face so pale it looked almost ghostly in the dim light, Penny asked him, "What are you doing down here? You're supposed to be in the church. You're supposed to be the best man."

"We all know that's not true," he said. Richard hadn't chosen him. But more importantly, neither had Megan. "I noticed the guy with the gun was missing," he said. "The one you stopped me from pummeling earlier." Penny had been right to stop him, though. He hadn't even noticed the other guys in the church. They could have been there earlier. And he could have started a shoot-out then.

"D," Penny replied. "He calls himself D. He was down here, too, with the waiter impostor. Megan tricked him into going up to check on the woman."

"Andrea," Megan supplied.

"She's fine," Gage said.

"Exactly," Penny said. "As soon as he unties her, all hell is going to break loose."

He didn't doubt it. The woman was furious that Megan had overpowered her and that they had tied her up. Releasing her would like releasing a wild animal from confinement.

Penny moved to walk around him, but he caught her arm and stopped her. "You need to leave with Megan," he insisted, "just like we planned."

She smacked his hand like he was a boy trying to sneak a cookie from the jar before dinner. "We also planned that you would be right at the altar with my daughter, that you would protect her."

"Woodrow is up there. And the minister is armed," Gage reminded her even though he felt a twinge of guilt that he had abandoned his assigned post. "And Nikki is armed. She can protect herself."

Penny shook her head. "No, she can't. She only thinks she can."

Gage resisted the urge to laugh. Penny Payne was legendary for her almost telepathic powers, for always knowing everything about everybody but most especially about her kids. How could she not know her own daughter? How could she have no idea how strong and resourceful Nikki was?

"I'll go back up there and make sure nothing happens to her," he promised. "You leave with Megan."

But he could see that it was too late. Penny didn't trust him anymore to protect her child. Before he could stop the wedding planner, she pulled away from him and hurried down the hall.

Megan tried to pass him to follow her. But he wasn't

taking any chances with her getting away from him like Penny had. He wrapped his arms around her and held her tightly. He wasn't about to let her put her life in danger again.

Megan gasped at the sensation of being pressed against the hard length of Gage's muscular body. Even through her heavy dress, she could feel his heat. And his tension…

"We need to hurry up," she said. "We need to help."

"You need to get the hell out of here," he told her. "That was the plan. To get you to safety. That's why I came down here—to make sure the man hadn't caught you and Penny before you escaped."

"He did, but we got away—"

"Only to try to rush right back into his clutches," Gage said.

"I might be safer in his," she murmured. She hadn't meant to say the words aloud, but they'd slipped out. And now they hung in the air between them.

Gage flinched like she'd slapped him. "I don't want to hurt you," he said.

"And you told me you would never lie to me." At least that was what he'd tried to tell her when she'd broken up with him. He'd tried to convince her that he hadn't been using her to get ahead at the Bureau like she'd been warned. But she hadn't listened to him. Maybe she'd been right not to. "I know you wanted to hurt me when you first showed up in the dressing room today."

"I did," he admitted. "But that was before I knew you were in danger."

She had been in danger then—in danger of making a horrible mistake. Then again, she hadn't known that

Gage was alive. It had taken her long moments of thinking she was seeing an apparition before she'd even believed that he was real and not a figment of her wishful imagination. But if she'd conjured him up, he wouldn't have looked at her like he had, like he'd hated her.

"*You* want to hurt me," she said because she didn't believe that he'd changed his mind. She didn't believe that he would ever forgive her. "But you don't want anyone else to hurt me?"

He groaned as if overcome with frustration. Then he kissed her. His mouth slid over hers, his lips tugging gently on her bottom one before he deepened the kiss. The tip of his tongue touched hers before retreating.

Her heart pounded, and her blood heated as passion overwhelmed her. But he pulled back, just slightly, just enough for her gasp for breath.

She had tried to communicate her feelings with a kiss. Now so had he. But she didn't understand what he was trying to say any more than she suspected he had understood her. She lifted her hands and slid them between their bodies, over his chest. Her palms tingled. She wanted to touch him, but instead she pushed him back. "We need to go upstairs to help them."

"You going up into the chapel will not help anyone," he said. "It will only put you in danger, too."

"I don't care," she said. And she didn't. "Not when the person who matters most to me is in danger!"

Gage flinched. Did he think she was talking about Richard? After their kisses, could he still think she cared about another man?

"My dad," she clarified.

And Gage's head bobbed in understanding.

Her dad had been always been everything to her, both

father and mother. Nurturer. Protector. He was the one whose shoulder she'd cried on when Gage had broken her heart and when she'd thought he'd died.

Gage might have been the one who mattered most to her if she thought he could ever love her again—if he ever had.

"I can't leave if my dad's in danger," Megan said. "And you know he is. The gunmen might be here because of him, because they want revenge against him."

"They might," Gage admitted. "Or they might have a whole other agenda..."

Him? Did he think they were there because of him? But why? Why would anyone think she mattered to him? She didn't even think that, even after that confusing kiss.

"It doesn't matter why they're here," she said. "It just matters that people I care about are in danger."

"People," he murmured.

"Nikki, Mrs. Payne..." There were other guests in the church, extended family. "And Richard." Richard had never done anything to her but be her friend.

He flinched again. He obviously thought she had agreed to marry Richard for love. But all she'd wanted was family. She'd hoped having one of her own might fill the hole in her heart that losing Gage had left in it.

"And how do you think you're going to help them?" he asked as he caught her hands in his. "You don't even have your gun anymore."

"The man—D—took it," she explained, her face heating with embarrassment that he'd snapped it from her grasp so easily.

He groaned again. "By now Andrea has it back, and you're the first person she'd use it on given the chance. You need to get out of here."

She shook her head. The curly hair she always fought so hard to tame tangled around her face. "I can't." Her voice cracked. "If I lose my dad..."

She didn't know what she would do. She couldn't imagine a world without him in it when for so much of her life, he had been her and her sister's whole world. No. She couldn't lose him.

Strong arms closed around her, and Gage pressed her against his body again. His hand stroked over her back, offering comfort. "He'll be fine," he assured her. "Woodrow Lynch wouldn't be bureau chief if he hadn't been a badass agent first."

But it had been years since he'd been in the field, years since he'd fired his weapon at anything other than targets. She knew her father missed it. But he'd given it up and accepted all his promotions and desk jobs because of her and Ellen, because he had wanted to be there for them and now for his granddaughters.

"I can't *not* do anything," she murmured into Gage's chest as tears sprang to her eyes.

"You can do something," he said. "You can go through that passageway and get help."

She pulled herself, albeit reluctantly, from his arms. "Of course."

But when she turned back toward the boxes Penny had begun to move, Gage caught her arm. "No, I'm wrong. That's a bad idea. You can't go out there alone. We don't know what might be waiting for you outside."

"Help."

"Or more people with guns," he said. "If not, there would be more guests upstairs. Somebody is keeping them out."

"I'll be careful," she promised. "You need to go back upstairs. You need to help my father and Nikki."

He sighed. "And stop Penny from taking them all on alone." But he didn't release her; his hand held her wrist yet—his fingers overlapping it. He stroked his thumb across her leaping pulse.

He looked like he was thinking about kissing her again. And she wanted his kiss even now, even when she knew they were all in danger. Maybe more now because she didn't know if she would be able to kiss him ever again.

But she pushed aside her selfishness and told him, "You better go." The music had stopped some time ago. The gunmen already knew that she wasn't the bride in the church. "We have no idea what's happening up there."

But then a shot rang out, echoing from above. And they knew nothing good was happening.

Chapter 13

Crazy bitch! Derek had been incarcerated long enough that he'd forgotten how mercurial Andrea could be. He tightened his grasp on her wrist, making sure the gun stayed pointed at the domed ceiling of the church in case she tried to fire again. She struggled against him, but fortunately she wasn't that strong, thanks to the stab wound in her shoulder.

"Calm down!" he yelled at her.

Eventually her anger subsided. But the moment he relaxed his grip, she tried to point the barrel down again.

"No!" she screamed. "That bitch deserves to die!"

"It's not her," he said.

She leaned closer to the bride she'd just tried to shoot and studied her. Her brow furrowed with confusion. "It's the other one, the bridesmaid."

The young woman shook her head, tumbling her curls

around her face. "No, no, I'm the bride," she insisted. Stubbornly. Stupidly.

"Where's the real bride?" Andrea demanded to know. "She's the bitch who stabbed me!"

Derek replied, "Ralph has her and the wedding planner tied up downstairs."

"Get her!" she ordered.

And his temper flared. His grasp on her wrists tightened until she flinched. "You are not in charge," he reminded her. Maybe he'd given her too much to do, because she obviously thought she was. Unfortunately, so did most of the men she'd hired to help them. They answered more to her than they did to him. And that just wasn't going to do. Maybe he should have left her tied up.

Then again, it might not be a bad thing if she were the one to pull the trigger. Then she would be the one going down for murder. He'd only be returned to jail for escaping and to serve out the last of his sentence for armed robbery. He could claim he had no idea she'd intended to take the wedding party hostage. But even if he faced new charges of kidnapping, the sentence wouldn't be as long as for murder.

During the five years he'd already spent in prison, he had been smug, thinking that he'd gotten away with murder...until he'd seen that picture. Then the joke had been on him when he'd realized that the son of a bitch had survived.

But Derek had been careful not to betray any recognition when he'd looked at him. He didn't want the bastard to know—until it was over—that Derek had gotten his revenge. Better he have no idea what the hell was really going on.

Unfortunately, with the way Andrea was acting, Derek

wasn't certain he was entirely aware of everything going on himself. He'd been attracted to the woman because she was smart. If not for her, he wouldn't have pulled off the robberies he had all those years ago. She'd helped him then. And she'd helped him escape.

But he wasn't sure she was helping him now.

She smiled at him, though it didn't quite reach her cold eyes. She was manipulating him with that smile and with her body, which she rubbed against his. "Please, D, tell Ralph to get her. I want her up here."

And neither of them could leave the chapel now in order to retrieve her. They had just taken everyone inside hostage. He hated sending Ralph downstairs. They needed all the guns they had because as he glanced around the chapel, he realized some guys were missing.

The rough-looking blond best man was gone, as was the gray-haired father of the bride. Where the hell were they?

He wouldn't have expected either of them to leave without a fight. They didn't look like the kind of guys who ran from danger but rather into it. They had to be planning something—something that was going to raise hell with their plan.

He shook his head. "This isn't right…"

"Please get her, D," Andrea implored him. Then she lowered her voice and reminded him in a whisper, "We need her—for the plan."

He wasn't sure if they'd be able to pull off the plan anymore. But he wasn't willing to give it up yet. So he nodded at the guy dressed like a waiter. Ralph started down the aisle toward the back of the chapel.

"Thank you," she said with a smile. She'd gotten what she wanted—or she soon would.

He released her wrist. And she swung the gun right back toward the substitute bride.

"You were there, too," she said, "when that bitch attacked me."

"Andrea!" He reached for her again. But this time he wasn't sure he would be able to stop her.

Her voice shaking with fury, she yelled, "You're going to die, too!"

Gage caught Megan again before she could slip past him and race down the hall to danger. She was struggling too hard for him to hold her tightly.

"Someone's been shot!" she said. "We need to go. Now. We need to help them."

"We don't know that anyone's been shot," he pointed out. "It could just be a trick." A ruse to draw them out. He knew the tricks dangerous men played to get people to do or say what they wanted.

"Or someone could be hurt and needs our help," she argued.

"Then we'll help them," he said. "But we can't do that if we get ourselves killed first."

Megan's safety was his top priority. She was the one in the most danger, for some reason. But the reasons didn't matter at the moment. All that mattered was keeping her safe. "You can't go up there with me," he said. "You need to—"

"I'm not leaving!" she said. "I can't—not until I know..."

If she'd lost someone she loved.

But was her fear for her father or for her fiancé?

That didn't matter, either. Sure, Gage had kissed her, but he would never make the mistake of trusting her with his heart again. He wasn't sure if he should trust her at all. Maybe he needed to drag her out through that tunnel himself to make sure she escaped.

But that shot reverberated inside his head. What if it had been Nikki or Woodrow or Mrs. Payne who'd taken a bullet?

He couldn't just leave them. He wasn't even sure what awaited them in the courtyard. If there were more gunmen outside, he wouldn't be able to get help.

No, he had no backup. Just like during those six months he'd spent in captivity, he could count on no one but himself. "I'll go upstairs," he said. "But I won't be able to help anyone if I'm worried about you."

Her face paled, and she drew in a shaky breath. "Of course."

"So you'll hide," he told her. "You'll hide so well that no one will be able to find you."

She nodded as if he'd asked her a question. But there was no question about it. He wasn't leaving her if he thought she would be in any danger.

"I'll hide," she promised. "Don't worry about me." Her brow furrowed slightly, as if she didn't understand why he was worried.

Did she believe, even after his kiss, that he wanted to hurt her? Even when he'd been furious with her, he hadn't wanted her hurt. He still wanted her...

Damn, maybe those six months had conditioned him for pain—because that was all she would bring him. In order to protect himself and not reveal how vulnerable he was to her, he said, "I'm worried that your father will kill me if anything happens to you. I promised him that I would keep you safe."

She nodded as if his explanation made sense. But then she said, "You don't work for my father anymore."

Giving up the job he'd loved working for a man he'd respected had been one of the hardest things he'd ever done. Losing her had been harder.

"I work for Payne Protection," he said. But that might not be for much longer if anything had happened to Nikki or Penny. His boss wouldn't just fire him; he'd kill him. "It's my job to keep you safe."

"I'll be fine," she assured him. "I'll hide—like you said. I'll make sure nobody finds me."

He nodded and turned to leave. Before he could walk away, she grabbed his arm. Maybe she'd changed her mind; maybe she wanted him to bring her to safety.

"If you're scared, I can get you out of here," he said.

She shook her head. "I'm not scared for me."

"Of course." And she wasn't, or she wouldn't have considered going up to that chapel where Andrea probably waited for her with a loaded weapon and a pair of scissors. "You're worried about your father. And Richard." He couldn't help the resentment that slipped into his voice with that last word. She shook her head again, and that curly, sexy hair tumbled around her shoulders. She was so damn beautiful.

"I'm scared for you…" She rose up on tiptoe and pressed a kiss against his lips. He couldn't help himself; he clutched a handful of that soft hair and held her mouth against his as he deepened the kiss. Passion pooled in his stomach, knotting muscles that were already clenched with adrenaline. Finally, he pulled back. And panting for breath, he rushed down the hall. He wasn't sure now if he was running to danger or away from it.

Because he knew Megan Lynch was the greatest threat to him. No one had ever been able to cause him more pain.

An elbow jabbed his ribs. A heel stomped on his foot. A woman struggled in Woodrow's arms, too, like the gunwoman had just struggled with her partner inside the chapel.

"Let me go," she mumbled against the hand he had clamped over mouth.

"Shh," he cautioned Penny.

They couldn't afford to draw any attention to where they hid in that coatroom just off the vestibule. He had pulled her into the room with him just as she'd tried to storm into the chapel. "You can't go in there."

Bursting in there, surprising already nervous gunmen, was certain to get her shot. "It's too dangerous," he said.

Maybe he'd gotten through to her, because she finally stopped struggling. But the second he released her, she headed for the door. He caught her shoulders and dragged her back into his arms.

"You think I'm going to stand in here and watch my daughter get killed?" she asked, her body bristling with outrage while it also trembled with fear.

He held her more closely, so that he felt her furiously beating heart against his. "She's not getting killed." At least not yet.

"The guy stopped his wife from shooting her," he pointed out. And as they watched through one of the lighter colors of the stained glass window between the coatroom and the church, the guy stopped her again. "If Nikki thought she was going to shoot her, she would draw her weapon."

But she'd left it holstered beneath her dress. Of course if she'd reached for it, Woodrow doubted the man would have stopped his wife. D would have let the woman blow her away. Nikki was so smart that she would have realized that, too.

"I also have a couple of other guys in there," he said. He wasn't certain how much help the minister or Tucker Allison would be. Neither of them had reached for their weapons yet, either, and he suspected it had nothing to do with Nikki's reasons.

They were just scared. Nikki, on the other hand, was fearless. She would make a damn good agent, a far better one than Tucker. She just had to survive this damn wedding. Concern for her was why he'd stopped himself from going any further than the coatroom. He could trust Gage to make sure Megan stayed safe; he needed to protect Penny's daughter.

"I need to go in there," Penny said as she renewed her struggle, pushing her breasts against his chest, her hips against his.

He swallowed a groan. How the hell could he even think about how good she felt now? When they were all in so much danger?

"You can't go storming in there," he said. "You'll get everyone shot—most especially yourself."

"So what am I supposed to do?" she asked, her voice cracking with raw emotion. "Just let my daughter die?"

"Penny…" Her pain reached inside him, twisting his heart around in his chest. And even though he had no way of knowing if he could keep it, he promised her, "Everything will be all right."

She shook her head. "That's easy for you to say. It's

not your daughter in there." Resentment joined the fear in her voice.

"No," he agreed. "It's not my daughter in there."

"Is that why you don't want me going in there?" she asked. "You know that when they see that I got loose, they'll realize she did, too?"

Panic stole his breath for a moment. "What? You two were caught?" Of course that explained why Penny wasn't out in the courtyard. Probably neither was Megan. "You didn't get outside?"

She turned toward him, and her eyes warmed. "Megan probably is now, though. Gage would have made her go."

He expelled a slight breath. "Thank you." Even as upset as she was, she had offered him reassurance. She was that sweet a woman.

But then her resentment returned as she turned away and peered through the stained glass window. "I never should have let Nikki act as a decoy."

"Our children don't always do what we want them to," he said. "Or what we think is best." And as he said it, his stomach lurched, because he knew Megan wasn't out in the courtyard.

Megan wasn't safe yet.

While Penny was focused on the chapel, Woodrow studied the door from the coatroom into the vestibule. He wasn't worried about anyone discovering them. The guy dressed like a waiter walked right past the room without glancing once in their direction.

Gage nearly passed, too, until Woodrow jerked him inside and demanded to know, "Why the hell did you leave her?"

"We heard the shot," Gage said. "And she wanted me to make sure you were all right."

Dread churned Woodrow's stomach. She wouldn't have left, then. She would be waiting somewhere, waiting to find out how he was. Or worse yet, knowing his loving daughter, she was probably on her way up the stairs to check herself because she had never trusted Gage.

Apparently, Woodrow shouldn't have trusted him, either.

Chapter 14

Megan tilted her head and listened. She could hear no sounds emanating from above the storage area where she stood frozen with fear and indecision. The chapel was almost eerily silent after that one startling gunshot.

Who had been shot? Or was it just like Gage suspected, a trick to draw them out? But it had only drawn out him—at her urging. Had she sent Gage alone into danger?

And worse yet, she hadn't told him how she felt about him. What if something happened and he never knew?

She'd spent those six months thinking that she'd missed her opportunity to let him know how much he really meant to her. And that last argument had echoed inside her head all those long months.

"I know you were just using me, trying to get ahead with my father," she'd said. "But that's okay. I was just using you, too."

"You were using me?" he'd asked. And his obvious surprise had made her angrier. She'd figured he'd thought her too ugly and stupid to be able to use anyone. But now she wondered if he hadn't just been confused.

"I used you for sex," she'd explained. "I knew you really didn't want a chubby, unattractive girl like me..." Or she'd thought she should have known. It had taken a few people pointing it out to her before she'd realized and accepted that a man like him would never want a woman like her unless he was getting something else out of it.

Like a quick promotion...

"Megan." He'd murmured her name and reached for her, like he'd intended to comfort her.

She'd jerked away, unable to let him touch her when she'd been hurting so badly. And out of that pain, she'd hurled those hateful words at him. "I never really loved you."

Only with her whole heart. But she'd lied, out of pain and wounded pride. Even then she'd seen that it had hurt him.

"Why?" she murmured.

Why would it have hurt him if he hadn't cared about her, if he'd only been using her? Wouldn't he have just laughed off her declaration like it hadn't mattered? He'd gotten the promotion he'd wanted—or she'd been told he'd wanted it. But if that was all he'd wanted, then why had he quit? Why had he walked away from a job he'd been willing to do anything—even romance her—to get ahead in?

Unless he hadn't been using her...

Unless he really had cared, maybe even really loved her. And she'd tossed that love back at him, unwilling to accept that it was real and that he'd been telling the truth. She'd wounded not only his pride but his heart as well.

Was that why he had reenlisted and put his life in danger? Because of her?

Just like he'd done now. He'd put his life in danger again because she'd asked him to check on the others. If anything happened to him... Guilt and fear overwhelmed her. It was a miracle he'd survived. She shouldn't have convinced him to tempt fate again.

She turned toward the boxes that Penny had begun to move. The door to the secret passageway was back there. She had promised Gage that she wouldn't risk going outside alone in case there were more gunmen in the courtyard. If only she hadn't lost Andrea's gun. Or even the scissors she'd used to stab the other woman. Maybe Mrs. Payne had something in her office that Megan could use as a weapon. Knowing Mrs. Payne and the fact that all of her children were bodyguards, maybe she even had a real weapon that Megan could use.

It was still eerily quiet upstairs. No more gunshots had rung out. So Gage hadn't fired at anyone or been fired at, unless someone had used Andrea's gun with the silencer on the barrel.

If that gun had been used, they all might be dead. Pain and panic gripped her heart over the thought of losing the men she loved: her father and Gage. Or the women she'd already come to care about: Penny and Nikki. She wasn't certain who else was in the chapel, who else could be in danger. She needed to know, so if she found a weapon, she would definitely head upstairs to help the others.

She hurried down the hall to Mrs. Payne's office. Despite living in Chicago, she had made the trip to the wedding planner several times, not because she'd wanted everything to be perfect but because Mrs. Payne had given her something she'd never had.

Sure, Dad had tried. He'd been the best mother he could be. But he was no Penny Payne. He wasn't capable of giving her the maternal understanding and female perspective that Penny had.

That was why she'd kept making the trip to meet with the wedding planner. So she knew which door opened off the hallway into Mrs. Payne's office. Before she could close her hand over the knob, someone grabbed her arm.

Even before she looked up, she knew it wasn't Gage. Her skin wasn't tingling. But her heart was racing. With fear. The man's grip was punishing.

"How the hell did you get free?" he asked her, his voice gruff with anger. He glanced down the hallway. "Where's the other woman?"

"I don't know." Megan breathed a slight sigh of relief. At least *he* hadn't caught Mrs. Payne. That didn't mean that she hadn't been caught, just as Megan had been caught.

"Where are you taking me?" she asked as he dragged her along the hall. His fingers pinched her arm, hurting her. But she held in a cry of pain.

He gave her an almost pitying glance. "I'm taking you to Andrea."

And Megan knew what that meant. He was taking her to her death.

As if he had a noose tied around his neck again, Gage couldn't breathe. There was too heavy a pressure on his chest, too much panic.

His gun drawn, he started forward, but a strong arm caught him and hauled him into a room down the hall from where the gunman had caught Megan outside Penny's office. Gage knew several ways that he could have broken that arm and the man to whom it belonged. But he knew it was Woodrow. So he didn't fight him.

"Shh," Woodrow cautioned him.

Needlessly. Gage knew how to be quiet. His life had depended on it. Now Megan's life depended on it. If the gunman realized he wasn't alone, he would kill her. Immediately. Before they had a chance to rescue her.

Gage shouldn't have left her. He should have known that she wouldn't hide. She wouldn't protect herself, not when she was so worried about her father.

Probably about Richard as well.

And knowing her, Penny and Nikki, too.

"We can't let him get her upstairs," Penny said, her voice soft but cracking with panic. "That woman will kill her for certain." She hadn't wanted to leave the chapel where her daughter was being held. But she'd been concerned about Megan. And Woodrow had insisted that they all stick together. There was safety in numbers.

Gage only needed the guy to get a little closer to him. Then he would act. He would do what he'd learned in the Marines—what had saved his life.

Megan struggled with the guy, fighting against the hand gripping her arm. The guy was big and he had to be hurting her. But she betrayed no pain. Only fear, her dark eyes wide with it. She knew, too, that if he delivered her to Andrea, she wouldn't live long.

Until that day Megan had broken his heart, Gage had had no idea how feisty she could be. She'd always been so sweet and loving with him. Then she had told him that she'd never loved him at all. And she must not have, otherwise, how could she have believed he'd only been using her? Why had she listened to that resentful Tucker? Why had she believed the petulant young agent over Gage?

Of course he had realized today that she hadn't known him any better than he'd known her. He had never guessed the depths of her strength. He saw it now as she continued to struggle with the man.

When the guy raised his hand to strike her, Gage started forward, but Woodrow held him back again. How could he let his own daughter get hurt?

Megan cringed in anticipation of the blow, but it didn't come.

The man tensed. Then Gage heard what Woodrow had heard—the crackle of static. As the guy reached for the walkie-talkie in his pocket, Megan pulled from his grasp and ran.

She was definitely stronger than he'd known. Was she fast enough to get to the secret passageway?

Gage moved to step into the hall again, but Woodrow held on to him, motioning for him to be quiet as a female voice emanated from the walkie-talkie.

"Ralph, did you get her?"

"Yeah, Andrea, yeah, I did," he quickly replied. He obviously feared the woman.

So did Gage. He'd already seen the hatred in her cold eyes.

"Then why haven't you brought her up here yet?" she demanded.

"I'll—uh—be up in a little while," he nervously stammered. "I'm—uh—just having a problem with the wedding planner." The problem obviously being that he had no idea where she was.

Fortunately, he was completely unaware that she was only a few steps away from him.

"Don't waste your time with her," Andrea replied. "The bride's the one we want."

And there was something ominous in her tone, something that insinuated she didn't just want Megan for revenge for the stabbing.

Megan was the key to whatever the hell their plan was.

Derek snapped the walkie-talkie out of Andrea's hand like he had snapped her gun out of the bride's hand. He couldn't believe Andrea had lost her weapon, that she had been overpowered.

Andrea flinched and glared at him.

Where was the love she'd professed when she had visited him regularly at the prison? He wasn't certain he could trust her now.

But she had helped him escape, and she had planned how to crash the wedding. She was the reason the plan had gone awry, though. She never should have forced her way into the bride's dressing room. Maybe the bride had been about to back out of getting married. There could have been another way to convince her than threatening her with a gun, one she'd lost in a struggle anyway. Then once Derek had freed her, Andrea had rushed into the chapel and fired his gun, the one without the silencer.

He pressed the button on the walkie-talkie for the man in charge of the reinforcements posted outside. Once the guy answered, he asked, "Do you see any sign of police?"

Someone must have reported the shot. The police would have to send at least one car to investigate. So he didn't have much time now, not if he wanted to avoid going back to prison.

"Not police," the guy replied, "but the landscaping crew showed up."

"Landscaping crew?"

"Yeah," the guy replied with a mixture of confusion and amusement, "a bunch of guys that all look alike. Gotta be a family business."

"Did you turn them away?"

"Yeah, I told them the wedding couldn't be disrupted." Not any more than it had already been.

Derek had thought about pulling a guy off perimeter duty to help him inside the church. But he had an uneasy feeling about the landscaping crew. If the wedding planner was as legendary as the blond guy had mentioned, why would she have scheduled a crew, with mowers and Weed eaters that could have disrupted the service, during a wedding?

She wouldn't have. That damn sure hadn't been a landscaping crew that had showed up.

"Don't let anyone near," he cautioned the guy.

"That's what Andrea told us."

Derek clicked off the radio.

"What's wrong?" Andrea asked.

Everything. But he just shook his head. "We need to get out of here."

"Ralph's bringing up the real bride," she said.

"If she's the only one you want," the substitute bride said, "can't you let the rest of us go?"

Andrea pointed her gun at the petite brunette. "You're not going anywhere!"

"That's fine," she replied without fear. "But what about the rest of the guests?"

Derek shook his head. "Nobody's going anywhere." If the police showed up, as he suspected they soon would thanks to Andrea's gunfire, he would need hostages.

He saw that realization in the brunette's eyes. Despite switching places with the real bride, she was smart. Maybe too smart…and way too courageous. He narrowed his eyes and studied her.

Who or what was she really?

"We need to search everyone," he said. "Make sure nobody's armed." He knew at least two men were: the best man and the father of the bride.

Where the hell were they? A movement in one of the pews drew his attention. Sunlight shining through the stained glass windows glinted off metal. Instincts kicking in, he turned and fired—once, twice, three times…

But he had Andrea's gun—with the silencer. No shots were heard. Only screams as the hostages reacted.

"Anybody else want to be a hero?" he asked as he swung his gun around, looking for any other shooters. At least nobody else had drawn a weapon. The bride started forward, though, trying to push past him. He shoved her back hard enough that she fell onto the floor.

Certain Andrea wouldn't let her move again, he started down the aisle to where the guy had fallen out of his pew onto the white paper runner which was now spattered with his blood. He leaned down and grabbed the gun the guy had dropped without ever having fired. The barrel was warm and slick with his sweat. He must have been holding it for a while, waiting for the opportunity to use it.

He should have waited longer. But the guy was young, probably early twenties or maybe older and he just looked like a kid. He moaned and shifted on the ground. Derek kicked his side, and the kid cried out.

"Who are you?" Derek demanded to know.

But the young man was too hurt to talk, his consciousness slipping away as the pain overwhelmed him.

Derek leaned down and patted his pockets. He found a billfold and pulled it out. It wasn't a wallet. It was a badge with credentials. He cursed.

Andrea, unwilling to the let the fake bride out of her sight, dragged her down the aisle with her as she hurried to Derek's side. "What? What is it?"

"He's an FBI agent." He'd just shot, probably mortally, an FBI agent. If the guy died, Derek wouldn't just go back to jail; he'd go to the electric chair.

"Why are you surprised?" the substitute bride asked as she dropped to her knees next to the young agent. She checked his wounds. Derek had hit him in the shoulder and the side. If he hadn't hit any organs, the kid might live if he didn't bleed out.

"Why wouldn't I be surprised?" he asked, although he noticed that Andrea wasn't. She hadn't reacted at all to the presence of a federal agent.

"If you somehow hadn't stopped guests from coming into the church," the young woman replied, "this place would have been crawling with FBI agents."

Alarm gripped Derek. "What? Why?"

She wadded the kid's jacket against his side and secured it there with his belt. Was she an EMT or an FBI agent, too?

She glanced up at Derek, and a slight smile curved her lips. "The father of the bride is Chief Special Agent Woodrow Lynch. Every agent in the Chicago Bureau was invited to his daughter's wedding."

In his mind, Derek heard the buzz of the cell door as it opened and then whistled closed behind him. He was going back to prison. That hadn't been part of the plan—at least not his plan. This felt like a trap. He glared at Andrea.

And she stepped back. "D—"

No. He wasn't going back to prison.

He would die first, but he damn well wasn't going out alone. He would take everyone in the whole damn chapel straight to hell with him.

Chapter 15

"The bride's the one we want." The words ringing in her ears, Megan ran for her life. The heavy dress hampered her movements. She tripped on the train and nearly fell, catching herself against the stone wall. The rough stone scraped her palms, but she held in a cry of pain.

The man wasn't running after her. He probably thought she was trapped in the dead end of the hallway. The hallway was her best chance of escaping, if she could find the door to the secret passageway.

She began knocking down boxes, hopeful she would find the door and be able to get inside before the guy caught her again. Her breath shuddered out as she discovered the wooden frame. She shoved the last box aside and reached for the door handle just as a shadow blocked her already faint light.

"What the hell is that?" the man asked.

Megan sucked in the breath she'd expelled and turned to face him. "N-nothing…"

"It's something," the man said. "Where does the door go?"

To freedom. To help. Both of those were eluding Megan now.

He pushed her aside and shoved open the door to see for himself. Peering into the dark hole behind the door, he remarked, "It's a tunnel. Is that where the wedding planner went?"

If only she had…

Megan nodded. "Yes. She's getting help."

He laughed off her bluff. "All she's going to get is killed. The church is surrounded with our guys. Andrea thought of everything. Nobody's getting inside this place and nobody's leaving."

"What do you want?" Megan asked. "Why are you doing this?"

The guy shrugged. "I don't know, lady. I just do what I'm paid to do."

"What are you paid to do?" she asked. "Kill? How much do you charge for that?"

He just glared at her.

"It can't be enough," she answered her own question. "Not enough to risk your freedom. To risk your life."

He shook his head. "Knock it off. You're not getting to me again."

She had to—it was her only chance of escaping him. "I won't have to get to you," she said. "The police will be here soon."

He snorted. "There's no way you were able to contact them. Andrea jammed the cell signal."

Of course Andrea had. Damn the bitch.

Megan offered him a condescending smile. "I heard that gunshot down here. You don't think anyone else heard it and reported it?"

His throat moved as he swallowed. And he tilted his head, as if listening for sirens.

Megan thought she'd heard screams just a little while ago, while she'd been running. She'd thought they might have been her own. She'd wanted to scream. Now she wanted to cry.

The guy shrugged again. "If the cops are coming, then we damn well better hurry."

"Yes," she agreed. "Let's you and I go out through the secret passage. Let's get out of here!"

He snorted. "Lady, that would get me killed for sure. if I double-crossed Andrea."

"Please, don't do this," she implored to his conscience, hoping that he had one. "You know if you bring me upstairs, Andrea will kill me."

"I don't care what she does to you."

Megan did, and she wasn't going to make it easy for him to do his job. Remembering another one of the games her father had taught her and Ellen—deadweight—she dropped to the floor.

"Get up!" he yelled at her. "Get the hell off the ground!" With his hand not holding the gun, he reached for her. Even though she lay flat on the concrete, he got his hand in her hair.

Tears streamed from Megan's eyes as the guy fisted his fingers in her hair and pulled. It hurt like hell, but she refused to budge until he pointed the gun right at her head. "Get up or I'll blow you away right here."

"But Andrea—"

"Andrea wants you dead," he said. "I'll just save her

the trouble of pulling the trigger. I'll kill you right here."
And he cocked the gun.

Megan closed her eyes and waited for the gunshot.

The barrel was so damn close to her head Gage was
worried that the gun might accidentally go off. But he had
no choice. If he did nothing, the guy would pull the trigger and kill her—right in front of him. And he couldn't
let that happen.

He moved quickly like he'd been taught in Special
Forces. The guy never heard or saw him coming. He
probably didn't feel a thing as Gage slid his arm around
his neck, caught his chin in his hand and twisted. He
heard the telltale snap. And the guy went limp in his
arms. Gage let his lifeless body slide down to the floor—
next to Megan.

Startled, she opened her eyes. Staring into the dead
face of her assailant, she let out a soft cry of surprise
and fear. Was she afraid of the man? Or would she be
afraid of Gage because of what he'd done? Of how easily he'd killed?

She turned toward him, and the fear left her dark eyes,
which widened with surprise. He extended his hand to
her, wondering if she'd take it after how he'd just used
it. But her hand closed over his. She pulled herself to her
feet before he could even help her.

And she threw her arms around his neck, clinging
to him. "Thank you!" she exclaimed. "Thank you! You
saved my life."

Before he could close his arms around her, she pulled
away. "But you shouldn't have come back," she said. "You
should be helping upstairs." Then her face paled, and she

began to tremble. Maybe it was shock. Her voice cracking, she asked, "Was it my dad? Was that who was shot?"

Gage had nearly forgotten about that gunshot—the reason she'd convinced him to go upstairs and leave her in the first place.

Before he could answer and ease her fears, another man replied, "I'm okay, sweetheart."

And Megan dodged around Gage to throw herself into her father's arms. "Are you really?" she asked. "You didn't get hurt?"

"No, no," he assured her. "I'm fine. But I'll be better when Gage gets you out of here." Over her head, Woodrow met Gage's gaze. There was so much in his expression: gratitude that Gage had saved her but also recrimination that he hadn't already gotten her to safety.

Guilt churned in Gage's empty stomach.

He wasn't the only one feeling guilty. It was on Megan's pale face when she tremulously asked, "Was it Nikki? Did she get shot?"

"No," Woodrow said. "Nobody got shot. Andrea fired one into the ceiling. That was all."

That had been all. They had no way of knowing what had happened since they'd come downstairs. A few moments ago, Gage had thought he'd heard the faint echo of screams, like someone had briefly opened a door to hell.

After the captivity he'd endured, Gage knew exactly what hell sounded like, the fear and pain of tormented souls. He didn't want the hostages in the chapel to have to endure the torture he had.

They had to rescue them.

But how? If the guy had been telling Megan the truth, it wasn't safe to slip out of the church, either. They were outnumbered and surrounded. But then, he'd been out-numbered and surrounded before and had survived.

"I'm the one Andrea wants," Megan said.

Her father offered a grim nod. "Yes, you are. That's why Gage needs to get you out of here."

Megan shook her head. "No, that's why I'm not leaving."

And Gage knew that the real threat to his safety wasn't outside. It was her—as it had always been. Worrying about her and fighting her stubbornness would kill him faster than any gunshot.

Penny's hand shook as she fumbled with the walkie-talkie. It wasn't the one Gage had taken off the man he'd killed. It was one of hers. She took another from the glass cabinet hidden behind the bookshelf in her office. Then she turned and passed it across her desk.

Woodrow fiddled with the one the fake waiter had used. He was careful to not press any buttons that might connect him with the gunmen in the chapel.

She was surprised that they hadn't called again. That Andrea wasn't wondering why Ralph hadn't brought Megan up to her yet.

Because he was dead.

She hadn't seen it happen, but she'd known when Gage and Woodrow and Megan had joined her in her office that it had. Gage had been grim. Woodrow had been re-lieved. And Megan...

She was in shock. Her face pale, her body trembling. She leaned against Gage, maybe consciously, maybe sub-consciously seeking his warmth and strength and pro-tection.

Penny glanced around her office. It was big enough

that it wasn't cramped with the four of them in it. She often hosted entire wedding parties in the space, so it was spread out. In addition to the desk she had a conference table and chairs and a couch against one of the walls.

Megan sat there now with Gage beside her, hovering protectively as if he thought someone might try to take her right in front of him.

Then someone nearly had.

She didn't know how Woodrow had handled it. How he'd watched that man threaten and hurt his daughter and not only not reacted himself, but he hadn't allowed Gage to react, either. That took a kind of patience and faith she didn't possess.

When she'd heard that shot earlier, Penny had rushed upstairs without even stopping to grab a weapon. She turned back to her open glass cabinet and pulled out one now. Years ago her husband had taught her to shoot, and then she had taught their sons.

She could help Nikki. If it wasn't already too late…

She'd heard screams earlier. Just because she hadn't heard a gunshot didn't mean there hadn't been one. A gun wasn't the only weapon that could kill someone. Megan had wounded the evil Andrea with a pair of scissors. Maybe she'd avenged her injury with another pair.

Penny waited for it, for that connection she had with all her children to let her know if Nikki was hurt. Or worse…

But her connection with Nikki had never been as strong as her connection with her sons. Or even with Nicholas Rus, her husband's illegitimate son. She could feel their anxiety and fear—even now.

Especially now.

She knew they knew that the wedding guests had been

taken hostage. They were no doubt working on a plan to save them without getting them killed.

Ordinarily, Nikki would have tried to be part of that plan. The boys would have excluded her for her protection. That might have been Penny's fault more than theirs. They probably knew that she'd never wanted her daughter working as a bodyguard.

She'd wanted Nikki to work with her—as a wedding planner. But working in the chapel had put Nikki in more danger than she'd ever been in as a bodyguard.

Woodrow's hand closed over hers and gently squeezed. "We'll rescue her. We'll figure out a way to get her safely out of the chapel."

She couldn't trust him. He wasn't telling her the truth, only what he thought she wanted to hear. And maybe she did want to hear lies—empty assurances that Nikki was all right. Nikki was Nikki.

Her fearlessness and her sassy mouth were her worst enemies. They always put her in danger, and now they might get her killed. But that wouldn't be Nikki's fault. That would be Penny's. She never should have enlisted her daughter's help.

She'd meddled so often in her kids' lives that it was second nature to her. This time her meddling might have gotten her daughter killed.

Chapter 16

Nikki's arm hurt from everyone grabbing it and dragging her along. At least Andrea had dragged her down the aisle toward the wounded agent.

What the hell had the young man been thinking? He'd pulled his gun so quickly that neither she nor the minister had had a chance to draw their weapons before Derek had fired. If they'd drawn their guns then, Andrea and the other two armed guys would have shot them.

She hadn't been able to do anything to prevent the shooting. But she'd tried her best to treat his wounds. Despite her limited first aid training, she had done everything she could for him before D had dragged her back up to the altar.

She wished he would have left her near the kid, so she could make sure they didn't lose him. Not that she could do anything else for him. She'd already pleaded her case for them to get him medical attention.

Andrea had laughed at her. "Do you think I'm an idiot?"

Nikki had laughed then, which had earned her another slap across the face. She tasted blood on her lip then licked it away as if it was nothing.

And it was in comparison to what they could do, to what they would do once they had Megan in the chapel. Maybe it wouldn't come to that, though. She'd heard the outside guy on the walkie-talkie with D.

That landscaping crew that all looked alike...

It had to be her brothers. The three of them—four with Nick—could have been quadruplets. They looked that much alike. Sure, the outside gunmen had turned them away, but they would find another way inside. They wouldn't give up.

And neither would she.

Beside her the groom sniffled. Irritated, she glanced over at him. He wasn't the only one crying in the church. But he wasn't crying for the kid that had probably lost his life, he was crying for himself.

To get him to shut up, Nikki murmured, "Don't worry. We're going to be okay." Her brothers would rescue her the same way they always had. And instead of dreading it, she almost looked forward to Logan's *I told you so.*

"What about Megan?" he asked anxiously. "Do you think she's okay?"

Maybe he really loved his bride. Nikki nodded. "Yes."

"But you heard them on the walkie-talkie—the guy they sent to get her had had her."

Nikki smiled, splitting her lip open again. "If he had her, they'd already be up here."

Richard's face flushed. "But what happened?"

She could only guess. "Gage and Woodrow."

A gasp of shock slipped out of Richard's lips. Had he forgotten about his best man and the father of the bride?

Nikki hadn't. She was counting on them. But of course she knew their primary focus was Megan, as it should be.

"They would die before either of them would let something happen to her," Nikki said. "She will be okay."

For a moment Nikki envied the other woman. Unlike Megan, Nikki had no father to protect her. No old lover to jump to her defense. But she did have her brothers, and she had no doubt they would get inside the chapel. She just hoped they made it in time.

The woman approached again and swung the barrel of her long gun toward Nikki's face. "What are you talking about?" she asked.

Nikki shrugged. "I'm trying to convince him it isn't bad luck to have our wedding hijacked."

"This is not your wedding," the woman said impatiently. "You were not the one in the gown when I went into the bride's dressing room."

Nikki shrugged. "I'm in the gown now." The gown she'd vowed never to wear. But knowing what it meant to her mother, she'd been careful to get no blood on it when she'd tended to the wounded agent.

Derek had joined them, his gun trained on her, as if he considered her the greatest threat.

She felt a flash of pride. But of everyone left in the church, she probably was, and he didn't even know she was armed. The agent drawing his gun had distracted D from searching all the other guests. He had visually inspected everyone, though. But he couldn't see her weapon, strapped to her thigh beneath her dress.

"Who are you?" he asked her.

"Nikki Payne," she answered honestly. She didn't

admit to being a bodyguard. Instead she said, "My mom owns the wedding chapel."

He snorted. "I doubt providing a bride is one of her services."

Nikki chuckled. "You'd be surprised."

His eyes narrowed into cold slits, he studied her face as he had earlier. "Oh, I am…"

And he shot a glance at Andrea. He had apparently realized that he didn't know his partner any better than he knew Nikki. "Why did you really switch places with the bride?"

Nikki nodded toward his lady friend. "Because of her." A muscle twitched along his cheek as he clenched his jaw. He was angry with Andrea—maybe angry enough that Nikki could drive a wedge between them. "I know she intends to hurt Megan."

Andrea laughed. "Hurt? You have no idea."

"Why?" Nikki asked. Because of Woodrow? She doubted that or Derek wouldn't have been surprised when he had learned the father of the bride was an FBI bureau chief.

No. Whatever they wanted had nothing to do with Woodrow Lynch.

Gage?

She turned back toward the sniveling groom. Had he put his bride in danger? She nearly laughed at the thought. It was more likely the other way around. Megan must have made enemies of her own.

"They want me," Megan said as guilt overwhelmed her. She never should have agreed to Nikki Payne taking her place. She never should have put anyone else in danger like that, no matter how much Nikki had insisted she could handle it.

What would they do to her when the fake waiter didn't deliver Megan like they were expecting? Would they do to her whatever they had intended to do to Megan?

Torture her? Kill her?

Nikki wasn't the only one in danger—the other guests were, too. Just because they hadn't heard any more shots didn't mean some hadn't been fired. Andrea's gun had a silencer.

Shivering with fear for what might have already happened, she said, "I need to go up there."

The others stared at her as if she'd lost her mind. Her father shook his head.

"Maybe they would leave," she said. And then everyone else would be safe.

"They probably would leave," Gage agreed, "either with you—or after they kill you."

She shivered again despite the warmth emanating from his body so close to hers on that couch in Penny's office. Until then she hadn't realized that she'd been leaning against him. Pride had her stiffening her backbone and pulling away from him.

"We're not going to let anything happen to you," her father assured her.

"What about everyone else?" she asked. Her concern wasn't for herself, not anymore. When she'd broken up with Gage all she had worried about was getting hurt, and because of her selfishness, she'd hurt someone else.

She had hurt Gage. And even if he was able to forgive her, she wasn't certain she would ever be able to forgive herself.

"We're working on a plan," Woodrow told her.

She loved her father and appreciated how protective he'd always been, but even so, he hadn't been able to stop her and Ellen from getting hurt. They'd been heartbroken when they'd lost their mother. Maybe that was why he had gone overboard, spoiling and coddling them.

She bristled now at his almost dismissive tone. Her father had treated her like a child long enough.

"No," she told him. "I'm part of this, too. You're not excluding me."

"That's why I'm excluding you," Woodrow said. "Because it's all about you…"

Her stomach lurched. Feeling like she might be sick, Megan jumped up and ran for the door.

"Megan!" her father called after her, his voice sharp with alarm.

She didn't want him to follow her. But she knew that someone had. And she knew who before she even turned around to face him. Instead she stared down at the body lying at the end of the hallway.

Gage had done that. He'd killed a man, for her. To protect her.

It had to stop. The danger. The death. It had to stop.

"You have to let me go," she told him.

His breath shuddered out in a ragged sigh. "I would like nothing more…"

His heart pounding with fear, Woodrow started after his daughter. "Stop," a soft voice said. Penny's voice was as delicate sounding as she was delicate looking. She wasn't strong. Physically.

Emotionally and mentally he suspected he had met no one stronger than she was. Sure, he'd had to stop her from charging into the chapel to save her daughter earlier. But she'd summoned control now. Control that awed him.

"I have to stop her," he said. "She's going to run up there and offer herself as a sacrifice. I can't let her do that."

He flinched as he realized what he'd said. He heard his own hypocrisy.

"You won't let your daughter do what you let mine?" she asked, her voice sharp now with bitterness.

He turned around and reached for her, his hands closing over her shoulders. "I'm sorry."

"It's too late now," she said.

He knew she was right. It was too late—for whatever they might have had between them. He'd destroyed any chance he might have had with her, if she ever would have given him a chance. Everyone thought she'd never remarried because she was still in love with her late husband. Just like everyone thought Woodrow was still in love with his late wife.

He figured the same thing that had held him back had probably held Penny back. Fear. He hadn't wanted to get hurt again. He suspected neither had she.

But he had hurt her.

"The damage is done," she continued. "My daughter has already been taken hostage."

"Your daughter is a trained and armed bodyguard," he reminded her. "Nikki's tough. She's strong. And more importantly, she's smart." Even though she was fearless, she would be careful. "She's like her mother."

Woodrow had never met a more impressive woman than Penny Payne. She was as brilliant as she was beautiful. He'd thought so on the other occasions they'd met, at the weddings of his agents. That was why he'd reached out to her for Megan's wedding.

Maybe he'd even used it as an excuse to see her again. It wasn't as if he'd really wanted Megan to marry Richard. But he'd thought marrying her friend might keep her safer than risking her heart again.

He'd never imagined how wrong it would all go…

"Megan's not like you," he said.

"No," Penny agreed. "She's like you."

He wished she was. But she wasn't his. Not biologically. When he hadn't been around to pay attention to his young wife, she'd sought attention from other men. Blaming himself, Woodrow had forgiven her, and he loved the daughter she'd made with another man as if that daughter was his own.

Penny had to realize that Megan wasn't really his. She'd mentioned how Megan had showed her a picture of his late wife. His youngest daughter looked nothing like him or like her mother. She must have looked like her biological father, whoever he was.

"You've taught her well," Penny said. "She's every bit as strong and smart as you are. She also has your over-developed sense of responsibility."

He groaned, but he didn't argue. Even though she didn't have any of his DNA, Megan was more like him than his biological daughter. Because Megan knew they wanted her, she would go—she would give up her life for the lives of others.

He turned back to the door. "I have to stop her."

"Gage already has," Penny assured him. "He would never let her put herself in harm's way."

That was true. Despite everything he'd been through,

or maybe because of it, Gage was the best man to protect Megan. And Penny.

"When they come back," he said. If they came back…

Maybe Gage had already dragged her out through the passageway. He'd never seen a man as tormented as Gage had been, watching the fake waiter threaten Megan. He'd been more upset than Woodrow—because Woodrow had known they would save her.

"You and Megan will leave through the passageway," he said, "just like we originally planned."

She snorted. And he knew why. They hadn't stuck to the original plan.

"Gage and I will go back upstairs," he promised. "We'll rescue Nikki and the others."

She shook her head. "No. We tried your plan," she said. "It didn't work. We'll switch to my plan now." She grabbed a bag and filled it with the guns and walkie-talkies she'd put on her desk.

"Penny!" He reached for her, trying to stop her as she passed him on her way to the door. "What the hell do you think you're doing?"

He could imagine her trying to pull a Dirty Harry or a Rambo, taking on all the gunmen by herself. For her daughter, she would do anything—except trust him. She would never forgive him for not making sure Nikki stayed safe.

"I'm going to end this," she said. "It's gone on long enough. It's time to take back my chapel." Her voice cracked with emotion. "And save my child."

And his heart ached. "You intend to do that alone?"

She shook her head. Tears glistening in her eyes, she admitted, "I can't…"

He suspected it was the hardest admission Penny

Payne had ever made. She was fiercely independent and protective of her family.

"I will help you," he promised her. He only hoped that they wouldn't be too late.

What had happened to the substitute bride when the fake waiter hadn't brought up Megan as they'd ordered?

Had they already killed Nikki in her place?

Chapter 17

"I wish I could let you go," Gage admitted. But he'd held on to her since that first day they'd met in her father's house. Even after she'd dumped him and broken his heart, he hadn't been able to let her go. During all those months of captivity, he'd been tortured more by her than by anything his captors had done to him.

He'd been tortured by memories of her, of her shy smile. Of how it brightened her eyes before curving her lips. He'd been tortured by memories of her hair, curling wildly down to her shoulders as it was now that it had freed itself from the knot into which she usually bound it. He'd remembered how it had felt against his skin, how her skin had felt against his...

Like warm silk.

His body hardened and heated with desire. He wanted her. He'd wanted her then. And he wanted her now.

"You can let me go," she said.

But he ignored her comment, and despite the heavy dress, he swung her up easily in his arms and carried her toward Penny's open door. Penny and Woodrow had left, probably for the chapel. Andrea and D would be wondering why Ralph hadn't brought up Megan yet.

They would know something had gone wrong. And they might react by getting rid of the hostages.

Penny's arsenal of guns and the walkie-talkies was gone, too. She'd emptied her secret closet, which stood open like her door had. She and Woodrow had gun power. But they needed him, too. They must have thought he'd stopped Megan and gotten her to safety. He needed to bring her to that secret passage where no one could find her.

But he was torn. She felt so good in his arms, against his body that ached for hers.

"You have to let me go," she murmured as he laid her down on the couch they'd been sitting on moments ago.

He shook his head. "I tried…" And he followed her down, covering her squirming body with his.

She moved beneath him, her breasts pushing against his chest, her hips against his. But then a soft moan slipped from her lips. "Gage…"

She tensed.

He forced himself to draw in a breath. But it didn't ease his desire. He could smell her now, the sweet scent that was hers alone. He could almost taste her, too.

"I've been wanting to ask you something," she said. And the shyness he'd known and loved was back in her husky voice.

"What?" What might she want to know? She could

probably tell, from the erection straining against his dress pants, that he still wanted her.

"Did you reenlist because of me?"

The question caught him off guard, and he wasn't certain how to answer. He didn't want to make her feel guilty or bad. It wouldn't do any good. It wouldn't change what had already happened.

"You promised that you would never lie to me," she reminded him.

"Yes," he agreed. "But you didn't believe me."

"I should have," she admitted. She stared up at him with tears glistening in her eyes. "I'm sorry."

He closed his eyes, unable to bear the beauty and the guilt on her face. "Megan..."

"Tell me," she prompted him. "Tell me the truth you promised me. Did you quit the Bureau and reenlist because of me?"

He had promised her honesty, and he had broken none of his promises—no matter what she had believed at the time. He wouldn't break any now, either. He opened his eyes and focused on her beautiful face. "Yes."

She gasped as if he'd struck her. "I had hoped that it wasn't my fault."

"It wasn't," he said. "You didn't tell me to do it. It was my choice."

"To leave a job you loved?"

"I didn't love it as much..." As he'd loved her.

Hell, he still loved her. That was why he had to stay away from her. He had nothing to offer her anymore.

The tears glistening in her eyes spilled over, sliding down her cheeks. He wiped them away with his thumbs.

"I'm so sorry," she murmured. "I was such a fool. I never should have listened to what people were saying."

"People?" He hadn't realized anyone but Tucker Allison had thought that he'd been using her.

"Tucker wasn't the only one," she admitted.

"Who else?" he asked. Had his friends betrayed him? Had they doubted him like she had?

Nick wouldn't have. No one knew him better than Nick, not even his sister. Annalise knew he'd loved Megan, though.

"It doesn't matter," she said. "Nothing matters but that I believed them. And I shouldn't have. I should have trusted you. I should have trusted what we had."

Feeling as if he was the one who'd been punched now, his breath shuddered out. "Maybe we didn't have what we thought we had. Maybe it wasn't real."

That was what he'd tried to convince himself of the past several months, but he had failed.

She reached up and skimmed her fingertips along his face. "It was real," she said. "It was…" She tugged his head down to hers and pressed a soft kiss against his lips.

He'd already wanted her. He'd never stopped wanting her. But the desire intensified. He kissed her back—deeply—passionately. His lips skimmed across hers then nibbled. Using his teeth, he gently bit the fullness of her bottom lip.

She moaned and opened her mouth for him. He slid his tongue inside, and she touched it with hers shyly before retreating. He kissed her again and again.

He wanted to take her right there on the couch in his boss's mom's office. But as he skimmed his fingers over her curves, the rhinestones on the dress scraped his skin and brought him to his senses.

She was wearing a wedding gown. She was another man's bride.

Not his.

She would never be his again.

But the least he could do was protect her. From the armed gunmen. And from himself.

"Gage," she murmured in protest when he pulled away. He easily tugged her off the couch. She turned her back toward him, as if she expected him to finally be able to get those little buttons free.

But he didn't want her free. He wanted her where she could get in no trouble, where she would be in no danger. Penny's bookcase stood open yet. Gage led Megan to it, passing the desk on which the wedding planner had laid out her arsenal. She'd missed a zip tie. It might have held something together. Or she might have intended to use it as Gage did. He wrapped it around Megan's wrists and pulled it tight.

She gasped in protest. "What are you doing?" she asked.

"Protecting you from yourself." And maybe he was protecting himself from her. But he was too proud to admit that, to admit to how close he had come to losing control and taking her.

He pushed her inside the secret closet. She was small enough to fit beside the glass cabinet that had held Penny's arsenal. It was all but empty now. Just a couple of guns left inside.

The wedding planner really did think of everything. Like her daughter had said, she even had a plan for armed gunmen invading her chapel.

"Don't!" Megan protested.

But Gage ignored her and closed the bookcase, locking Megan inside. The little key charm Penny had used to open the case was still inside the lock. He left it there. It wasn't like anyone would notice it.

And from inside Megan couldn't reach it, even if she had been untied. She wouldn't be able to escape. She wouldn't be able to put herself in harm's way. And knowing that would help Gage. He couldn't afford any distractions now, not when he was about to risk his life.

But hell, he would much rather risk his life than his heart again. And if he'd stayed on that couch with Megan, he would have lost his heart entirely.

Anger coursed through Megan, heating her already hot skin. She had wanted Gage so badly, her head clouded with love and desire, that she hadn't realized he'd been tricking her. He'd tied her up. He'd hidden her away.

She strained against the binding around her wrist. But the zip tie was tight, the plastic so hard that it bit into her skin—just like Gage had nipped her bottom lip.

So seductively…

Had it all just been a ploy? A way to distract her so that he could tie her up and tuck her away? Maybe none of it had been real, the kisses or his admission.

She shouldn't have trusted him, just like Richard had warned her. When she'd broken up with him for Gage, he'd told her that they would stay friends because he knew she would need one. He knew that Gage would break her heart, that he had an ulterior motive in going after her.

She'd been hurt but realistic enough to suspect that Richard was right. She was no great beauty. No exciting lover. But with Gage, she actually had been. Making love with him had made her needy and bold. She'd touched him and kissed him. She'd climbed all over him, sliding his erection inside her, riding him…

A moan slipped out as she felt needy all over again. Her skin tingled, and her body ached. She wanted him even after what he'd done. How he'd tricked her…

Had he tricked her before? Had he just been using her like Tucker and Richard had warned her?

She had begun to doubt that. She'd begun to believe that Gage really had loved her. He'd quit his job, he'd re-enlisted—because of her. He'd admitted that now. And he really had no reason to lie to her.

So if he'd been telling the truth…

Had Richard been lying?

But what reason would he have had? He wasn't a jealous man, like Tucker Allison, who had obviously been jealous of Gage and his success in the Bureau. Richard had never been in love with her, so he'd had no reason for jealousy. Just concern because he had been her friend.

Guilt flashed through her. She'd been so worried about Nikki Payne taking her place that she hadn't given Richard much thought. He was her friend. And he was in every bit as much danger as Nikki and the other guests.

But then Richard wasn't likely to put himself in danger. He wouldn't try to play the hero like Nikki or Gage would. He probably wouldn't do or say anything at all. If he wasn't the groom, the gunmen might have never noticed him.

Derek pushed the button on the walkie-talkie. "Ralph? Ralph?"

"Where the hell is he?" Andrea demanded to know. "He should have brought her up a while ago." Her long body that he'd always found so sexy was tense almost to the point of being sharp—like her voice when she asked, "Do you think she got away?"

"I think she'd be here if she hadn't." And so would Ralph. Unless he couldn't...

"What the hell happened?" Andrea asked—as if he'd been there.

He hadn't, but he suspected he knew. "The father of the bride, the bureau chief..." How the hell had he not known that? Of course he'd been locked up in prison with limited access to the outside. Andrea had done the research. How had she not known? "And the best man... I suspect he's an agent, too."

"Not anymore," the petite brunette remarked from where she sat on the floor.

"Got fired for banging the boss's daughter?" Andrea asked with a smirk.

Nikki Payne shook her head. "Quit to reenlist. He got deployed almost immediately and then went missing for six months. But he survived those six months of captivity and torture and escaped on his own. He's like Rambo."

"Just because he survived torture doesn't mean he's Rambo," Derek replied with a glance at the groom. "Some people are just like cockroaches—hard to kill."

Sweat streaked down the groom's face.

"That's not the case with Gage," the girl said. "He's a killer. It doesn't matter how many guns or guards you have around here. He'll take them all out."

Andrea laughed.

But Derek's blood had chilled with her ominous warning. And he shivered instead.

Andrea tugged him aside. "Are you letting her get to you?" she asked. She lifted her gun. "If she is, I'll shut her up—permanently."

He pulled down the gun. "No."

For some reason he liked the young woman; he respected Nikki Payne's spunk and sass. She was the kind of woman he'd thought he'd married.

Only now he realized Andrea was a stranger to him. Just like someone else was pretending to be...

He gestured toward the profusely sweating groom. "Does he really think I don't recognize him?"

"He doesn't look the same," Andrea said. "Are you sure it's him?"

"It's him," he said. He had recognized him from his engagement notice. Seeing him in person, he was even more certain. "You confirmed it."

Andrea nodded. "Of course."

She'd found the plastic surgeon who had treated Richard's burns. Even the blowtorch hadn't been able to get Richard to admit where he had stashed the loot from their last heist. It had been the biggest.

Would he give it up if they tortured his bride instead? Andrea thought so, but Derek was beginning to doubt it. Richard was nervous but not scared. He wasn't terrified for himself or for his bride.

Derek wanted him scared, scared like he'd been years ago. Derek lifted his gun, but like he'd done with hers, Andrea held the barrel of his. "No. You can't shoot him."

"I went to prison because of him."

She shook her head. "He never testified against you. You went to prison because you were matched to the security footage on the jewelry store cameras."

"Security footage he was supposed to hack in and erase." That was why Richard had been involved. He'd been their computer hacker, their security expert. He'd never held a gun or driven a getaway vehicle. But they wouldn't have gotten into the places they had without his help. He was good—too good to have made a simple mistake like he'd claimed when the security footage had hit all the news outlets.

Derek tried to lift his gun again. He wanted to shoot the bastard—a lot of times. He wanted to take out his knees, then drill holes into his arms until he fired the kill shot right between the bastard's little beady eyes.

"I know you want to kill him," Andrea said.

Want wasn't a strong enough word. He *needed* to kill him.

"But this isn't just about revenge," Andrea reminded him. "We're here for something else."

"But where are they?" Did Richard even have them? Or had he pawned them and blown all the money already?

"We'll find them," Andrea said.

Derek sighed. They had to at least try. Without them they wouldn't be able to get away like they planned—to a country with no extradition.

Glancing down the aisle at the lifeless FBI agent, he sighed. He had already killed. He would drop a lot more bodies to find what he was looking for...

Chapter 18

Except for some rare instances usually involving her kids and Woodrow's agents, the majority of the weddings at Penny's white wedding chapel went very well. Her staff had as much to do with it as she did. She had her own caterers, waiters and bartenders in the reception area of the basement. It was where she'd brought her bag of guns and walkie-talkies.

"We knew something was up," Jimmy the bartender said. "The waiter claimed you'd hired him because you needed extra staff."

Penny shuddered, grateful that the guy hadn't killed Jimmy for asking too many questions.

"He's the only one down here who's a stranger, right?" Woodrow asked.

Penny already knew. She'd recognized everyone else in the hall.

Jimmy replied, "Yeah. But I don't know where he's gone."

"He's no longer a threat," Gage said as he joined them in the reception hall. He glanced around at the fairy lights and flowers. It was beautiful. Was he thinking of how Megan would have married another man here? Or of how she should have been marrying him?

"Where's Megan?" her father anxiously asked. "You didn't send her alone through the tunnel?"

"Of course not," Gage replied. "I stashed her where no one will find her, though."

Behind the bookcase, Penny instinctively knew. She imagined Megan was not happy in the small space. Hopefully, she wouldn't be there long.

"Who's this guy?" the bartender asked, his eyes narrowed with suspicion.

"Gage Huxton," Penny said. "He works for my son Logan."

"A bodyguard," Jimmy said with a slight sigh of relief. "And this guy..." He pointed to Woodrow.

"Father of the bride," Penny said. "And an FBI agent— he's in charge of the Chicago office."

"Okay, we can do this then," Jimmy said.

Penny wasn't so sure she could ask so much of her staff. "It's still going to be dangerous," she warned him and the waiters, waitresses and chefs who'd gathered around them.

"You said Nikki's up there," Jimmy reminded her. "That she's in danger."

"I wondered why our phones weren't working..." one of the waitresses murmured.

"Cell jammer," Penny said. "We can't call out and we can't go out. All the doors are blocked."

"So we can't call for help and we can't expect any help to get in," Jimmy said. "Sounds like we have no choice."

"You do," she assured them. "You can hide."

Like Gage had hidden Megan. There were more nooks and crannies than the bookcase in her office and the secret passageway at the end of the hall. She could find safe places for all of them.

Jimmy shook his head. "No. We can't. Nikki's in danger. She's family."

That was the way Penny had always felt, like her staff was family. That was why she struggled with the thought of putting them in danger.

Woodrow had no such struggle. "Let me tell you the plan then," he said. And like a colonel, he began directing his makeshift army of her trusted waitstaff.

But the only real soldier of the group was the most impatient. "We've got to go," Gage said. "We can't waste any more time."

He was probably eager to get back to Megan. But there was no guarantee that he would. There was no guarantee that any of them would survive. They all started off after Gage anyway. When she moved to follow, Woodrow caught her shoulders. Staring down into her face, he ordered her like he had the others, "You are staying here."

She shook her head. "I can't ask my staff to risk their lives unless I'm willing to risk mine."

"I'm not willing to risk yours," Woodrow told her.

She could have said something about his risking Nikki's. But she knew he hadn't done that lightly. Nikki had been insistent and convincing that she could handle the danger far better than Megan could.

Penny would be insistent and convincing, too. "I am going," she said. "Nobody knows this place like I do."

"We know where we're going," Woodrow said. "And we know what we're doing."

"And I know where I'm going and what I'm doing, too," she insisted as she tried to tug away from him and step around his long body.

His hands tightened on her shoulders, easily holding her in place. "You're stubborn," he said. "Do I need to lock you up like Gage did Megan?" As big as he was, he could probably easily toss her over his shoulder.

But Penny wouldn't go down without one hell of a fight. She ignored the flash of excitement she felt over a physical struggle with Woodrow Lynch.

"Your daughter is safely locked away," she said. "Mine's not. Mine is up there with that crazy woman who already tried to shoot her."

"Penny—"

She shook her head. "But she hasn't been shot," she said with a little breath of relief. "Not yet."

He looked at her as if he wanted to believe her, but he'd been in law enforcement long enough to be a cynical man. And he'd seen Nikki at her most stubborn and fearless.

If anyone would have tested the gunmen, it would have been Nikki. If anyone had been shot, it hadn't been her.

"I would *know*," she said.

Maybe Woodrow would think she was crazy—like some others did. But she had never hidden who she was. "I would *know* if one of my children was hurt."

"You're saying you're psychic?"

She shook her head again. "If I was psychic, I never would have called Nikki to help me." She would have known the danger in which she would be putting her only daughter. "But I have a special connection with my kids. I know when one of them is hurt."

He nodded. "You're empathetic."

She grabbed up one of the guns left atop the prettily set table.

"And impatient," he added.

"I am also a damn good shot," she said. Her husband had taught her when they were first married. Then she had been the one to teach their sons, because her husband had died before he could. "You need me up there."

Woodrow was beginning to think that he just needed her too much to let her put herself in danger. She was also too strong and determined for him to argue with her anymore. Before she could pass him, he caught her shoulders and swung her back around to face him.

Ready to fight, she opened her mouth. And he kissed her. His lips slid over hers, stroking back and forth. He enjoyed the friction—the sensations that he hadn't felt in so long. His blood heated; his pulse beat faster. He'd never been so excited by just a kiss. But then, Penny Payne was special. He'd known it the first moment he'd met her.

Finally, he pulled back and stared down at her.

"Why did you do that?" she asked.

He could have told her that he'd meant it just as a distraction. But he knew that was a lie. He just hoped he wasn't lying when he assured her, "We'll get Nikki out safely."

"You don't know that's possible," she said. "Don't make promises to me that you can't keep."

Another man had done that to her. He'd promised—in this very church—to be faithful. But he'd fathered a child with another woman. He'd betrayed her in the worst way a spouse could be betrayed.

Woodrow knew her pain. He'd experienced it himself. It didn't matter to him that Megan wasn't his child. And he'd been careful that no one else realized the truth. But he worried that Megan suspected. She might not have remembered her mother, but she'd seen photos. Hell, she'd seen Ellen, who looked exactly like her. Blonde. Like Woodrow had been before he'd gone gray. And blue eyed. Like Woodrow. He worried that was why Megan had always considered herself unattractive—because she didn't look like them.

But she was his. No matter that she didn't have his DNA, he loved her like his child. He loved Penny Payne, too, but in an entirely different way.

"I don't make promises I don't intend to keep," he told her. He'd promised his dying wife that he would raise Megan like his own. And he'd kept that promise. Not out of obligation. But love. He would keep this promise to Penny for the same reason—because he loved her.

He held her chin in his hand, his fingertips stroking over her silky skin, until she met his gaze. She stared at him for a long moment before she finally nodded, accepting that he spoke the truth.

He drew in a breath, heavy with the responsibility he'd just accepted. But before he could turn away, she reached up and kissed his lips.

With a smile, Gage glanced away from the older couple. He'd figured something was going on with Woodrow and Penny Payne. He hadn't known for certain what it was until he'd gone back to see what was keeping them and caught them kissing.

There was attraction between them, but it was more than that. It was deeper. It was real.

Watching Woodrow and Penny made Gage long to see Megan before they headed up to the chapel. He wanted to make certain she was all right, that she hadn't cut her wrists trying to get off the zip tie. That she wasn't panicking in the close confines of the cramped closet.

And more importantly he wanted to see her again, to look deeply into the fathomless depths of her dark eyes. He wanted to touch her again, the silkiness of her skin, the softness of her hair. He needed to be with her—just one last time—in case he didn't return from his mission.

But if he took her out of her hiding place, he doubted he would be able to get her back in. She would be like Penny, insistent on putting herself in danger.

As much as he wanted to see her again, it was better that he not risk it. It was better that he not be distracted with thoughts of her, either. With how beautiful she looked in that damn wedding gown...

With how badly he'd wanted to get her out of it, and not just so that she wouldn't marry another man. Despite everything he'd gone through because of her, he wanted her. But she wasn't his.

Even though her wedding had been hijacked, she'd intended to marry another man. Gage had to push that thought from his mind, too, or he might not try as hard to save Richard as he would the others.

And if he let her groom die, he doubted Megan would ever forgive him. She must have cared about the guy to have been his friend even before she'd become his fiancée. She wouldn't want to lose him.

Would she care if she lost Gage? She hadn't last time.

Or she wouldn't have been in this church—about to marry another man.

Gage had to remind himself of that. While he loved her, she had never really loved him. She'd said so herself.

Chapter 19

"Gage!" Megan shouted his name. She wanted to hurl obscenities at him, tell him that she hated him for tricking her.

For tying her up.

For shoving her in a closet.

But no matter what he'd done, she would never be able to hate Gage Huxton. She loved him too much.

And still she'd failed to tell him that. She'd apologized for doubting him. But she hadn't owned up to her lie. She hadn't admitted the truth. That she had loved him with all her heart. That she loved him still, even as much as he infuriated her.

Anger coursing through her, she struggled against the zip tie, wincing as the plastic cut her skin. Maybe she could rub it against something. Her wrists bound behind her back, she ran her hands over the glass case, trying to find a sharp edge. She couldn't feel one, but maybe she could find a way to break the glass.

She turned. But in the tight space, her bodice scraped against the glass. The rhinestones scratched the surface, etching deep, so deeply that the glass cracked and then fell to the floor at her feet. It narrowly missed her polished toes peeping out of the front of her white satin pumps.

A gasp of surprise slipped through her lips. How the hell had that happened?

Then realization dawned. She remembered how Andrea had looked at that dress. She must have realized what Megan just had. Those bits of sparkle weren't rhinestones.

She wasn't the one they were really after. It was the damn dress. And all this time her father and Gage had been blaming themselves. She had seen the guilt on their faces. There had also been tension between them, so they'd probably been blaming each other as well.

But this whole thing had had nothing to do with them. They weren't responsible for the danger she was in—and that everyone in the church was now in.

She was. She had made a horrible mistake. And if something happened to either of the men she loved, or to anyone else, she would never forgive herself.

Nikki strained, but she was only able to catch bits and pieces of Andrea and D's intense conversation. But she saw the way they kept looking at Richard and she filled in the blanks.

"It's you," she said. "You're the reason they're here."

He shook his head, and some of his sweat spattered

onto the marble floor. Like the young agent's blood had spattered the white runner.

Was he dead? Had a man died because of Richard?

"I thought you were just some computer nerd," she mused. She was a computer nerd, too. While Logan had refused to let her do field bodyguard work, he'd put her in charge of the Payne Protection Agency's internet security. She didn't just protect their systems, though. She'd learned to hack everyone else's. Hacking was far more dangerous than her brothers knew. "What the hell did you do?"

"Nothing," he said. But his face flashed with the lie, and his beady little eyes glanced away from her.

"You did something," she said. "You know who these people are."

She saw it in their faces now, the recognition. They knew him. She wanted to know him, too. She doubted he was who he'd claimed, because, as protective as Woodrow Lynch was, he would have checked out his baby girl's fiancé. Just like her brothers would have checked out anyone she dated, if she'd ever really dated.

"Who are you really?" she asked. She deserved to know the real identity of the man who was probably going to get her killed.

He shook his head and spattered more sweat.

A droplet landed on her cheek, and she grimaced, repulsed. Better sweat than tears.

"I'm not that man anymore," he said. "He's dead."

"He should have been," D said as he joined them, his gun pointed at Richard's face. "How the hell did a little wuss like you survive what I did to you?"

Richard sat up straighter, and it was as if his shoulders widened. As if he grew…

It had all been an act—the cowering, the slouching…

"You made the mistake of thinking just because I'm smart I'm not tough, too," Richard said.

If she hadn't wanted to kill him herself, Nikki could have commiserated with the guy. She'd battled the same prejudice.

"Oh, I'm not sure how smart you are," D said. "Putting that engagement notice in the newspaper was one hell of a mistake."

Richard stroked his fingers along his jaw. "Really. You recognized me?" He glanced beyond D—at Andrea, whose face paled.

Something was going on, something more than even D realized.

"The plastic surgeon fixed the scars," D said. "But he didn't change you enough that I wouldn't know you when I saw you again."

Richard sighed. "I never thought I'd see you again."

"I'm sure you didn't," D agreed. "Not after you left that footage on the security camera so I'd be caught."

A smirk spread across Richard's face. "I see you learned to cover up your tattoos now. Not too smart to have such identifiable ones, at least not in your business."

"What is your business?" Nikki asked.

"None of yours," Andrea answered for them. "Come on D," she said. "Let's get out of here. The cops will be coming soon."

"Yeah, because of that shot you fired," he said, and he stared at her with suspicion. "You did that because you want the cops to come. You want me to go back to prison."

"Of course not!" she said. "Why would I have broken you out if that was what I wanted?"

Nikki suspected Andrea was one of those women who didn't know what she wanted beyond attention. And she didn't particularly care what man gave it to her as long as she got it. She snorted in derision.

Andrea ignored her. But D glanced down at her. "What?"

"The police are the least of your worries right now," she said. "Those landscapers, the ones your guy said look all alike?"

D nodded. "What about them?"

"They're my brothers."

Andrea laughed now. "That's cute. You think your big brothers can come save you."

"I know they will," she said. "They'll save us all and send you two either to prison or to the morgue." She offered a pitying sigh.

Andrea laughed again, albeit nervously.

"Who are they?" D asked. "FBI?"

"One of them was," Nikki replied. "Nick worked for the father of the bride. He's the FBI agent who cleaned up the corruption in River City. My brother Cooper was a Marine. The twins were cops. Now they're all bodyguards with the Payne Protection Agency."

D flinched as he recognized the name. Even in prison he must have heard about them. Her brothers had sent a lot of criminals to join him behind bars.

"But they're the least of your concerns," she said. "Gage Huxton is the one you should fear."

"Gage?"

"The blond guy," she said.

He glanced around as if he expected Gage to pop up out of a pew. "Rambo?" He smirked as he repeated it.

Nikki laughed. "Yeah, he's a former FBI agent, former Marine and now he's a bodyguard. And trust me, protecting the bride is the assignment he takes more seriously than any of his other ones."

D shuddered as if he'd seen a ghost or feared he was about to become one.

"We need to get out of here," Andrea implored him again.

He shook her off his arm. "I'm not leaving him alive," he said as he shoved his gun against Richard's head. "And I'm not leaving without the diamonds."

It was going down now. Nikki moved her hand, shoving it beneath the skirt of her dress. But before she could reach her holster, D grabbed her arm. "You're a bodyguard, too," he said. "Just like your brothers. That's why you switched places with the bride—to protect her." He turned his gun on her now. "So who's going to protect you?"

She lifted her knee, ramming it into his groin and dropped him to his knees. She heard other guns cock and she ducked, bracing herself for the flurry of gunfire. It came—from everywhere. The balcony, the vestibule.

It was like a war, with shots going everywhere. Before she could reach for her gun, someone was grabbing her, dragging her behind the altar toward the groom's dressing room. Nikki didn't dare lift her head.

She knew she wasn't being rescued. She was being taken hostage and used as a human shield against all those flying bullets.

Help had finally arrived—for everyone else. It would do no good for Nikki.

Gunfire exploded around him with blasts of light and sound, Gage waited for the paralysis that had gripped him before. Any time he'd been in a gun battle since his escape, he'd frozen, reeling with flashbacks to those other battles lost.

But he moved now, his instincts guiding him like they had for his escape. He aimed and squeezed, taking down the gunmen guarding the doors to the vestibule. Then he turned toward the outside doors just as they opened and fired on the two guys who'd begun to rush inside. They never made it through the doors, which closed on them, leaving them outside—wounded or worse.

As the guy standing near the altar advanced down the aisle, firing on them, Gage shoved Woodrow aside and fired back. The guy dropped, but maybe he'd just fallen over the body lying on the runner. Gage advanced slowly, cautiously, his barrel pointed directly at the man's head.

D was lying on that runner, blood pooling beneath him. It turned the white fabric a dark crimson and ran across the marble tiles, too. Gage had hit him. Hell, he must have struck an artery. He dropped to his knees beside him. But there was no saving him.

"I'm dying," D said with an eerily calm acceptance.

Gage nodded. "Yes, you are. Help's coming..." After all the shooting, the police were certain to arrive.

"I'll be dead before they get inside." There were more men outside, more men fighting. Gage could hear the gunfire. He waited to flash back again, especially when he stared down at the dying man. He waited to see the faces of other men, of fellow Marines he hadn't been able to save, of enemies he'd had to kill in order to survive. But he saw only the man who lay before him.

"I think I knew you'd do it," D said. "The first time I saw you. I think I knew that if anyone was going to take me out, it would be you..."

"Am I the reason you're here?" Gage asked.

The guy shook his head, and blood trickled from the corner of his mouth. "No."

"Woodrow?"

"Who?"

"Are you here because of me?" Woodrow asked as he leaned over the dying man, too.

Derek shook his head again, and more blood gurgled out of his mouth.

"Then what do you want?" Woodrow asked. "Why did you put my daughter in danger?"

D's thin lips curved into a slight smile, and he remarked, "You have no idea who the real danger is..."

"So Megan's still in danger?" Gage asked, his heart beating in his throat. He was more nervous now than when he'd been in the gunfight.

Now D nodded, or he tried. He only moved his head slightly before the last of his life slipped away.

He was a horrible man. Gage knew that. But he felt a pang of regret that he'd killed him. Now he might never know the real reason they'd taken the church hostage. All he knew was that Megan was still in danger.

And despite their best efforts, the church wasn't secure yet.

He turned toward his former boss and mentor. He could stay and help him. Or...

Woodrow read his look and urged him, "Go. Get Megan out of here."

That was what he wanted, what his instincts were screaming at him to do.

"But we don't know if there was any truth to what he said."

Woodrow nodded in agreement. "We can't trust him. But we can't trust anyone."

No, they couldn't. Gage straightened up. He would go. He would make certain that Megan got to safety this time.

But would *she* trust him? Would she leave with him this time? Or was she already gone? Sure, he'd tied her up. But he knew about the games Woodrow had taught her and her sister when they were kids.

He knew she knew how to escape being tied up. Had she freed herself from the bookcase? If she had, she might do something stupid. She might trust someone she shouldn't.

He had to get to her—before anyone else did.

Chapter 20

"She's gone." Penny's heart sank as she realized Nikki was nowhere in the chapel. No matter how many times she kept peering around the pews for her, she could catch no sight of her beautiful girl.

Some people cowered in the pews, weeping with fear or maybe relief now if they realized they'd been rescued. Penny knew she wouldn't find Nikki cowering or crying. Even as a child Nikki had rarely cried. She probably hadn't wanted to betray any weakness in front of her older brothers.

Penny turned back to Woodrow where he crouched beside the two men lying in the aisle of her church. She didn't really want to look at them, to know that they were gone. That Nikki might have gone that way, too.

When Woodrow met her gaze, she let her resentment spill over in a glare. If he hadn't insisted that she wait in the vestibule until the shooting was over, she might have seen what had happened to her daughter.

"Maybe she ran out," Woodrow suggested.

Other guests had run out during the shooting. But Penny knew her youngest. She was every bit as stubborn as her brothers—maybe even more so. Nikki wouldn't have run away from danger. She would have run straight into it. Her foolish girl knew no fear.

Penny shook her head. "No, there's no way she would have run away."

"Then she has to be here," Woodrow said, reaching out to squeeze her shoulder. His blue eyes held such concern—and something else.

Unable to hold his gaze and acknowledge his feelings and maybe her own, Penny looked down. Then she shuddered at the sight of those bodies lying in the church aisle. She recognized D, the gunman who'd died as violently as she suspected he had lived.

"Who is he?" she asked about the young wedding guest. He had been sitting on the bride's side.

Woodrow uttered a ragged sigh. "He worked for me," he admitted. "But he shouldn't have. He had no business being an agent."

Tears stung Penny's eyes over the loss of such a young life. She suspected he'd been trying to impress Woodrow when he'd drawn his gun. Instead of getting praise, he'd taken a bullet. Or two. He hadn't died in the recent gunfire, because someone had already tried to treat his injuries.

Nikki...

Somehow Penny just *knew* that Nikki had pressed the jacket against the wound and bound it with the belt. She wouldn't have been able to not help unless she'd been too injured to help herself. Then she might be where Penny couldn't see her.

Penny stepped over the bodies on the bloody runner and hurried down the aisle toward the front. There was no blood near the altar. No bride or groom, either.

Richard was gone, too. But she cared less about him than about Nikki. There was something about him... something that had made her uneasy. She'd known Megan shouldn't marry him. But she'd thought that was just because Megan's heart belonged to another man.

Woodrow had followed her, and he peered around too. "I don't see the woman."

"Andrea." She'd left her husband to face the gun battle alone? Left him to die alone? "Doesn't anyone honor their commitments anymore?" she murmured.

"No," Woodrow said. "But maybe he told her to leave. Maybe he wanted to protect her." Like Woodrow had tried to protect her.

Penny snorted. "A woman like her doesn't need protection. People need to be protected from her, especially Megan." The woman had been insistent that the fake waiter deliver the real bride to her. Maybe she'd gone downstairs to get her herself.

Woodrow nodded in agreement. "Gage went down to make sure Megan is safe," he admitted.

She knew. Gage had passed her as he'd been leaving the chapel and she'd been entering. He'd barely spared her a glance he'd been so anxious to get back downstairs. But he'd looked pale—haunted.

"Was it Gage?" she asked as she gestured back at the gunman lying in the aisle as well as the two in the vestibule.

Woodrow nodded. "I understand now how he survived those six months. He's almost superhuman."

Nikki wasn't superhuman. She was just a very petite girl. Would she survive?

"Where is she?" Penny murmured, tears of frustration stinging her eyes. In the distance sirens wailed. Help was coming. But would it be too late?

Then something else wailed, closer than those distant sirens. Someone else, actually—it was a woman screaming. Penny wasn't certain that it was Nikki. She had never heard her daughter scream before. Every maternal instinct in her reacted, and she ran toward that scream.

The scream struck Woodrow like a blow to his heart. He wasn't sure if it was his daughter or Penny's who'd cried out in such fear. But he didn't care.

He ran toward that scream. Fortunately, his legs were longer than Penny's, and he passed her before she could burst through the closed door of the groom's dressing room.

He didn't want her getting hurt by what was happening or what she might see. She was already upset over the bodies of the strangers lying in the aisle of her beautiful little chapel. She didn't need to see her daughter if Nikki had been hurt.

Or worse.

Now more shots rang out again, echoing inside the church. Those people who'd stayed behind ran now, stumbling in their haste to escape. Falling over those dead bodies. But they had no reason to be fearful. The gunfire and the screaming emanated from the groom's dressing room.

Woodrow reached for the handle and found the door locked.

Inside that locked room, the woman screamed again. Woodrow stepped back then rushed forward, slamming his shoulder and hip against the door. Wood splintered as the frame cracked and the door sprang open.

"Nikki?" he called out for her. She had to be the one inside the room. Gage had hidden Megan away. No harm could have come to her.

Penny's daughter was the one in danger—because of him, because he'd agreed to let her sacrifice her safety to protect Megan. If something had happened to her, Penny would never forgive him.

And he would never forgive himself.

Nikki wasn't one of his agents. She wasn't even a real bodyguard. She'd had no business taking on such a dangerous assignment.

"Nikki!" he called out again.

But his only reply was the rapid retort of more gunfire. It flashed and banged, so close that he felt the burn and vibration of it. Then he realized why he'd physically felt the gunfire; he'd been hit.

Most of Woodrow's fifty-five years had been spent as an FBI field agent—some before that, like so many of his best agents, as a Marine. Despite all the dangerous missions and assignments he'd carried out, he had never been shot before. Maybe he was wrong, though. Since he had never been shot before, he couldn't be certain that he had been now. Maybe he was just experiencing shock, like the numbness the agents felt after taking a bullet in their vest. But Woodrow wasn't wearing a vest beneath his tuxedo.

He hadn't thought he would need one for his daughter's wedding. He should have known better. He should have known that bad things could happen anywhere, even in Penny Payne's beautiful little wedding chapel.

Heat radiated across his chest. Was it his blood? Or was he having a heart attack as well? He reached up and clutched his chest. And blood oozed between his fingers.

His knees began to shake, threatening to fold beneath him. He stepped back—out of the doorway—so that he wouldn't be hit again.

It might not have mattered. He knew sometimes that all it took was one shot. One shot to kill…

Locked away behind the bookcase, trapped beside the glass cabinet, Megan shouldn't have been able to hear the gunfire. For some reason it was louder inside her confined space, as if the weapons were being fired directly over her. The chapel was above the other area—the dead end of the hallway where she could have escaped through the secret passage. Or she could have run right into the arms of her captors.

That was why Gage had locked her up, for her safety. But she didn't feel safe. Each shot had her flinching as she expected the bullet to penetrate her flesh. She was safe, thanks to Gage. It was everyone else who was in danger.

Gage.

Her father.

The Paynes.

Richard? Was he in danger? Or was he the danger? She stared down at her dress. How had she not noticed? Because she hadn't paid that much attention to the dress.

She had wanted to wear her mother's dress, but Richard—who didn't care any more about fashion than she did—had insisted on designing her wedding gown. She'd been surprised, but if—as he'd claimed—he'd wanted everything to be perfect, she wasn't going to argue with him.

Of course she'd known nothing was perfect, because she'd thought Gage was dead. He hadn't been then. She had no idea about now.

He'd vowed to protect her, and that would probably prove his most dangerous mission ever. She wasn't the one everyone wanted, but she had what they wanted.

Why had Richard done it? She needed to get out and warn Gage and her dad and Nikki—if it wasn't already too late. Richard wasn't who any of them had thought he was.

They might already know that. Another gunshot drew her attention up, and she noticed the speaker above her. Mrs. Payne, who thought of everything, must have had a sound system installed so that she could stay apprised of what was happening even when she was down in her office.

While Megan could hear the shots, she couldn't hear anything else. No voices. She didn't know if someone had been shot. Or killed...

She could only imagine the worst.

The worst was Gage, his beautiful green eyes open but unseeing, lying lifeless inside the church. Gage dying without ever knowing how much she had loved him. Without knowing that she would always love him...

She couldn't lose him.

Not again...

She struggled again against the zip tie then remembered that she'd broken the case. Finding the jagged edge of glass of the cabinet, she ground the plastic against it.

The glass scratched her wrists. But she ignored the pain, and in seconds, the zip tie snapped free.

She uttered a ragged breath of relief that echoed inside the small room. She could get out now. But there was no handle inside the cabinet, no way to get that bookcase to slide open again.

Maybe if she just pushed on it…

As she pushed, someone else pulled. Someone had found her. She had no time to turn and reach for a weapon before the bookcase slid open. She had no time to protect herself from the danger that awaited her.

She was the one who had what everyone wanted, the reason people were willing to risk prison and death.

And they would have no qualms about killing her to get what they wanted. She had no time to grab a gun from the case and load it. So she did the only thing she could— she propelled herself at the person who'd found her, intent on defending herself. But she wasn't fighting for her life. She was fighting so that she could help the others.

She was fighting for Gage.

Chapter 21

Fists pummeled his chest and shoulders. Feet kicked his shins and knees. Gage grasped the struggling bundle of lace and brocade and rhinestones, clutching Megan close.

"Hey, hey, calm down," he told her. He'd had no idea how angry she could get. This was even worse than when she'd broken up with him. Then she hadn't been angry so much as cold. "I shut you in there for your protection."

And for his, too. If he'd thought she was in any danger, he would have been distracted, so distracted that D might have killed him instead of the other way around.

He felt a flash of regret, not so much that the man had died but that he'd died with his secrets. Gage still had no idea why he'd taken the wedding hostage.

Megan stilled—finally—the fight leaving her body. And she gasped his name on a breath that whispered across his throat.

So when she'd been struggling with him, she hadn't known it was him at all. She'd thought he was someone else, someone who might have hurt her. And she'd fought him. She'd fought him for her life.

He moved his hands to her face. Cupping it in his palms, he tipped it up to him. Tears glistened in her brown eyes. She must have been so afraid. He leaned down and brushed a kiss across her lips. "It's okay... it's just me."

Her breath shuddered out against his mouth, and she deepened the kiss. Her arms slid around his neck, and she clutched him closely. "You're okay!"

And he realized she hadn't been afraid for herself at all. She'd been afraid for him. "Yeah, I'm fine."

But she pulled back and ran her hands over him, as if she didn't believe him, as if she had to check for herself. If he'd been shot, he hadn't realized it. He felt no pain, or he hadn't until she touched him. But he felt a different kind of pain, the kind from desire overwhelming him. He wanted her. He *needed* her.

But he needed more to make certain that she was safe. D's words rang in his head. *You have no idea who the real danger is...*

"You're not hurt," she said.

But she was. He gently grasped her hands and lifted them. Blood smeared her skin and trailed down her wrists to saturate the cuffs of the lace sleeves of her gown.

She must have struggled so hard to break the zip tie that she'd hurt herself. Guilt and regret gripped him. "I'm sorry," he said. "I shouldn't have tied you up."

He hadn't known how determined she would be to escape—so determined that she would hurt herself.

She shook her head. "I did this on the broken glass."

He glanced behind her at the cabinet. She'd struggled even harder than he'd realized. "Why would you fight so hard to get free?"

"I wanted to help," she said.

"Help…"

"I heard all the shots—" her voice cracked with fear "—and I thought you were hurt."

He shook his head. "None hit me." He'd fired more than he'd dodged. But the gunfire hadn't stopped. It rang out now, echoing inside Penny's office.

"What about my dad? Or the Paynes…"

He waited for her to ask about Richard, but she didn't. And relief eased the tightness on his chest. He hadn't looked for Richard. He didn't know if her groom had been shot. Or worse.

Once he'd stopped D, he hadn't cared about the others, especially after hearing the dying man's warning. He'd cared only about her—about making sure she was safe.

"We have to get out of here," he said. "It's still too dangerous."

More of the men from the outside must have come into the church. It was only a matter of time before they searched the basement.

He could shoot at them like he had earlier. But he didn't want her getting caught in the cross fire. When he slid his arm around her, she tensed against him.

"No," she said. "We can't leave."

"We have to—"

And she began to struggle again. Now that she knew it was him, she didn't kick or hit. But she wriggled, pushing her hips against his groin and her breasts against his chest. He groaned as his body tensed—with desire.

"Megan," he warned her. "Be still…"

"I'm not leaving," she said. "Not until I know my dad is all right."

"Your dad told me to get you out of here," Gage said.

"You don't work for him anymore," she reminded him. "You don't have to listen to him."

"Your dad isn't the reason I want to make sure you're safe," he said.

Her face flushed, maybe from her struggle, maybe from embarrassment. "That's right. You're a bodyguard now. And protecting the bride is your assignment."

Protecting her wasn't a job to him; it was a necessity—such a necessity that he ignored her struggles and lifted her. Slinging her over his shoulder fireman style, he carried her from the office and down the hall toward that secret passage. While he kept his hand locked around hers, he had to let her down to get inside the narrow tunnel. He couldn't carry her through it. He couldn't even stand upright himself. He had to hunch over, but still his shoulders and back scraped the stone walls.

Going through it reminded him of his escape from captivity. The confined space, with its musty dankness, cut off his breath. He also knew that if anyone caught them—on either end—they just had to shoot into the tunnel to kill them both. They were more vulnerable here than they'd been anywhere else.

He'd gripped her hand to tug her along behind him. And it gave him some comfort, having the warmth and softness. This time he wasn't alone. But he'd rather be alone than risking her life with his.

"Gage," she murmured. "Are you all right?" She must have heard his erratic breathing or maybe even the crazy fast pounding of his heart. It beat so hard that his body shook with it—trembled. Or maybe he'd been gripping her hand too tightly. She was already injured. He forced himself to ease his grasp.

She squeezed his hand, offering a reassurance he hadn't had those six months. A comfort he'd been denied. God, how he'd needed her then.

Even more than he needed her now. But he was glad he'd been alone, glad he'd endured those atrocities by himself. He never wanted her to experience the pain that he had. He didn't even want her to know about it.

It was too late for the fear. She was afraid. Even though she offered assurance, her hand trembled in his. She was scared, too. She must have realized what he had.

That they weren't safe.

He'd been right to question the wisdom of escaping this way. Because there was no light at the end of this tunnel, only the dark shadow of the man who waited for them, his gun barrel trained on them. At least Gage was first. The bullets would hit him before they hit her.

Megan blinked against the brightness of the afternoon sunshine. She'd only been in that tunnel a few minutes, but it had been so dark.

She focused and turned to Gage, who knelt on the bricks of the little courtyard. He gasped, gulping in air like they'd been in that tunnel for days instead of minutes. His skin was pale, too. And she realized this tunnel had only affected him because of whatever memories it had conjured up of the nightmare he'd already endured.

"Oxygen! Someone bring some damn oxygen," a dark-haired man called out. She recognized Nicholas Rus. Fortunately, so had Gage before he'd fired his weapon at him.

Someone ran toward them, but it wasn't an EMT. Slender arms circled Megan, clasping her close. "Thank God you're all right," Ellen said. "I was so worried…"

Ellen always worried about her, like a mother hen. But this was the first time Megan had actually given her cause to worry.

"I'm fine," she assured her. But she wasn't so sure about Gage. She pulled away from her sister to stand next to him. "Are you all right?"

Drawing in a deep breath, he nodded. Then he regained his feet and his strength, his shoulders squared and his chin lifted with pride. He'd visibly shaken off the vestiges of the nightmare.

"I'm fine," he said. Then he turned to his best friend and remarked, "No thanks to you. Where the hell was the cavalry when we needed them?"

"I couldn't reach him," Ellen said. "His phone kept going to voice mail." Tears brightened her eyes. "And you'd told me not to call 911, to trust only Nick."

What had Gage gone through that he trusted no one but his best friend? Was it what he'd endured when he'd been captured? Or was it because of her? Because he'd trusted her and she'd broken his heart?

She realized now what she'd done when she'd doubted him, when she'd believed other people over him. But she'd had no idea then that she shouldn't have trusted Richard. She still couldn't believe—she had to be wrong…

"That was a mistake," Gage said. "But I didn't think he'd be irresponsible enough to shut off his damn phone—"

"I had no choice," Nick said. "Your sister would have killed me had I been taking calls while she was in labor."

"What?" Gage asked, his eyes wide with shock. "Annalise had the baby? Is she okay?"

Nick nodded. "She's just furious at you for not answering your phone, though."

"There's a cell jammer—"

"I know," Nick assured him. "Even before I listened to Ellen's voice mails, I knew something was wrong. Penny would have been at the hospital, too, if she'd been able to leave the chapel."

"They're still inside," Gage said. "She and Nikki"

"And Dad," Megan said.

Tears glistened in Ellen's eyes again. They were blue, like their dad's. Their mom had had blue eyes Megan recalled from the photos she'd seen of her. Only Megan had dark eyes and dark hair. She'd figured out in science class what that likely meant, but she'd never had the guts to ask anyone for confirmation. She hadn't wanted to know.

It didn't matter if Woodrow Lynch wasn't biologically her father like he obviously was Ellen's. He was the only parent she had ever known. She couldn't lose him. But what if it was too late?

Her heart pounding with fear as she recalled all those shots, she started toward the little white church.

Gage caught her, holding her back. "We just got you to safety. You are damn well not going back inside."

"But—"

"It's too dangerous," he insisted.

That was why she wanted to go back inside. "It's too dangerous for Dad, then." And he was alone, because he and Gage had insisted on protecting her. He had to know that she wasn't his, but he'd never loved her any less because of it. Maybe he'd even loved her a little more.

Nicholas Rus chuckled. "Nothing's too dangerous for your dad," he said. "He's the toughest guy I know."

Gage nodded in agreement. These men—warriors in

their own right—respected her father immensely. She expelled a slight breath of relief.

"He's safer than you are," Gage said. "The guy—D—"

"Derek Nielsen," Nick finished for him. "He escaped from prison just a few days ago."

Gage turned to him. "How do you know?"

"One of the guys we caught out here told us who was running the show."

Gage shook his head. "I don't think it was him."

"It's his wife," Nick said. "Andrea Nielsen."

Megan shivered as she remembered the dangerous woman.

Gage shook his head. "Just before he died, Derek told me and Woodrow that we didn't know who the real danger was."

"He died?" Nick asked but then answered his own question with a nod. He knew how Derek had died—at Gage's hand. "What did he mean?"

"That we can't trust anyone," Gage said. "I need to get Megan out of here."

"No," she protested. "I'm not leaving until I know that Dad is okay."

"If anything happens to you," Ellen said, "he won't be. It'll destroy him." She knew. She had to. As an RN, she'd taken many science classes. She understood genetics and that Megan likely shared no DNA with Woodrow Lynch. But they shared love and an incredible bond. He'd always tried so hard to protect her. That was probably why he'd never told her the truth. Hell, maybe he hadn't wanted to face it himself.

"You know that," Ellen said. "And you know that he would trust Gage to protect you." She turned to him. "I trust you," she said, but she gave him a hard stare. "Don't let anything happen to my baby sister."

"I won't," he assured her.

"Do you know where to take her?" Nick asked.

Gage nodded. "I know where the Payne Protection safe house is." His arm around Megan, he began to guide her from the courtyard.

But she dragged her heels across the bricks. She needed to tell them about the dress—about Richard. But then what Gage had said to his best friend reminded her of what was most important: "Don't worry about us," he said. "Worry about getting into the church and making sure everyone else is safe."

Nick nodded. "We will."

That was the most important thing. She would tell Gage about the dress and let Nick and the others focus on getting everyone out the church.

Before he left his friend to that job, Gage asked, "Hey, what's my nephew's name?"

Despite the situation, Nick grinned as he replied, "Woodrow Gage Payne."

He had named his son for her father. He would make sure he was all right. She didn't have to worry, but she still had that knot of apprehension in her stomach. Maybe she wasn't afraid for her father, though.

Maybe she was afraid for herself because as Gage suspected, she was pretty sure she was still in danger as long as she had the damn dress.

Nikki leaned down and felt for a pulse. There was none. She'd thought she might have killed someone before. But her brothers hadn't admitted if it had been her gun or her brother Nick's that had fired the kill shot.

They'd told her it didn't matter. They'd been protecting her—like they always had—in case she wouldn't be able to handle taking a life.

There was no doubt now. She had killed someone.

Andrea stared up at her, her last expression one of hatred and shock. Maybe she hadn't thought Nikki had it in her to take a life, either. But with the way Andrea had been wildly firing around the room, she'd had no doubt that the other woman would have killed her had Nikki not killed her first.

She glanced down at herself, looking for holes or blood in her mother's old wedding gown. Surely, she'd been shot, too. With all the bullets she'd fired, how the hell had Andrea missed her?

She heard a gasp and glanced down. Had she been wrong? Was Andrea alive yet? She reached quickly for the woman's weapon, making sure she couldn't pull that trigger again. But she hadn't been wrong. Andrea was definitely dead, but even in death, she tightly grasped her weapon.

The gasp she'd heard became a cry, one of fear and alarm. And she turned toward the doorway where her mother stood. Penny's eyes were huge in a face that had gone deathly pale.

"Mom!" Nikki exclaimed. "Are you okay?"

If Penny had showed up earlier, she might have been shot in the cross fire.

When Andrea had dragged her into the groom's dressing room, she'd closed and locked the door behind them. It was broken now.

Nikki dimly recalled it flying open. But Andrea had been standing between her and the door; she'd fired at it before swinging back toward Nikki.

That was when Nikki had shot her. She must have struck her right in the heart, which had shocked Nikki nearly as much as it had Andrea. She would have doubted that the woman possessed a heart at all.

There was no doubting her mother had a heart. Was she this upset over the dead woman? Or over Nikki firing the bullet that had killed her?

"It's okay, Mom," Nikki assured her. "I had no choice. I had to shoot her."

Penny nodded. "I know. But you didn't do it soon enough."

Nikki glanced down at her dress again. There was no blood. "I'm fine. I didn't get hit." She stepped forward over Andrea's dead body. "Did you?"

Her mother wouldn't have been able to break down the door. But then she wouldn't have needed to. Her mom had keys to every lock in the chapel. She would have just used one of them. Then dread clutched Nikki's stomach. And she knew. Someone else had been hit.

Penny shook her head and tears spilled over, sliding down her face.

Was it one of her brothers? Had they finally managed to get inside only to get shot?

"Who?" Nikki asked. She stepped closer to the broken doorjamb and peered around her mom. She saw Logan and Parker standing near the doors to the vestibule, talking to some uniformed policemen.

Garek and Milek Kozminski—Payne Protection bodyguards and brothers-in-law—were there, too. But they kept their distance from the police. They had their reasons for not trusting them. They stood in the church aisle, staring down.

Where was Cooper? Where was Nick?

She stepped closer, and her mother launched herself into her arms, seeking comfort. Nikki was stunned. She'd never had to comfort her mom, not even when her dad had died. Of course she'd just been a child then, and her mom had been acting strong for all of them. Even when Penny had been confronted with the evidence of her father's affair when Nicholas Rus had showed up in River City, she hadn't needed comfort. She'd offered it instead to Nick and to Nikki.

Now Penny trembled in Nikki's arms. Was it Nick? Was he the one who'd been shot?

She peered around her mother again. Some EMTs leaned over a body lying just outside the dressing room door.

"Who is it?" she demanded to know.

"Woodrow," Penny's voice cracked with emotion. "Woodrow has been shot."

Now regret and remorse gripped Nikki. She wasn't upset that she'd killed Andrea. She was upset that she hadn't killed the bitch sooner. She might have taken out a good man with her. A man who obviously meant a lot to her mother.

Penny had already lost too much. She couldn't lose this man, too.

Chapter 22

As the metal door slid closed behind them, Gage breathed a sigh of relief. The condo had been converted from an old warehouse to living space. It was all exposed brick and metal and polished concrete floors. He cared less about how it looked than about how secure it was with a security system only the Kozminskis—renowned jewel thieves—had been capable of cracking. Since they had designed it, no one else could get inside. No one else had been able to get to Gage's sister when Nick had brought Annalise here.

Gage had brought Megan for the same reason that Nick had brought Annalise: to keep her safe. But could he? Even if they rounded up all the hired gunmen at the church, he doubted she would be safe yet.

You have no idea who the real danger is...

Megan shivered, as if she'd heard his thoughts. Or maybe she was just cold. He touched the buttons on the security panel. Not only did it make sure no one would breach the doors or windows, it turned up the thermostat as well. "It'll warm up in here soon," he promised her.

She shook her head. "It doesn't matter. We can't stay here."

"Yes, we can," he said. "Nobody can get inside. You're safe." At least she was safe from whatever dangers lurked outside. She wasn't safe from him. He wanted her.

How the tunnel had affected him had proven to him that he wasn't the man he'd once been. He was getting better. He hadn't flashed back during the shoot-out. But he'd nearly crumpled in that tunnel. If not for her hand holding his, he might have.

Despite this temporary comfort, he couldn't count on her fixing him. It had been months since he'd escaped, and he hadn't been able to fix himself. Sure, he was better. But he would never be whole again. He would never be the man he'd once been. That was why he could never be with her; it wouldn't be fair to put her through that.

"We need to go back," she said.

"And get in their way?" he asked. "Every agent with Payne Protection is at the church." But for him. "They will get everyone safely out of there."

She released a shuddery breath and nodded. "I know. I know my being there would probably only put everyone in more danger." Her big brown eyes glistened with tears of guilt and concern.

"So you accept that you're still in danger?"

Biting her bottom lip, she nodded again.

His stomach tightened as need coursed through him. He wanted to bite her bottom lip—gently—to pull it inside his mouth and nibble on it. He wasn't strong enough now—after that damn tunnel—to resist the temptation. He lowered his head and did exactly what he'd just imagined.

He kissed her just as he'd wanted. Deeply. Passionately. And she kissed him back, her fingers sliding over his nape, holding his head down to hers. She nibbled on his lips, too, and shyly slid her tongue into his mouth.

And now he wanted more than kisses.

He wanted her—wanted to bury himself inside her—to feel connected with her the way they used to connect. When they'd made love, he had never felt closer to anyone than he had to her, so close that they'd been part of each other.

Her hands slid away from his neck and she stepped back until his arms—that he hadn't even realized he'd wound around her—dropped back to his sides. He drew in a deep breath as he fought for control. He couldn't connect to her as he once had. He wasn't the same man.

And she was engaged to someone else. If the gunmen hadn't laid siege to the chapel, she would have been married to Richard. She would have been leaving for her honeymoon.

The thought struck him like a blow, nearly doubling him over with pain. She wasn't his.

"I'm sorry," he said. He shouldn't have kissed her. He had no right. Not anymore.

While that hadn't stopped him at the church, he'd known then that he couldn't go beyond kissing her. There had been too much going on.

Too much danger…

The danger wasn't over yet, but it couldn't get to them here. The only danger was Gage acting on the desire he felt for her.

"Don't be scared," he told her.

She glanced at the heavy steel door. "You said we're safe here."

"We are," he agreed. "I don't want you to be scared of me."

"I'm not," she replied—too quickly.

"You should be," he said.

She'd seen him snap a man's neck. Had been there when he'd freaked out in the tunnel. And she had to know that he'd taken out more than one man with his gun during the shoot-out. She would be crazy to not be afraid of him.

Her lips curved into a slight smile, a sad smile. "I used to be afraid of you," she admitted.

"When?" he asked.

She had never betrayed any fear. But then she was far braver than he'd ever known.

"The first time we met," she said. "At my father's house, you terrified me."

"Then?" He laughed at the thought of anyone fearing him then. Compared to the man he was now, he'd been a clueless kid then. Harmless. "Why?"

"Because of how you looked at me," she said.

He could imagine how that had been—like he'd wanted to eat her alive. He suspected he was looking at her that way right now, because he wanted her even more now than he had then.

Even though the condo had begun to warm up, she shivered again. "No one had ever looked at me that way before." Her throat moved as she swallowed. "Or since…"

Gage finally let himself ask the question that had been burning him up with jealousy. "Then why did you agree to marry Richard?"

"Because I was afraid of you," she said. "I was afraid of how you made me feel, of how easily you could hurt me."

He shook his head. "I never would have hurt you." Not then. He wasn't sure what he was capable of now; he wasn't the same person he'd once been. That was why he couldn't risk getting into a relationship with her again, even if she was interested.

"And I felt safe with Richard," she continued, "like he couldn't hurt me…"

He heard the doubt now. "You don't believe that anymore?"

As if bracing herself, she sucked in a breath. "I need to tell you something."

Nerves clenched his stomach muscles again. "What?"

"I'll tell you," she said. "But first you have to get me the hell out of this dress!"

Megan's heart leaped like the passion in Gage's green eyes. His pupils dilated. And he stepped closer to her. He must have thought she wanted out of her dress in order to be naked with him. She opened her mouth to explain. But as much as she wanted the dress off, she wanted Gage even more.

His arms remained at the sides of his tense body, and he shook his head. "This is a bad idea…"

It was. She knew that for all the reasons she'd just told him. She was afraid of him, not of what he would do to her but of how he made her feel. Too much.

"I can't stay in this dress," she said.

He drew back as if she'd doused him with a bucket of ice water. "Of course. Yeah, you've wanted out of that dress all day."

And that was before she'd realized what it was all

about; she'd never wanted to wear it in the first place. "Please," she implored him. "Help me get it off."

He reached into his pocket and pulled out a knife. With a flick of his thumb, the blade popped out. "Turn around," he told her.

She immediately spun around, presenting her back to him. He tunneled his fingers into her hair and lifted the heavy weight off her neck. But that left him with only one hand to wield the knife, so she replaced his hand with hers, holding her hair up and out of his way.

"I wish I hadn't lost all of my pins earlier," she remarked.

"I'm glad you did," he said.

Heat flashed through her as she remembered all the times he had pulled down her hair. He'd preferred it curling wildly around her shoulders, had claimed that it was incredibly sexy.

"It's in your way," she pointed out. That was why she'd always bound it, to keep it out of her way. And because it made it so clear to her that she wasn't genetically related to her father.

"It's fine," he said, and his fingertips skimmed along her spine.

Even through the heavy material, she could feel his touch. But it wasn't enough. She wanted the fabric gone. She wanted nothing between his skin and hers. But most especially not this dress.

"I'll cut through these little loops around the buttons," he said.

"You should have used that knife earlier," she said.

The buttons pinged as they dropped onto the wooden floor. And she sucked in a breath. "Wait!"

What if the buttons were like the rhinestones that

weren't really rhinestones? They spun away and rolled across the floor, disappearing beneath the leather sofa and chair.

"Did you change your mind?" he asked. "Do you want to keep it on?"

She could finally breathe again without the tight bodice squeezing her breasts. Expelling a ragged sigh of relief, she vehemently replied, "Hell, no!"

He chuckled, or at least she thought that was what that rusty sound was. But maybe she'd been mistaken, because when the dress dropped away and she turned back to him, he wasn't laughing at all.

His face was tense, a muscle twitching along his tightly clenched jaw. He stared at her in that way that only he had ever looked at her—with desire. But it was more than desire. It was need.

She recognized it because she felt it herself. She had to tell him about the dress. When he reached for her, she forgot all about it and the diamonds on it. He lifted her out of the mound of material. Sweeping her up in his arms, he carried her through a doorway off the living room.

He didn't release her, not even when he laid her down on a bed. Instead he joined her, his hard, long body pressing hers into the mattress. And he kissed her. His lips pressed against hers, deepening the kiss.

She lifted her hands, clutching at him. Holding him to her, she kissed him back and rubbed her breasts against his chest. While she wore only the white silk bra and panties she'd had on beneath her gown, he wore a tuxedo. The black jacket, the loosened tie and vest. It was too much. She needed to feel his skin against hers. Wishing she had his knife to undo the buttons, she reached between them and pulled his shirt loose.

But he caught her hands.

"Gage," she murmured in protest. He couldn't leave her like this, wanting him so badly that she trembled with need.

He groaned and leaned his forehead against hers. "I don't think I can stop…"

"I thought you were."

He shook his head. "I was just getting rid of this." He pulled off his jacket, dropping it to the floor beside the bed. He was more careful with the holster and gun inside it, laying them on the table next to the bed. His other clothes followed until he was completely naked.

The blinds were drawn in the bedroom, so the only light spilling in was from the living room. But despite the shadows, she could see the scars on his body.

As he caught her staring, he tensed. "I'm sorry," he said. "I forgot." And he reached for his shirt.

She caught his hand, forcing him to drop it back onto the floor. "I'm glad," she said.

"That I got hurt?"

He hadn't just been hurt. He'd been tortured.

"I'm glad that for a few minutes you were able to forget what you've been through," she said. Because she didn't think she would ever forget what he'd endured, how she'd nearly lost him.

As she stared up at his face, she wondered if he was really back. Or if the Gage she had loved was gone forever.

"I won't ever really forget," he said. "I won't ever really get over what I went through—what I saw—what I had to do to survive."

She shivered.

"I'm not the man you remember," he said. He reached

for his shirt again, intent on putting it back on to hide his scars. And maybe to hide his injured soul from her.

She stopped him again, her hand on his. Then she leaned forward and kissed him. "You're not the same," she agreed. "But neither am I."

His lips curved into a slight smile. "But you don't know me anymore."

"I know that you're the man that I want." Not just to-night but always.

He nodded. "We both need this," he said, as if he was trying to convince himself. "We've been through hell today." And he closed his arms around her, drawing her body against his scarred one.

But even with the scars, he was still beautiful—all straining muscles. She rubbed against him.

He unclasped her bra and pushed down the cups until it fell away from her. Her nipples rubbed against his chest until he pushed her back. Then his tongue rubbed over her nipples, teasing them.

Heat pooled between her legs. "Gage..."

"It's been so long," he murmured. "I'm not going to last."

But he took his time with her. He pulled off her panties and made sure she was ready for him, his fingers moving in and out of her. She shuddered as she came.

It had been a long time. She hadn't been with anyone since him. She'd told Richard she wanted to wait for their wedding night. But she knew now—even if she'd still be-lieved Gage dead—that she wouldn't have been able to make love with him. She hadn't loved him.

She'd loved only Gage.

He pushed her back onto the mattress and parted her legs. Then he was there, nudging against her core. She arched and stretched, trying to take all of him. She bit her lip as he thrust inside her.

He tensed. "Did I hurt you?"

She shook her head. "No, it's just been a while."

His brow furrowed, and he stared down at her with surprise. And hope.

"There's been no one since you," she told him.

"You don't have to lie to me," he said.

"I only did that once," she said. "When I told you I never loved you. That was the only lie I've ever told you."

He closed his eyes as if overwhelmed and murmured her name. "Megan…"

He'd said he wasn't the same man he'd been. But he felt the same to her—felt as perfect as he always had—as if they'd been made for each other.

She moved beneath him, the tension building tightly inside her as the passion—the passion she'd only felt with him—overwhelmed her.

He moved slowly, sliding in and out of her while he kissed her lips. And her neck. And her shoulder. As he kissed her, he touched her. He teased her breasts with his fingers, making the nipples tighten and tingle.

"Gage…" She was so close—to losing her mind.

Then he moved his hand between them, flicking his thumb over the most sensitive part of her. And she came, screaming his name.

His body tensed, shuddering, as he filled her. He moved so that he dropped onto the bed next to her.

She shuddered in the aftermath of the orgasm. Because she felt cold suddenly—separate—where a moment ago they had been so close they'd felt like one.

Then his arm slid under her shoulders, and he rolled

her up against him. His other hand reached across his body to wrap around hers, his palm against her hip.

"Gage?" she whispered. She peered up at his face. His eyes, those beautiful green eyes, were closed. And his jaw, shadowed with stubble a few shades darker than his hair, was clenched yet but not nearly as rigidly as it was when he was awake.

She suspected that after what he'd been through during those long months he'd been missing, this was as at rest as Gage ever was anymore. So she didn't have the heart to wake him up—to tell him what the rhinestones on her dress really were.

Megan settled her head on Gage's shoulder. She knew she was still in danger because of that damn dress. But here—in his arms—she felt safe. Her only wish was that everyone else was, too.

The mother of men who routinely put their lives on the line to protect others, Penny had spent more than her share of time in hospital waiting rooms. She'd never paced the floor over a man who hadn't been a relative. Nick didn't count. She hadn't given birth to him, but he was her son, same as Logan and Parker and Cooper. The Kozminskis, Milek and Garek, were her boys, too. They all waited with her, their eyes full of concern for her. And confusion.

They had no idea why she was so upset. Neither did she. It wasn't as if she knew Woodrow Lynch that well. They'd met a little over a year ago, but he lived in Chicago and she in River City. They'd never even been out on a date.

He'd never asked. But if he had, she wasn't sure she would have accepted. She hadn't wanted to be in this position again. She hadn't wanted to love a man that she risked losing because of what he did, of who he was.

She'd never had the chance to pace a waiting room for her husband. He'd died before he'd ever made it to the hospital, like Derek Nielsen had. So she'd been spared this nightmare of waiting, of worrying.

Losing her husband had been fast, like ripping off a Band-Aid. That could be why it hadn't hurt like this. And even though she'd forgiven him his betrayal, she'd never completely trusted him again, not enough to love him freely anymore.

Not that she loved Woodrow Lynch. She couldn't. She hardly knew him. Sure, he was a great father. That was obvious with how much his girls loved him. Ellen wasn't pacing like she was. She was too weak from morning sickness. She slumped in a chair with her husband's arm around her shoulders. They'd brought their kids to her mother-in-law earlier, when Gage had turned them away from the chapel.

It wasn't just family in the waiting room, though—his and hers. All of Woodrow's agents had come to hospital, too. They not only respected their boss, they loved him.

No agent loved him more than Nicholas Rus did. Actually, it was Nicholas Payne now. He had finally done what she'd asked. He'd taken his father's name. And he'd given his new son Woodrow's name. Nick stepped into her path so that she had to stop pacing. But the minute she stopped, the fear caught her, overwhelming her. Nick's arms closed around, holding her as she fell apart.

She couldn't lose Woodrow—just as she'd realized she loved him, too.

Chapter 23

Something soft brushed against Gage's chin and his neck and his chest. He opened his eyes and glanced down to find Megan's head on his shoulder. His heart swelled in his chest, love overwhelming him. He loved this, loved waking with her in his arms. This was how they used to sleep whenever he had convinced her to stay over at his place. It had always felt so natural to him—so right—to sleep with her in his arms, her head on his chest.

Maybe that was why he'd struggled so hard to sleep since his escape. It hadn't been because of the nightmares but because she hadn't been with him. He couldn't remember the last time he'd fallen asleep so quickly or slept so soundly. Glancing at his watch, he realized that it had only been a couple of hours. That much uninterrupted sleep was a big deal for him.

He couldn't get used to it, though, couldn't get used

to having her back in his arms. Even if she wanted to be with him again, he wouldn't let her make that sacrifice. Because he loved her, he couldn't put her through life with a man as broken as he was now.

It wasn't as if she really wanted to be with him again. She had just been through a lot today and had needed someone. He'd been there for her.

Where had Richard gone?

Had he made it out of the chapel alive? Had everyone else? Gage reached for his phone, which was in the pocket of the tuxedo jacket lying on the floor on her side of the bed. So he had to roll across her. His body tensed as she stirred beneath him. He wanted to bury himself inside her, wanted to feel as close to her as he had just those couple of hours ago.

Her thick lashes fluttered just before she opened her eyes and stared up at him. At first she looked surprised, like she hadn't expected to find him in bed with her. He studied her, waiting for disappointment. After all, he wasn't the man she had really wanted, the one she had agreed to marry.

Why had she agreed to marry Richard?

She'd admitted they'd never had the passion that she and Gage had. That passion flared now in her eyes, and her skin flushed. She reached up and linked her arms around his neck, pulling his head down for a kiss.

Like before, he couldn't resist her, not with her naked body lying warm and soft beneath his. She was already wet and ready for him, so he slid inside her. She lifted her legs and locked them around his waist, matching his rhythm as he thrust inside her.

She moaned then screamed his name as she came. Her inner muscles clutched at him as her body shuddered with release. The tension that had been gripping him snapped, and he joined her in ecstasy.

He tried to pull back, but she held on to him, as if unwilling to release him. Being connected with her was all that he'd remembered: so right, so humbling…

Love filled his heart, and he wanted to tell her how he felt. But it wasn't fair. He couldn't ask her to take a risk on a man like him, one who'd been so damaged not just physically but mentally as well.

He drew in a steadying breath and pulled away from her. He grabbed up his jacket from the floor and found his phone. Seeing the dark screen, he cursed. The cell jammer had drained his battery. Fortunately, a charger had been left next to the bed. He plugged it in.

"It's so dead that it's going to take a couple of minutes before I can get it to power up," he said. "Then I'll call Nick and find out what all happened at the chapel."

She nodded then drew in an unsteady breath. "That's good. I need to tell you something before you talk to Nick."

"What?" he asked. Somehow he didn't think she was going to profess her love for him.

"I know why the gunmen showed up at the church."

He tensed. There was something about her tone that raised his suspicions. He and Woodrow had been blaming each other for the gunmen showing up at the church. But what if it had been because of her?

"Why?" he asked. "Why did they want you so badly?" Not that he could blame them. He wanted her badly, too, so badly that even after making love with her twice, he wanted her again. "What did you do?"

"I didn't do anything," she said with a trace of defensiveness. "It wasn't really me they wanted."

"I heard—"

She pressed her fingers across her lips. "They didn't want *me*. They wanted my dress."

He snorted. "That thing?"

She had looked beautiful in it. But she would look beautiful in a gunnysack as well. The dress itself had been ostentatious and gaudy, not something she would have chosen to wear at all.

"Yes, that thing," she said. "I thought the rhinestones were tacky."

"Then why did you pick it?"

"I didn't pick it," she said. "Richard did."

His stomach knotted with anger. Gage never would have told her what to wear, especially not for her wedding day. All he would have wanted was for her to be comfortable and happy.

"And those rhinestones," she said. "They're not rhinestones at all."

"What are they?"

"Diamonds."

He snorted again. "Yeah, right."

"How do you think I broke that glass cabinet in Penny's closet?" she asked.

"Kicked it—hit it, I don't know," he admitted.

"With the rhinestones."

"But rhinestones…" Then he realized she was right. Only diamonds could have cut the glass. He cursed. "What the hell—how did they get there?"

He glanced through the open bedroom door to where the dress lay on the hardwood floor of the living room. It sparkled in the late afternoon sun shining through the skylight above it. There were a lot of rhinestones sewn into the heavy fabric. If they were all diamonds, a fortune lay there.

No wonder the gunmen had laid siege to the church. The risk they'd faced would have been worth it had they gotten the dress. But to get the dress, they would have had to get Megan, too.

He'd managed to protect her at the chapel. But she was still in danger because she had the dress. He had to keep her safe. So he reached for her again, wanting to wrap his arms around her and hold her close so no one could get her.

But she pulled away from him. Taking a sheet with her as she left the bed where they had made love, she wrapped it around herself. She could be shy like that, even after they'd made love. He suspected there was something more to her wanting to cover up.

She felt exposed. Or foolish.

She had been such a fool. Would Gage ever forgive her for all the mistakes she'd made? Instead of trusting him, she had trusted the wrong man, and it had nearly cost her life as well as the lives of other people she cared about.

"Is your phone charged yet?" she asked. She needed to know for certain that her father was all right and that the Paynes were, too. Nikki had risked her life taking Megan's place. But fortunately she hadn't taken her dress.

If she had...

Who knew what the gunmen and Andrea would have done to her? Of course given Andrea's disposition, she might have hurt Nikki anyway, just out of spite.

Gage glanced at his cell and nodded. "It's charged enough to power up now." But he didn't reach for it.

"Are you going to tell me how the diamonds got on your gown?"

His green eyes were narrowed with suspicion as he stared at her.

And Megan shivered. "I didn't put them there," she assured him.

He sighed. "Richard..."

She nodded. "It has to be. He had the dress designed. He found the seamstress. It had to be him."

"How the hell would he have gotten his hands on that many diamonds?" Gage mused aloud. "Unless he stole them..."

"He must have," she agreed.

"The danger is not from who you think." Gage muttered the words.

She shivered again. "What?"

"Those were D's last words," Gage said. Regret flashed in his green eyes.

"He died."

Gage nodded. "He said he knew that I would be the one—" He cleared his throat. "That if he died, I'd be the one."

"I'm sure you had no choice," she said.

"Like the guy who was trying to bring you upstairs to the chapel."

She narrowed her eyes and studied his face. Was he worried about what she'd think? He was nothing like the men he'd killed. "You had no choice," she said again. "He would have killed me."

Gage nodded and released a ragged sigh. "Yes, he would have."

"And D must have realized he'd given you no choice,

either," she said. "Or he wouldn't have given you a warning."

"That was a warning," Gage agreed.

"It must have been about Richard."

A muscle twitched along Gage's tightly clenched jaw, and he nodded. "It must have been. So they knew each other."

"And I didn't know him at all," she said. "He's not at all who I thought he was…" She'd thought him a harmless nerd, not a thief.

But what if that wasn't all he was? What if he was a killer, too?

"Never thought I'd see *you* in a wedding dress," Logan remarked as he joined Nikki in the corner of the hospital waiting room.

She glanced down at the gown, surprised she was still wearing it. She had forgotten all about it. "I never thought I'd wear this dress, either," she admitted. But despite her reservations, it had brought her luck.

If she had switched dresses with Megan, she doubted she would have gotten out of the chapel alive. Because she'd figured out where the diamonds Derek wanted were.

Those weren't rhinestones on the real bride's wedding gown. "Where are Gage and Megan?" she asked.

Logan glanced around the waiting room. "I don't know."

"I couldn't reach him on his cell phone," Nick said as he joined them.

Nikki looked around for her mom, whom Nick had been comforting earlier.

"Ellen told the hospital that it was fine for Penny to

go see Woodrow." They had only been allowing family members back since he'd come out of surgery. They'd gotten out the bullet, but he'd lost so much blood that it was still touch and go. He might not make it.

Regret struck Nikki's heart. If only she'd taken down Andrea earlier...

But Andrea wasn't a threat anymore. Richard Boersman was, though.

"We need to get a hold of Gage," Nikki said.

"Yeah," Nick agreed. "He would want to be here. And of course Megan needs to be here, too. She doesn't even know about her dad."

Nikki shook her head. "They can't come here. They're still in danger."

"We rounded up everyone at the church," Logan said. "How could they still be in danger?"

"The danger is not from who you think," Nick murmured.

And Nikki shivered. "I will never get used to you having that same freaky sixth sense Mom has."

"It's not that," Nick said. "Gage said those were the escaped convict's last words."

"He warned him." She wasn't surprised. While the guy had obviously had no qualms about killing, he'd also had a warped sense of honor, too. If not for him, Nikki would be dead. His wife would have killed her when she'd stormed into the chapel after he'd untied her.

If only he hadn't untied her...

"So Gage knows she's not safe yet," Nikki said.

"That's why he got Megan out of there," Nick said. "He got her to the safe house."

Nikki expelled a breath of relief. "That's good." But it

wasn't enough. "We still need to talk to him. Warn him about Richard."

"Richard?" Logan repeated the name.

"The groom," Nikki said. "Didn't you meet him at the church?"

Logan shook his head.

"You didn't see another guy in a tuxedo? Short, nerdy-looking guy?" she asked.

Parker stepped up and shook his head. "There was no one wearing a tuxedo but Woodrow."

And he'd been lying on the floor, bleeding. Nikki shuddered as she remembered. She'd been so busy consoling her mother and worrying about Chief Special Agent Lynch that she hadn't even thought to look for Richard.

"Gage was wearing a tux, too," Nick said. "But nobody else that we saw inside the church."

Nikki cursed. "He must have gotten away." Or worse yet, he'd followed Gage and Megan. "Until we catch him, Megan isn't safe."

She had what he wanted. His diamonds.

He had endured Derek torturing him and hadn't given them up. He wouldn't let anyone get between him and his fortune. Not Megan and not Gage.

Chapter 24

"They already knew about Richard?" Megan asked as Gage clicked off the cell phone.

Fortunately, he'd taken the call in the living room while she'd been getting dressed in the bedroom. Since Payne Protection often used the condo as a safe house, the closet was stocked with clothes in an assortment of sizes.

He'd found a pair of jeans and a black sweater that fit. He turned to where she stood in the bedroom doorway. She wore a red sweater dress with tall suede boots. She looked so damn sexy.

He forced himself to focus on her question and nodded. "Yeah, they already knew about Richard and the diamonds." He glanced at where the wedding dress spilled out of a box sitting on the leather couch. But they'd shared with him something he hadn't known, something that made him feel physically ill.

Woodrow was hurt. Badly.

He wasn't certain how to tell Megan that her father might not make it. He wasn't certain if he should even tell her at all. Because if he told her, she would want to go to the hospital.

And it wouldn't be safe for them to leave until Richard was caught.

"How did they know?" Megan asked.

"Nikki overheard an argument between Richard and Derek Nielsen in the church," he said.

"Derek Nielsen?"

"D," he explained. "Remember, Nick told us his name outside the church." He was surprised that he'd remembered, though. He'd been so shaken from going through that damn tunnel. "Derek just recently broke out of prison. He was serving a fifteen-year sentence for armed robbery."

"Let me guess," she said. "Of a jewelry store?"

He nodded.

"I don't understand how Richard was involved."

"Nikki figured he was the one who bypassed the security system so that no alarm went off. There were actually several robberies where someone hacked the security systems and the stores were robbed."

"Richard?"

He nodded. "The Kozminskis—they're bodyguards with Payne Protection, too—recognized D at the church. They knew he was responsible for several more jewelry store robberies than the one for which he was serving time."

"How do they know?" she asked.

"Have you heard the saying it takes a thief…"

She nodded. "But you said they're bodyguards."

"They are."

"And thieves, too?"

"Not anymore," he said. "But they keep a foot in that world. It's a good thing, though. It gives us information we wouldn't be able to get without them."

"Did they know anything about Richard?" she asked.

He nodded. "Not by name. But they knew Nielsen recruited some college kid several years ago and had him hacking the stores' security systems. But then there was a glitch with Derek's last robbery. Some security footage of him showed up, and he was arrested."

Megan gasped. "Richard betrayed him."

"There's another saying," Gage began.

"There's no honor among thieves," Megan finished for him.

"Except the Kozminskis," he quickly added. He would trust those guys with his life, and he might have to if they were the backup bodyguards Logan was sending to the safe house.

"What is it?" Megan asked.

"What's what?" he asked, stalling for time.

He wasn't sure how to tell her what he needed to. She loved her father so much; she would be devastated if he didn't survive his gunshot wound.

She narrowed her eyes and studied his face. "What are you not telling me?"

"Megan…"

"I know there's something you're not telling me," she insisted.

He still needed to stall for time, at least until his backup arrived at the condo to see if Richard was lurking outside. Gage had whisked her away from the church quickly, and he hadn't noticed anyone following them. But he had underestimated Richard once. He wouldn't make that mistake again.

So to stall, he asked the question that had been bothering him. "If you can read me that well," he said, "how could you not know that I was telling you the truth about how I felt about you?"

She sucked in a breath. "You want to talk about that now?"

He nodded.

"I told you that I was wrong," she said. "I shouldn't have doubted you. I shouldn't have listened to Tucker or Richard."

He flinched.

"What?" Annoyance pulled her full lips into a frown. "What is it?"

"Tucker…"

"What about Tucker?"

"He died." Gage couldn't believe it. But his name had been on the list of casualties Nick had run down for him. "He arrived early, so he made it inside the church. Then Nikki said he tried to draw his weapon when Derek had ordered all the guests to be searched." He must have gotten scared, or he'd been trying to play the hero he'd always wanted to be.

Stupid kid…

Megan's lashes fluttered over the tears brimming in her eyes. Then she stalked over to the dress and pounded her fist against the side of the box. "He didn't deserve to die, especially not over these damn things."

Seeing how upset she was about Tucker, Gage dreaded telling her about her father. But he needed to let her know. She would never forgive him if Woodrow didn't make it and she didn't get to see him again.

One last time…

* * *

No one had ever scared her like Gage could. When he'd started flirting with her, she'd been afraid because she'd never had a man like him—so handsome and sexy—interested in her before. She hadn't trusted his attraction to her was real. He'd scared her even more when he'd reenlisted and disappeared during his deployment. That had nearly scared her to death.

But this—the fear she felt now because he kept avoiding her gaze—scared her nearly as much. He had information that he knew would upset her so much that he was reluctant to share it with her.

"What is it?" she asked again, as she had so many times before. "Just tell me!"

"Megan…" The reluctance was there in his deep and raspy voice. He really didn't want to tell her.

So she started guessing, knowing that when she hit on it he would betray himself. "Did Richard get away?"

He nodded. "Yeah, nobody even saw him at the church. He must have escaped during the shoot-out."

She grimaced as she remembered all the shots she'd heard emanating from the speaker in that small closet in which Gage had locked her. "Tucker died and Derek," she said. "Was anyone else killed or hurt?"

The look on his face chilled her blood. "There were more casualties!"

He nodded. "The woman—Andrea."

She gasped. She'd been afraid of the woman. But she hadn't wished her dead. She hadn't wished any of them dead. "That's too bad."

"Nikki had to kill her."

"That's even worse." She couldn't imagine how Nikki felt. "Is she okay?"

He expelled a breath but nodded. "*She's* fine."

Panic clutched her heart. Someone else obviously was not fine. He wasn't willing to come right out and tell her. So she had to keep asking questions. "And Mrs. Payne? Penny?"

He nodded again.

Realization dawned on her, making her sick. "My dad!" she exclaimed. "He got hurt."

Gage nodded yet again.

Tears stung her eyes. Everybody had kept telling her that he was so tough, that he could handle anything. That was the only reason she'd left with Gage before knowing if everyone had survived the shoot-out inside the chapel.

"I shouldn't have left the church," she said, berating herself. She'd thought her staying there—when all everyone had actually wanted was that damn dress—might put other people in danger. But she shouldn't have left until she'd known everyone else was out of trouble.

"How badly is he hurt?" she demanded to know.

Gage flinched as if it hurt him just to think about it. He had always thought so highly of her father. All Woodrow Lynch's agents respected and loved him. He wasn't just a boss to them. He was a friend—a mentor—a *father*—to them as well.

"How badly is he hurt?" she asked again.

Was he just hurt or was he dead?

"He was shot," he said. "Andrea shot him before Nikki killed her."

And now she wished Nikki had killed the woman earlier. Or that Megan had. Maybe she should have plunged those scissors into the woman's cold heart instead of her shoulder.

Megan trembled with both anger and fear. How dare she...how dare she hurt Megan's father...

"He's been through surgery. They removed the bullet. It was close to his heart, did some damage to one of his lungs," Gage said. And now he spoke almost too freely.

She felt sick thinking of the physical damage that had been done to her father. He'd always been so strong, so invincible.

"And he lost a lot of blood," Gage continued.

"Is—is he going to make it?" she asked.

He fell silent again, and his green eyes looked down. He was unwilling to meet her gaze.

"Gage!" she yelled. "Tell me!"

"They don't know," he admitted, his voice ragged with his own emotions. She saw it then. He hadn't just respected her father. He'd loved him, too. He had loved working with him.

If not for her, she doubted Gage would have quit the Bureau. He would have kept working with her father. She had put this all in motion.

If she hadn't broken up with him...

If she hadn't agreed to marry a man she hadn't loved...

It was all her fault. She'd already lost Gage through her stupidity. She couldn't lose her father, too.

Images played behind Woodrow's closed lids. The flash of the gunfire as the bullet fired. He waited for the pain he'd felt, but he was numb.

Was he dead?

Had he died?

What about Penny? She'd been right behind him. Had she been shot too?

Megan was safe. Gage would make certain of that.

He'd promised to get her to a secure place. He would protect her with his life.

Woodrow would have done the same for Penny—if he'd had the chance. He struggled to move, but something lay against his side, something warm and soft that lulled him into a feeling of security himself. But he wasn't safe. He'd been shot once. Even though he'd tried to stay awake, consciousness had slipped away from him.

He had no idea if he'd been shot again. Or if anyone else had...

"Penny..." he murmured her name as he fought to regain consciousness.

"Shh..." a soft voice soothingly replied. "I'm right here. I'm right here."

And when he finally dragged his lids up, he saw that she was. She was the warmth and softness he'd felt as she lay next to him in the narrow hospital bed. He'd never been as comfortable as he'd been with her lying beside him.

He was sure it had nothing to do with the drugs that were pumping into his veins through the IV in his arm. It was all her: Penny Payne.

Her face was flushed as if she was embarrassed he'd caught her in his bed. Her curls were rumpled like her bronze dress, and her makeup slightly smeared beneath her eyes, making dark circles look even darker. But she had never looked more beautiful to him.

"You're all right?" he asked.

She nodded. "Yes. Are you?"

"I'm alive?" It was a question; he wasn't sure. His body still felt curiously numb but for his heart that swelled with love.

For her...

He wanted this, wanted to go to sleep every night with Penny in his arms, wanted to wake every morning with her lying beside him.

Her lips curved into a smile, one full of relief. And she blinked back tears. "Yes, you're alive."

"You sound surprised," he mused.

She shook her head. "No, I never had any doubt you'd survive."

"Liar."

Her lips curved into a bigger smile. He couldn't resist; he leaned forward and kissed those lips. Her breath escaped in a ragged sigh against his mouth.

"I was so scared," she admitted. "I hoped but I didn't know."

"Like you always know everything," he teased.

She shook her head. "Not everything…"

Panic clutched his heart. "Is Nikki okay?"

"Yes," she said. "You were right about her. She's far tougher than I ever realized. She shot and killed the woman who shot you."

"Did she get hurt?" He remembered all those flashes of gunfire.

"Not a scratch on her."

"She's not just tough then," he remarked with surprise. "She's damn lucky."

Penny's lips curved into a smile again. "She thinks it's the dress."

"The dress she was wearing?"

"My old wedding dress."

"Then it is lucky."

"I'm not so sure," Penny admitted. "I didn't have the storybook marriage I thought I'd have."

"Neither did I," he admitted.

"I know."

And she would. She must have realized that Megan wasn't his. It didn't matter, though. He didn't love her any less. He didn't blame her for what her mother had done. Hell, he didn't even blame her mother. He'd never been there for Evelyn, not like she'd wanted or needed him to be. His job had always mattered more to him than she had.

Now Penny...

If she wanted him to quit, he would do it in a heartbeat. He knew now that nothing mattered more than love. But maybe he'd only realized that because he was truly in love for the first time in his life.

Before he shared his feelings with her, he had to know. "Did everyone else make it out all right?"

She nodded. "Yes."

He released a ragged breath of relief. "So it's over..."

Her eyes—those beautiful warm brown eyes—squeezed shut, as if she didn't want him to see the truth in them.

"You said everyone made it out all right."

"Yes, but it's not over," she said.

Then he remembered what Derek had told him and Gage. *The danger is not who you think...*

He groaned.

She sat up and looked at the machines hooked to him, monitoring his condition. "Are you okay?"

"Yes." But he wouldn't be able to tell her what he wanted to tell her until he knew this was over. "Physically, I'm fine. But if something happens to one of my daughters..."

She squeezed his IV-less arm. "I know."

No parent knew better than she did, not with the danger her kids routinely faced.

"Nick and my other boys," she said, claiming her husband's illegitimate son in the way he had claimed Megan—wholeheartedly, "they're working on finding Richard."

"Richard?"

"Yes, he worked with Derek and double-crossed him. That was how D wound up behind bars and Richard wound up with the fortune in diamonds Derek had stolen."

He sucked in a breath.

And she touched his chest.

He couldn't feel her fingers though through the heavy bandages wrapped around his torso. Now he knew where he'd been shot. He expelled that breath in a shaky sigh of relief that he'd survived.

"Are you sure you're all right?" she asked.

He nodded. "I'm just shocked. I checked Richard out. And he has no record."

"He'd never been caught," she said.

Woodrow shook his head. "I don't understand…"

"What?" she asked. "You couldn't have known. No one suspected what he was capable of."

"But why wouldn't Derek have turned him in?" he wondered. "If he'd given up his partner, he might have gotten a reduced sentence."

"From what Nikki overheard, Derek thought he was dead. Apparently, he tortured Richard to find out where he'd stashed the diamonds. He'd thought he'd gone too far and Richard had died."

"But he survived." Woodrow regretted that after all the fear the man had caused Megan and might still cause her. Realization dawned as he remembered what he had discovered about the man who could have been his son-in-law, probably would have been had Derek not broken out of prison and hijacked the wedding.

"I know he had a lot of plastic surgery five or so years ago," Woodrow said. His hacker had hacked the hacker's medical records. "It was due to burns, though. I figured they were just from the fire Megan had mentioned Richard had been in."

Instead he had been tortured. Derek Nielsen must have been determined to get those diamonds. But Richard had been even more determined to keep them. He'd been willing to give up his life over them.

"Nikki figures Andrea helped him," Penny said, "that she was playing both of them."

But she was dead and so was Derek Nielsen. And hopefully Richard was long gone.

"I'm sure he left the church and headed straight to the airport," Woodrow said.

Penny shook her head. "I doubt it. He won't leave without the diamonds."

"So he'll retrieve those from wherever he stashed them, and he'll leave."

Her face, which had been flushed with color when he had awakened, grew pale now.

"What?" he asked. The numbness was beginning to wear off because he felt a pang of fear now—in his heart.

"The diamonds were on Megan's wedding gown."

He knew what that meant. Richard wouldn't leave without the diamonds and probably not without Megan, either.

"Gage will protect her," Penny assured him.

Woodrow trusted Gage. But Richard Boersman was

more dangerous than any of them had realized. And even more desperate.

He had been willing to give up his life once for those diamonds. He would definitely be willing to do it again. And Woodrow suspected that for those damn diamonds, Richard would have no qualms about taking a life or two.

Chapter 25

Gage had been through some epic battles in his life. But no one had ever fought him as hard as Megan was. He tightened his arms around her, lifting and carrying her away from the security panel.

"You can't keep me here," she shouted at him as she pummeled his shoulders with her small fists. "You can't treat me like a prisoner."

He had said those same words himself before, so he knew exactly how she was feeling. His heart ached with sympathy for her. He didn't want to hurt her—like he'd been hurt. He only wanted to protect her. "I can't let you leave until we know where the hell Richard is."

"Richard won't hurt me," she said.

Gage wasn't so sure.

She must have seen the doubt on his face because she insisted, "He won't. He just wants the diamonds."

"Why did he sew them on to your dress?" Gage wondered.

"What was the reason?" Megan shrugged. "I don't know. And at the moment, I don't care. I just want to see my dad." Her voice cracked with emotion, and tears shimmered in her dark eyes.

"You will see him," he promised. "We'll leave as soon as my backup bodyguards arrive." But even then he wasn't certain it was a good idea to take her out of the safe house. Nobody had any idea of what Richard was capable. And Gage couldn't figure out why the hell he'd had the diamonds sewn on to Megan's dress. What was the purpose of that?

No, it was too risky, and Gage wasn't willing to take any chances with Megan's life. Refusing to bring her to see her father would be taking a chance with his life, though. She might kill him.

"You're lying to me," she accused him. "You have no intention of bringing me to see him."

"It's too dangerous," he told her.

She shook her head. "No, it's not. But what does it matter if it is? Why do you care?"

She was asking something else—something else he couldn't answer honestly. He couldn't tell her how he felt. He couldn't burden her with his feelings because there were too many now—too many nightmares—too much damage.

So he reminded her instead, "It's my job. Protecting you is my assignment."

She sucked in a breath. "That's all I am to you?" She glanced over his shoulder to the bedroom where they'd made love.

"That was a mistake," he told her. "I crossed the line. I shouldn't have."

"Do you do that on all your assignments?" she asked.

He thought of his first one, of the elderly lady with Alzheimer's and nearly smiled. "No…"

But he couldn't let her think that it meant something that he had with her. He couldn't let her think they might have a future together. After what he'd been through, he couldn't offer anyone a future.

"It didn't mean anything," he said. "I could *never* be with you again." Because he had nothing to offer her… but nightmares and uncertainty.

She flinched and nodded. "I knew that. I knew that you would never be able to forgive me."

"Megan…" She broke free of his grasp and ran to the control panel again.

He gave her a moment to figure out she couldn't escape, just like his captors used to give him…until the day he'd proven them wrong. But security in the Kozminskis' condo was high. You didn't need the code just to get in; you needed it to get out, too.

When she began to type in numbers without hesitation, Gage realized she'd watched him enter the code and she'd remembered it.

Cursing, he rushed forward just as the metal door began to open. She slipped through the narrow space and ran out. What the hell did she think, that she was going to walk to the hospital? Hail a cab? She had no car keys, no money for a cab.

"Megan!" he called after her. "Come back here! You can't leave."

She ran faster, turning the corner of the warehouse without so much as a glance back at him. Even if she had money for the fare, there were no cabs or buses running in this area of town. Once industrial, it was mostly abandoned now but for the warehouse Milek Kozminski had converted into the condo and art studio space.

"Megan!" he yelled.

But she didn't answer him. He figured she was just being stubborn until he turned the corner. Then he saw why she hadn't answered.

There was a hand clasped over her mouth and a gun pressed to her head. Richard had caught her—right next to the open door of a black sedan.

Gage hadn't drawn his gun, but he wore his holster. All he had to do was reach for it. But would Richard shoot before he could?

"Let her go," Gage advised him.

"You'd like that, wouldn't you?" Richard asked, his voice full of resentment. "You stole her from me once, but you're not stealing her again."

"You love her that much?" Gage asked hopefully. Richard wouldn't hurt her if he loved her.

The other man laughed. "Love? I leave that for fools like you. I don't love her."

"Then let her go." Because Gage loved her. Losing her once had nearly destroyed him. Losing her again…

He couldn't imagine it. It would be a nightmare beyond any he'd endured.

"I need her!" Richard said.

"But you said you don't love her." Then Gage realized why the other man claimed to need her—because he needed what he thought she had. "She doesn't have the diamonds anymore."

Richard's face flushed. "What? Where are they?"

"In the condo," Gage said. "Or they were."

"What do you mean?"

"I left the door wide open. Anyone could have walked off with them now." And Gage couldn't have cared less. Money mattered nothing to him.

"You better hope not," Richard said. "Or I will pull this trigger."

Megan's eyes widened with shock. Obviously, she had never considered her fiancé capable of such violence. But then neither had Gage.

"You don't want to hurt her," Gage said. "Or you won't live to see those diamonds again."

Richard's face flushed an even darker shade of red. "You tough guys..." He shook his head. "Like Derek. He thought he was tougher than me, too. He thought he could break me. But I broke him. I sent him to prison and he didn't even know."

"Because you did it behind his back," Gage said. "You were underhanded, just like you were with Megan, hiding who you truly were from her."

Richard chuckled. "It was easy to fool her, thanks to you."

"Me?"

"You distracted her for me so she didn't ask too many questions. Then she felt so guilty about dumping me for you that I could manipulate her into doing whatever I wanted," he boasted.

"Like wearing that ugly damn dress."

"That dress is worth millions," Richard said. "Maybe even billions!"

"Then let her go," Gage said. "And get your damn diamonds."

"Oh, I'll get them," Richard assured him. "But first I need to do this."

Gage didn't know what he was going to do, but that it would be bad. So he reached for his weapon. But he couldn't draw it fast enough.

Richard pulled his trigger first, firing the bullet right into Gage. Then he chuckled and asked, "Was that straightforward enough for you?"

Megan screamed so loudly it either penetrated Richard's hand or knocked it away from her mouth. Gage lay facedown on the sidewalk in front of her. Richard had just shot him—in cold blood.

How had she never realized how cold-blooded he was? She'd thought the reason she had felt no passion with him or from him had been her fault. Now she knew. He was a heartless monster.

"Should I make sure he's dead this time?" Richard asked as he lowered the barrel of his gun toward Gage's head.

She screamed again and did what she should have moments ago—she grabbed his arm. He fired anyway, but the shot missed Gage. Or at least she hoped it did. She saw no blood spread across his back. But his sweater was black. Maybe he had been struck.

Richard was stronger than she'd known. He easily pulled free of her grasp and turned on her with the gun. "You can't help him," he said. "But you can help yourself."

She didn't care about herself, not if she lost Gage. And she might have already lost her dad. "You're crazy if you think I would help you!" Then she saw the madness in his eyes and realized that he was crazy.

"You were going to help me," he said, "before *he* came back from the dead." He pointed his barrel at Gage again.

"No!" she shouted at him, to draw his focus back to her. "I would have never helped you with anything illegal."

He grinned, a mocking grin. "By marrying me, you were going to help me get those diamonds out of the country."

"But I didn't even know you had them."

"You had them," he said. "And you would have worn that dress through airport security."

She never would have worn that dress on a plane. The minute she'd put it on she had changed her mind about marrying him at all, even before Gage had appeared in her dressing room. "They would have found them then."

"You think airport security would have searched the daughter of an FBI bureau chief?" And he would have made damn certain they knew she was. He chuckled. "Never."

"That's the only interest you had in me," she realized. "My father."

He didn't even bother denying it. In fact he uttered another mocking little chuckle that confirmed it.

"He might be dead," she said. "Andrea might have killed him."

He cursed. "That stupid bitch. She's an idiot. She screwed everything up with her petty jealousy. She just had to see the woman I was marrying." He shook his head in disgust.

"She's dead," Megan informed him.

"The cute little brunette killed her?" he asked.

Megan nodded.

"Figured Andrea was too stupid to let that go."

"Let *me* go," Megan urged him. "Just get in your car and drive away." Then she could get help for Gage.

Maybe he hadn't been injured too badly. But he lay so still on the pavement.

"Not without the diamonds," Richard said. "We're going to get those and then maybe I'll think about letting you go."

She didn't believe him. Finally, she recognized when someone was lying or telling the truth. Too bad she'd figured it out too late to listen to Gage. If she hadn't left the condo, they would be safe inside it. Together. He wouldn't be bleeding on the concrete. This—like everything else—was all her fault.

Actually, it wasn't all hers. It was Richard's. He had manipulated her long enough. If only she could get to Gage's gun.

But it must lie beneath him. She couldn't see it. There were other weapons back inside the condo, though. Payne Protection had an arsenal there.

"Then let's get the diamonds," she urged him.

His hand on her arm, he jerked her forward so that she nearly stumbled over Gage's body. Her heart lurching, she stepped over him. Richard kicked him as he crossed his body. Gage didn't move or even grunt in pain.

Tears stung her eyes. She'd lost him again and this time for good. She wanted Richard to pay for that, for taking the life of a good man.

He dragged her along the sidewalk back to the condo. The metal door stood open, how Gage had left it. He hadn't cared about the diamonds lying just inside on the couch. He'd cared only about her, about keeping her safe. Of course it had been his job to protect her. It was her fault that she'd kept making it so hard for him.

But that was really the only thing that was her fault. Everything else was on Richard, on his treachery and greed. It gleamed in his eyes as he caught sight of the wedding dress spilling out of the box on the couch.

"There they are, just like he said." He turned back and pointed the gun at her face.

"You need me," she reminded him. "You need the bureau chief's daughter to help you out of the country."

A smirk spread across his face. "Yeah, right. Like you'd help me…"

"I would," she said. But she had never been a very convincing liar. Why had Gage believed her when she'd told him she'd never loved him? Maybe he'd had some of the same insecurities she'd had.

"I can't fly out of the country," he said.

"Why not?"

"That little brunette, she overheard me and D talking," he said. "She knows."

"Then you're trapped."

He gave her another condescending smile. "With this much money, I can get my hands on anything I want. You were only my plan A."

He *would* have a plan B. He was brilliant. It was one of the things she'd admired about him, his intelligence and how understanding he'd been when she'd dumped him for Gage. But he was so smart that he'd intended to manipulate her the entire time.

"I don't need you anymore." He turned the gun barrel toward her.

"Richard…"

"I'm doing you a favor," he said. "This way you don't have to mourn Gage Huxton all over again. You can be with him—for eternity."

Megan squeezed her eyes shut just as the shot rang out.

* * *

No matter how many painkillers they'd pumped through his IV, Woodrow had found no relief. He couldn't sleep, not without Penny by his side. She had been gone too long.

He was only allowed one visitor at a time, so she'd been giving everyone else a turn. Ellen. His son-in-law. The only exception had been Nick. He'd been allowed to bring in his newborn son with him.

"Why the hell did you saddle him with a name like Woodrow?" he'd teased his best agent as the guy had cradled his baby in hands that were nearly as big as the infant himself.

The only man who could have been a better agent had quit before he'd had the chance to prove himself. He'd proved himself at the church, though.

Where the hell was Gage?

Hopefully, keeping Megan safe. He knew Gage would give up his life before he'd let anything happen to the love of his life. Fortunately, he'd found her when they were young. They would have a long life together.

It had taken Woodrow too long to find Penny. And getting shot had proved to him that he couldn't waste another minute. Sure, he'd been hesitant to say anything to her until they knew everyone else was safe. But it didn't matter.

It wasn't like he was going to wait until Richard was caught. The guy was smart. He could elude the authorities for years. And Woodrow wasn't willing to wait years. Not now that he'd finally found his true love.

His door creaked open, and he turned toward it with a reassuring smile. He'd presented that face to every worried visitor. As if thinking about her had conjured her from his dreams, Penny stepped through the door. His smile widened into a grin of delight.

Her curls were still tousled. The circles beneath her eyes might have grown darker. She was still the most beautiful woman he had ever seen. She didn't smile back. In fact her brown eyes were dark with worry and regret.

She didn't have good news for him.

Pain jabbed his heart as he realized that. He shook his head and implored her, "Wait!"

She paused half in, half out of his hospital room.

He gestured her inside, and the door closed behind her. "I want you," he said. "I just don't want whatever you have to tell me."

She gasped. "Woodrow…"

"Just wait," he told her. "Before you tell me whatever it is you have to tell me, I want to ask you something first."

"But…"

He gestured her closer until she stood right next to his bed. Then he pulled her down beside him, like when he had awakened and found her pressed against his side. "I think you brought me back," he said.

"What?"

"The surgeon and doctors are all surprised that I made it," he said. "They said I lost so much blood that they didn't expect me to wake up."

She gasped again and trembled against him.

"But I had to come back," he said. "For you…"

Tears glistened in her eyes.

"It took me fifty-five years to find you," he said. And he lifted and pressed her small hand against his heart. He couldn't feel it through the bandage, but he knew it was there. More importantly, he knew she was already inside it. "I wasn't going to give you up without a fight."

"I'm glad," she murmured. And her lips curved into a slight smile. "I was worried that I'd already lost you."

He shook his head. "Not a chance."

"That's why I told myself I couldn't fall for you," she said. "Because you're too great a risk. I could lose you like I lost…"

"Your husband?"

She shook her head. "I lost him before he died. I lost the illusion of what I thought we had. It wasn't this. I know that now."

"Me, too," he said.

She nodded. "Megan…"

"She's not mine. Biologically."

"It doesn't matter," she agreed. "With the child…"

But with the spouse, the trust was irrevocably broken. He had forgiven, but he'd never forgotten. Just as he imagined she had.

"I will never betray you," he promised. "I would never put you through what I was put through."

"I know."

"And this bullet thing…" He sighed. "That was a fluke. My first gunshot wound in all my years with the Bureau and the Marines."

"Maybe I'm bad luck," she suggested with a smile.

"You're good luck," he said. "I doubt I would have survived if I hadn't wanted to be with you."

She snuggled against his side, clutching his shoulders. Then she lifted her face and pressed her lips to his. "I didn't want to fall for you," she said. "But I did."

"I love you," he said. "And I want to marry you."

The regret was back in her dark eyes. "Woodrow, I need to tell you—"

He pressed his mouth to hers and then his fingers. "It doesn't matter. Nothing matters except you becoming my wife. I want to be with you through good times and bad. If the bad starts now—" and he had a sick feeling that it had "—then I want to go through it with you. Please, Penny, say that you'll marry me."

Tears streaked down her face. Any other woman might be too afraid after all she'd lost to risk her heart again, especially on a man like him. But she was the bravest woman he knew. And she nodded. "Of course I will marry you."

His breath shuddered out in a sigh of relief. And he kissed her again—deeply. "I love you. I want to marry you as soon as we can get a license."

"I can see to that," the wedding planner assured him.

"But first you want to tell me what you came in to say." He braced himself. Whatever it was, no matter how bad, he would be able to handle it with her love and support.

"Richard found Megan and Gage at the safe house," she said. "He got there before any other Payne Protection bodyguards arrived for backup."

He sucked in a breath. "And?"

"There was a shooting."

He cursed and clutched his arms around her, holding her close.

"Who did we lose?" he asked. Because he knew that someone had died.

Chapter 26

The young doctor gasped as Gage pulled off his sweater. "Oh, my God, what happened to you?"

Gage glanced down at the blood trickling from the wound on his shoulder. It had nearly stopped bleeding now. "It's just a scratch," he said. "The bullet barely grazed me."

Fortunately, Richard was a lousy shot, but Gage had played dead to buy himself some time. He might have wound up dead for real if Megan hadn't prevented Richard from shooting him again. She'd saved his life, which had enabled him to save hers.

He shuddered as he remembered Richard pointing that gun in her beautiful face. Shooting him had been a risk, though. Richard could have squeezed the trigger out of reflex as he went down.

So Gage hadn't given him the chance to even get his finger on the trigger. He'd fired as soon as Richard had lifted his gun.

While Megan hadn't been shot, she wasn't all right. She'd barely said anything since the shooting. Nick and the other Payne Protection bodyguards who'd showed up at the condo had asked her questions, but she'd either nodded or shaken her head. She hadn't said anything to them after she'd asked them about her dad.

"I'm fine," he said, dismissing the doctor's concern for him.

The only reason he'd agreed to come to the hospital had been for her, so she could see her father. And for a doctor to see her and make sure she was all right. Gage's gunshot wound had gotten them back to the ER faster than her shock would have, though.

"You need to check her out."

The dark-haired doctor glanced at Megan, who stood near Gage's gurney. Her skin—usually such a warm honey tone—was unnaturally pale except for the droplets of Richard's blood that had spattered across her face. The doctor noticed the blood and asked, "Was she shot as well?"

"No," Megan replied. "I wasn't."

But Gage flinched as he remembered how close she had come to getting shot—to getting killed. Damn Richard. But he couldn't hurt her ever again.

"I think she's in shock, though," Gage said.

She shook her head and tumbled her curly hair around her blood-spattered face. "I'm fine."

She wasn't. And they both knew it. After what she'd seen, she might never be fine again. Too bad she'd opened her eyes right as the bullet had struck Richard. Gage had had to take the kill shot—or risk Richard killing her.

"She's been through a lot."

The doctor looked from Megan back to Gage, his smooth dark brow beginning to furrow with confusion.

"She was at that wedding chapel that armed gunmen invaded earlier today," Gage explained.

The doctor's eyes widened. "There was a shoot-out there. Is that where the blood came from?" He gestured at her face.

Gage wasn't going to waste time explaining about the second shooting. So he simply replied, "She was the bride."

She was supposed to marry the man Gage had killed. How did she feel about his killing her groom? How did she feel about him now? He could tell nothing from her face.

The doctor looked at her with more concern now. "Your father came through the ER just as my shift started early this afternoon." His face was easy to read; he didn't think Woodrow had had a chance when he'd seen him.

"He made it," Gage said.

Nick had assured him of that when he'd showed up at the condo with Garek and Milek Kozminski. They'd been so sorry for not getting there sooner. But Gage had brushed off their apologies. They'd brought good news.

"He's tough," Gage said and offered Megan a reassuring smile. He suspected she was still worried. She wouldn't believe her father was okay until she saw him for herself.

"I don't need stitches or a tetanus shot," Gage told the doctor as the young man probed his wound. "Just stick a bandage on it."

"Looks like you've been through a lot, too," the doctor remarked as he swabbed the injury with alcohol, cleaning it before taping on the bandage Gage had requested. "Where did all the scars come from?"

Gage didn't answer. Hell, he wasn't even sure where he'd been.

The young man peered closer at the ridges of healed flesh along Gage's torso, shoulders and arms. "Looks like you were tortured." Then as he glanced up and met Gage's gaze, his face flushed with embarrassment at his lack of tact. "I'm sorry…"

Gage shrugged. "It's fine."

"He was a Marine," Megan said. He heard both her pride and her regret.

One was *always* a Marine. Even her father. That was how he'd survived getting shot. But Gage didn't explain that to her. He didn't say anything.

The doctor spoke again. "Thank you for your service."

Gage glanced at Megan and murmured, "The worst wounds leave no marks…"

The worst wounds leave no marks…

"You're never going to forgive me, are you?" she asked as they rode the elevator up from the hospital lobby to her father's room. He'd been moved from ICU to a private room. While she was relieved about that, she was still scared over how close she'd come to losing him. And scared that Gage was still lost to her…

"Forgive you for what?" Gage asked, as if he truly had no idea.

"For breaking your heart."

His lips parted in a soft gasp. "Do you know what that means?"

"You were talking about me," she said, "when you talked about the worst wounds…"

He grinned. "Well, that, too. But it means that you actually believe I loved you. Or how else could you have broken my heart?"

Loved. Her heart cracked at the past tense. He didn't

love her anymore. And after what she'd put him through, she doubted he ever would again.

"I was stupid," she said.

"You were not stupid," he said—as if he needed to defend her to her.

"Yes, I was," she insisted. She had been so stupid. How could she have ever considered a cold-blooded con artist like Richard a friend?

"You were insecure," Gage corrected her. "That's how people like Tucker Allison and Richard got to you. You never saw yourself as you really are."

"How am I really?" she asked, because she felt like a fool.

"Beautiful…"

She snorted.

Then his hand shot out, hitting the stop button on the elevator control panel. The car jerked to a stop, launching Megan into his arms. Gage caught her and held her tightly, kissing her with such passion. His lips moved over hers, gliding first before sucking her lower lip into his mouth. He nipped it lightly before sliding his tongue over the sensitive flesh. He groaned, and his arms clutched her closely against him, molding her soft curves to his hard muscles. His erection pressed against her.

The passion and need were real. He was attracted to her. But was it just attraction?

When he finally pulled back, she panted for breath, and her heart pounded erratically.

"Do you get it now?" he asked.

She smiled suggestively. "No, but I'd like to…"

He laughed. And whatever torment he still carried with him appeared to lighten as his green eyes twinkled.

"Oh, I'd also like to," he agreed. "But I have to do something else first." He restarted the elevator.

"See my dad," she agreed as the doors opened. But once he returned her safely to her father, would he consider his mission completed, and would he leave, never to see her again?

Before she could ask him, he stopped at the nurses' station. "Woodrow Lynch?"

An older nurse looked up from her computer monitor and uttered a weary sigh. "Yes. But he's had too much company and not enough rest. We need to cut off visiting hours for him early."

"I'm his daughter," Megan said.

The nurse pursed her thin lips as if she didn't believe her.

"She is," Gage insisted in a gruff voice that brooked no argument. They had never discussed it. But he'd been to her house. He'd seen photos of her mother and of her father when he was younger. He had to know she couldn't biologically be Woodrow's child. But he also knew that they were family no matter what the DNA.

"Are you Megan?" another, younger nurse asked as she joined them at the desk.

Megan nodded.

"And you're Gage?" she asked.

He nodded. "Yes."

"He's been waiting for them," this nurse told the other one.

The older woman, with her brush-cut short gray hair, glared at her. "But he's had too much company and is only supposed to have one visitor at a time."

"He was shot at her wedding," the younger nurse said. "He won't rest until he knows they're all right."

The older nurse pursed her lips again disapprovingly but nodded her agreement. Like it mattered. Megan had been through too much to let anyone keep her from her father.

And the same went for Gage. If he tried to walk away, she wouldn't let him. She'd persist until he gave her another chance. She would never give up on them again.

The younger nurse gestured at them to follow her, and she led them down the hall to a closed door. "Sorry about her," she said. "I think she's jealous."

"Jealous?" Gage asked.

"Of the love…"

And when she opened the door, they saw the love— Penny curled up against Woodrow's side in his narrow hospital bed. Penny tensed and tried to ease away, but Woodrow kept his arm around her shoulders. Despite having been shot, he looked happier than Megan had ever seen her father.

Tears of joy and relief stung her eyes. She rushed forward to hug him. "I'm so glad you're all right!"

He clasped her head in his hand, holding it against his, as his breath shuddered out in a sigh of relief. "Me, too, my beauty. I'm so glad you're all right."

"What?" Gage asked with his arms outstretched. "I gave you my word that I would keep her safe. Did you doubt me?"

"He wasn't the one doubting you," Penny said. "You've been doubting yourself."

Gage chuckled, and it sounded a little less rusty than when Megan had heard it before. "Damn you," Gage cursed her with a wealth of affection in his gruff voice. "For always being right!"

"It's a pain in the ass, isn't it?" Woodrow said. "Don't

know what I was thinking to propose to this woman. It's going to be a hardship to have a wife who's always right."

"You're engaged!" Megan uttered a squeal of pure delight. No wonder her father looked so happy. He was going to marry a wonderful woman. She hugged Penny, too.

Penny touched her cheek, tipping her face to hers. "Are you sure you're okay with this?" she asked. "This feels like horrible timing after what happened at your wedding."

"I'm so happy something good came out of such a horrible day," Megan said.

Penny nodded in agreement then she glanced up at Gage. "Is our engagement going to be the only good thing?"

Gage shrugged. "I guess that's up to Woodrow."

"Me?" Her father tried to mimic Gage's gesture of stretching his arms out but winced. He was going to be okay. But it was going to take him a while to heal completely. "I already proposed."

"Yes," Gage said. "But will you let me?"

Megan's pulse quickened. Could he be asking what she thought he was asking?

Her father grinned. "Convince me you're worthy of my daughter."

"I love her," Gage said. "I've always loved her."

Megan turned to him, unable to believe what she was hearing. "Loved—you said," she reminded him. "Past tense—as in you did once but don't anymore."

"I never stopped," he said then uttered a ragged sigh. "God knows I tried…"

She flinched. "I'm sorry," she murmured. "Sorry for everything…" If only she hadn't been such a fool… "You quitting the Bureau—reenlisting—it was all my fault." How could she expect him to forgive her when she couldn't forgive herself?

Gage pulled her into his arms, his hands smoothing over her back. "I'm the one who's sorry," he said, and he leaned his forehead against hers, staring deeply into her eyes. "I acted like an idiot with wounded pride. I shouldn't have run away. I should have stayed and fought for you."

She nodded and lightly tapped his chest with her fist. "Yes, you should have."

"I will," he promised. "I won't give up on us again."

"Neither will I," she said.

"It won't always be easy," he warned her. "I'm not myself yet. But with you, I'm more myself than I've been since we broke up. And for you, I will work on getting completely whole again."

How had she ever doubted his love, even for a moment?

Then she remembered. "But you were going to let me marry Richard…"

"That's why," he said. "I thought he would be the better man for you. I thought I was too broken, that the sleepless nights and my nightmares, the flashbacks… I thought it would all be too much for you. I didn't want to put you through what I'm going through."

"That was noble," her father said, as if he agreed with Gage's reasons for not wanting to be with her again.

Megan snorted. "That was stupid. And rude…"

Gage stepped back as if she'd slapped him. "I thought—"

"You thought I wasn't strong enough to help you through this," she said.

He nodded. "You're right. I was stupid and wrong. And you proved that to me. You proved to me how strong you are."

Until today—her wedding day—she hadn't even realized how strong she was. That she was capable of stabbing someone with scissors or tricking armed gunmen…

But she knew not thinking her strong enough hadn't been the only reason for his hesitation.

"You probably also thought I didn't love you enough," she said. "And that is my fault."

He shook his head. "I never should have believed you that day. I should have known that you were just saying you never loved me to protect yourself—that you were scared."

"Not anymore," she said. "Back then I was so afraid of getting hurt. But I had no idea what pain was until I thought I'd lost you forever. I don't want to ever go through that again."

"So you'll marry me?"

"You haven't asked," Penny pointed out, but there was amusement in her voice. She pointed to the floor, apparently wanting Gage to drop to his knees.

"And I haven't given my permission," Woodrow said.

Gage turned to his former boss. "Sir? I promise you that I will spend the rest of my life doing everything in my power to make your daughter happy."

Her father nodded. "You have proven to me over and over again that you're a man of your word, Gage Huxton. Your word is good enough for me. You have my permission."

Gage nodded, too, and there was a hint of moisture in his green eyes. Megan knew her father meant a lot to him.

Woodrow reached out and squeezed her hand. He stared up at her and asked, "What about you, Megan? Is his word good enough for you?"

Like they had, she nodded. She would never doubt Gage's word again. "Yes."

Her father released her hand—as if letting her go. She turned back to Gage, who had dropped to his knees as Penny had directed. Tears rushed into her eyes; she had to blink them back to focus on his handsome face.

"Will you marry me?" he asked. "Will you be my wife?"

She opened her mouth to reply. But he pressed his fingers over her lips.

"I promise that you will never doubt my love again," he said. "I will make sure that you always feel secure and safe with me."

"I do," she told him. "And I will marry you, Gage Huxton. I will be your wife." She threw her arms around his neck and held him closely while Penny and her father cheered.

"What the hell's going on in there?" Nikki Payne asked of the nurses who stood near the door of Woodrow Lynch's hospital room.

The younger nurse smiled. "More love."

The older one snorted but blinked back tears as she hurried away, as if embarrassed at getting caught either at the door or with tears in her eyes. The younger one pushed the door open a little farther so that Nikki could see inside to the two couples embracing.

"Two engagements today," the younger nurse said as she closed the door again. She glanced down at the diamond on her own hand. "My fiancé could have learned something from these two guys about romance." She blinked back tears of her own and hurried off.

Nikki was happy for her mother. So happy…

While Penny had always had all of them—and whatever other kids she'd emotionally adopted as her own, like the Kozminskis—she had still been alone. She had been the only parent. She had been the one offering comfort and never receiving it.

Woodrow had apparently been the same, raising his daughters alone as both father and mother. He'd also been a father figure for all of his agents. Like Penny, he had been there for everyone else while no one had been there for him with support, with comfort, with love…

That was all in the past now for both of them.

Just like all Gage and Megan's pain was in the past. After all they'd been through, they would never break up again. Their love was stronger now—unbreakable—like Gage had been in captivity.

Wrinkling her nose and blinking against the sting in her eyes, Nikki turned away from the closed door. She would be back—with a bottle of champagne so they could really celebrate.

She was happy for them even though this wasn't what she wanted for herself. She had never been the girly girl. She'd never wanted to play Cinderella or Sleeping Beauty. She'd never needed a prince to rescue her. She'd never wanted to marry and have kids. She'd just wanted to kick ass like her brothers.

She hadn't wanted love for herself, but she'd at least believed in it—until she'd learned of her father's betrayal. Then she'd doubted that it was ever real.

Until now…

She blinked harder, fighting back the moisture blurring her eyes. She had no doubt that Megan and Gage were truly, deeply in love. And she had no doubt that her mother had at long last found her true soul mate in Woodrow Lynch.

Real love existed.

For other people…

Just not for Nikki. Not just yet, but maybe someday soon.

* * * * *

CAPTIVE BUT
FORBIDDEN

LYNN RAYE HARRIS

CHAPTER ONE

Late November, London

THE President of Aliz was hiding in the ladies' room.

Veronica St. Germaine lifted her head, frowning at her reflection in the mirror. She really should go back out there, but she was tired of smiling, tired of shaking hands and making small talk, tired of feeling desperate and overwhelmed and so very out of her element.

Yet she knew she had a job to do.

For Aliz. Her people needed her, and she would not fail them. They'd entrusted her with their welfare and she would not return empty-handed.

She couldn't.

Momentarily, she would go back to the hotel ballroom and paste on a smile. Just as soon as she regained her center of calm.

She couldn't quite say what had triggered her need to escape. Perhaps it was the huge crush of curious faces, the suggestive looks from some of the men, or even the knowledge that she was surrounded by men in black suits who would dog her every step for the next two years of her life.

That was what she hated most of all—the loss of her autonomy. In truth, it sparked unpleasant associations she would rather forget. Until the age of eighteen, her life had been so tightly regimented that she'd not had even a single friend.

Veronica took a deep breath and pulled a lipstick tube from her purse. Another moment, and then she had to return to the elegant party.

She'd been traveling for the past two weeks, trying to drum up investment in her country. It wasn't an easy prospect. Aliz was beautiful, with beaches and coastline and balmy breezes, but it was also poor after so many years of mismanagement. Investors wanted to know that if they poured money into the country, it wouldn't be in vain.

She was here to convince them Aliz was a good bet.

And it was much more difficult than she'd anticipated. In so many ways, she wasn't prepared for this job. She'd said no to running for office, but Paul Durand—an old friend of her father's—had convinced her she was the person who could make everything right again.

She'd laughed at the idea—who was she to be president of a nation? She was famous in Aliz, but she was infamous the world over. There was a difference between the two, but Paul hadn't listened.

He'd spoken with such passion, such conviction. And he'd convinced her she was the one person who could do the most good for Aliz. Her notoriety, far from being undesirable, was an asset in the public arena.

She reminded herself of that now. She'd done many things wrong in her life, but she would do this right. Aliz needed her. And she was not the same person she'd been when she'd fled her father's house ten years ago.

Then, she'd been headstrong, selfish and a touch naive.

She'd been looking for adventure, and she'd done everything to excess once she'd escaped her father's control. It had been inevitable that she would become a bad girl, a diva, a spoiled debutante. Some would even include wanton seductress on that list, but all she would say was that she'd allowed herself the freedom to take lovers when it had suited her.

A dart of pain lodged beneath her breastbone. Her last relationship had not ended so well—though it wasn't the man who'd caused the pain that even now threatened to consume her.

If she stopped fighting for even a moment, the pain would win. Because it was her fault it had happened. Her fault the tiny life growing inside her had never had a chance.

She'd always felt impervious, as if no one could hurt her because she refused to let them, but she'd learned there were many kinds of hurt. Some hurts snuck up on you like a scorpion in the night and left you gasping and aching and wondering how you'd never known it could happen to you.

Veronica swiped a hand beneath her eyes.

Not now. She would not dwell on it now.

The lights flickered overhead. It had been snowing heavily for hours. Perhaps the power would go out after all. She resolutely sucked in a breath and bent toward the mirror to remove all traces of tears from the corners of her eyes. Then she stood and smoothed a hand down her gown.

Her pity party was finished; it was time to return to the ballroom before the power went out and she was left in the dark alone.

Veronica bit back a cry as the door to the ladies' room suddenly swung inward. No one should have gotten past the bodyguard stationed outside.

But the intruder was a man, dressed in an all-too-familiar black suit.

She pivoted angrily. This was too much. She would not have her private moments intruded on by her security staff.

Except this man was not her guard, nor was he wearing the typical black suit of one of her people.

"Who are you?" she blurted, her heart beginning to hammer in her throat as she faced him.

The man was tall and clad in a tuxedo that appeared to be custom-fitted. The fabric looked expensive, with a hint of shine that came from how tightly the cloth was woven. His dark hair curled over his collar, his golden skin so exotic and beautiful.

She'd seen this man by the bar, talking to her old friend Brady Thompson. She relaxed infinitesimally. If he knew Brady…

"I am Rajesh Vala."

The name meant nothing to her.

His hands were shoved casually into the pockets of his trousers. The door swung shut behind him, and then it was just the two of them in the small anterior suite of the powder room. Mirrors lined three walls, giving her the impression there was more than one man in the room with her.

She swallowed, the pulse in her neck tapping a rhythm he surely could see.

He said nothing, as if he were waiting for her to speak. But she couldn't. She could only stare. He was Bollywood-handsome, with his tanned skin and honey-gold eyes, and she found herself thinking of tigers. Sleek, gorgeous, deadly.

Her heart kicked up again and she found her voice. "What have you done with my bodyguard?"

His scorn was not promising. "Your security is sadly lacking, Madam President. The most inept criminal could get to you with little trouble. And that's a problem."

"My security is fine—"

He took another step closer, his hands sliding free of his pockets like an animal unsheathing its claws. Instinctively, she backed away, her bottom hitting the ledge she'd rested her purse on only a few moments ago.

He held up his hands. "I'm not here to hurt you."

"Then step aside and let me leave."

His sensual lips parted in a mocking smile. Her heart stuttered, then tripped forward again. *Too handsome and flashy. Too, too dangerous.*

She had no use for men like this. No use for *any* man, she silently corrected, not for a long time now. Not since she'd realized there were consequences to be paid.

"I'm afraid I can't do that just yet, Madam President."

"I beg your pardon?" Veronica said, as coldly as she was able to. She'd learned, over the years, to brazen her way through when necessary. Sometimes all it took was the perception of authority to actually imbue authority. "That is not your decision to make."

Again the concentrated power of the leashed tiger reflected in his eyes. "Ah, but it is."

A chill rippled down her spine like the beginnings of an avalanche. Understanding unfolded within. She'd seen this man with Brady, but she had no idea who he really was.

What he was capable of.

Why he was here, now.

Her pulse throbbed even faster. "What have you done to my bodyguard? If you've hurt him…"

His head tilted. "He is special to you?"

Veronica clasped her tiny purse in both hands, holding it in front of her body like a shield. A very inadequate shield. A sudden, overwhelming urge to walk over and wipe the superior look off this man's face rolled through her. She would not act upon it, however.

"He is my countryman, and he's in my employ. Yes, I care about him."

"I see. Admirable of you, Madam President. But tell me, why are you not so careful with your own person?"

Veronica gave her head a little shake. She almost felt as if she'd been drinking, when in fact she'd had nothing stronger than sparkling water, so completely did this man befuddle her senses. "I beg your pardon?"

"Once more with the begging? I'm surprised. I understood that you were far more fierce than this."

A current of anger spiked in her belly. "I'm afraid you have me at a disadvantage, Mr. Vala. You seem to know so much about me, and I know nothing of you. Other than I saw you talking with Brady Thompson in the bar."

"So you *were* paying attention."

Veronica ground her teeth in frustration. "I would appreciate it very much if you could stop talking to me like I'm a two-year-old and tell me what you want."

Rajesh Vala laughed. The sound startled her. It was rich, deep. Sexy. It curled around her, slid through her. Disconcerted her.

"Very good, Veronica. No wonder they elected you. You project competence, regardless of whether or not it's true."

She refused to rise to the bait, though a worm of hurt burrowed through her composure. But what did she expect? She'd spent years being the kind of person no one would ever take seriously.

"If you truly know Brady, then you'll know you aren't impressing me at the moment. What is the purpose of the exercise, Mr. Vala?"

His golden eyes sparkled. Those sensual lips twitched. She found herself focusing on them, thinking how they would feel pressed against her own.

The thought shocked her. She hadn't felt the slightest hint of interest or attraction for any man in over a year. She simply wasn't ready for it.

To say this was an inconvenient time for those feelings to return was an understatement.

"No purpose, other than to see how good your security is. It isn't." He leaned against the wall, arms folded across his chest. It was such a casual pose.

But it was deceptive. She had the impression that he wasn't relaxed at all. That he could spring into action at any second. Could strike without warning.

Like a scorpion in the night.

"The guard?" she demanded again.

"He's fine. He might even be achieving his own personal Shangri-la right about now. Depending on his staying power, of course."

She felt her face redden and she glanced away. Since when did she blush over innuendo? She was Veronica St. Germaine, notorious trendsetter. She'd once attended a party in Saint-Tropez wearing a dress that had been airbrushed onto her body. She'd literally been naked, other than the paint.

And this man made her blush?

"He was quite easily distracted, by the way. The charms of lovely Tammy, an Irish lass from Cork, were too much to resist, it seems."

"You're despicable."

"No. I'm thorough. And quite adept at staying."

Her ears were on fire. She was no longer certain what they were talking about. Security? Sex? Her mind was opting for sex and her body was reacting to the suggestion.

It'd been too long since she'd had sex. That had to be the only reason he could make her flush like an innocent virgin.

"I can't imagine that Brady approves of your methods," she said coolly. It was the first thing she could think of to say that might bring the conversation back from the brink.

"Not always. But he knows I'm the best."

She wanted to sit. The heat was going to her head, making her feel faint. Or perhaps her dress was too tight. Whatever the case, she was moist with perspiration. She sank onto the bench, uncaring what he might think, and clasped her hands in her lap. Though what she really wanted to do was grab one of the fluffy white towels stacked on one corner of the vanity and dab her forehead with it.

"The best, Mr. Vala?" A sudden thought occurred to her. Brady had told her just this morning that she was too wound up—but he wouldn't hire a gigolo to relax her, would he? A gigolo who outfoxed her bodyguard and caught her in the ladies' room? A bubble of laughter escaped before she could stop it.

God, it was ridiculous. And maybe, just maybe, Brady truly was that crazy.

"I am a...security consultant," the man said, watching her curiously.

Did he think she would pat the bench and suggest they get cozy together? Was Brady so insane as to think she had bodyguard fantasies? That a handsome, too-sexy tiger in a tuxedo could rock her world in the ladies' powder room of an expensive hotel and she'd suddenly be relaxed and ready to face the challenges awaiting her?

Once, no doubt, that would have been true. But she was a different person now. She had to be.

She found the strength to stand again. "I'm not in the mood, Mr. Vala, but I thank you for the diversion. If you could get out of my way, I'll say good-night now and return to the ballroom."

His brows drew down. She had the feeling she'd insulted him somehow.

"Perhaps you didn't hear what I said," he replied, taking a step toward her.

"Oh, I heard you. And I'm not sure what you and Brady cooked up between you, but I'm not that desperate. Or that stupid."

He stood so close now. So close that if she reached out, her fingertips could slide down the sleek fabric of his lapel.

His scent stole to her. Sharp and clear, like rain and warm spices. Like a sultry Indian night.

The lights dimmed for a long moment before brightening again. The tiger didn't move, his gaze never leaving her face. She felt trapped—and safe, paradoxically.

"The power will probably go out," he said. "We should get you back to your room. It is the safest place."

"The safest place for what?" she asked, her voice little more than a cracking whisper, as her imagination ran wild and her skin grew hot and prickly.

Again, he looked at her curiously. "For you, Madam President."

Cobras. They had cobras in India. Cobras that mesmerized their prey before striking. Was he less of a tiger and more of a cobra? Was she mesmerized? Was that why she felt so languid and warm, why she wanted to close her eyes and lean into him? Why she wanted to take what she thought he was offering and then pretend it had never happened?

Deliberately, she took a step back, breaking the spell. This was insane. And she had to put an end to it. There was too much at stake.

"I'm sure you're quite good, but I've a duty to perform and no time for casual sex on the bathroom counter. Please tell Brady I was happily satisfied, if that's what you need to do to get paid. I'll find my own way back to my room."

He stared at for her a long moment—and then he threw

back his head, a sharp bark of laughter springing from his throat. She was so startled she couldn't move. And then she felt the bite of heat flooding her again. A different kind of bite this time.

"This is definitely a first," he said, the humor evident on his handsome face. It transformed him somehow, made him less frightening and more real. More human. "But I am not here for your, uh, satisfaction, I assure you."

For some reason, that statement made her angry. As if he'd never consider such a thing with her. As if the thought were repulsive, when men had always clamored for her attentions.

She drew herself up. "You come in here talking in innuendo and half-truths—what do you expect me to think?"

She clung to the anger because the alternative was to melt into an embarrassed puddle. He probably had a wife and ten children at home, even if he was too perfect for words and wore no wedding band.

A sudden, sharp stab of something—*pain, Veronica, pain*—pierced her chest at heart level. She knew she was not the sort of woman who inspired visions of picket fences, warm kitchens and laughing babies.

And it had never bothered her until recently, until she'd almost had her own baby.

Baby.

Funny how that word snuck up sometimes and squeezed the breath from her chest. She closed her eyes briefly, swallowed the bile rising in her throat.

I'm sorry, sweet baby...

"Are you unwell?" he asked.

She sliced a hand through the air impatiently, shoving the pain down deep into her soul. "I'm fine."

The lights flickered again. He looked up, frowning.

"We really should return to your room before the power goes out."

"*We* aren't going anywhere," she snapped.

He looked at her as if he pitied her. "That is not your choice to make."

Veronica stared at him for a moment, undecided, while anger built into a solid wall inside her. How *dare* he? How absolutely *dare* he?

Energy exploded inside her like a wave collapsing and racing toward shore, until it sent her striding forward, intending to push past him if necessary.

He anticipated her, caught her bare arm in one strong hand. The shock of skin on skin sizzled into her core, and Veronica gasped. It was too much, too many raw emotions welling to the surface all at once. She couldn't bear it, couldn't bear to be touched by him.

She twisted hard, her open hand swinging up to connect with his cheek.

She missed. At the same time, her body spun out of her control—and then she was pressed against him, her back to his front, one strong hand clasping her wrists together behind her back while the other snaked around her waist and held her tightly.

Fury welled inside her as she jerked uselessly against the bonds of his iron grip.

He was so solid, so warm and hard. It took her a moment to realize that her bottom nestled in the cradle of his hips. That his body was responding to the way she squirmed against him. If she weren't wearing heels, she wouldn't be tall enough.

But right now, she was.

Her skin was hot, so hot. She wanted to press back against him, wanted to feel his heat pass into her cold body.

The thought horrified her so much she pulled forward

in his grasp, trying hard to minimize the contact between them. Her back arched, her breasts straining against her gown as if they would pop free at any moment.

"Let me go," she groaned.

"I'm here to protect you," he said, his warm breath whispering against her ear. A shudder traveled the length of her spine. She had no doubt he'd felt it.

"Protect me from what? From you?" she flung at him as the evidence of his arousal grew against her.

He managed to put a little distance between them, though not much. The loss of contact disconcerted her in ways it shouldn't. What was wrong with her?

"From yourself," he growled in her ear. "From the incompetence of your staff."

"A funny way you have of doing it," she snapped, trying so hard to concentrate on what was wrong with this picture instead of what felt right.

His touch. His breath in her ear. The scent of him. The solid feel of him standing behind her. Veronica fought for control. "I have protection, in spite of what you might think. That man will be fired immediately. Another will take his place."

"Very good, Veronica. I'd thought you would be soft on him."

"I'm never soft," she said as another tremor passed over her. His fingers began to slide slowly across her abdomen.

"Are you quite certain?" His voice was seductive and beautiful in her ear. So much in that sentence. So much she couldn't begin to speak to.

"You can let me go," she repeated.

"I'm not so sure." His fingers moved slowly, so slowly. The pressure of them against her body was light, yet she felt them as if she was naked and he was stroking her like a lover.

She closed her eyes, swallowed hard. *My God...*
The lights flickered once more....
And then snapped out, plunging them into darkness.

CHAPTER TWO

THE sudden silence was crushing. Veronica could hear his breathing, but nothing else.

"Now what?" she asked, her voice so loud to her ears. Catching at the end. Sounding husky. Needy.

For this man? A stranger to her?

It was unfathomable, and yet nothing was as it should be. Nothing had been as it should have been for months. In truth, her entire life had spun out of control and had yet to spin back.

"We wait," he said, his fingers stilling.

"For what? Don't you have a flashlight or something? For all your fine talk about being the best, you seem unprepared."

"I am definitely prepared," he growled in her ear, his breath tickling the fine hairs on her nape.

"Prove it," she said, her voice even huskier if that were possible. Dear God, what was she up to? There was no way on earth she was truly egging this man on, was there? She might find him amazingly attractive—devastatingly so— but she was not about to lift her gown and wrap her legs around his body in reality.

No matter what Brady seemed to think she was capable of. No matter what she might have done a little over a year ago when confronted with a man of such beauty and power as this sexy tiger in black.

The old Veronica would have made *him* blush.

"I'm beginning to understand you," he said in her ear. "You challenge those around you as a way to deflect attention from yourself. And yet you've been elected to a very public position. Odd, is it not?"

A stone dropped inside her stomach. It was too close to the truth. Too close to who she'd been before she'd lost her way. "Save yourself the trouble of trying to analyze me, Mr. Vala."

"Don't you think you should call me Raj now?" His hand around her wrists was hot, his skin still burning hers with his touch. Though it was dark, she closed her eyes.

Raj. It was exotic, like him. She wanted to say it aloud, wanted to try it on her tongue.

But she would not.

"I see no need," she said. "As soon as the lights come back on, I don't ever intend to see you again."

"You need me, Veronica. Whether you wish to admit it or not."

She swallowed. "I don't need anyone." She'd made sure of it over the years—and she'd only been wrong once.

His hand dropped from her waist. A moment later, she felt the tips of his fingers sliding along her spine where her dress opened, leaving a trail of fire in their wake. "Mr. Vala…"

"Raj."

"Raj," she said, giving in to his demand because she hoped it would stop the insane stroking of her skin. It did not.

She *wanted*. And yet she couldn't allow this side of her nature to surface, not now. Not ever again. The only way to protect herself from harm was to suppress her feelings. Feelings of need, of loneliness, of desire.

Human feelings.

No.

Veronica sucked in a shaky breath, fighting for control. "This isn't very professional, is it? Do security consultants usually attempt to seduce their charges?"

The torturous track of his fingers ceased. Her heart hammered in the thick darkness. She'd scored a hit, but it didn't make her feel any better. In some ways she wanted to take the words back, wanted him to continue the light stroking of her skin.

He did not. "Forgive me," he said, his tone clipped—but whether it was with anger at her or himself, she wasn't certain.

A moment later she was moving sideways, falling—but just as she was about to grab for him, about to wrap her arms around his neck so she didn't fall, he eased her down on a bench and let her go. She searched the blackness for him, but could see nothing. Panic filled her until she willed it away.

"Don't leave me here," she said, nearly choking on the words as she did so. She hated to admit weakness, hated to admit she did need him, at least for the time being.

"I'm not leaving," he replied, his voice coming from across the room. But she could hear the door easing open. He was going to leave her alone in this dark, lonely room. She would be lost, as lost as she'd been at sixteen when her father had locked her in a closet to punish her for trying to run away.

Blindly, she shot upright…and fell forward as her foot hit a nearby table.

Somehow, she managed to catch herself, but not without bending her wrist too far. She cried out as needles of pain shot through her arm.

"What are you doing?" Raj demanded.

She groped her way back onto the bench, relief flooding her as she held her wrist, sucking in deep breaths to keep from crying. "I thought you were leaving."

"I told you I wasn't." His voice sounded closer now. A second later, light illuminated the small room.

She blinked up at him. "You have a light."

"Yes."

"Why didn't you use it to begin with?"

"Because I needed to be sure no one was outside first." He bent in front of her, his dark head close as he took her arm in his hands and probed her wrist. She didn't bother to ask how he knew she'd hurt herself. Veronica hissed as he found the tender spot. "It's just a light sprain," he said.

Then he stood and the light blinked out again.

"Why do we have to sit here?" she asked. "Why can't we use your light and go to my room?"

"So now you want my help," he said softly, almost teasingly.

"You have the light," she replied, as if it were the most logical thing in the world to say.

She felt movement, felt a solid form settle on the bench beside her. He reached for her arm, finding it so surely that she swore he must have a cat's night vision.

His fingers danced over the skin of her wrist, his thumbs pressing in deeply, making her gasp—and yet it felt good, as if he were easing the sprain out of her by touch alone.

"This is what we are going to do," he said. "We're going to spend the next twenty minutes here, while pandemonium reigns in the hotel, and hope the lights come back on. If they don't, we're going to your room."

She hated being told what to do, and yet she'd tacitly

agreed to it when she'd panicked over being alone in the dark. "Did Brady hire you?"

His soft snort was confusing. "In a manner of speaking. I've done work for him in the past. Protecting his celebrity clients."

She had to bite back a moan as his fingers worked their magic on her. "I appreciate your diligence, Mr. Vala, but Brady should have known better."

"He cares about you."

"I know," she said softly. Brady was a true friend. She knew he'd always wanted to be more than that, but she'd never felt the same in return. In spite of it, their friendship flourished. Brady was a good man, the kind of man she *should* have been interested in. Life would have been a whole lot easier if she had been.

The pressure of Raj's fingers was perfect, rhythmic. Why did she always want the kind of men who were terrible for her? Men like this one, handsome and dangerous and incapable of seeing past the facade of her outward appearance to what lay beneath?

It was her fault they could not. She'd spent so many years building a wall, becoming someone interesting and compelling and, yes, even shocking, that she no longer knew how to be herself with a man. She had no idea if the real Veronica was even worth the trouble.

And she wasn't planning to try and find out.

Raj's voice startled her. "After what happened tonight, do you still trust your staff?"

A chill slithered down her spine. That was something she hadn't wanted to think about. Because how could she admit that she didn't know? That she was out of her depth and uncertain where to turn?

She thought of the letter she'd gotten that morning, and shivered. It had been so simple, one word in cut-out letters: *slut*. It had been nothing, really. The work of a former rival. Who else would go to the trouble?

But the one question she'd kept asking herself today was how had the letter penetrated her security and found its way onto her breakfast tray?

She'd interrogated her secretary. The guard on duty. The maid. The porter. No one seemed to know.

Then, in a moment of weakness, she'd told Brady about it. She regretted that now, as it was surely the impetus for him to call this man.

"Yes, I trust them," she said, because she could say nothing else. Was she supposed to run scared over a simple letter? Her bodyguard abandoning his post tonight was an unrelated incident. That didn't mean the rest of her staff was incompetent.

"Then you are either naive or stupid, Madam President," Raj Vala said.

"I am neither one," she replied, bristling not only at the way he'd pronounced her incompetent, but also at the condescending tone he'd used to say the last two words. As if he didn't think her worthy.

She might not be, but it wasn't his place to say so. He was not Alizean. "Not everything is as straightforward as you might think. There are many options to be considered."

His thumbs worked magic. Tingles of sensation streaked up her arm, over her scalp. Down into her core. She couldn't stop the little moan that escaped her.

Damn him. And damn her reawakened senses.

Wrong time. Wrong place. Wrong man.

It was the situation, she told herself, the fact she now found herself alone with a dynamic, sexy stranger who touched her as if he had a right. Because she'd allowed no man to get close to her since the miscarriage, she was now suffering from sensory overload.

"Would you like me to tell you the best option?" he asked.

"Do I have a choice?" she snapped.

"You always have a choice," he replied evenly. "Except in instances where your immediate safety might be at stake."

She wanted to tell him to go to hell. Who was he to walk in here and try to take over this aspect of her new life as if he had a right?

But he kept rubbing, soothing her sore wrist, and she didn't say a word because she selfishly didn't want him to stop.

A minute later, the fingers of one hand slid up her arm, over her jaw, her chin, across her lips. She didn't know why she allowed it—

No, that wasn't quite true. She allowed it because it felt shockingly perfect to let him touch her. He made her feel normal, and that was something she hadn't expected to feel ever again. It felt surprisingly good to be touched after all this time.

She trembled at the featherlight stroking of his finger across her mouth, and she bit down on her lip to keep from nibbling him in return.

Oh, he was good. Good enough that she began to wonder if he hadn't missed his calling in life. Gigolo seemed a perfectly acceptable occupation for a man with his skill set.

"Then tell me this option," she stated, hoping she sounded businesslike and cool as she dragged her attention back from the summit. "Let's see how good you are."

His fingers slid along her jaw now, so light, so erotic. His soft laugh was a sensual purr in his throat, and she knew she'd made a mistake. A dreadful, heart-pounding mistake.

"It's quite simple. You need to acquire a lover, Madam

President." His voice was so sexy, so mesmerizing, his slight British accent combined with another she couldn't quite place.

Everything inside her stilled. Her stomach clenched painfully. *Of course.*

He might be here to help her, but he wasn't above helping himself, either. Men like him made her sick. Always wanting something in return. Brady might truly care, but this man did not.

"It's out of the question," she said, her voice tight. "I don't want to hear another word of this—"

"Ah, but you will listen. Because you're smart, Veronica." His fingers continued their damning track across her skin. She felt his presence in the dark as a solid wall of heat, and she tilted her head back, sensing somehow that he loomed over her, that his mouth was only inches from hers.

She should pull away, and yet she couldn't seem to do it. "Flattery will get you nowhere."

"Why deny the truth? You know it as well as I do."

Heat suffused her from the inside out. Somehow she managed to scoot backward on the bench, to put distance between them. Was she that transparent? "I have no idea what you're talking about."

But she did. Because he touched her so lightly, so expertly, that her body was tightening like a bowstring.

There was definitely something there, something between them...something that would combust if she let it. Part of her desperately wanted to let it...

"Yes, you do," he said softly. His tone was that of a lover.

Did he feel it, too?

"Maybe..." she breathed.

But his next words shattered that illusion.

"Your presidency is too new, Aliz is in turmoil and you aren't safe."

Every word was like a blow. Embarrassment flooded her in bright, white-hot waves. She'd been preoccupied with the way he made her feel when he touched her, and he was nothing but business. Damn him for making her forget, even for a moment.

"Those things are none of your concern," she said evenly, thankful he couldn't see her flushed face. Thankful there was no light to give her away. "Nothing you can do will fix it overnight."

"This isn't a game, Veronica. You can't quit this party when it no longer amuses you." Raj heard her draw in a breath. He'd probably insulted her, but he didn't give a damn.

Because Veronica St. Germaine was precisely the sort of woman he had no sympathy for.

She was a slave to her passions, her wants, her desires. She was the worst kind of person to be entrusted with the welfare of a puppy, let alone a nation—yet here she was.

And here he was, damn Brady to hell. Raj hadn't wanted to do this job, but Brady had begged him.

For old time's sake. And since Raj owed at least a measure of his success to Brady's faith in him when he'd been fresh out of the military and working his first security job so many years ago, he couldn't say no.

So now he was sitting in the dark with a too-sexy, spoiled society princess and arguing over whether or not she needed his help.

He should just kiss her and put the matter to rest. He wasn't unaware of her response to him. He also wasn't unaware of her reputation as a woman who pursued her appetites relentlessly, be they clothes, shoes, fast cars or men.

And at least one part of his anatomy didn't mind the prospect of being an object of her desire.

Not that he would allow himself to go down that road.

It'd been a long time since he'd personally guarded anyone, but he had never allowed himself to get involved with a client. It angered him immensely that he'd nearly violated that creed with her.

He didn't know why he'd allowed himself to succumb to the temptation to stroke his fingers along the creamy skin of her exposed back. She was not the kind of woman he would ever get involved with. It wasn't that she wasn't desirable—she definitely was—but she was self-centered and destructive. Poisonous.

"I know this isn't a game!" she barked. "Do you really think I don't?"

He'd heard those words before. Or ones very like them anyway. He knew all about people who had no control over their impulses. People who claimed to want to conquer their addictions, but inevitably slid back into them when life got too hard or too boring or too hopeless.

He had no sympathy for her. She'd taken on this task, and she deserved no pity if it was turning out to be too difficult. After all, her people would get none if she faltered. "It's a big responsibility you've accepted. Not quite your usual thing, is it?"

He could feel the fury rolling from her in waves.

"You know nothing about me, Mr. Vala. I'd appreciate it if you'd keep your pop psychology to yourself."

She was cool, this woman. And blazing hot on the inside. He was beginning to understand the public fascination with her.

He'd made sure to have his people prepare a dossier on her before he'd ever come to the hotel tonight. He hadn't read the entire thing during the limo ride over, but he'd skimmed enough to get an idea.

A dilettante in the worlds of fashion, music and television, she'd designed a line of clothing, recorded a hit album and had her own late-night talk show for a brief time in America.

She'd been a darling of the tabloids. Her face and figure were splashed on more magazine covers worldwide than were the royals. It was astounding.

Until about a year ago, she'd regularly appeared. Then she'd dropped out of sight. Working on a new project, her spokesperson had said at the time, though the speculation had been that she was nursing a broken heart after a failed affair.

When she'd emerged from hiding four months later, she'd been relegated to a small blurb on the pages she'd once dominated. It had been shortly afterward that she'd declared her candidacy for president.

It wasn't difficult to figure out why she'd done so, because suddenly she was back on top, a darling of the media once more.

He understood where that kind of need for attention came from, but he had no patience for it. People like her destroyed those foolish enough to get close to them.

Or those who had no choice—like children.

More than once he'd watched his mother spiral into the depths of her selfish need for attention, unable to stop her. Unable to prevent the crash. He'd survived that life, but he certainly hadn't come away unscathed.

"A lover could get close to you without suspicion," he said. "It would be a way to provide extra security without anyone on your staff questioning the addition."

"You aren't listening to me, are you? I don't like you, and I can't take a lover. Even a false one."

He didn't bother to point out that she did like him. That she'd been sending him signals from the moment he'd entered the room. Frustration hammered into him. Why was he arguing with her? He'd done what he'd promised Brady he would do. He'd tried to help. Now he could take her back to her suite and leave her there in good conscience.

Except it wasn't in his nature to give up so easily, especially when he believed she truly was in danger. Her country was in turmoil, and it was well-known that the previous president hadn't been too happy with the outcome of the election. Aliz was a democracy, but only just. And Monsieur Brun had been in power for twelve years before he'd lost to this woman who had no political experience whatsoever.

Disgruntled loser was an understatement.

"You need protection, Veronica. That threat should never have gotten through the layers surrounding you. It will escalate, believe me."

He could feel her stiffen beside him. "There's been no threat."

"That's not what Brady says."

Her breath hissed out. "I *knew* it. It was *one* word, made of newspaper letters and glued to a piece of paper. That's hardly a threat!"

Every instinct he had told him otherwise. It was an ugly word, the kind of word that was filled with hate and derision. Spoken in anger was one thing. Deliberately pasted together and sent? "Did you keep the letter?"

"I threw it away."

He'd expected as much, though it would have been better if she had not. "Has it happened before?"

"Before I was president?"

"Precisely."

She let out a frustrated breath. "No. But that doesn't mean anything. Everyone has enemies."

"But not everyone is the president of a nation. You have to take every anomaly, no matter how small, as a legitimate threat. You have no choice now."

"I realize that." Her voice was ice.

"Then you must also realize that we wouldn't actually be lovers," he said, as much to himself as to her. "That's not why I'm here."

A shame, really. She was an extraordinarily sensual woman. He'd watched her work the room from his position at the bar earlier. She'd slain men with her smile, with the high, firm breasts that jutted into the fabric of the purple dress she wore. With the long, beautiful legs he'd glimpsed through the slit in the fabric when she walked.

Her platinum-blond hair was piled onto her head, and her dress dipped low in the back, revealing smooth, touchable skin. Men had tripped over their tongues as they'd gathered around her. He'd watched it all with disdain.

Until he'd gotten close to her. His visceral reaction had been strong, his body hardening painfully. It was nothing he couldn't handle. He was accustomed to want, to deprivation and pain. The military had made sure of it. Denying himself pleasure, no matter how much he might want it, was easily done.

"Even the appearance of it would be too much," she replied, her words crisp and lovely in the French accent of her homeland. "I am the president. I have an image to maintain."

"You're a single woman, Veronica. You're allowed to date. And Aliz's is not the sort of culture that would take you to task for it."

"Aliz has had one crisis after another. They need a president who is focused on their welfare, not on her personal life."

He found the words ironic coming from her, but he allowed it to pass without comment.

"They also elected you because you are glamorous and exotic to them. You've achieved fame on the world stage, and they are proud of you. If you become simply another staid politician, you will disappoint them. They want you to fix things, but they also want you to be the Veronica St. Germaine they know and love."

"You can't know that," she said angrily. "You are saying whatever you think will further your personal agenda."

A current of annoyance rippled through him, only partly because it was true. "My personal agenda? I'm doing you a favor, Madam President, in trying to protect your lovely behind."

"How dare you suggest I should be grateful when you keep trying to give me something I don't want?"

What she needed was a hard dose of reality.

He grasped her shoulders, pulled her closer to him. He did it for effect, not because he wanted to kiss her. Not because he'd been dying to kiss her from the moment she'd turned to him when he'd entered this room.

Never because of that.

Her palms came up, pressed against his chest. "What are you doing?" She sounded breathless. Not scared, not angry. Breathless. Anticipating. Wanting.

If he were a weaker man, she would be the ruin of all his fine control.

"We're alone and you're at my mercy," he said, making sure his voice was harsh rather than seductive. "If I'd come to harm you, no one would stop me."

"I'm not helpless," she replied. "I took a self-defense course."

Raj laughed. He couldn't help it. Self-defense was good. Everyone should take a self-defense class. And yet…

"There are people against whom your average self-defense techniques don't work. Because those techniques rely on surprise, and some people cannot be surprised. Some people are trained killers, Veronica."

Like he was, he silently added. Six years in the Special Forces had taught him that much and more.

He felt the shiver go through her body. The idea was reprehensible to her. As well it should be.

"Everything you say is for one purpose," she said, her breath soft against his face.

It wouldn't take much to claim her lips. To plunder them with his own and taste their sweetness.

"But you and Brady have got it all wrong. No one is out to harm me."

His grip on her tightened. "Are you willing to bet your life on that?"

CHAPTER THREE

VERONICA's pulse skipped and bobbed like a white-water raft sailing toward a massive waterfall. But whether it was his insistence she was in danger or how closely he now held her, she couldn't be sure.

He gripped her so tightly that she could feel the strength of the leashed power in him. A shiver skimmed over her. He'd scared her with his talk of danger—but she wouldn't let him know it.

His hands splayed over her back. She could feel his breath on her face. She thought he might kiss her just to prove his mastery—and part of her longed for it.

Another part wanted to run as far and as fast away from this man as she could get. For whatever reason, he affected her. She'd thought herself immune to men after Andre—handsome, flashy, selfish Andre—but Raj was proving her wrong on that count.

She'd made the right decision when she'd told him she didn't need his help. No way on this earth was she allowing him to pretend to be her lover. One way or another, it would be disastrous.

She strained in the dark to hear him, to feel him, to guess his intent. His breath was on her lips. If she tilted her head, would their mouths touch? She told herself not to do it, and yet her head moved anyway.

Abruptly, he released her.

"Come," he said. "It's time to take you back to your room."

The light flashed on again, and she realized it was coming from his cell phone. His handsome face was in shadow, but she could see the gleam of his eyes as he stood and held out a hand to her.

She took it, let him pull her up, her pulse skittering wildly the instant he touched her.

"I'm not stupid," she said, feeling the need to defend herself. "If I thought there was any real danger, I'd hire you in a minute. But there isn't. The security I have can handle the day-to-day issues that arise."

The steady look he gave her said he didn't believe it for a second. "Instead of justifying it to me, perhaps you need to ask whether or not you're being honest with yourself."

Then he turned and opened the door instead of waiting for an answer. Not that she had one to give. He went through first, and then motioned her to follow. She stayed close behind him as they worked their way toward the upper floors.

The hotel was in disarray, but the staff had managed to get the emergency lights working in the main hallways and stairwells. Exit signs also provided light, though meager, and she heard scraps of conversation about the generator and its failure to provide backup power. Raj said nothing, simply led the way through the hotel until they came to her room. She was only surprised for a moment that he knew which room was hers.

Of course he knew. Brady had told him everything.

Before she could ask him how he planned to get inside with the power out and the card reader down, he had the door open.

"Behind me," he said.

It was on the tip of her tongue to thank him for his help and tell him to go, but she said nothing. Instead, she did what he told her to do. Regardless of how she felt about him—or about Brady's meddling—it was clear that Raj knew what he was doing. She felt safe, at least for the time being.

He gave her the motion to stay where she was, then went into each room of her suite in succession before returning and giving her the all clear.

Veronica let out a long sigh of relief—not that she'd expected anything to be wrong. She was just glad to be back in the privacy of her room again. She kicked off her platform stilettos, her feet sinking into the plush carpet. "Thank you for escorting me," she said. "I'd offer you a drink, but it's getting rather late. Tell Brady you tried your best. He knows how I am."

Raj fished out a lighter from somewhere and lit the candles that were sitting on the tables. She'd thought they were merely decorative and, in truth, had forgotten all about them. Then he shrugged out of his tuxedo jacket and threw it across the back of a chair.

"I'm not leaving just yet."

A hot bubble of anger popped inside her. She wanted to be alone, wanted to strip out of her gown, put on her pajamas and watch a little bit of television—assuming the power came back on—before she fell asleep. "I didn't ask you to stay."

He lifted his mobile phone and tapped a few buttons. "Until your security returns, I'm staying."

"That's really not necessary. I'll lock the door behind you."

"Forget it," he said, turning away from her to talk to someone on the phone.

Veronica sank onto the couch and folded her arms over

her chest. Damn the arrogance of the man. But she already knew it was useless to order him to leave. Useless to do anything but wait.

If she were lucky, Brady would come looking for her—and then she could give them both a piece of her mind. She'd had quite enough of being told what to do lately. She had to conform to a schedule as president, had to take meetings and attend functions, had to let her day-to-day activities be far more structured than they'd been since she'd lived on her own.

But she'd agreed to do those things when she'd decided to run for office. What she hadn't agreed to do was let a dark, sexy stranger intrude on the very small slice of privacy she had remaining.

Her gaze drifted to Raj. She couldn't hear what he was saying, but he seemed engrossed in his call. He was even more golden in the candlelight than he'd been in the low lights of the powder room. So handsome. So dangerous. Like the tiger she'd first envisioned when he'd filled the small anteroom and made her aware of him on a level she wished she weren't.

A ring glinted on his right hand, a signet made of gold. She hadn't noticed that before.

His white tuxedo shirt stretched across his chest, and onyx studs winked at her in the flickering light. He reached up and loosened the stud at his neck before yanking the bow tie off and tossing it aside.

She started at the small wedge of bare skin he'd revealed. He glanced up then, straight at her, and she twisted away, cursing herself for getting caught. A moment later he ceased talking and tucked the phone into his trouser pocket.

"Was that Brady?" she asked.

"No."

Frustration knotted her stomach. Since she didn't know what else to do, she reached up and began to unpin her hair, dropping the pins onto the glass side table with a *clink, clink, clink.* Then she threaded the fingers of both hands through her hair, loosening the glossy mass.

When she stopped, Raj was watching her. He stood in the same place he had been, his gaze hard.

Her stomach flipped, her pulse humming with energy. She looked away and began to remove her jewelry.

"Have you been doing this kind of thing long?" she asked. If he insisted on staying, then the least she could do was bore him with questions. Maybe he'd decide to leave her alone after all.

"A few years."

"How exciting." She slipped off the jewelry—bracelet, necklace, rings—and dropped everything on the table with the pins. "Who's the most famous person you've ever worked for?"

"Confidential information."

She glanced up at him, her heart squeezing as she took in the masculine beauty of his face once more. "Ah, of course."

"Are you trying to interview me, Madam President?" he asked, one corner of his mouth twitching with humor.

She swallowed. Humor was not at all the effect she'd been going for. Veronica pulled her feet up beneath her and began to absently rub one instep while her blood beat in her temples, between her breasts. "Not precisely. But if we're to be stuck here together for the foreseeable future, it seems a way to pass the time."

It took her several moments to realize that the side slit in her gown had dropped open to reveal the curve of her legs. She resisted the urge to cover herself, though she suddenly wanted to do so. But she would not let him think she cared that his hot eyes skimmed her form.

"How does one get into the bodyguard business anyway?"

"You've certainly grown chatty," he observed, meeting her gaze once more. She felt heat rising in her cheeks, but she didn't look away. Then he shrugged and shoved his hands into his pockets. "I was in the military. It seemed the logical thing to do when I got out."

"Oh, I see. And do you work for a company that sends you out on these jobs?"

"In a manner of speaking," he said.

The humor was back, but this time she didn't know why.

"If this *were* a job interview," she pointed out, "I don't think I'd be inclined to hire you based on these answers. You're almost monosyllabic."

He sank onto the chair opposite, his big form sprawling comfortably—as if he belonged here, in her suite. As if *he* were the one in charge and she merely a supplicant.

She didn't like that he made her feel inconsequential simply by being in the same room.

"Fortunately, this is not an interview," he said. "You don't need me, as you've pointed out." His golden eyes speared her so that, once more, she was mesmerized. "And I don't do interviews. No one hires me. I decide if I'll help *them*."

"My, my," she said, her face growing hot for some reason. "Aren't you special?"

He leaned forward then, his gaze raking her. She only hoped he couldn't see the *tap, tap, tap* of her heart.

"That's the way *your* world works, Veronica. But not everything is a competition, and not every desire needs to be indulged. I know my worth based on what I've done in the past. I don't think I'm entitled to anything because I deserve it. I've earned it."

She didn't know whether to be outraged or embarrassed. Heat flooded her, made her want to grab a magazine off the table and fan herself. She did not. She'd made her proverbial bed, after all. It was no surprise when someone forced her to lie in it.

But she would not apologize for her life, not to this man. He could know nothing of what she'd been through. No one could.

"Until you walk a mile in someone else's shoes, perhaps it's unwise to make assumptions about them," she said, her smile as brittle as she felt.

He inclined his head a fraction. "You do that so well."

"Do what?"

"Indignation."

She thought of a million responses, discarding them each as she did so. It was no use. There was no point in trying to make this man understand. He meant nothing to her and, after tonight, their paths were unlikely to cross again.

Veronica got to her feet and stared down at him coldly. Imperiously. *Bastard.* "I believe I've had enough of this charming conversation," she said by way of dismissal. "I'm going to bed."

"If this is how you intend to handle affairs of state, Aliz is in a great deal of trouble." His words were mild, his tone nonconfrontational—but his eyes accused her, burned her.

"You are hardly an affair of state," she said, picking up one of the candles from the table, proud that she kept herself from trembling with fury as she did so. "And I'll not stay here and listen to you insult me. You've made up your mind about me. I see no need to waste my breath in pointing out the flaws in your logic."

He flicked a hand in the direction of the bedroom. "Go,

then. It's far easier to run from your problems than to confront them."

"In this case," she said, "I believe it is."

Then she turned and strode away, holding her hand in front of the candle to keep it from blowing out. She closed the bedroom door firmly behind her. Fury churned and roiled in her stomach, burning like acid. Why did she let him get to her? He meant nothing to her. His opinion meant nothing.

He was no one, she reminded herself, nothing more than hired muscle. She didn't let her Alizean bodyguards irritate her half so much, so why was she allowing this man to do so?

Veronica shrugged her shoulders to ease the tension and began to get undressed.

It was a relief to shrug out of the beaded gown and into her flannel pajamas. The Christmas elves marching merrily across the fabric cheered her. She'd thought they were whimsical and cute and she'd bought them impulsively. They were warm and cozy, and she didn't regret it in the least.

Veronica went into the bathroom and washed off her makeup, then returned to the bed and jerked back the covers without removing all the fluffy pillows. Something slightly heavier than a pillow came away with the last tug and bounced down the bed, landing in the middle. She didn't remember leaving anything on the bed when she'd left the room tonight.

Curiously, she lifted the candle.

At first, she wasn't sure what the dark blob was. But then her breath caught in her throat. She wanted to scream, but her vocal chords had seized up. Her mouth opened and closed, like a fish gulping water.

"Raj," she finally squeaked. "Raj. Raj! Raj!"

Each time she managed a little more breath, his name a little louder on every exhalation.

Until the door whipped open and he was at her side. He gripped her arms, bent his head until he was at her level. He looked concerned, intense. She realized he was speaking. Asking her what was the matter. If she were hurt.

She shook her head, turned away. She couldn't look at that…thing…again.

She knew the moment he saw it. He stiffened. Swore.

Then he hooked an arm behind her knees and swept her up against his chest. She didn't protest. She didn't want to protest. Another moment and he was striding from the room. She buried her face in his shirt and let the tears fall.

CHAPTER FOUR

HIS brain had switched into work mode, but his body was very aware of the woman clinging to him so tightly. Raj carried her into the living area, intending to put her on the couch and cover her with a blanket, but her arms were wrapped so tightly around his neck that he knew she wasn't about to let go.

Instead, he settled into one corner of the couch with her on his lap and started to make phone calls. Red-hot anger was a thick brew inside him. It was only a doll on her bed, but someone had gouged out its eyes and splashed what had to be red paint across its body. The alternative was too horrible to contemplate.

Someone had sent a message tonight. An ugly, brutal message if the way Veronica clung to him, her silent tears dampening the fabric of his shirt, was any indication.

No matter what he thought of her, she didn't deserve that kind of ugliness.

He let her cry, one arm firmly around her while he called in one of his security teams. He would have them sweep for any other signs of intrusion before he let Veronica stay here another night. Whether she liked it or not, he was definitely involved.

He considered having her moved to another hotel altogether, but he wasn't entirely convinced that someone on her staff wasn't behind the threats. In that case, moving would do no good. He fully intended to have them all investigated, starting immediately.

He finished the calls and laid his phone on the couch beside his leg. Veronica was curled up in his arms, her face pressed to his chest. She was wearing multicolored pajamas with elves on them—not quite what he'd expected when he'd burst into her room as she'd cried his name.

She'd scared him. He hadn't known what to expect when he'd answered her cry, though he was relieved it hadn't been worse. The doll had apparently been shoved beneath the pillows on her bed. When she'd pulled the covers free, the doll tumbled loose. He cursed himself for having missed it, but the truth was that he couldn't have known.

He would check her quarters more thoroughly in the future.

She held him tightly, but he could feel that she was beginning to be uncomfortable doing so. Her body was stiffening, her fingers opening and closing on his shirt periodically.

She didn't like being dependent on anyone. He'd guessed that about her earlier when she'd been so insistent she didn't need his help. She was proud, and used to getting her way.

A few moments more, and she began to push herself upright. He tightened his grip on her, surprised that he wanted her to stay in his arms, that she felt good there, but immediately let her move away. This changed nothing between them. She was still spoiled, still selfish and self-destructive.

He was here to do a job, nothing more.

She got to her feet, her back to him, and scrubbed her sleeve across her face. His heart pinched. But he was a professional and he would view these events dispassionately. He couldn't do his job if he were emotionally invested.

"Thank you for not saying I told you so," she said a few moments later, her back still to him. The candles flickered, and he found himself wishing she would turn around. That she would look at him.

"What was that about, Veronica?"

She shrugged. It was supposed to be a casual gesture, but it failed miserably. "I wish I knew."

He wanted to be gentle with her, yet he couldn't afford to leave anything unexamined. Her life might depend on it. "I think you do."

Her shoulders drooped. "I'm not prepared to discuss it," she said softly.

In that moment, he had to admit that he admired her more than he'd thought possible. She could have lied, could have insisted she didn't know what he was talking about. But she didn't.

"I don't know who could have done it, and that's the truth," she continued.

Raj stood and put a hand on her shoulder, squeezed. "You don't want to talk about it. I can respect that—for now. But there may come a time when you have no choice."

She turned to him then. A sharp stab of emotion pierced him at gut level. Her face was so fresh and young, so innocent. She'd removed all her makeup and stood before him with red-rimmed eyes, the tracks of her tears gleaming in the candlelight.

He wanted to pull her into his arms, tuck her head against his chest and tell her it would be okay. Instead, he kept his arms rigid at his sides.

"Thank you." She dropped her gaze away, as if she suddenly couldn't look at him. For some reason, that bothered him. She'd been so fiery earlier, so confrontational. She hadn't backed down once. This Veronica was too timid, too defeated.

He didn't like it.

Raj put a finger under her chin, forced her to look at him. Her eyes glistened, but she didn't cry. He could tell that she was finished with crying. Determined.

"Will you let me help you now?" He phrased it as a question, though as far as he was concerned there was no question.

Her throat moved. "Yes," she said, her voice uncertain, thready. She repeated it, the word stronger this time.

"A wise decision," he said.

Her expression hardened, just for a moment. "My staff can't know."

He'd already considered that. If someone in her employ *was* doing these things, it wouldn't do any good for them to know she had extra security.

"Then we're back to the original plan," he said. "Can you do it?"

Her eyes flashed. But she thrust her chin out and gave a firm nod. "If that's what it takes, yes."

He grinned at her. That's the Veronica he'd been looking for. "Then we'll begin tonight."

Her eyes dropped, boldly taking in his form. Then she met his gaze again, one eyebrow quirking. "You're a bit overdressed for the part, considering what I'm wearing."

His body went from zero to sixty in half a second. He couldn't help it, though he was thankful the room was dark enough she couldn't tell.

"We'll improvise," he told her. Because he most certainly wasn't stripping down to his silk boxers.

She wrapped her arms around herself, once more the vulnerable, helpless innocent. He reminded himself that she was neither of those things, though she was certainly frightened—and with good reason.

He put his hands on her shoulders. "You can trust me utterly, Veronica. I won't let anything happen to you."

She let out a shaky sigh. "I know that."

Suddenly the suite was flooded with light. Veronica brought her hand up and covered her eyes. Raj squinted as he made his way over to the wall and flipped the switch, plunging the room into candlelit darkness again. Then he turned on a couple of lamps while Veronica blew out the candles.

She put her hands on her hips, frowned. "Perhaps we should have kept the candles. More romantic."

Someone pounded on the door and Veronica jumped, squeaking as she did so.

Raj went and peeked through the hole, then jerked the door open when he saw it was Brady.

"Where is she?"

Raj stepped back. "She's here."

Brady burst into the room and rushed to Veronica's side. Raj watched them carefully as Brady swept her into a bear hug. "I'm so glad you're well," he said before he set her down again.

She smoothed a hand over her pajamas. Self-consciously? Probably, since Brady had found her alone here with him and she was clearly dressed for bed. Though how she could think elf pajamas were the least bit suggestive, Raj wasn't sure.

"I'm fine, Brady."

Brady shoved a hand through his hair. He was a tall man, though not as tall as Raj, and he'd remained lean throughout the years. Brady's hair was graying at the temples, but that was the only change Raj had noted since the last time—before tonight—that he'd seen the other man.

Brady threaded his fingers through Veronica's and brought her hand to his lips. Raj didn't like the tight pulse of envy that shot through him at the casual gesture.

"I had a call I had to take," Brady said. "And then the lights went out. I had hoped Raj had you safe, but when I came to your room the first time, you weren't here."

"We were, um, elsewhere," she said, not quite meeting his gaze. "But I'm fine. Raj is a very good bodyguard."

Brady's expression was fierce. "I'm glad you think so. Clearly, the one you had tonight was no good."

She looked angry suddenly. Deliberately, she pulled her hand from Brady's grip, crossing her arms over her chest. "So you knew about that?"

"I don't question Raj's methods," Brady said. "He's never failed me."

Veronica slapped him on the shoulder. It wasn't hard. It was the kind of slap Raj imagined a sister would give to her annoying brother.

"That's for not telling me what you were planning," Veronica said, her brows two angry slashes in her face, though her tone was gentler than Raj had expected it would be.

Brady, however, looked like a puppy who'd peed on the carpet. He knew he wasn't in big trouble, but he was in trouble nevertheless. And he didn't like it.

Poor Brady. The way he looked at Veronica, spoke about Veronica—he seemed to want more than her friendship, but he'd decided to be satisfied with what she gave him. Even now he looked at her as if she was the sun and he one of the lucky planets in her orbit.

Typical with women like her, Raj thought sourly. She drew men like flowers drew honeybees.

His mother had been exactly like that before she'd lost her beauty from the drugs and drinking.

Until then, however, she'd managed to keep them both warm and dry by dragging him to stay with her various "boyfriends."

There'd never been a shortage of men willing to take her in. They'd taken him by extension. Some had ignored him. Others had resented him. And at least one had threatened him.

"I knew you wouldn't approve," Brady was saying to her.

"I wouldn't have," she admitted. "But Raj has managed to show me the error of my ways."

Brady's gaze slewed to him. "Has he?"

Veronica was looking over Brady's shoulder at him with wide eyes. She gave her head a little shake, as if to warn him. Raj knew what she wanted from him. And he had no problem complying, because the fewer people who knew about the doll, the better.

Raj shrugged. "She was stubborn at first, but I pointed out that if I'd come to kill her, I'd have been able to do so with very little trouble once I'd got rid of her bodyguard."

Brady heaved a sigh as he turned back to her. "I knew you'd be sensible, Veronica."

"She is very sensible," Raj said as Veronica's cheeks turned pink. No doubt she was remembering how *in*sensible she'd been until she'd discovered the doll. She turned and went to sit on the couch, once more the cool, imperious lady.

An imperious lady in elf pajamas. He had to bite down on the inside of his cheek to keep from laughing at the incongruity.

"So what now?" Brady asked.

"I'm staying close," Raj said. "Veronica doesn't want her staff to know she has extra security, so we've decided to pretend there's a bit of a…uh, relationship."

Brady blinked. His gaze raked over Raj, as if just now realizing he was without his tie and jacket, and then he turned to Veronica. She heaved a sigh. "Don't look at me that way, Brady. It's the only way to keep this a secret. Raj will pretend to be my newest boyfriend. It makes the most sense."

"Is that wise? You're the President of Aliz now," Brady said.

Veronica tilted her head back and threaded her fingers through that glorious platinum hair. "Yes, well, I'm allowed a bit of a personal life. And besides, it's not really true. Raj is undercover."

Brady seemed to take the news in stride when it came from her. Naturally. "I suppose you're right." Then he turned to Raj, his eyes sparking. "Raj, a word, if you don't mind?"

Veronica rolled her eyes. "For God's sake, you're the one who orchestrated this in the first place. It's all strictly professional—isn't that right, Raj?"

Raj's blood hummed. Electricity crackled in his veins, but whether it was irritation with his old friend or something to do with Veronica, he wasn't quite sure.

"You know I don't get involved with clients, Brady. Have I ever let you down?"

The other man shook his head. "Not so far."

Raj heard the undertones that seemed to say, *But this woman is different. Irresistible. You'll get involved, and you'll slip up somehow at the job.*

"Do you want my involvement or not?" Raj said mildly.

"I do, but I thought you had people for this."

Ironic, since Raj had originally suggested one of VSI's teams and Brady had said he wanted Raj personally. "A team won't be able to uphold the necessary fiction. The client wants it kept quiet. This is the best way."

Brady gave him a look that held volumes of meaning. "Whatever it takes to keep her safe."

"That's the idea."

Brady stayed awhile longer, chatting with Veronica, while Raj kept in contact with his people. Her staff was scattered throughout the hotel, but they were beginning to make their way back.

There were only eight people with her. A small number, but Aliz was a small country. Besides, it would make it easier to have them watched.

Within half an hour, they'd all trickled back to Veronica's suite. He sat by and watched Veronica interact with them, surprised that she seemed so cool and controlled as she did so. He'd had the doll removed and the room checked thoroughly, so nothing was out of place.

He watched for signs of guilt or surprise in anyone, but there seemed to be nothing. The guard who'd abandoned his post arrived, but his guilt was most certainly of a different nature.

Veronica's chief of staff, a man named Georges, dealt with the man quickly and effectively. He was ordered to pack his bags and told he would be returning to Aliz on the next available flight.

And then everyone was gone again. Brady said his goodbyes as Raj sipped the coffee that Martine, Veronica's secretary, had prepared for him. Veronica walked with Brady to the door. He gave her a kiss on both cheeks, and then—after shooting Raj another meaningful look—he was gone, too.

"Ready for bed, darling?" Raj said, setting down the coffee.

She looked at him haughtily. He almost laughed. But he was glad to see her be strong, glad that she wasn't succumbing to the terror and uncertainty. She'd played her part quite well tonight. Once her people had returned, she'd acted as if nothing had happened. He—and whoever had put the doll there for her to find—were the only ones who knew.

"Don't get carried away with your part," she told him.

And then she sagged against the door, raised a shaking hand to her head. Raj was moving before he ever realized he'd stood.

Veronica's heart crashed against her rib cage as she watched him. He moved like a cat, so sleek and deadly, coming straight for her. She was frozen in place, watching the way the fabric of his shirt stretched across his chest, molding the hard curves beneath. Her mouth went dry at the thought of what lay beneath the crisp white material.

She rubbed her palm over her eyes. What was she doing thinking of him naked when some maniac had gotten inside her room and put a defiled doll on her bed?

"Don't go there," he said firmly, reaching her side and putting an arm around her shoulders. "Don't give it power over you."

"I'm trying," she whispered. Because it was so cruel, so evil. Reminding her of what she'd lost.

Of what she'd destroyed.

Because she was the one responsible for what had happened to her baby, wasn't she? If she'd known she was pregnant sooner, she wouldn't have continued to drink cocktails or stay out until the early-morning hours, partying with her so-called friends because she couldn't bear to be alone.

It didn't matter what the doctor told her. She knew it was her fault.

"You need to sleep," Raj said, his arm firm around her. She wanted to turn into his embrace, wanted to bury her face against his solid chest again. She'd felt so safe for those few minutes earlier when she'd done so. "When was the last time you had a good night's rest?"

Veronica shrugged as he herded her toward the bedroom. "I don't remember. I sleep, but not well."

She hadn't slept well in months. Not since she'd realized what a truly horrible person she was.

"Then get into your bed and try."

She stopped at the threshold to the bedroom. "I can't sleep in there tonight."

He skimmed a hand along her jaw, the touch warm and light. It made her insides tighten. Heat—glorious heat—leeched into her bones. How could she need his touch when she didn't even know him?

"I'm not going anywhere. You'll be safe."

"I don't really want to sleep with you, Raj," she said, though she realized it was a bit of a lie. Right now, she was tempted to seek oblivion in his arms, tempted to drive away her memories by using his body for one hot night of sex.

"We aren't sleeping together," he replied. "But I'll be here nonetheless."

"Where are you planning to sleep, then?" she asked.

"The couch folds out."

She swallowed. He would be here, sharing the same space but not quite sharing it. She had to admit that she felt safe at the thought—as well as a bit unnerved.

"It's happening so fast," she said, shaking her head. "By tomorrow, every newspaper and tabloid will be simultaneously writing about our grand affair and our inevitable breakup."

"Not quite yet. We have a day or two with this snowstorm keeping everyone busy."

She snorted. "I wish I had your confidence. Not that it

matters," she said. "I don't really care what they say, so long as you find whoever did this."

"I will," he said in that sexy voice of his that sent little whirlpools of heat spiraling down her spine.

Veronica dropped her gaze again, unable to keep looking at him. Up close, those golden eyes made her long for things she had no right to long for. Made her reckless, dizzy and willing to do things she hadn't ever thought she'd do again.

"I don't want to sleep in that bed tonight. Do you suppose we could trade?"

His sigh was long-suffering. "We can't trade because this is the exterior room. But you can have the fold-out bed. I'll take the floor."

She lifted her head again, her eyes meeting his. He was so solemn, so serious. "I can't ask you to do that."

He shrugged. "It's fine. I'll drag the covers from the other bed. Believe me, I've slept in worse places than on a floor."

She helped him remove cushions and unfold the bed from the couch. Once that was made, he disappeared into her bedroom and came back with a pile of blankets and pillows that he laid out on the floor nearby.

She felt guilty as she climbed into the cozy bed, and yet she couldn't bear to sleep in the other room. She'd thought she could, but she couldn't.

And tomorrow, she was going to play the diva and demand another room. At least her reputation was good for something.

"Raj," she said once the light was out and everything was quiet again.

"Yes?"

"Where did you sleep that was worse than a floor?"

"You don't really want to know."

"I wouldn't have asked otherwise. Though if you don't want to say, that's a different matter."

She heard him sigh. "I was in the military, Veronica. The Special Forces. I've slept in mud, blood, blazing deserts and freezing blizzards. A floor in a posh hotel is heavenly."

"I still feel badly for taking your bed," she said.

"Then invite me into it."

She couldn't help but smile. "You say that to shut me up. I heard what you said to Brady."

"Maybe I lied."

Her heartbeat throbbed in the darkness. "I don't believe you."

"Invite me into your bed and find out."

Flames licked her skin at the thought. "Good night, Raj," she said, punching her pillow and turning onto her side.

She wasn't sure, but she thought he laughed softly. "Sleep well, Veronica."

There wasn't much chance of that now that he'd planted the image in her head of the two of them in this bed together. Skin against skin, heat against heat, soft against hard.

She practically moaned at the thought.

CHAPTER FIVE

LONDON was beautiful in the snow, especially Hyde Park with all its trees and open expanses. Though it was dark, the snow made everything bright and fresh. Veronica knew that it wouldn't necessarily look so pristine during the day when all the warts and blemishes of humanity shone through.

But for now, she could enjoy it as her limousine crawled its way toward Mayfair and the exclusive party she'd been invited to there.

Tonight, she hoped to persuade Giancarlo Zarella, the Italian hotel baron, to bring one of his exclusive resorts to Aliz. Where Giancarlo went, others would follow.

But rather than concentrating on the Italian and going over the information about him that she'd been given, she kept thinking of Raj. She had not seen him since this morning.

He'd shaken her awake early, telling her they had to put the bed away before her secretary arrived with the morning dispatches. She'd been bleary-eyed, but she'd obeyed.

Or, rather, she'd mostly watched while Raj fixed everything. Then he led her into the bedroom and told her to climb into the bed. In the gray light of morning, the bed hadn't looked so frightening. She'd complied, falling asleep immediately.

When she'd awakened a second time—with a hotel maid delivering her breakfast tray and Martine standing stoically near—Raj was gone. Brady arrived a bit later, and once she'd answered her dispatches and sent Martine on an errand, she'd quizzed Brady.

Raj Vala was not simply a bodyguard. He was self-made, the owner of Vala Security International, a very successful firm that provided elite corporate and internet security.

According to Brady, Raj was a loner. And he was every bit as hard and ruthless as she'd thought he would be, with a military Special Forces background and the drive to be the best in everything he did.

Raj, Brady assured her, would make sure she was completely protected from harm.

After last night, she tended to believe it. She took her phone from her purse and checked her text messages. She would not ever be caught without a personal phone again.

The text from Raj was still there, still brief and to the point: he would meet her at the party. She smoothed a hand down the sleek ice-blue Vera Wang dress she wore. It was strapless, slit up one side, and shimmered as if it had been sewn with millions of tiny lights.

She told herself she'd chosen it to appeal to Signor Zarella, but the truth was she'd been thinking of Raj. Her hair was tousled and long, flowing artfully around her face and over her shoulders. She checked her makeup in the small mirror she'd tucked into her purse and breathed deeply to control the racing of her heart.

It wasn't like her to be nervous. She'd always loved parties, always loved getting dressed up and going out with other people who laughed and talked and helped her feel as if she were catching up on everything she'd missed growing up.

Except that now, part of her wished she could be anywhere but here. The thought of mingling with yet another crowd failed to cheer her the way it once would have.

The limo arrived at the Witherstons' grand Georgian town house, and Veronica deliberately turned her thoughts to Giancarlo Zarella. She had a duty to perform. Obsessing over her personal issues wouldn't help her to get it done.

Her bodyguard—a different man from yesterday—preceded her from the car. Three other Alizeans exited a car that had been following and formed a loose band around her. They were all very serious about their jobs today.

After they went inside and Veronica gave her thanks to the host and hostess, her security team peeled away until she was left with one man following at a discreet distance.

Inside the ornate ballroom, she was swept into the whirl and chatter of the crowd. Men and women introduced themselves in dizzying succession, her hostess having appeared from somewhere to guide her through the maze. She was still hoping to talk with Signor Zarella when Mrs. Witherston gave a little gasp.

"Madam President," she said breathlessly, "allow me to introduce you to Raj Vala."

Veronica turned sharply, her gaze clashing with Raj's. He was smiling at her as if he'd never seen her before in his life.

"Pleased to meet you, Madam President," Raj said.

"Likewise, Mr. Vala," Veronica replied, following his lead.

But her heart began to beat double time as she took him in. He was far too handsome in his bespoke tuxedo, the white shirt once more setting off the golden color of his skin and eyes.

Truly, it should be against the law for a man to be so striking.

The jazz ensemble struck up a tune and Raj reached for her before she realized what he was about. "Do me the honor, Madam President?" he asked, as Mrs. Witherston tittered like a Regency matron.

"Of course," she said as she put her hand in his. What else could she say? What else did she *want* to say?

Raj swept her into the swirling crowd, one hand firmly against her back, the other clasping hers. The pressure of his touch comforted her, made her feel as if she'd come home again after a long time away.

She hated it. Hated how her body reacted, how her mind seemed to want to attach significance to this man. He might be able to keep her physically safe from harm, but he could not keep her safe from himself if she insisted on lying helplessly in the tiger's claws.

She knew better, and yet she turned into a puddle each time he touched her.

"How have you been today?" he asked.

"Well," she said. "You?"

His eyes seemed to search her face, as if he didn't quite believe her. "I was busy taking care of a few things. But now I'm all yours," he said, a devilish grin lifting the corners of his sensual mouth.

"Oh, all mine," she cooed. "How delightful, Mr. Vala."

"I thought we had gone beyond that."

"How could we? I've only just met you."

Her heart skipped a beat at his sudden smile. "Ah, yes, of course. I thought we could use this opportunity to begin our 'official' relationship."

"Why not?" she said, returning his smile. "It's certainly more dignified."

"But perhaps it's not the first time we've met," he said, his gaze skimming her face as he brought her hand up to his mouth and kissed it. "Perhaps we are old souls who have known one another before. Perhaps we are meant to be."

Veronica stumbled, but quickly caught herself. Raj was frowning. "It's the shoes," she said. And the fact she was tired from a restless night and unnerved to be in his arms again. "I'm fine."

"Good," he said. They moved across the floor together, their steps as fluid as silk. In her peripheral vision, she could see people stopping, pointing, heads leaning together as they talked about her and Raj. Ah, well, that had been the plan, had it not?

And yet it disappointed her in some respects. Now that they would be publicly linked, it was as if the innocence of their budding relationship had been eroded.

What relationship?

"Are we falling madly in love now?" Raj asked, jolting her out of her thoughts.

"Madly," she agreed, playing the game. "I've never felt like this before."

"Neither have I."

The words they said had no meaning, and yet she couldn't help but want to assign meaning that wasn't there. Had she ever been truly, madly in love before? She'd thought she'd been in love, but she'd usually realized the disappointing truth at some stage.

And she was positive that no man had ever felt that emotion for her. Lust, yes. Love, no.

"When we finish dancing, I suppose you will remain by my side the entire night?" she asked. "Enraptured by my presence?"

"The proverbial wild horses could not drag me away, Madam President." He lifted her hand to his lips again. The feather touch of his mouth against her skin sent a shudder rolling through her body. Hot need sizzled into the deepest parts of her.

Too bad this really wasn't Regency England, because then she would be wearing long gloves. She wouldn't be able to feel the sensual pressure of his mouth on her skin, wouldn't have to fight the focusing of all her senses upon that one spot. It was an exquisite torture to endure.

"Too bad our love is doomed to fail," she said, needing to counteract the drugging affect of his touch.

Again with the killer smile. "Then let us enjoy it while it lasts," he purred. "It's much more fun that way."

The evening went much as she'd thought it might. Raj did not leave her side. To all appearances, he was smitten with her. And she returned the favor, smiling in his direction, seeking him out if he walked away for the barest moment. Her eyes were pulled to him as if he were a magnet and she the metal.

It made talking to Giancarlo Zarella a bit difficult, but she finally managed to get the Italian alone at a table for a few moments. He seemed interested in Aliz, his eyes gleaming speculatively as she talked of incentives and subsidies.

"You would levy no taxes against us for the first year of operations, you say?"

Giancarlo was handsome, but she found herself comparing him to Raj and judging him lacking. "So long as you invest the money into building up the resort and hiring Alizeans to staff it."

"Make it two years, and I will consider it," he said shortly.

Veronica leaned in. "One year is what I can promise. But I pledge to work on reducing the tax burden in your next five years in Aliz."

Giancarlo laughed. "You drive a hard bargain," he said.

"But then you know just how to twist the knife enough to get me to notice. I will think on it, I promise you."

After that, Veronica felt as if nothing could puncture the balloons lifting her up tonight. She had no guarantees, but she felt as if she'd made a good start with Giancarlo. He would be in touch, she was certain. He left her at the table with an apology as someone beckoned him from another table a bit farther away.

"Did you get what you wanted?"

Veronica jumped at the voice. Raj was frowning down at her. He seemed troubled, but not alarmingly so. "I did," she replied. "Or so I think."

He took her elbow and helped her up. "Good. I think it is time we leave, then."

Veronica blinked. The jazz ensemble was playing an upbeat version of a classic Christmas carol. "Time we leave? I'm not finished here yet."

"How many hearts do you plan to capture tonight?" he asked. His voice was teasing, but his eyes seemed hot and intense. Serious. "You've had a long few days. It's time you rest."

"I can decide that for myself. You weren't hired to oversee my schedule, you know." She knew he was merely trying to protect her from harm, and yet the memories of her life with her father were too strong to dismiss. She would not be so controlled ever again. Keeping her safe wasn't the same as wrapping her in a cocoon.

His jaw hardened imperceptibly. "Actually, it goes with the territory. Or didn't you realize that?"

"I decide when I leave," she said. "And I'm not ready yet. Unless there is a real threat at this moment and time, which I will acknowledge is your responsibility. Is there?"

He looked angry. "No," he said shortly. "There is no immediate threat."

"Then we stay."

One eyebrow crooked. The superiority of that look infuriated her. "Then don't blame me when you encounter people you might wish you had not."

"And what's that supposed to mean?"

"It means that Andre Girard just arrived."

Her heart skipped a beat at that name falling from Raj's lips. It was wrong somehow. Horribly, horribly wrong. For a moment she wondered if he knew what had happened between her and Andre, but then she told herself it wasn't possible. Only a very small handful of people knew the true story.

"Andre is old news," she said, more to convince herself than him. "I will not leave a party simply because he's here, too."

At that moment, Raj changed tactics. He slipped an arm around her waist, anchoring her to his side as he smiled down at her, his head dipping so close to her own that if she tilted her head back just slightly, their lips would meet. Her heart thundered in her breast so hard she was certain he could see it.

"I'm glad he's old news," he said softly. "Because he's on his way over here."

Veronica couldn't speak as a shiver skidded along her nerve endings.

"I don't care," she finally managed to say.

"Good," Raj said. "Neither do I."

Then he dipped his head and kissed her.

Veronica couldn't have prepared herself for the sensations zinging through her even if she'd had a year to do so. Raj's mouth on hers was firm, the pressure exquisite. The barest slip of his tongue along the seam of her lips, and she was opening to him, taking him inside, tangling her tongue with his.

He made a sound of approval low in his throat that vibrated through her. Her core was melting, softening, aching. It was both surprising and alarming.

She knew there were reasons she shouldn't be seen kissing this man so publicly, but she couldn't think of even one. He scrambled her senses with his nearness. Made her long for more of the same. Made her want bare skin on bare skin, bodies tangled and straining together toward a single goal.

His fingers splayed over her jaw, tilted her head back so he could better access her mouth. The kiss seemed to go on and on, and yet she knew it had to have been only a matter of seconds before it ended.

She was staring up at him now, her lips stinging, her pulse throbbing in places she'd thought dead and buried until he'd walked into her life just twenty-four hours ago.

Raj was so cool, so unaffected. His golden eyes were hot, but that was the only sign he'd been at all moved by their kiss. He took a step back, his arm looped loosely around her.

"So you've found a new victim, I see."

Veronica turned. Andre smirked at her, a pouty supermodel clinging to his arm. Andre was slick and handsome, as always. But he didn't move her, not anymore. What she'd once thought was a fun and witty personality was now tarnished and dull.

Or, rather, her eyes had been opened to his true nature.

"Andre. I would say it's a pleasure to see you again, but we'd both know that was a lie."

Andre laughed. "It was good while it lasted, no? And just look at you now," he said. "President of Aliz. However did you pull that one off, darling?"

Veronica refused to rise to the bait. It was what he wanted, but she relished denying him his wish. "The usual way. I ran against the incumbent and the people decided I was the better choice."

"Ah, yes." His eyes narrowed. "So much more interesting than motherhood, I would imagine."

Veronica kept smiling even as a hot dagger of pain twisted in her gut. She wanted to turn into Raj's chest, hide until Andre was gone, but she would not. She would not give her former lover the satisfaction of reacting.

She'd known he would take the shot. From the moment Raj had told her Andre was here, she'd known what would happen. She could feel Raj's curiosity sparking, but she had to ignore it. Andre was her problem, not his.

"I believe there are rewards in many things," she said.

Andre's gaze flicked to Raj. "Careful, my friend. She's not at all what she seems. You think she wants what you want, until one day she surprises you by wanting something else. If you're lucky, you will escape before then."

Raj's grip on her waist tightened. "Veronica is an amazing woman," he said. "Too bad that you couldn't see it. Good for me, though. So thanks for being an idiot."

Warmth flooded her. She knew he was only playing a part, but she was still grateful to him for saying it. He could have said nothing, but he'd chosen to defend her. When was the last time anyone had done so?

She'd been so devastated after she'd lost the baby. And yes, she'd turned to Andre, thinking he might feel her pain, too. But he hadn't cared one bit. He'd considered it a lucky escape.

Andre's smile was patently false. "Suit yourself," he said. "But don't say I didn't warn you."

Then he turned and walked away, the model trotting along dutifully.

Veronica let out the breath she hadn't realized she'd been holding. It had gone better than she'd expected, though perhaps she should have realized that Andre would never make a scene. It simply wasn't his style to get overly worked up about anything.

"What did you ever see in that guy?"

She met Raj's critical gaze. He looked at her as if she'd grown a second head and he was trying to reconcile it. Veronica shrugged self-consciously. "He was charming when we first met. We had fun together."

Belatedly, she pulled out of Raj's grip, the memory of their kiss still sizzling into her brain. He let her go easily enough, and it made her wonder if she was the only one who'd been affected by the contact. That kiss had stripped away all her barriers while it lasted. It had scorched her to the depths of her soul.

Raj, however, looked completely cool and controlled. As if it had meant nothing to him.

Veronica lifted her chin. She was tired and she'd had enough for tonight. Enough with pretense and drama. Enough with being *Madam President*. She'd done what she came to do. "I'm ready to leave now."

To his credit, Raj only said, "I had thought you might be."

It took a while to say her goodbyes, but eventually they were in the foyer and Raj was helping her into her coat while her bodyguard stood by. She'd assumed he would put her into the car and follow separately, but he climbed into the warm interior with her. The guard went into the front seat, and then they were rolling away from Mayfair, the darkened London streets still alive with sound and traffic even at this late hour.

The kilometers ticked by in silence, other than the street sounds coming from outside. Veronica turned her head and watched as snow drifted silently down. She thought about making small talk, but could suddenly think of nothing to say.

"You will have to tell me eventually," Raj said, his voice like the crack of a gun in the silent car, though he spoke in a normal tone. It was the sound coming after so much silence that startled her and made her lift a shaking hand to her throat to fuss with her scarf.

"Tell you what?" she managed to respond. Her voice was even. Calm. She was proud of that.

Raj's fingers suddenly threaded into hers, closed tightly. They both wore gloves, but the pressure of his grip was warm, soothing. Comforting.

He squeezed softly, as if he were imparting strength. "About the baby."

CHAPTER SIX

SHE didn't say anything for so long that he wondered if she'd heard him. But of course she had. She sat stiffly, her head still turned away from him. In the light of one of the buildings they passed, he saw her throat move.

Raj pulled off his glove and put his fingers against her cheek. She turned to him, her eyes filled with tears. His fingers were wet and his heart constricted at the pain on her face.

"I don't want to talk about this with you," she said, her voice barely more than a whisper.

"I'm sorry," he said softly. He didn't want to push her, and yet he had to know. "But it could be important."

She closed her eyes, shook her head slightly. Her platinum hair gleamed in the dim light, and he thought of her last night, standing by her bed and calling for him. How vulnerable she'd looked, how innocent. Such a contrast with the woman he'd gotten acquainted with on paper.

Her chin dropped, as if she were surrendering. He found a box of tissues in a nearby compartment and handed them to her. She snatched a few into her hand and dabbed at her face.

"How can it be important?" she finally said. "No one really knows about it."

"Someone does. Andre does."

She sucked in a breath on a half sob. "Of course he knows. He was the father."

Somehow, though he'd expected it, that news sliced through his gut like a sword. He didn't want to think of Veronica with Andre Girard, didn't want to imagine that she could have loved the man once. But she must have done so.

"Was he angry?" He still didn't quite know what they were talking about, but he could tease the details from her if he worked gently enough.

Her laugh was bitter. "Angry? God, no. More like relieved. He didn't want a child, so he's not in the least bit upset there isn't one."

"I'm sorry for your loss, Veronica." He squeezed her hand again. He wanted to pull her into his arms and hold her tight, but he wasn't sure she wanted him to do so. Instead, he sat and waited.

"You're good," she said, dabbing at her eyes again. "You've managed to get me to talk about it after all. No matter that I don't want to."

"I have no wish to cause you pain," he said. "But I need to understand who could want to hurt you. Whoever it is knows about the baby. And this person sees it as the perfect way to get to you."

Her free hand clenched into a fist on her lap. "I wish I could understand why. It has nothing to do with anyone but me and Andre."

"Was there another woman? A jealous ex, perhaps?"

"There's always a jealous ex. But why would anyone care enough to be so cruel when we're no longer together? We weren't even very serious, but then I got pregnant and—"

"And what?" he prompted when she didn't continue.

She bent forward as if she were in pain, rocked back

and forth, her face turned away from him. It alarmed him. His throat felt tight as he waited.

A sob escaped her, but she stuffed her fist against her mouth and breathed hard, as if trying to cram the rest of them down deep.

Raj put an arm around her, pulled her toward him. She turned instantly, buried her face against him.

"I'm sorry," she said, her voice muffled and broken.

"It's all right," he said softly. "It's all right."

A lump formed in his throat as he watched the lights of storefronts go by. He had no idea where they were, or how long they were silent, before she pushed away from him and dabbed her eyes.

As if she hadn't just cried her heart out. As if she hadn't turned to him for comfort while she did so.

She was an enigma to him. Soft and hard at once. Strong and weak. Filled with sadness and pain. Not at all what he'd expected from the party girl in the tabloids.

If anything, he realized how very fragile she was beneath the layers of steel she cloaked herself in. He had no right to try and break through those barriers.

"I lost the baby soon after I learned I was pregnant," she said. She shook her head, swallowed hard. He could hear the audible gulp as she pushed her sobs down deep again. But then she speared him with a look. "I won't break, Raj. I'm stronger than you think. And I won't let anyone use this to stop me from doing what's best for Aliz."

Her mind worked much more quickly than he'd given her credit for only yesterday, when he'd watched her work the crowd from his position in the bar. He'd thought her pampered and shallow, but he had to admit that she had depths he'd never guessed at.

"Who is the woman in the tabloid reports?" he asked.

"Because I can hardly credit she's the same person as the woman sitting beside me now."

"Oh, no, she's definitely the same. Some of it is exaggerated, of course. But much of it is true." He wondered if she knew she was rubbing her thumb along the underside of his palm. The pressure was light, but it made him want to strip her glove off and see what her touch would feel like on his skin.

"I can hardly believe it," he said, trying to lighten the conversation once more.

"That was my version of acting out," she said quietly. "My rebellion against my father. The worse I behaved, the angrier he got. Did you ever act out, Raj?"

Her question surprised him. A dart of pain caught him behind the breastbone. "I think everyone has," he said.

Except that he hadn't. Not really.

He'd always had to be the adult in the house, especially once his mother started experimenting with drugs the summer he turned twelve. If he hadn't made sure they had food and a roof over their heads, however temporary, they'd have starved or frozen to death.

He'd known nothing but responsibility from the time he was young. He'd been stripped of a normal childhood by his mother's addictions and constant need for attention.

Acting out had been the furthest thing from his mind when all he'd cared about was food and shelter. Not that he could admit that to Veronica. It made him seem pitiful—and he definitely wasn't pitiful.

"Yes, I suppose so," she said. "Some of us worse than others, perhaps. But those days are over now, at least for me. I have too many things I want to do in life. I've wasted enough time."

Raj stifled a laugh. "You're twenty-eight and the president of your nation. How have you wasted time?"

Her smile was unexpected. It shook at the corners, as if she were still on the verge of tears.

It made him want to kiss her again. A white-hot bolt of need shot through him as he watched her mouth.

"That's true, yes. But I'm realizing what I really want. I'm only sorry it took me so long to figure it out."

"And what is it you want, Veronica?" Because he knew what he wanted right this minute. He wouldn't act on it, of course. Kissing her at the party had been one thing. Kissing her now that they were alone was another altogether.

"You will laugh."

"I won't."

"You will, but it's okay. I want a home. A real home, with a family. Maybe it'll just be a cat or a dog, or maybe I'll find a man I adore, who adores me in return. But I want the dream, the happy-ever-after where I like who I am and someone agrees with me."

Raj swallowed. Home. Family. He had no idea what those things were, really, other than a roof and four walls, and people whose happiness and welfare you were responsible for. "It's a nice dream. I hope you get it."

"You think it's ridiculous," she said.

"No."

"You do."

He sighed. "It's not that. It's just that I doubt you've ever been without a home. You want to imbue the word with more than it needs. You want it to fulfill you emotionally when, really, that is your responsibility."

Her thumb had stilled in his palm. Gently, she disentangled her hand from his and he knew he'd gone too far. Or maybe he'd gone far enough. It was better if she had no illusions about him. Better if they nipped this growing attraction in the bud and kept their relationship on the professional level it was meant to remain on.

"You're a cynic," she said. "I hadn't realized it."

"Not a cynic. A realist. Home isn't a magical place. It's shelter. It's having enough to eat, being warm. You have always had these things in abundance. Not everyone is so lucky."

She bowed her head. "No, you're right. I've never gone without the necessities. But I was talking of something more. Something intangible."

The car drew to a halt then and the door opened. They'd arrived back at the hotel she'd moved to earlier in the day. He thought he should say something more, should soothe her somehow—but he was at a loss. Instead, he exited and held his hand out for her.

"I thought you would understand," she said as she joined him on the curb, gazing up at him, her lovely face puzzled.

"I do," he said, because he had to say something. "I just don't happen to agree. Be thankful you've never slept on the street, or wondered where your next meal was coming from. Be thankful you've never had to fight for a dirty blanket to keep warm with because it was that or nothing. You are free to be you, wherever you happen to be. You already have what you need."

She sucked in a breath. The air misted around her face as she let it out again. She looked sad. "I hadn't quite thought of it like that."

"Many people don't."

"Maybe because it's easier to think that if only we have X, then Y will happen."

He was surprised at how readily she accepted the idea. And it made him feel somewhat guilty, as well. She'd been through a lot recently. More than she'd told him, and it wasn't his right to make her question the ideas that comforted her.

"I'm sorry, Veronica."

Her brows drew together. "For what? For speaking the truth? For reminding me of all the advantages I've had?"

He put his hands on either side of her face, gloried in the soft catch of her breath. She wanted him as much as he wanted her. It was enough. It would have to be enough, because he could not act upon it. Even if she weren't under his protection, he couldn't take her to his bed.

Because she'd been through too much pain and loss, and because she wanted more than he could give. He could see it in her eyes. Hell, she'd just said it aloud. Veronica was a woman who wanted a family.

The one thing he felt unqualified to ever provide. Family wasn't for him.

"I'm sorry for making you question what you want," he said. "There's nothing wrong with building a safe place in your head, and with trying to get there. Sometimes, X does lead to Y."

"You're really sweet," she replied softly.

He wanted to laugh. Sweet? Him? No way. "If it makes you happy to think so, then, yes, I'm sweet."

She giggled, then slapped her hand over her mouth as if she were surprised she'd done so. It was as if she'd let him see the real Veronica for a moment, the one beneath the pain and mystery. He'd had glimpses of her before, but never so natural as this. A sharp pain settled beneath his rib cage and refused to go away.

"As sweet as a tiger," she said a moment later. "A tiger who's just eaten and won't be hungry for a while."

He couldn't help but return her smile, though his chest ached. She was infectious like that. "Oh, I'm definitely hungry," he said. "But I have excellent self-control."

"I'm glad to hear it." She ducked her head so their eyes no longer met. And then she delivered what would have been the death blow had he been a weaker man. "Because I seem to have none at all when it comes to you."

A moment later she was striding into the hotel, leaving him standing numbly on the sidewalk. Aching. Wanting. Cursing himself.

Veronica woke up in the night, gasping for breath, the tail of some dream fading away. The air was dry, so dry, and her throat hurt. She didn't care how cold it was, she needed to open a window, needed that fresh bite of outside air to cleanse her. She stumbled to the window and found the mechanism—then she was cranking the window up and the air rushing in made her gasp again.

But it felt good. Clean.

She stood at the sill, shivering, but feeling refreshed nonetheless. She couldn't even remember the dream now.

The door to her bedroom burst open, a bright light searing into her brain. It happened so fast she wasn't able to let out even a squeak of surprise. The light winked out again and a voice asked, "What in the hell are you doing?"

Raj's voice. Relief slid through her, made her weak. If he'd been out to harm her, as he'd pointed out so recently, no one could have stopped him.

"What does it look like I'm doing?" she said.

Raj crossed the room so silently that when he arrived at her side, she jumped. Then he was cranking the window closed again.

"Hey," she said. "I want it open."

"Too bad," he replied. "It's not safe."

She could only blink into the blackness. But then light flooded the room as he snapped on her bedside lamp. The bright spots left from the light he'd shined when he'd first entered still marched across her vision. Big green splotches that made him indistinct if she looked directly at him. She turned her head, peered at him sideways.

He loomed, big and solid and oh, so unapproachable. He was completely different than he'd been earlier. He'd charmed her, held her, soothed her. Kissed her.

And now he was back to treating her as if she was something unappealing that he'd found on the bottom of his shoe.

Her temper sparked. "Do you mean to tell me that it's not safe if I open the window a crack on the tenth floor of a hotel? For a few minutes?"

"Precisely."

She popped her hands onto her hips. "What kind of world do you live in, Raj? Because I'm not sure I want to be a part of it."

"You already are," he said. For the first time, she noticed that what she'd always assumed to be a mild British accent had taken on a distinctly American twist. "It's your world, not mine. You entered it when you ran for president. You bought it when you got elected."

What had gotten into him? Before she could dwell on it, something else occurred to her. "How did you know the window was open?"

"A small sensor," he said matter-of-factly.

A sensor. He'd put sensors in her room. She was familiar with that tactic. She'd been thinking of him when she'd dressed with such care tonight, and he'd been busy thinking of how to control her.

Her blood ran cold. She'd snuck out of her father's house once, when she was sixteen. He'd been so furious once he'd caught her that he'd had the place wired like a military compound.

Oh, yes, she knew about sensors.

Veronica worked hard to control her temper. What had happened to her as a teenager had nothing to do with now. She was someone who needed protecting, someone with big responsibilities. Raj had only been doing what she'd agreed to let him do.

"You could have told me," she said tightly. "I wouldn't have opened the window if I'd known."

His look was dark. "Most people don't open the window at 3:00 a.m. in the middle of winter."

"I won't be caged in," she said, panic rising in her throat as her insides clenched in fear. "I won't be controlled."

"Then you should have considered another career path," he said coldly.

She hugged her arms around her body. Her vision was still splotchy, but she could see that Raj was still in his tux. Or, partially in his tux. The jacket and tie were missing, and the top couple of studs were gone. His sleeves were rolled partway up his forearms. She realized that she'd never seen his bare arms before.

A shiver rippled over her.

Raj swore. "You'll catch a cold," he said gruffly as he came and put an arm around her, herded her toward the bed. "I thought you had more sense than this."

"I'm fine," she protested.

"Then why are you shaking?" he demanded.

She couldn't answer, not without giving away the secret of how he affected her. Because, though she was slightly chilled, it wasn't that making her shiver.

She wanted to shrug away from his touch, but couldn't. She was still so angry with him—and yet there was that electricity between them, that spark and fire that sizzled along her nerve endings the instant he touched her. It took her forcibly back to that moment outside the hotel when he'd told her he was hungry. Her insides had turned to jelly then. Her legs had wobbled. She'd wanted to take his hand and lead him to her bedroom.

She hadn't done it because she'd been confused. Did she want him because she felt close to him after the conversation in the car? Because she'd told him about the baby and she'd felt vulnerable? Because he'd held her hand and said he was sorry?

She wasn't sure, and in the end she'd done nothing.

But right now all the same thoughts and needs were crashing through her again. And she was asking herself once more how she could want this particular man when she'd wanted no man for over a year now.

Because he was wrong for her.

He was beautiful, strong, proud, fierce. And too wild to ever be tamed. No woman would ever own this man, and she was no longer willing to be the sort of woman who was temporary.

But oh, how her insides rippled and churned at his nearness. How her heart wanted the one thing that was forbidden to her.

He pulled the covers back and held them.

"Get in," he said. She obeyed because she was starting to shiver in earnest now. But she hardly believed it had anything to do with the ten seconds of fresh air, and everything to do with him.

"Don't think I did it because you told me to," she said when he dropped the covers on top of her.

His mouth twisted. "I would never think that, Veronica. You would just as soon die of exposure than do what I say. If you've gotten in bed, it's because you wanted to."

She closed her eyes. "Too right."

"Don't open the window again."

"I understood the first time," she said. "Raj?"

He turned back to her. "Yes?"

"Will you stay and talk to me for a little while?"

He didn't move, and she wondered if he would tell her no. But then he nodded, came over and sat on the edge of the bed farthest from her.

She didn't know why she'd asked him to stay, except that she'd suddenly not wanted to be alone. She couldn't remember her dream, but it hadn't been a good one. She felt restless, keyed up, anxious.

There was a time when she couldn't stand to be alone at all, when she'd had twenty-four-hour parties full of all the laughter, music and chatter she'd been denied growing up. She was no longer that person, but she still sometimes felt the weight of silence pressing in on her.

She deserved that silence, considering what she'd done. But tonight she couldn't handle it.

Veronica reached up and turned out the light, needing the anonymity of utter darkness. She could feel the solid presence of Raj nearby. Just like yesterday, it was comforting. She put a hand to her head, rubbed one temple. It was all the travel, all the days spent in hotels—all the days spent being serious and worrying about Aliz—that made her grateful for his company now.

She waited for him to speak, to say anything at all, but he didn't. She huffed out a sigh. "You aren't talking."

"Neither are you." She felt him move, the bed dipping as he slid up against the headboard and stretched out his legs.

"Where did you grow up?"

He muttered something beneath his breath. "Tell me about you. It's far more interesting."

"I disagree," she said. "I want to know why you sound British but sometimes use American phrases."

He blew out a breath. "My mother was American."

"See, that's interesting. Did you grow up in India?"

"No."

"Is it a secret?" she prompted when he said nothing else.

"No. But it's not important."

Veronica sighed. "Fine. Don't talk about it, then."

"I won't."

"I grew up in Aliz," she said, because she needed to say something. "I never left until I was eighteen. And then I didn't go back until my father's funeral two years ago."

"I'm sorry for your loss."

"Thank you. We weren't close, but we were...working on it...."

She'd tried to make her peace with her father. They'd been speaking more frequently in the months before his death. She sometimes couldn't believe he was gone. Though she understood now what had motivated him to be so overprotective, she'd had a hard time forgiving him for it.

"It's good you were trying."

"I think so." She turned on her side, facing Raj. She could see the outline of his profile in the dim light coming from the bedside clock. "What you're really wondering is why the people elected me president since I hadn't actually lived in Aliz for many years."

He didn't hesitate before answering. "I wonder why you ran, not why they elected you."

She thought of her father, of Paul Durand. Of the hope and delight she'd seen in the eyes of those Alizeans who believed in her ability to change things for the better. "I thought I could do something good for the country."

"I think you probably can," he said. "I think you already have."

For some reason, that made her throat tight. "I'm try-ing," she said. "It's very important to me."

She thought he laughed softly. "Veronica, I don't think there's anything in this world you can't do once you set your mind to it."

"I'm sure there are a few things," she said, her eyes stinging as her voice caught. *Damn it.* This was not at all what she'd intended when she'd started talking.

But this was how it had been since she'd lost her child. The yawning cavern snuck up on her when she least ex-pected it, threatened to consume her.

Beside her, Raj swore again. And then he was mov-ing, closing the distance between them and gathering her to him. She didn't protest, though she knew she should. How many times did she have to lose her composure in front of him?

Instead, she buried her nose in his pristine shirt and breathed him in. She loved being close to him.

"I'm sorry," he said. "I shouldn't have said that."

"No," she replied, her fingers curling into his shirt. "You were paying me a compliment. I liked it."

She could hear his heart thudding in his chest. It beat faster than she'd have thought. For some reason, that made her happy. Raj Vala—strong, amazing, sexy Raj—wasn't unaffected by holding her close. Perhaps he was a little bit human after all.

"But it made you think of what you'd lost."

She swallowed, unable to tell him the rest of it. Unable to say that she blamed herself and always would. "You can't guard what you say in hopes I won't."

His grip on her tightened. "I wish I could say some-thing. Do something. I'd take away the hurt if I could."

She knew he meant it, and it touched her more than she

could say. A lone tear seeped from her closed eyes and trickled down her cheek.

"Just hold me," she said. "It's enough."

CHAPTER SEVEN

RAJ knew he was losing the battle with himself. He closed his eyes and tried to pretend he was somewhere—anywhere—but here, in her bed, holding her close and listening to her soft breathing. He felt the bite of moisture on his skin, knew she was crying. He wanted to make it stop, wanted her to sleep again. He didn't know how to make it happen.

She didn't make any sound, but her body trembled in his arms.

"Veronica," he said, his voice strangled, "it'll be okay. Someday, it'll be okay." He wasn't stupid enough to think that the kind of loss she'd suffered was something she would get over quickly. How could she? How could anyone?

Andre Girard was a fool. And Raj had a sudden desire to hunt the man down and make him suffer the way Veronica suffered. She shouldn't have to go through this alone.

"I know," she said, her voice so soft and sweet, hovering on the edge of control. "I get upset sometimes, but it's normal."

He didn't know what was normal and what wasn't—but he couldn't stand that she was in pain. He tipped her chin up with his fingers, lowered his mouth to hers.

He meant it to be a soft kiss, a sweet kiss. A kiss of comfort.

He should have known it was impossible.

Later, he wouldn't be able to recall who'd taken the kiss deeper first. But it didn't take more than a moment for it to happen. She clung to him, her mouth warm and inviting, her soft sigh like fuel to the fire stoking low in his belly.

He was harder than he'd ever been in his life. And he knew he was about to lose the battle between his head and his groin. He tried to remind himself of all the reasons he shouldn't be doing this…and came up empty.

He tightened his fingers in her hair—that glorious, lustrous fall of platinum silk—and gently pulled her head back as he broke the kiss. He had one chance left. One chance to end this free fall into insanity.

"Tell me no, Veronica. Tell me to get out, and I will. For both our sakes, tell me," he urged her. Because he was powerless so long as she clung to him. So long as she seemed to need his touch, his kiss, he was absolutely powerless to stop it.

He shouldn't be. He should be able to get up and walk away. He'd suffered unbelievable agony while training for the Special Forces, and he'd never broken. He'd endured.

But he couldn't endure her. She'd broken him, at least temporarily.

One word from her, and he could regain his strength. He could disentangle himself, distance himself. One word was all it would take.

"I can't," she said. "I don't want to. I want you to stay."

He groaned, and the sound reverberated through her body. Veronica's heart thundered in her ears. Heat prickled along the pathways of her nerves, slid deep into her senses, melted her core. She'd terrified herself with the words she'd spoken, and yet she'd known they were the right words.

She was ready for this again, ready for the intense pleasure of being with a man. With Raj. There were so many reasons why she shouldn't, why she should have said no as he'd told her to do, but she couldn't.

She simply couldn't.

He'd touched something inside her that had lain dormant for as long as she could remember. It was both shocking and compelling. Why now? Why him?

Why?

"I can't promise you anything beyond tonight," he said roughly. "You have to know that, Veronica. That's why you have to make me leave."

She reached up and spread her palm along the shadow of his jaw. He needed to shave, but she loved the rough texture.

"Just give me one night, then," she replied, surprising even herself with the request.

But he was untamable, this tiger. He needed to be free. She understood that. She would take what he could give her and then she would free him.

Veronica swallowed hard. For a moment, doubt assailed her. What was she doing? What was she getting herself into? Could she handle one night of passion between them? Was she really prepared for this?

But then he kissed her again, and she knew she was ready. Her body was on fire for him. Sizzled and sparked for him. Her pajamas—silk tonight—felt like sandpaper next to her sensitive skin. She wanted them off, and she wanted to burn herself up in his embrace.

In the dark of night, when no one would ever know.

When tomorrow came, she would deal with the aftermath.

His hand slid against the silk of her top, his fingers

spreading to cup her breast. She moaned as he found and teased her nipple beneath the fabric. In answer, she tugged his shirt from his waistband, shoved her hands beneath it until she was touching the hot, smooth skin of his torso.

His groan whipped the froth of her excitement even higher. She struggled against the blankets, wanting to be free of them so she could wrap her body around his. He obliged her by grabbing a handful and yanking them down.

And then she was throwing a leg over his hip, pulling him to her. He rolled until he was on top of her, until that hard part of him she wanted so much was pressed intimately against the silk of her pajamas. In spite of the fabric between them, sensation streaked from her scalp to her toes when he flexed his hips and thrust against her.

His mouth—his beautiful, magical mouth—made love to hers so thoroughly that she never wanted to stop kissing him. For some men, kissing was a bothersome prelude to the main course. For other men—for this man—kissing was an erotic act in itself.

She'd never been kissed like this before.

Never.

But she wanted more than his kiss. Veronica pushed his shirt up as high as she could make it go. She wanted their clothes gone, wanted to feel bare skin on bare skin. Raj broke the kiss, reached over his shoulder and tugged the shirt over his head with one hand. She could hear the studs snapping, the fabric tearing.

It was sexy and wild and she loved it. Her heart hammered, her pulse tripping as if she'd mainlined a vat of caffeine.

But oh, was he worth it.

His mouth found hers again, but his chest was now bare and she could run her hands over him. The hard planes and smooth skin, the dips and hollows of solid muscle that rippled beneath her fingers. So sexy.

Quickly, he unbuttoned her shirt, the fabric falling open until her breasts were exposed to his sight. She could see his eyes gleaming in the dim light coming from outside the windows. Her nipples peaked as he watched her. She was shameless. Utterly shameless.

"Raj," she said, his name a plea on her lips.

"You're beautiful, Veronica," he said softly, kissing her once more.

And then he was sliding his tongue down the column of her neck, kissing the sweet spot where the nerves in her shoulder seemed to connect to the hot, throbbing center of her. She arched her back, gasped.

Raj said something against her skin, but she didn't hear what it was. The vibrations rolled through her, crested in her core. If he kept doing that, she thought she might explode.

Impossible, but exciting. So exciting.

When his mouth closed over her nipple, she thought that was the end. How could she stand this much pleasure?

This much pain?

Because she couldn't help but think of all that had happened in the months since the last time she'd been with anyone. She'd changed so much. Fallen to the depths of despair. Risen again as she'd determined to go on with life.

Raj seemed to sense her turmoil. He chose that moment to slip his fingers beneath the waist of her pajama bottoms, and her temperature spiked. He made a noise of approval when he found the lacy top of her panties. Fire streaked through her. And *want,* so much want.

She thought she would die if he didn't touch her.

But he did, finding her swiftly, his fingers clever and

sure as they stroked her while a long moan vibrated in her throat.

"Veronica," he groaned against her breast. "So sensitive, so responsive."

She couldn't speak, couldn't tell him it was all because of him, because she trusted him. Wildly, she thought that she hardly knew him—and yet she knew enough. He was a good man, a strong man. He was reliable, even if he was ephemeral.

He was exactly what she needed when she needed it.

She would not think about tomorrow.

It didn't take long for her to reach the pinnacle; her body tightened so painfully—then flew free as she gasped his name.

His fingers stilled.

And then he was removing her bottoms, tossing them aside and pushing her legs apart. She thought he would unzip his trousers, would plunge into her body and join them together finally—but he did no such thing. Instead, he slid down until his mouth—that clever, beautiful mouth—hovered above her most sensitive spot. She could hardly breathe in anticipation of what came next.

She was not disappointed. His tongue slid over her, again and again, nibbling, sucking, flicking, while she grasped handfuls of the bedding and thrust her hips upward.

This time when she came apart, stars exploded behind her eyes. Her breath was sucked from her body as her back arched off the bed. She was absolutely helpless beneath the onslaught of pleasure.

He didn't stop there. He took her to the top again, then pushed her over the edge until she was ready to beg him to stop, to let her breathe, to let her recollect her senses and reorder them again.

It was simply too much. It was primal and raw, and as much as she wanted to stop, she also wanted to go on. She wanted to reach the next peak, and the next. But she wanted to soar with him instead of alone.

He must have felt something of her desire, because he kissed his way up her body again—her torso, her breasts, her shoulder…oh, that shoulder!—and back to her lips, capturing them for a long, lingering kiss.

Then he surprised her when he rolled to the side and tucked her against him. Confused, she pushed herself up with one hand splayed against his glorious chest. He was so dark in the night, so powerful and protective. She shivered in anticipated delight.

"We aren't finished yet," she said.

His laugh was strangled. "Yes, but I've realized I have no protection. This is not what I came here for tonight."

She leaned down and kissed him. "I'm on the pill," she said against his lips. "I had to take it after…well, after I needed my hormones to stabilize. They were all over the place for a while."

His fingers came up and stroked along her cheek. It was a sweet gesture, so simple and honest. She loved it.

"You slay me, Veronica," he said. "And you deserve far better than I can give you. I'm humbled that you trust me, but you've just convinced me that I can't take advantage of your vulnerability."

She pulled away and sat up. She was completely naked, but she didn't care. Let him look. If it made him uncomfortable, so much the better. Frustration was a hot stew in her belly. And disbelief. Could he really be serious?

"You're the most arrogant man I've ever met, Raj Vala. And I've met some arrogant ones, believe me. What makes you think for one instant that I don't know what I want? That I can't make my own decisions? That I'm somehow blinded by your fabulousness and not in control of my own mind?"

"I didn't mean—"

"You did," she said firmly. "Because you're so wonderful, of course, and no woman can resist you. Therefore, it's up to you to be noble and deny my poor, weak female mind what it thinks it wants."

"You aren't thinking," he growled, "or you wouldn't want this. In the morning, you would regret it."

"That's my problem, isn't it?" she snapped, anger and sexual frustration building to a peak inside her. "You're here to protect me from an outside threat, not from myself."

"I want you, make no mistake. And if I were a bastard like Andre Girard—or any of those other men you've taken to your bed—I'd seize what you're offering me and to hell with your peace of mind."

"Fine," she said, scrambling from the bed and whirling to face him. She was absolutely on fire with anger. And humiliation. She'd thrown herself at him, and he'd turned her down flat. After making sure she had an orgasm or two—alone. It was ridiculous, but she felt so worthless right now.

"Clearly, you know what's best for me. Now get out and let me sleep."

He was so still and quiet that she didn't think he would respond, but a few seconds later he exploded off the bed, grabbing his torn shirt and coming to loom over her. "You'll thank me tomorrow," he snarled.

She started to snap back at him, but something stopped her. Sometimes you had to pull the thorn from the tiger's paw, right?

She put a palm on his chest, slid it up to his jaw. He shuddered beneath her touch, a great golden cat on the edge of control. Boldly, she reached for him, cupped her other hand around the bulge in his trousers.

"Veronica…"

"I'm a grown woman, Raj. I know what I want." She took a step closer to him then, her bare breasts coming into contact with his naked chest. "I need this," she told him. "Yes, you're the first after my loss, but that's why it has to be you. I do trust you, and I'm afraid I'll never find the courage again if you don't—" She sucked in a breath, her voice on the edge of breaking. It took her a few moments to regain control. "If you don't make love to me. Please, Raj."

He closed his eyes and tilted his head back. She could see the column of his throat move as he swallowed. "God, you're killing me," he groaned.

She pressed her lips to his breastbone, gloried in the silken feel of his skin beneath her mouth. He didn't stop her. Deliberately, she unsnapped his trousers. Pushed them down his hips until they slid the rest of the way on their own.

Finally, finally, she could cup him in her hand, nothing between them. He was so hard, like marble. So soft, like silk. She stroked him, squeezing softly.

"You win," he said on a sharp intake of breath. "You win."

And then he hooked a hand behind her knees and swept her into his arms. Carried her to the bed and lay her across it. Automatically, her legs went around his hips as he followed her down. Her body throbbed for want of him. He cupped a breast in his hand, tweaked her nipple as he kissed her again.

Then she felt him. Slowly, inexorably, he slid into her body. It burned, and she suddenly gasped with the pain of it.

He stopped moving. "Am I hurting you?"

She realized she was gripping both his biceps in her

hands, her nails digging into him. Tears pressed at the back of her lids and she swallowed them down.

"It's been a long time," she said. "It's, um, more difficult than I'd thought it would be."

He swore softly. Started to withdraw.

"No," she cried out, tightening her legs around him. "I need you, Raj. I need you."

His breath sucked in, as if he were in pain, too. Which, she thought, he probably was, though it was a far different pain from what she was experiencing.

"We'll take it slowly," he said, and her heart swelled with feeling.

He put his hand between them, found her. Sweet, singing need began to hum in her body again as he stroked her. Softly, sweetly, as if he had all the time in the world. As if there was no dawn and no sunset, no appointments, no pressures. As if she was the world and he her servant within it.

It took longer to hit the peak this time, but she did, her body opening to him as he took the opportunity to slide farther inside her.

"Okay?" he asked.

"Kiss me," she said.

He did, his mouth so warm and giving that she lost herself in the kiss once more. She could feel him moving again, and though her body tightened a bit at the intrusion, the pain was far less than it had been.

She didn't know how long they lay entangled like that, but finally Veronica tilted her hips up and took him the rest of the way inside. She could feel him throbbing deep in her body, could feel the tight control he wielded over his needs as he held himself so still.

"Poor Raj," she whispered. "What a project I've turned into for you."

"You aren't a project," he said fiercely. Protectively.

She loved the conviction in his tone, loved how honorable he truly was. The feelings swirling in her heart and soul were beginning to confuse her. Frighten her. Deliberately, she shoved them away.

"Make love to me," she said.

He began to move so slowly once more, until she was a mass of tight nerve endings and shuddering tension. Until she was begging him to take her faster. He took his time obliging her, but when she didn't shrink from him, when she didn't cry out or flinch in pain, he turned up the intensity.

Again and again, he took her higher, their bodies straining together, sweating, skin sliding on skin. Exquisite. Torturous.

The pain was still there, but so slight she hardly noticed. The pleasure was far, far stronger.

And then it crested until she cried out, her entire body shuddering beneath him, wanting still more but unable to last a moment longer. His control was so exquisite, so perfect, that she knew when he gave himself permission to follow her into the abyss. He lifted her to him, his body pumping into hers one last time before he was still.

He propped himself up, careful not to crush her. In the darkness, she could still make out his features. Could see the troubled expression he couldn't mask.

"Thank you," she said, because it was all she could think to say.

"Are you all right? Did I hurt you?"

"I'm fine."

Physically, that was true. Emotionally was another story. So many emotions crashing in on her. She'd made love with him, and though she didn't regret it at all, the weight of the feelings she'd been carrying for so many months—

wondering if she were damaged somehow, if she would ever feel as if she were whole again, if she would ever be able to be with a man without dissembling—was immense.

"You don't sound fine," he said. And then he rolled over and took her with him until she sprawled half on his body and half off.

"It's a bit overwhelming," she admitted.

"I get that a lot," he said smugly, and she knew he was trying to make her laugh.

It worked, damn him. "Arrogant bastard."

His fingers stroked along her spine. "Seriously," he said after a few moments. "Are you okay?"

"Yes," she said on a sigh. "I am."

It was not his finest moment. Raj lay awake long after Veronica had dozed off and contemplated the mess he'd made. What the hell had he done?

He'd never, ever slept with someone he was guarding. It had been wrong to do so, and yet he'd been powerless to resist her request.

Hell, he hadn't wanted to resist. Since the moment he'd seen her from the bar of the hotel, he'd wanted this woman with the kind of craving that abhorred him. The kind of craving that drug addicts used to justify their excesses.

That thought did not cheer him in the least.

But she'd been all gorgeous, sexy femininity, with an alluring laugh and a come-hither look that fooled every man she bestowed it upon. He'd known better than to fall for it, yet he had.

Beneath the facade, she was amazing. Serious, smart, funny and sad. Sadder than any woman he'd ever known, with the exception of his mother. He hated that sadness, wanted to take it away from her forever.

He pressed a hand to his chest. There was a dull ache

there, the kind of ache he'd gotten whenever he'd come home from school to find his mother high again.

Whenever he'd been able to go to school, that is. He'd missed most of his middle school years with all the moving they'd done. How he'd ever gotten into—and graduated from—high school was as much a mystery to him as anyone.

That he was even thinking of those days right now was not a good sign.

He considered slipping from the bed and returning to the living area, where he'd been on the computer when she'd opened the window and triggered the silent alarm he'd set, but the bed was warm and she was soft and sleeping. Her head lay on his chest, her silky platinum hair a shiny tangle that he itched to shove his fingers into.

He would not move, would not risk waking her when she was sleeping so soundly—especially when she'd told him she didn't usually sleep very well.

Eventually, he fell into a light doze, his mind filled with thoughts of her—of the soft cries she'd made as he'd taken her, of the way her body opened to him, moved with him, the way she'd found her pleasure and cried out his name.

Beneath the surface, he was troubled. Troubled because she'd trusted him. She'd flat-out told him earlier that she wanted someone who would love her, who would give her a family, and though he knew he wasn't that man—couldn't ever be that man—he'd accepted her trust and taken her body because he was too weak to say no.

Because she'd gutted him with her trust and her need and he'd been powerless.

A few hours later, in the dim light of dawn, he felt her stir. Her hand slipped along his chest, her fingers spreading wide, as if she were learning him by touch. Her mouth pressed against his skin, and his body hardened instantly.

He should have gone back to his bed on the couch, but it was too late. He knew, even as her fingers found him, wrapped around him, that he was not pushing her away.

He should, he definitely should—but he couldn't. Instead, he lay there, let her stroke him, purr against his skin. He groaned her name when she climbed on top of him and took him inside her inch by slow inch.

She was so warm, so wet, and he closed his eyes, let himself feel the pleasure of her fingers splayed against his chest as she rode him slowly, so slowly he thought he would die of anticipation.

"Raj," she said. "Oh, Raj."

Once more, she broke his control. He threaded his fingers in her hair, pulled her down to him, kissed her thoroughly, his tongue sliding against hers, his lips molding hers as she began to make little noises in her throat that drove him insane.

He flipped her over, slid so deeply into her body that they both groaned with the pleasure.

"Don't stop," she said, as if sensing that he was at war with himself. "Please don't stop."

He didn't. Not for a very long time.

CHAPTER EIGHT

VERONICA woke alone. Martine stood by the bed as usual, a maid and a breakfast tray close by. Veronica pushed herself upright, disappointment hollowing her stomach as she blinked in the bright morning light.

She ran her hand over Raj's side of the bed, came away cold. He'd been gone for a long time.

Ridiculously, she thought of their fiction—which was no longer fiction, and yet her lover had left her. Perhaps he didn't want to be seen with her after all.

The thought made her head throb.

Instead, she ate her breakfast, listened to Martine detail her morning appointments and took a shower. She dressed carefully in a bright pink cashmere sweater dress, deciding at the last minute to be a little naughty and pulling on tall, suede boots to complement it.

Then she brushed her hair into a thick ponytail and went to face the day.

She drew up short when she entered the living area to find Brady.

And Raj, she realized. He stood by the window, looking all dark and broody and distant.

"Good morning, gentlemen," she said, her heart beginning to throb as Raj turned toward her. She couldn't tell what he was thinking. His expression was hooded, his feelings a mystery to her.

Part of her cried out in protest. How could he have made love to her the way he had and be so distant now? How could he not look at her with heat simmering in his eyes? She felt as if her feelings must be written all over her face, and yet he was as unreadable as stone.

She shot a glance at Brady. He was oblivious to the undercurrents, thank God. He walked over and gave her a hug, then took her by the hand and led her to the couch.

"You need to sit down, Veronica," he said.

The first prickles of alarm dotted her skin.

"What's going on?" Her gaze slewed from Brady to Raj.

"I'm sorry, Veronica," Raj said, his sexy voice so impartial and cool. Not at all the voice of the man who'd whispered in her ear last night. Who'd told her she was beautiful and amazing as he'd thrust deep inside her.

Her heart squeezed tight at the memory. She wanted that man back, the one who was tender and loving and worshipped her body so beautifully that he'd given her back something of herself. He'd made her feel as if she deserved to be treated special. As if, for a short while, she wasn't a horrible woman who'd lost her child because she'd been careless.

He'd made her feel whole.

"There's been a coup in Aliz," he continued. "The chief of police has seized all the government buildings in the capital. He's calling for your ouster and the restoration of the former president."

"He can't do that," she said numbly. But he could. He had. She rose, her limbs shaking with sudden fury. "I won't let him."

"Sweetie," Brady said, but she held her hand up to silence him.

Raj, however, did not remain silent.

"I know what you're thinking. But it's too dangerous for you to return. You need to remain here."

"And do what?" she demanded, fury swirling inside. "Do nothing?" She shook her head. "I can't sit by and let them get away with this. I won't."

Raj's eyes flashed. "They won't get away with it," he said. "But it'll take time to sort it out. In the meantime, you're in danger, especially if you try to return to Aliz."

But he didn't know her country, didn't know her responsibility. She wasn't backing down, wasn't abandoning the people who had elected her. She couldn't.

"I'm returning to Aliz," she said. "With or without you."

"Very well," he said. So cool, so casual. Even when he lost the battle, he appeared to be in complete control. It irritated her.

"Just like that?" she said. "No arguing? No attempts to persuade me otherwise?"

He inclined his head. "Just like that." Then he turned and walked toward the door.

Her chest ached at the thought he was leaving her after what they'd been through together. So easily, as if it meant nothing.

Which it probably hadn't. He'd told her he couldn't give her anything else. It was her fault if she wanted to believe more was possible.

"You aren't just going to leave her, are you?" Brady called out angrily.

Raj stopped and turned back to them, hand on the door. "No. I'm going to pack."

Three hours later, they were airborne. Veronica sat in a plush leather seat and gazed out at the snowy English land-

scape below. She knew she owed the speed of their depar-
ture to Raj.

Without him, she'd still be waiting on a chartered plane
since Aliz did not maintain a government fleet. Instead,
Raj had let her use one of VSI's company jets. She and her
staff were on their way home, thanks to him.

He sat across the aisle from her, engrossed in whatever
was on his computer screen at the moment. He'd barely
said a word to her in the three hours since he'd come into
her suite and told her of the situation in Aliz.

She'd been mortified to have to hear it from him when
she should have known before he did.

Yet another sign that Raj was powerful and connected.

His fingers tapped something on the keys, and a current of heat swirled in her belly. Those fingers had touched
her so expertly, had drawn such need and passion from
her that thinking of it now made her wet. She wanted him
again, in spite of everything.

He must have sensed something, because he looked up
at that moment, his gaze turning swiftly to capture hers.
She didn't bother to pretend she hadn't been staring. Her
heart skipped a beat. Her nipples began to tighten against
the cashmere of her sweater dress.

His gaze slid down, then back up again, his eyes glittering with heat and need that mirrored her own. A thrill
shot through her. He still wanted her. Maybe one night
hadn't been enough.

It was impossible, though. There was a bed on this
plane, but there was no way they could retreat to it.
Between her staff, his team and the flight crew, there was
no hope of privacy.

And once they reached Aliz, who knew what would
happen?

He snapped his computer closed and pushed up from

his seat. Then he was sinking into the seat beside hers, and her skin was prickling with his nearness. Her blood was singing with heat and need.

She picked up the vodka cocktail the flight attendant had brought to her—she'd hoped it would calm her nerves—and took a small sip. The vodka wasn't strong, but it kicked back nevertheless, burning her throat in a good way.

"Thank you," she said.

"You've already thanked me at least fifty times," he replied, his voice low and containing an edge she didn't quite recognize. "I couldn't let you go alone. They would devour you in a matter of minutes."

She met his gaze, her heart turning over at the intense look in those golden eyes. "Maybe I was thanking you for last night."

He didn't say anything for a long moment. "Just when I think you can't get to me," he said, shaking his head.

"I get to you?" For some reason, that made her stomach leap.

"In the worst way," he replied seriously.

Veronica frowned. "I'm not sure that's very flattering."

He picked up her hand where it rested on her lap, threaded his fingers through hers. Her pulse shot into overdrive. Her core throbbed with need for him, her body tightening painfully. When he lifted her fingers to his lips and kissed them, a shiver rocketed through her.

"Raj…"

"I want to spread you out on silken sheets, Veronica," he said, his voice pitched for her ears alone. "I want to lick you everywhere, kiss you, thrust into your body."

She closed her eyes. "I can't take this. Don't talk to me like this."

"I want to take you hard, soft, slow, fast. I want to take

you often. And I want you to wear those damn thigh-high boots you've got on while I do it."

Veronica was drowning in need and frustration. "Stop," she choked out. A few rows away, Martine looked up at Veronica's cry, met her gaze. Just as quickly she turned away again, a red flush spreading across her cheeks.

Veronica wanted to tell Martine it was okay, but she couldn't speak. Because at the moment Raj drew one of her fingers into his mouth, sucked it in and out so slowly as fingers of fire raced along her nerve endings. She bit her lip to stop a moan. He kissed her palm, then leaned forward and took her mouth in a hard, sensual kiss.

She didn't care who saw them. She cupped his jaw, kissed him back with all the passion and fire he aroused in her. If they were alone, she'd have him undressed and inside her before the next few moments passed.

"Now what do you think?" he whispered in her ear. "Flattered or not?"

"Yes," she breathed, heart racing. Martine was engrossed in a magazine now, and Veronica took another sip of her cocktail while Raj leaned back on the seat and shot her the most sexy grin imaginable.

"I'm hard for you," he said. "Another minute of that and I'd be lifting that Barbie-doll-pink dress and to hell with everyone else."

"Another minute of that and I'd let you," she replied. And then she laughed. "Barbie-doll pink? How do you know that, Raj?"

"How else? Barbie was my favorite doll," he said—and then he winked as she gaped at him.

"You say things like that just to make me laugh."

He shrugged. "Sometimes." Then he picked up her hand again, threaded their fingers together. "My mom moved us around a lot when I was growing up. One of the things I remember, when I was about eight I think, was this little girl in my class. She was blonde, like you, and she had these enormous pigtails. She was the prettiest thing I'd ever seen, and she carried a pink backpack with a Barbie face on it."

"You must have liked her."

"I did."

She thought of him as a love-struck little boy and smiled. "So what happened? Did you write one of those notes to her where you asked her to circle 'yes' or 'no'?" she teased.

"No. But she did invite me to her birthday party. I remember the invitation was pink, with Barbie dolls on it."

"Was the party pink-themed, too?"

"I don't know," he said. "I never got to go. We moved again."

She imagined the disappointment he must have felt when he couldn't go to the party. "I'm sorry you didn't get to go."

"I probably wouldn't have liked it anyway. There'd have been a pink cake, no doubt, and pink balloons everywhere. And what if I'd been the only boy invited?" He gave a mock shudder.

"The horrors," she agreed. And then she sighed. "At least you got to go places. I never did."

She thought of her vast bedroom with the purple walls, the piles of toys and the utter loneliness that had so often assailed her. She'd had a nanny, but even Mrs. Petit couldn't completely fill the emptiness created by the vacuum her father had placed her in. A vacuum made all the worse by the fact they'd had a normal life until her mother had died in the accident.

Veronica had spent the past several years of her life trying to fill that emptiness; it'd gotten her nothing but heartbreak.

"One thing I've learned in this life," he said, "is that the grass always looks greener on the other side of the fence—though it usually isn't."

"Maybe so," she said. "But sometimes it just might be."

"It does no good to think like that, Veronica. It only leads to regrets. And they might be false regrets."

She turned to look out the window. They were over water now, winging their way toward the island of Aliz in the Mediterranean. "I have enough regrets to last me a lifetime."

She could feel the weight of his stare on her, but she didn't turn. Tears were suddenly pressing against the backs of her eyes. Stupid, stupid tears. If she looked at him, she wasn't sure she could stop them from falling.

But why? What was it about him that made her want to unburden her soul to him every damn time?

She sucked in a breath, nibbled on her thumbnail. So quickly, she'd grown to trust him. So quickly, she'd grown to care about him. And she still knew next to nothing about him.

"You can cry if you need to," he said, so softly that she almost didn't hear.

How did he know? She turned to face him again, resolutely burying the tears and forcing herself to smile.

"Not at all," she replied. "I was just thinking."

He didn't look convinced. "It's a long trip, Veronica," he finally said. "Why don't you rest?"

"Nonsense. It's only a couple more hours. And we really should discuss what happens when we arrive." She had to concentrate on that, on the moment the plane landed and she set foot on her home soil again. She'd only been gone two weeks, and she'd set in motion much that would be ruined if she didn't quickly get this situation under control.

Giancarlo Zarella would never agree to build a resort in Aliz if they couldn't maintain the rule of law.

Raj's eyes sparked. "There's nothing to discuss," he said. "I'll handle it."

Veronica blinked. "You'll handle it? Handle what? I think we should at least discuss the possibilities."

"No," he said, his voice harder than it had been only moments ago.

A current of anger swirled in her belly. "No? I'm not a child, Raj. I have a right to know what your plans are."

He got to his feet, every inch the imperious lord and master. Then he shoved a hand through his hair—and she realized that he looked as if he hadn't slept much lately.

Her fault, no doubt.

"We'll discuss it before we arrive," he said.

Veronica bit down on the spike of temper. Perhaps he was still finalizing his plans and didn't want to share them yet. Or maybe he had no idea what to expect when they arrived. She could wait another hour. She'd trusted him this far, and he hadn't failed her yet.

"Fine. But I expect a full report quite soon."

His mouth was a hard line. "You'll get it, believe me."

Veronica awoke with a start, confusion crashing through her. Then she remembered that she was on a plane, flying back to Aliz. After Raj had walked away, she'd closed her eyes for a few minutes. She hadn't expected to fall so soundly asleep.

Or maybe she had, considering how little sleep she'd gotten the night before. A flight attendant materialized at that moment. "Madam President, would you like something to eat?"

She started to refuse, then realized her stomach was growling. But they would be in Aliz soon, and she could wait. She sent the man away with a request for water instead and turned to raise the window covering that someone had lowered.

Her blood froze as myriad stars glittered against a sea of black. It was wrong, all wrong. It shouldn't be dark yet. Aliz was only four hours from the U.K., and they'd left early enough to arrive before nightfall.

Veronica unsnapped her seat belt. Before she could rise, Raj was there. His hands were shoved in the pockets of his camel trousers. His navy shirt was unbuttoned partway, exposing a tanned V of skin, and his dark hair curled over the collar, so carefree and sexy, as if he belonged on a beach instead of here.

Her heart beat sharply. "Where are we, Raj? Where are you taking us?"

Part of her already knew she'd been betrayed, but the other part—the part that had trusted this man with her body and soul last night, that still wanted to trust him—refused to believe he could be so duplicitous. It was a mistake, that's all. She'd simply miscalculated, or they'd had to go a different route for some reason.

There was no way he was forcing his wishes upon her. No way he was taking her somewhere against her will. He wouldn't do that.

"We're going to my home in Goa," he said, and her stomach went into a free fall.

She was stunned, as if she'd been running fast and suddenly smacked up against a brick wall.

"Goa? Isn't that a bit far from Aliz?" She sounded so bitter, so terribly bitter. Fury was bubbling in her veins like a volcano preparing to erupt—she felt as if she would burst apart at the seams if she had to stay on this plane a moment longer.

But what choice did she have? What goddamn choice?

He had her right where he wanted her—and he was *controlling* her, taking away her autonomy, locking her up. Revulsion mixed into the vile stew inside her, rose into her throat so that she wanted to retch with the bitterness of it.

She would not do so. She would not crumble, not now.

"I'm sorry, Veronica," he said, though he didn't look sorry at all. "But it's necessary. You can't go back to Aliz just yet because it's not safe for you there. The chief of police controls the government—and all the weapons, I might add. If we landed, he could execute you—all of us—before the next sunrise."

She was a block of ice. Her teeth began to chatter, though she tried very hard not to let them. It was no use. Raj swore, sinking down into the seat beside her and gathering her into his arms before she could stop him.

He was so warm, so solid. And she wanted to melt against him, wanted him to hold her while she thawed, while she drew his heat into her body.

But she couldn't. She couldn't accept comfort from him when he'd betrayed her. She'd trusted him, given him something of herself that she'd been unable to give in a very long time, and it meant nothing to him. He'd betrayed her so easily.

Veronica shoved him as hard as she could. "No," she said between clenched teeth. "Let me go. I *hate* you."

"I'm sorry," he said again, his grip not loosening. "I had to do it. I won't let them harm you."

An angry sob tore from her throat before she could stop it. And then she was fighting like a madwoman, shoving hard, screaming her fury. He let her go and she scrambled back, away from him, pressing herself against the wall, her knees drawing up to fend him off if he tried to touch her again.

He did not do so.

His gaze was troubled, but unrepentant. There was a long red scratch down his cheek, but she refused to care. If it hurt, so much the better. He deserved it.

"How dare you?" she snapped. "How dare you think you have the right to decide *for* me?"

His eyes flashed, and then his expression hardened. "Go ahead and have your tantrum, Veronica, but would you put them in danger, too?" he asked coldly, jerking his head toward the rear of the cabin and the men and women who sat there, pretending not to stare at them. "You have no idea what that man is willing to do, no idea what awaits you— or them—and yet you would have me take you there? You might risk it on your behalf, but can you risk it on theirs?"

She hated that he made her feel guilty, hated that he sounded sensible. Hated that he turned this against her when he was the one who'd betrayed *her*. She drew in a shaky breath, trying so damn hard not to cry—because she was furious, damn it, not because she was weak—and glared at him.

"No one would hurt them," she said. "They've done nothing wrong. I'm the only one who need fear reprisal."

"You don't know that," he said, his words measured. "You only think you do."

Then he stood and looked down at her, his presence so big and imposing and infuriating. She wanted to tear his eyes out.

And she wanted to kiss him. The force of the longing took her breath away.

Veronica closed her eyes and turned her head, her cheek pressing against the cold, vibrating wall of the airplane cabin. *No, never again.* Her body might not realize that everything had changed, but she did. She could never, ever trust him again.

"Go away," she said. "I don't want to talk to you."

She didn't think he would go, but when she cracked open an eye after a long silence, he was gone.

And she felt emptier than ever.

CHAPTER NINE

IT WAS early morning when they landed at Dabolim Airport on the Bay of Dona Paula. The aquamarine water sparkled like fire-tipped diamonds in the morning sunlight as the plane came in for a landing. After the snow in the U.K., the blinding blue sky was insufferably cheerful.

Veronica didn't feel in the least bit happy, however, though the sky was clear and the landscape looked impossibly green and verdant and warm.

She had changed into something a bit more suited to the weather in Goa—a tangerine silk sheath and a pair of nude peep-toe pumps, since she'd not packed sandals for her official trip across the mostly chilly United States and Europe.

When the cabin door opened and she stepped out onto the stairs, the heat and humidity wrapped around her senses and eased the chill in her bones. It was certainly welcome after wintry London, but Aliz would have been warm as well—not quite this warm, but not as frigid as northern Europe, either.

There was no press awaiting them, which was both a surprise and a relief. She felt far too off balance just now to deal with the media hounding her. Somehow, Raj must have managed to keep their destination a secret. How long he could do so was another matter altogether.

Martine was beside her as they descended the stairs. Georges was behind them, and the rest of the staff followed. In spite of the situation, she held her head high, determined to maintain the dignity of her office. For their sakes as well as her own.

She'd spoken with them last night, after she'd managed to regain some of her balance, and been surprised that no one seemed to disagree with Raj's plan. The security staff had understandably been dismayed at the turn of events both in Aliz and in London—when they'd climbed aboard Raj's plane and put themselves at his mercy—but somehow he'd won them over in spite of it. Now they were content to let him run the show.

She was not. She was furiously, murderously angry.

Ahead of them, Raj stood near a fleet of Land Rovers, talking with one of the drivers. He'd changed into a pair of khaki pants, sandals and a dark T-shirt that stretched over the hard muscles of his biceps and chest, delineating every line and bulge. Her heart throbbed painfully, her body tightening in response.

She hated that she couldn't stop her reaction to him. She wanted to smother it, and bury it down deep. Instead, the slight soreness between her legs reminded her of all they'd done together, of the silken slide of his body within hers. The driving pleasure. The bliss of orgasm.

Stop.

His betrayal, coming so hard on the heels of their intimacy, stung all the more. She'd *trusted* him—and he'd shattered that trust into a million shards.

He looked up then, his eyes shaded behind mirrored sunglasses. Though she couldn't see them, she knew he was looking directly at her. Her body sizzled under his regard, her nipples tingling, her core flooding with heat.

Damn him!

He separated himself from the driver and came to her side. Martine fell back, out of earshot. Veronica wanted to turn and tell her secretary there was no need, but she refused to do so lest Raj think she couldn't handle him on her own.

"How are you this morning?" he asked.

A riot of emotions tore through her at the silken sound of his voice. She hardened her heart and kept looking straight ahead. "Furious," she spluttered.

"But alive," he added, and she whipped her head sideways to glare at him. The red mark on his face was fading. She hadn't drawn blood, so it would disappear soon. She wanted to reach out and touch him, soothe him—and she wanted to mark him again. The feelings warring inside her were so tangled that it hurt to try and sort them all out.

"You say that like you know for certain what would have happened in Aliz. You don't, so I would appreciate it if you would admit there were other possibilities."

He shrugged, further inflaming her. "It's possible. But what I do is plan for the worst—and then avoid it."

"Or perhaps you create the worst," she said. "Aliz had a chance before you abducted me. Now, no one will come to her rescue."

She didn't truly know that, but she was too angry not to say it.

His frown turned down the corners of his sensual mouth. "And who is making assumptions now? I hardly think it's my actions you need worry about. It's Monsieur Brun's and the chief of police's."

Her heart skipped a beat at the former president's name. He had not liked her, that was certain. He'd attacked her in the media for months before the election, and he'd said the most vile things. That, however, was politics.

"Have you had more news?"

"None yet. The police have shut down communications for the time being. Nothing is getting out now."

She could hope that somehow Signor Zarella remained ignorant of the situation, though she didn't count on having that kind of good fortune. News of the coup had already made it to CNN, and it was only a matter of time before more news started to trickle out of Aliz again.

"I should be there," she said.

"You should be anywhere *but* there," Raj replied.

They'd reached one of the Land Rovers. He opened the door for her and she climbed in. When he got in beside her, she turned away from him, her pulse kicking up at his nearness. Martine and the others settled into the other cars, and then they were on their way, rolling south through lush country filled with palm trees, tall grasses and jade-green rice paddies. In the distance, gray shadowed hills rose up as a backdrop to the lush landscape.

It was exotic and beautiful, as were the brightly colored saris of the women they passed on the road. Goa was a mixture of the modern and ancient, and she found herself studying everything with the kind of interest of someone who'd always longed to go places. She'd traveled plenty over the past ten years, but she'd never come to India…an oversight she was sorry for now that she was here.

They passed the crumbled ruins of something that looked like a medieval fortress, and she craned her head as it faded away behind them again. It had seemed so odd, so strangely European in this setting.

"The Portuguese settled in Goa in the sixteenth century," Raj said, correctly guessing at her thoughts. "They only recently left. Much of their architecture is still evident in the villages and towns. Their influence can be found in the food, and there are even a few churches that remain."

She didn't want to look at him, but she did anyway. "You are originally from here?"

His expression seemed distant, a bit sad perhaps. "My father was Goan, though I did not know him. He and my mother divorced when I was two."

"But you have a house here."

"Yes. I wanted to see my heritage, or half of it anyway."

"Do you have family nearby?"

"If I do, I don't know them. My father died in England when I was a child. Any connection to family was lost a long time ago."

"Where does your mother live, then?" She didn't want to talk to him, and yet she couldn't seem to stop herself. She remembered that his mother was American, and she was curious. He seemed so exotic, as if he belonged here, and yet he was actually more American, or European, than he was Indian.

"She's in a home," he said, his eyes so distant and troubled. "Her mind is gone now. She doesn't know who I am."

In spite of her anger, a swell of emotion threatened to clog her throat. "I'm sorry, Raj. That must be terrible for you."

"She did it to herself," he said. "Drug use."

He said the words so matter-of-factly, but she knew they hurt him. She could see it in his expression, in the way he stared into the distance, as if he didn't see her beside him. What must he have suffered, watching his mother go through something like that?

She didn't remember her mother. She had impressions sometimes of a soft, laughing woman that were so fleeting she wondered if she'd imagined them. Her father had never talked of her mother once she was gone. He'd simply smothered his daughter in an attempt to keep her from leaving him, too. As if death could be cheated by imprisonment.

They rode the rest of the way in silence, finally turning and climbing steadily up a hill until they reached a sprawling estate that perched over the Arabian Sea below. The land was dotted with tall swaying palms, green grass that tumbled down to white-sand beaches and bordered by the sparkling sea that went on forever before finally curving into the horizon.

It was beautiful, far more beautiful than she'd realized it would be. The sea view reminded her of Aliz, and a pang of emotion clawed into her belly as she thought of her nation. What was happening there now? Would she ever see her home again?

A woman in a bright turquoise sari edged in gold and shot through with green threads emerged from the house, followed by a cadre of servants, who collected luggage and issued instructions. Veronica's gaze kept straying to the sea, and when she finally looked back again, she realized that she and Raj were alone.

"The view is even better from the terrace," he said.

"Where is my staff?"

"They've been shown to the guest cottages. Don't worry, they will be quite comfortable there."

"I'd like a guest cottage, too," she said, her heart suddenly picking up speed again at the prospect of being left alone with him.

"You will stay in the main house," he said. "With me."

"I'd rather not." She lifted her hand to shade her eyes as he moved, the light off his sunglasses reflecting the sun and sending a bright shaft of light into her vision.

Then he was before her, so close—too close—and the brightness was gone.

"You have no choice," he replied. "It is for your safety."

A shiver of dread washed over her. And then there was something else. Something warm and electric. Something he caused by standing so near, by filling her senses with his scent and his presence.

"And who will keep me safe from you?" she said softly.

One corner of his mouth lifted in a faint smile. A predatory smile. "That is entirely up to you, Veronica. I won't touch you unless you ask me to."

"I won't," she declared. "I'd rather curl up with a cobra."

He laughed. "This is India. That can be arranged."

Veronica followed him into the house, the brightly clad woman appearing once more as soon as they were inside. She spoke to Raj in a language Veronica didn't recognize. He said something in return, slowly she thought, as if he were figuring out the words.

And then the woman was turning and sweeping down the hallway like a dazzling exotic bird flying away.

"Your room is this way," he said, leading her down a hall to a polished wooden door. Iron hinges and studs decorated the edges, and carvings of elephants, tigers and flowers marched in profusion across the surface.

Raj opened the door without seeming to notice its beauty and held it for her. She preceded him inside, and found her luggage already waiting at the end of the bed. Double doors were open to the outside, leading onto a terrace. She went out, drawn once more by the sea view. She hadn't realized how tense she'd been over the past few weeks, but something about this place calmed her. In spite of her fear and anger, she felt strangely calm beneath all the emotion.

A breeze lifted her hair, blew it across her face. She pushed the strands down again and breathed deeply. She wasn't precisely free here, but at least he hadn't shut her into a room with four walls, tiny windows and one door.

She could come and go as she pleased, though she didn't fool herself that she wouldn't be watched or that she could leave this estate and keep on going right back to the airport and thence to Aliz.

She wasn't that free.

She didn't have to turn to know he was standing behind her. The hair on her arms had prickled as he drew near. Even now, her body was zinging with electric sparks. Longing was a palpable force within her.

If only she were here under different circumstances. If only. The story of her life, really.

She had merely to lean back, and she would connect with his solid form. He would put his arms around her as she tilted her head to the side, gave him access to her neck. His mouth would skim along her throat, her shoulder, and then he would turn her in his arms and kiss her.

She closed her eyes, her chin dropping as the weight of her need pressed down on her. And the weight of her sadness.

"You should have consulted me," she said bitterly. "You should have treated me like I was capable of offering an intelligent opinion on the subject. Bringing me here against my will was wrong."

He sighed. "You left me no choice. You were determined to go to Aliz, no matter what anyone said to you."

"It was my choice to make, not yours."

"We will never agree on this subject, Veronica."

She turned then, taking a step back. He regarded her with golden eyes that made her heart skip. So beautiful. So exotic. He'd always been exotic, and yet this setting made him more so.

"What happens now, Raj? I'm here with you, but I still have a responsibility to the people of Aliz. I can't simply give up."

"You aren't giving up. Your people have issued statements on your behalf. World pressure will be brought to bear on Monsieur Brun."

She blew out a breath. "I don't like waiting," she said. "I've never been very good at it."

He reached out, lifted a tendril of her hair, rubbed it between his thumb and forefinger. "I can wait," he said, his voice a deep, sensual growl that vibrated into her belly. "I can wait as long as it takes. Sometimes, the reward is much sweeter after the waiting."

Every cell in her body was attuned to him. Her breath had stilled, her heart, her blood—everything silent, waiting…waiting for a touch that never came.

He dropped her hair, stepped back. "Dinner is at six," he said. "Wear something simple—but stunning."

"Why?" she asked, the pulse point between her legs throbbing now. "Will there be guests?"

"Perhaps." And then he left her alone on the terrace, the breeze gently caressing her, tormenting her. If she closed her eyes, she could almost imagine the tendrils of wind were his fingers, skimming oh so lightly along her skin.

At precisely six o'clock, Veronica emerged from her room, dressed in a simple black gown that was strapless and long, skimming her form down to her ankles. One side was slit to her thigh, and she'd chosen to wear tall crimson heels with jeweled straps. For jewelry, she'd kept it simple. A diamond pendant and earrings, a lone diamond bracelet.

She hadn't heard any cars arrive, but she'd napped until nearly five-thirty before she'd awakened with a start and hurriedly gotten dressed. Now, as she glided through the sprawling house, following her nose toward the delicious scents of curry and spice, she realized there was no sound except the occasional distant voice speaking in Konkani.

The dining room was empty, but a long wall of wooden doors was opened to the terrace. She stepped out, expecting to find a small gathering of people. Perhaps Raj had invited powerful friends who could somehow help her.

But there was no one. Nothing except a long wooden table set for two with hibiscus blossoms and gleaming crystal, china and silverware. Torches flickered around the perimeter and the sound of the sea washing the beach drifted up from below. A lone man stood at one end of the terrace. She knew who it was even before he turned.

Her heart caught at the sight of him in an ornate green silk *sherwani* coat over traditional trousers. His dark hair had been cut since she'd last seen him this morning, the ends no longer curling over his collar. He looked like a maharaja, so exotic and handsome and regal that he took her breath away.

"Where is everyone?" she asked, because she could think of nothing else to say.

He came forward and poured a glass of wine for her. She accepted it, her body reacting with a shiver as his fingers brushed against hers ever so lightly.

"It's just us tonight," he said, his voice wrapping around her senses, caressing them.

"My staff?"

"Dinner in their cottages, I assume."

She'd met with them earlier when she'd spent part of the afternoon making phone calls about the situation in Aliz. They were all tired, all stressed by what had happened. And perhaps a bit regretful that they'd been with her in London. If they'd been at home in Aliz, they'd be swept into this change from the inside and simply riding the wave until it came to rest onshore. But because they were with her, they were now outsiders, too.

Veronica took a sip of the wine, frustration and guilt hammering through her.

"Don't beat yourself up, Veronica," Raj said gently.

"What makes you think I was doing so?"

He shrugged, his golden eyes gleaming in the torchlight. "Call it a hunch."

"Is anyone else coming?" she asked, and then felt stupid since he'd just informed her it would only be the two of them.

"No," he said, the corners of his mouth lifting in a faint smile.

He pulled a chair out for her and then sat in another nearby. At that moment, a waiter came outside with a tray. There were many small silver dishes containing food in red sauces, green sauces and bright amber sauces. There was also creamy *raita* and naan bread, as well as fragrant basmati rice. Fried fish, fried prawns and salads of purple onion slices with tomatoes and cucumber rounded out the variety. And then there was chutney and thin, crispy yellow *papadum*.

If she weren't so hungry, she'd get up and go back to her room. She was supposed to be angry with him, not companionable. But the food smelled too good, and the night air was warm and fresh.

And she just didn't feel like fighting with him again after the stress of the past twenty-four hours.

"Fish curry is a Goan specialty," he said after she'd filled her plate with a bit of everything.

She took a bite and the flavors exploded on her tongue—the spice, the fresh fish, the tomatoes and hints of coconut milk. "It's delicious," she said.

It was awkward at first, but eventually they started to talk about subjects that weren't sensitive in the least. They avoided anything personal, avoided Aliz or what had happened between them last night. There was even a discussion of Bollywood movies—Raj hadn't seen many, and Veronica was surprised.

"I was born in Britain, but raised in America," he explained. "And then I joined the military. I haven't spent a lot of time watching any movies, much less Indian ones."

"How did you like the military?" she asked, dipping a piece of naan into a masala sauce before popping it into her mouth.

He didn't look at her. "Well enough," he said. "It got me where I am today."

She could picture him in military fatigues, silver dog tags hanging from a chain around his neck. He was tall, broad, tough—the kind of man to whom a weapon was an extension of his body and not just a foreign object. It's what made him so good, she realized. And so lonely.

"So where is home for you? Where is the place you most identify with?"

She wasn't sure, but it seemed as if he stiffened. And then he was looking at her sharply before he smoothed his expression. "I'm a mutt," he said. "I have no specific home."

"A mutt?"

"Someone of mixed ancestry, like a dog that you can't quite tell what the dominant breed is."

"But you live in London," she said, trying to approach it from a different angle. "Is that the place you prefer over the rest?"

"I don't prefer anywhere. I go where I want to go."

"Like here?"

"Precisely."

She took another sip of wine. "But what about when you're ready for a family? Where will you settle then?"

His eyes were hard, glittering. "Don't, Veronica," he said. "Don't take this conversation down that road."

She tilted her chin up to glare at him icily, though her stomach was doing flips. "Don't flatter yourself. I was simply making conversation, not trying to set up house with you."

He shoved a hand through his hair and leaned back on his chair. The torches crackled, the sea churned, and he was silent for a long moment. "It's complicated," he finally said. "I'm complicated."

"Aren't we all." She said it as a statement, not a question, and he looked at her, appraising her.

"You certainly are," he said softly. And then he took a drink of his wine. "Family is not for me," he said. "It's not what I want."

Her heart pinched in her chest. Yes, she did want a family—a husband, children—but she didn't want them right this moment. Nor was she naive enough to think that one night of sex with Raj made him her ideal man, her love for all time. But the fact he could state so emphatically that a family was out of the question...

Yes, it bothered her. Because it seemed as if men never thought of her in terms of family life. They thought of her for sex. For uncomplicated, uncommitted relationships based on physical attraction.

There was nothing deeper. There never had been. And that saddened her.

She set her napkin on the table, pushed back and got to her feet. "Thank you for a wonderful meal," she said. "But I think I've had enough excitement for one day. It's time to turn in."

"Veronica," he said, standing, holding his hand out as if to stop her.

She turned slightly, her gaze not on him but on a point

behind him. "It's okay, Raj," she said. "I understand. I'm just tired."

"It has nothing to do with you. I just don't feel the need for those things. I'm happy the way I am."

"Are you?" she said, her voice stiff even though she tried to make it casual.

He looked as if he pitied her. She hated it, because she knew what he was thinking. It made her wish she'd never told him about the baby. She didn't want his pity. She didn't want anyone's pity. She didn't deserve it.

"Not everyone needs the same things out of life. I have money and freedom. I need nothing more."

"How lonely that sounds," she said. "And what happens in twenty years when you wake up and realize you have no one who cares?"

He shook his head slowly. "You'll find him, Veronica."

"Find who?" she asked, quaking inside.

He reached out and skimmed a finger along her cheek. "The man who will love you the way you want to be loved."

CHAPTER TEN

HE SHOULD have left her alone, should have let her nurture her anger with him and left it at that. He shouldn't have planned to have dinner with her, shouldn't have asked her to dress up for him, and shouldn't have sat for more than an hour talking with her about anything and everything, listening to her bright laughter and falling just a little more under her spell with every word.

Raj shook his head as he stood on the terrace and let the wind whip through his clothes. It was hot and humid, but the breeze took it all away, for a short time anyway.

Why couldn't he simply leave well enough alone? He'd hurt her when he'd taken her body, and he'd hurt her when he'd betrayed her trust and brought her to Goa against her will. Tonight, he'd hurt her again when he'd been unwilling to tell her why he didn't feel at home anywhere, why he couldn't settle into a family life.

Things with Veronica had gotten out of control much too quickly. He'd broken his own code of conduct when he'd gotten involved with her, and he was willing to break it again for one more night in her arms. The truth was that he'd sell his soul for one more night with her.

He wasn't proud of it, but there it was.

She wasn't like other women. He'd had relationships, some lasting for several months as he'd stayed put in one location or another, but he'd never felt as if his skin was itching on the inside, as if only one woman could soothe the restlessness that plagued him.

It was simply the circumstances of their meeting, he told himself. He'd expected a spoiled, useless brat who'd somehow fooled an entire nation—but he'd found a thoughtful, intelligent woman who hadn't led a perfect life, but who wanted very much to do a perfect job.

He admired that. Admired her. Two days ago, he'd have never thought that possible.

She'd experienced great sorrow in her life, but she hadn't let it beat her down. Her spirit was unbroken, though perhaps sorely tested.

She'd trusted him, in more ways than one, and he'd broken that trust. He didn't like the way that made him feel.

With a curse, Raj strode into the house and to her bedroom door. She'd only been gone for a half an hour or so. She might be in bed, but he would bet she was still awake. He knocked softly.

When she didn't answer, he knocked again, more loudly. Still nothing.

His heart kicked up. There was nowhere she could go really. They weren't on an island, but there was nothing for miles—and he did have security on the perimeter. He'd given her the illusion of complete freedom, but he wasn't so incautious as to leave her unguarded.

Even here.

With a curse, he pushed on the handle…and the door swung inward. The doors to the terrace were wide-open, the white curtains blowing in the breeze. She wasn't in bed, or in the en suite bath. He slipped out onto the terrace—a different terrace than the one they'd had dinner on, facing a different direction—but she wasn't there, either.

She was still on the premises, or security would have

alerted him. He eyed the path that sloped down to the beach and knew instinctively where she'd gone.

Heart lodging in his throat, he took the path at a run and skidded down the hill. Veronica was not so stupid as to try and escape, was she? Because though she wouldn't get away, she might very well harm herself in the process.

And he couldn't stand it if anything happened to her.

At the bottom of the hill, the path abruptly ended in sand. He stood, looking in both directions, his ears straining to hear anything over the sound of the sea caressing the shore. A flash of something caught his eye and he took off in that direction.

He was only a few feet away when he heard singing, and he crashed to a halt. Relief flooded him as she turned her head, the moonlight catching her blond hair.

"Veronica," he said, and the singing stopped.

"I couldn't sleep." She turned to face him, her pale arms wrapped around her chest. "How about you?"

He wanted to laugh in agreement, and he wanted to snatch her into his arms and hold her tight. "You're still in your evening gown," he said, noticing with a jolt the way her creamy thigh split through the fabric as she took a step forward. Her feet were bare, her legs so long and perfect. He could still feel them wrapped around his waist, could feel how they'd trembled and stiffened when he'd brought her to orgasm.

He wanted that again.

"It doesn't matter," she said.

"I'm sorry." It was the thing he'd wanted to say, the reason he'd gone to her room in the first place.

"For what, Raj?" Her voice sounded tremulous, as if she were trying very hard not to allow any emotion to escape.

"For everything," he said. "For bringing you here. For making love to you—"

She laughed, the sound bitter. "Of course," she said, "of course. Because it would be better if you had not done so, correct? I corrupted you, corrupted your squeaky-clean morals—"

"Stop it," he said harshly. "I made love to you because I wanted to. But I shouldn't have been so weak. I should have resisted."

"Yes, of course." She turned toward the sea again, but he could see the lone tear that slid down her cheek. "I'm not the sort of woman a man resists, am I? But I am the sort he regrets."

"I don't regret it," he growled. But he did. He regretted that he'd been so weak in the first place, that he'd been unable to resist and that he'd hurt her in the process.

"Don't bother explaining," she said. "I understand."

He reached for her, his fingers closing around her bare arm. She was delicate, like spun glass in his hand. He feared that if he held her too tightly, she'd break.

"You understand nothing," he said, turning her to face him. He was careful not to pull her closer, though he wanted to.

"Oh, Raj," she said, her voice carrying to him on the sea-scented breeze, "I'm not sure either one of us understand."

"Then tell me what I need to know," he replied. Because he very much wanted to know what made her tick. There was the baby, her loss—and yet there was more. He wanted to know everything, though a small voice told him it wasn't a good idea.

The less he knew, the better in the end.

Her hand came up, her fingers sliding along his jaw. Her touch was like fire, like ice. She burned him, and he wanted nothing more than to keep burning.

"I'm so angry with you," she said, "and yet I can't help but want you, too. Why is that? Why can't I resist you?"

Her admission sent a current of hot possessiveness through him. His body hardened. He turned his head, kissed her palm. She did not pull away. Her sky-blue eyes sparkled in the night, diamond-tipped with tears.

He had done that to her. But no matter how much he wanted her just now, he couldn't make her cry again. Because she would. He would walk away in the end, and she would cry.

And he didn't want that. Somehow, he had to find the strength to let her go.

Before this got any more complicated than it already was.

"I only want what's best for you, Veronica," he said. "If I had let you go to Aliz and something happened, I would never forgive myself."

Her laugh was strangled. "My God, you sound just like my father." Her hand dropped and her head tilted back. Her gaze sparkled up at him. "He kept me locked up until I was eighteen, until I was old enough to leave home and do what I wanted to do. His excuse was that he loved me. And he did, I know that. But it was horrible, Raj, horrible to be kept prisoner to someone else's fears for so long."

So much about her made sense now. Her wild life, her rebellion, her refusal to take a backseat while someone else steered the cart. She wanted a say because she was frightened of giving up control. He could understand that. Could empathize with it. He thought of her last night, on the plane, and felt guilty.

"This isn't the same," he said gently—justifying his actions, yes, but also because it was true. "There is a real threat to your safety, especially if you return to Aliz while it's in chaos."

She pushed a lock of hair that had blown into her face back over her shoulder. Her brows were pinched together, her eyes narrowed.

"I know that," she said finally. "I was angry with you— I'm still angry that you didn't consult me—but I know you did what I asked for when I accepted your help."

"Your safety is my priority, Veronica. No matter how angry I make you, or how much you might hate me for it."

She shook her head, looked away. "I don't hate you. Though it might be easier if I did." She drew in a long breath. "You kept me safe, and you did so when I was determined to put myself—and my people—in danger."

"I'd do it again, if the circumstances were the same."

"I know that, too." Her head dropped as she fixed her gaze on the sand at her feet. He wanted to pull her close and kiss the top of her head, but he did not do so. He stood with arms hanging at his sides.

He felt…useless in some ways. He'd brought her here, but he hadn't yet found who'd sent her the note or placed the doll on her bed. She was safe, but for how long? If her government was restored and she returned to Aliz, then what?

She wouldn't need him anymore. He would never see her again, except as a photograph in a newspaper.

She looked up, her eyes shining with unshed tears. "I wish I'd met you earlier, under different circumstances. Maybe neither of us would have any regrets then."

He couldn't stop himself from reaching out and lifting a strand of her hair. He loved the silken feel of it, the bright pale color. In the moonlight, it hung down her back like ropes of gossamer ribbon.

"Life is filled with regrets," he said.

He couldn't imagine not being able to touch her like this. He didn't want to imagine it.

She let out a deep sigh that slashed into his control. "Oh, Raj, if we don't learn from our mistakes, then what is the point?" He froze as she reached for him, her hand wrapping around the back of his neck while the other gripped his arm to steady herself as she stood on tiptoe.

He didn't resist as she pulled him down to her, didn't resist as her lips brushed his. He didn't close his eyes because he wanted to see her face while she kissed him. Her lashes dipped down, fanning long and silky beneath her eyes as her mouth skimmed across his.

The pressure was light, so light. Unbearable. He wanted to crush her to him, wanted to slide his tongue between her lips and feel her response.

"It's too late," she whispered against his mouth a moment later. "As you've pointed out more than once, you aren't the right man."

She took a step backward, breaking the contact, and then turned and started down the beach. He watched her as she found the path back up to the house, his heart a lead weight in his chest. He'd wanted her to realize the truth, hadn't he?

She had finally done so. And he wanted to howl.

Veronica found her way blindly up the side of the hill, then stumbled into her room and slapped the doors closed. Tears pricked her eyes. She was tired of fighting them, so she let them fall.

She'd lied. She'd stood there and lied to him when she'd told him he wasn't the right man. Because he was the man her heart wanted, though she tried to deny it. She'd realized it tonight, and she'd been running from the truth of it when she'd gone down to the beach.

How could she be so stupid? How could she have allowed herself to fall for him?

It was too soon.

He was too much.

He stunned her, quite simply. He was insightful, tender and tough. He made her feel safe. He'd even made her feel loved, though she knew he didn't love her.

But he was also wild, untamable. She'd known it, and yet she'd insisted on lying in the tiger's jaws. When he chewed her up and spit her out, she had no one to blame but herself. She stood in the middle of the room, tears falling as she dashed them angrily away, and wanted to scream. She'd been just fine until he'd come into her life! She'd been getting through the days, trying to heal, trying to live.

He'd ripped everything open again, made her feel, made her ache and want and need and love.

After a while, Veronica went into the bathroom and washed her face with cold water. Then she stripped off her gown and dropped it on the bed.

The bed was huge, a solid carved four-poster with white filmy netting hanging from it—and no way was she staying here tonight. No way was she sleeping in this giant bed, with Raj in the same house, knowing she couldn't go to him.

Knowing he would not come to her.

Veronica found a thin silk robe in her luggage and wrapped it around herself. Then she slipped into the hallway and toward the front doors. She would go down to the cottages, find Martine's quarters and sleep there tonight. If she were not under the same roof with Raj, she could breathe again. She could think and feel and not ache so much.

She found the front door and jerked it open—

Raj was standing on the other side, his hand poised over the handle. They stared at each other without speaking. He wasn't wearing a shirt, and her heart lodged in her throat. A pair of pajama bottoms sat low on his hips, the drawstring tied just loosely enough to allow his lean hip bones to protrude.

Not to mention the ridges of his abdominal muscles, so hard and tight beneath his broad chest. Her mouth went dry. Her brain refused to function. She tried to speak, but no sound came out.

"Going somewhere?" he asked, one eyebrow lifting sardonically.

"Yes," she managed to respond, her voice croaking out as if she'd been traveling across a desert with nothing to drink. She swallowed. "I was going to find Martine."

"Isn't it a bit late to dictate a letter?"

She couldn't admit to him that she'd wanted to escape this house. Wanted to escape him. It would give him too much power over her. As if he didn't have enough already. As if she weren't teetering on the edge of something that would change her forever.

"I thought of something important," she lied, lifting her chin.

"It's a distance to the cottages." His gaze slipped down her body. "And there are things you might not wish to meet in the dark. Especially dressed like that."

"I went to the beach in an evening gown," she pointed out.

"Not as far. Or as rich with vegetation."

She wanted to argue, but she took a step back, defeated. She wanted out, but she wasn't stupid. Who knew what manner of creatures waited on the path to the cottages? Bugs? Stinging bugs? Cobras?

Veronica shivered.

Raj came inside and closed the door. Locked it.

Her heart thundered in her ears. He was so close. Once more, so close. He smelled delicious, like the sea and wind and India.

"You're upset," he said softly.

"I'm not."

He lifted a finger, skimmed her cheek, tipped up her chin so he could look down into her eyes. The light in the entry came from the living area, warm and golden and spilling through the prism of glass that divided one area from another. Her breath stopped in her chest. Time seemed to stretch out between them, so fine and thin, like the thread spun out by the mythical Fates.

But would one of them cut it, or would it continue to spin?

"You make me want things I shouldn't," he said, his voice so husky and deep.

Her heart pounded in her temples, her throat, between her legs. "Who says you shouldn't? You? Are you not in control of your own destiny?"

His laugh was part groan. "You make it sound so simple, like one simply reaches a decision and starts down a new path."

"Don't they?"

"You know it's not true. You know that life throws things at you, and you do the best you can to deal with them. If you're lucky, you figure out what works for you, and you stick with it."

It was her turn to laugh. "And how is that working for you, Raj? Because I have no idea what I'm doing from one day to the next sometimes. Maybe I should try your method."

His expression was troubled in the dim light. "You confuse things, Veronica."

A pinprick of pain pierced her, the hurt rippling outward as if someone had thrown a rock into a pond. "Don't patronize me. I'm not stupid, and I'm not confused."

"You confuse things for *me*," he said. "You make me question myself."

"Everyone should question his paradigm from time to time."

"Are you questioning yours?" he asked, taking a step closer to her. "Am I still the wrong man?"

His mouth was so close now, and her body was sizzling with heat and memory and need.

"You're completely wrong," she said. "I don't want you at all."

His smile was self-assured. Feral and sexy. "You're lying, Veronica."

He tilted his head, studying her. She endured his scrutiny, her heart thundering, her skin begging for his touch.

Oh, God, she no longer cared. She just wanted him to touch her, to give her the bliss he'd given her two nights ago. She wanted to feel loved again, even if it wasn't quite true.

She thought she would go mad waiting.

"What do you plan to do about it?" she said, a heaviness settling in her abdomen, between her legs.

He smiled again, only this time it was filled with regret. "Nothing. The desire will have to be enough for both of us."

Furious tears stung the backs of her eyes. "Bravo, Raj. Once more, you're willing to sacrifice yourself on the altar of altruism for my sake. Whatever would I do without you to make decisions for me?"

His growl was not what she expected, but it sent a thrill through her belly nevertheless. "You can't have it both ways," he snapped. "You can't tell me I'm wrong for you and then look at me like I'm the only man who has what you need. So tell me what you want from me or get back to bed."

CHAPTER ELEVEN

TELL me what you want.

Such a simple statement, and so complicated all at once. So many things she wanted, and only one thing she would get from him. Only one thing he was willing to give.

Or perhaps he wasn't.

Perhaps he was simply trying to humiliate her. Perhaps the best thing she could do—for herself, for both of them—was to turn and go back to her bedroom.

Heart in her throat, she turned away and took two steps. And then, because she was frustrated and angry and hurt and confused, she turned back. Stood there staring at him while he stared back, no one saying anything, no one moving.

So many emotions and thoughts crashing through her—and one very big one that said, *Why are you doing this? Life is too short to play games. You know what life can do to you when you don't take it seriously.*

As soon as she thought the words, she understood something very fundamental about Raj. It was as if someone had pulled back a curtain and shown her an illuminated tablet upon which this particular truth was carved: he was accustomed to denying himself.

The little boy who'd never written that note to the Barbie-pink girl, who'd never gotten to go to her party or ask her to be his girlfriend, was standing here now, unwilling to take a chance. Because tomorrow might change everything. Because tomorrow he might move away again, and the party would happen without him. The girl would find another boyfriend. Nothing stayed the same in Raj's world, and he'd learned it was better not to get attached to anything just in case.

Her blood sang as if she'd just been shown a priceless secret. She understood what motivated him. She understood and she knew what she had to do.

Veronica untied the belt at her waist and let the robe slide down her shoulders to pool at her feet. She was only wearing the black lace thong she'd worn beneath the strapless gown, and nothing else. Her breasts pebbled as she stood there for what seemed an eternity, waiting for Raj to react.

"Veronica," he said. Choked, really.

"I know what *I* want," she said. "But I don't think you do. You think you have to deny yourself. But you don't, Raj. It's okay to want things. It's okay to want *me*. I don't expect anything out of you."

"You do," he said, his voice still strained. "You want the kind of life I can't give you."

She swallowed. "I don't think either one of us is ready for more at this point in our lives."

Though part of her ached for more, she didn't deserve it. She had to be real with herself. Because he would despise her if he knew what sort of person she really was. And she couldn't bear it if he did.

She closed the distance between them. They didn't touch. The heat emanating from his body touched her instead—enclosed her, enveloped her. He was on fire. It made her wonder how much she would sizzle when he actually made contact.

Then she slid her palms up his arms while his eyes glowed hot, over his biceps and hard pectoral muscles. His nipples were small, tight, and she tweaked them with her thumbs while he growled deep in his chest.

And then she told him what she wanted right now. The words she used were graphically, shockingly raw.

She surprised herself. Surprised him if the way his eyes widened were any indication.

But then he was dropping to his knees in front of her, pressing his face to her bare belly, kissing a trail down her abdomen. Hooking his fingers into the material of her thong, he slipped it down her legs until she could step out of it.

Then he lifted one of her legs and put it over his shoulder while she gasped.

"Raj, not here!"

"Yes, here."

She gripped his shoulders to keep herself upright, but his mouth on her body, on her most sensitive spot, soon had her panting and gasping and thrusting her hips to increase the pressure. When she came a split second later, her knees buckled. Only his strong grip kept her standing.

And then he was on his feet, backing her against the wall. She wrapped her arms around his neck, kissed him, their tongues tangling urgently as he shifted her against him until her legs were wrapped around his waist and his hard shaft was at her entrance.

Veronica cried out as he plunged into her body. But it wasn't pain that caused her to do so. Somehow he knew, because he didn't hesitate to thrust again and again, harder, until she dragged her mouth from his and tilted her head back to moan her pleasure.

Oh, this was exactly what she wanted—what she

needed. Raj, here like this. Raj, inside her, part of her. *Raj, Raj, Raj...*

"God, Veronica," he said, and she knew she'd been speaking aloud. She'd been telling him what she wanted, saying his name...

His mouth found her throat, his lips and tongue and teeth sending a shiver of delight racing down her spine, over her nerve endings, into her molten core. She was close, so close.

Raj made a sound of frustration. "Need more," he said, the words hot against her skin. "Need more of you."

And then he strode across the room, their bodies still joined, taking her somewhere, though she didn't know where until they were falling together and her back hit something soft.

He rose above her, his dark face so handsome and sexy as he worked to hold on to his control. She could see the restraint in his eyes, could see how he held a part of himself back, how he was still worried about hurting her in spite of his need.

"Give me all of you," she said. "I want all of you, Raj."

"Veronica—" Her name was a groan—so raw, so torn.

"I don't want you to hold back. If this is all we have, I don't want to miss anything."

They both knew it wasn't about the physical. That part was perfect. Amazing, hot and wonderful. His gaze was wild, his body throbbing inside hers, and yet she still wondered if she'd carried it too far, if he would withdraw and leave her lying here alone.

He was capable of it, she was certain, no matter the cost to his pleasure.

But then he groaned, his head dropping until his forehead touched hers, and she knew he'd surrendered. He kissed her, their mouths fusing so sweetly, so perfectly. He was still so hard inside her, but he didn't move. He simply kissed her, skimming the fingers of one hand over her face, as if he were learning her shape and texture by touch alone.

A tear leaked from her eye, slid down her temple. He kissed it away, kissed the tender skin of her cheek, the bones of her face. Love swelled inside her heart until she thought it would burst. She wanted to let it out, wanted to tell him how she felt, and yet it terrified her.

She was in love with him, and she couldn't tell him. So bittersweet, so shattering.

Veronica thrust her hands into his hair, curled them into his skin, slid them over his body. She wanted to know every part of him, the golden skin and eyes, the hard, sensual lips, the straight, regal nose. The hardness buried deep inside her.

"Oh, Raj," she gasped as he flexed his hips and sensation bolted through her, from her fingertips to her scalp, her toes to her nipples. Every part of her was alive and on fire for him.

"I love the way you say my name when I'm inside you," he growled. "So sexy, so needy."

"I am needy," she said, arching her back, trying to get him to move again. "I want more."

He withdrew from her, surged forward again. "More of this?"

"God, yes."

This time he obliged her, thrusting into her again and again, her body soaring as he drove her toward completion. There was nothing left between them. No barriers, no secrets, no lies—nothing but raw, hungry emotion. Their bodies rose and fell together, giving and taking, taking and giving.

She wanted to feel like this forever, and yet it had to end. Finally, she could hold back no longer. The pounding pressure started a ripple of sensation deep inside that engulfed her senses. The only word she could say, the only one that would form on her tongue, was his name.

And then he was tumbling over the edge right behind her, grasping her buttocks and lifting her to him as he came. Her name on his lips sounded so raw it gave her a thrill. His breath in her ear was rapid, as if he'd been running.

Veronica closed her eyes, her heart racing in time with his, blood pounding and body singing. She was happy. Right this moment, she was so incredibly happy. She felt as if she was flying and she didn't want to look down, didn't want to see the scorpion waiting to strike. She didn't want this to end.

But it would. She knew it would.

"You've killed me," he said. "Sacrificed me for your selfish pleasure. I'm done in."

Veronica laughed, ran her fingers up the damp skin of his back. "Oh, yes, my evil plan is complete. I intend to drain you, Rajesh Vala. Leave you an empty husk, unable to ever get it up again for any other woman."

She said it jokingly, and yet the thought of Raj with another woman pierced her to the bone.

"Don't do that," he said softly, skimming his lips along her jaw, the shell of her ear. "Don't put something between us that doesn't exist."

She shuddered beneath him, her heart pinching tight in her chest. "I'm simply being realistic," she said. Because there would be other women in his life, once she was gone. He was too sensual, too male. He couldn't be tamed—but he could be caught, for a short time anyway.

He tweaked her nipple, made a sound of approval when she gasped. "This is what's real, Veronica."

A short while later, he carried her to his bed and proved that he was perfectly capable of sacrificing himself for her pleasure yet again.

Raj came awake as the sea breeze blew into the windows and rustled the filmy netting. The covers had been flung off long ago. Beside him, Veronica was curled into a ball with her back to him. He traced a fingertip along her shoulder, her hip. Already, his body was stirring, wanting her again.

She was a fire in his blood, this woman. She had been since the first moment he'd seen her. He spared half a thought for Brady, but she'd never been Brady's to begin with. Veronica had chosen *him,* and he would not feel guilty for it.

He kissed her shoulder, cupped a breast in his palm. She came awake with a smile, turning sleepily in his arms.

She was as hot for him as he was for her. Thank God. Pushing him onto his back, she straddled him and sank down onto him with a groan. He closed his eyes, his body pulsing inside hers. He could live this way. He could wake every morning like this, Veronica undulating her hips and making him crazy with need.

He gripped her thighs, slowing her movements before it was over too fast. When he looked up at her, her pale hair was swinging around her breasts as if she were Lady Godiva riding through the town square. Her nipples were hard little points that he wanted to suck.

Except that he couldn't move. If he moved, it would be over too quickly.

She arched her back, lifted her arms and pulled her hair off her body. "Oh, yes," she said, her voice little more than a throaty whisper. "Like that. Just there."

He suddenly wanted to shatter her control, wanted to

prove he could, wanted her wild and wriggling beneath him. He wanted to know that she was his, that he was the one who made her quiver and sigh and cry out with pleasure.

With a quick movement, he flipped her over, driving deeper into her body. Her legs wrapped around his hips, her teeth biting into her lush lower lip as she arched toward him.

He lost whatever thread of control he'd been holding on to, driving into her until she shattered beneath him with a sharp, hard cry. But he didn't stop there. He couldn't. He kept stroking into her until she caught on fire again, until his body was burning up with hers, until they both plunged over the edge and crashed onto the rocks below.

Mine, he thought. *Mine.*

It was sometime later when he woke a second time. Veronica was asleep again, her lush body pale in the morning light. Her skin was red in places, and he realized he needed to shave. He climbed from the bed with a yawn and a languid stretch before making his way to the bathroom and turning on the shower.

If he had any strength at all, he'd make love to Veronica in the shower. He imagined holding her against the slippery wall, imagined driving up into her body, and was half tempted to go wake her when he began to harden.

Instead, he got dressed and headed for the dining room. Breakfast would be waiting, as well as his morning reports. He took a seat at the table and tore into the fragrant *dosa*.

It had taken him several visits to convince the housekeeper that he didn't want a traditional English breakfast every morning when he was in residence. Now that he'd been coming to Goa for the past few years, they'd slipped into enough of a routine that he could expect masala *dosa* in the mornings unless he specifically asked for full English.

He flipped through the reports, finding nothing he didn't already know in any of them. The doors to the terrace were open, and air fragrant with the spices being used in the kitchen blew gently through the house.

"Good morning."

Raj looked up from the report he'd been reading. Veronica waltzed into the room, her hair a gorgeous mess pinned on top of her head, her lips full and swollen from his kisses, her skin glowing. She'd slipped into one of his shirts, which she'd rolled at the cuffs, the tails hitting her about midthigh.

He'd always thought it a not-so-subtle attempt at claiming ownership when a woman put on one of his shirts the morning after sex. As if she were saying he belonged to her now that they'd spent the night in bed.

But with Veronica, all he could think was that she belonged to him and that his shirt was a lucky bastard.

"Don't gape, Raj," she said, grabbing a piece of *dosa* and a cup of chai that seemed to magically appear when she did, before she turned and went to stand in the open door. Beyond, the sea sparkled in the sun.

Raj went to stand behind her, breathing in the scent of her hair. Aching to touch her again, right now. Right here.

"It's so lovely. I don't think I've ever felt more relaxed." She turned and winked up at him. "But I don't think the relaxed part has anything to do with the view."

"It's a very nice view," he said—though he didn't mean the scenery.

She laughed and pulled the V of his shirt closed where it had gaped over her breasts. "Such a man."

"Definitely."

She took a sip of the chai and sighed. "It's odd to think it's nearly Christmas, isn't it, when it's so warm?"

"I like it warm."

She turned to him. "You don't like a traditional Christmas, with snow and hot chocolate and a big evergreen tree?"

He shrugged. "Actually, I don't care for Christmas much. It's too commercial."

She blinked. "But what about presents? Surely you like presents."

"It doesn't have to be Christmas for presents."

"No, that's true. I just remember such fabulous Christmases when I was a little girl. When my mother was still alive, my father would take us to Switzerland or Bavaria. He'd rent a chalet, and we'd ski and do all the traditional things. It was wonderful. I never feel like it's Christmas unless I'm cold." She grabbed a slice of mango from the table. "What's your favorite Christmas memory?"

A dart of pain pierced him. He started to make something up, to give an answer that would satisfy her and let her keep chattering happily away.

But he couldn't seem to do it. The urge to speak the truth built in his gut until he was nearly bursting with it.

"I don't have any. My mother couldn't afford Christmas."

She'd done her best when he was small, finding some cast-off toy at the thrift shop or signing him up for whatever local program gave to needy children. But the older he'd gotten—the further she'd sunk into her addiction and depression—she'd given up even trying.

Veronica's sky-blue eyes grew cloudy. She reached out, squeezed his arm. "I'm sorry."

"It's fine. I'm not a kid anymore. It doesn't matter."

"But you must have been sad when you were little. I'm sorry for that."

He slipped a hand into the small of her back, pulled her

in tight. His body wasted little time in reacting to the soft, warm feel of her pressed against him.

She tilted her head back to look up at him. He traced a finger along the beautiful line of her mouth. "It was a long time ago. And I can think of a few things you can give me if you really want to give me presents."

She ran her free hand up his arm, threaded her fingers into the hair at his nape. She looked troubled still—but then she smiled a wicked smile and he forgot everything but her.

"Oh, I imagine I could think of a few of my own."

Veronica couldn't remember ever being as happy as she was with Raj. It was her second day in Goa, and he'd taken her into one of the small villages along the coast. They were currently strolling through a market, hand in hand. She knew they had security.

Except the men Raj employed weren't dressed in suits and sporting headsets. They blended in, unlike her own staff had done in London.

She enjoyed it because it made her feel carefree. It was an illusion, but she was determined to take pleasure in it anyway.

"We can't stay long," Raj said as they meandered between stalls filled with fresh fruits and vegetables— tomatoes, cucumbers, onions, squashes, coconut, mangoes, nubby jackfruit—and dried spices and chilies that were so colorful she wanted to stop and stare at them so she could remember just how vibrant colors like orange and red and brown could truly be.

The women wore colorful saris, the men *kurtas* and sandals. There were goats, cows, the occasional painted elephant and a few Western tourists in their T-shirts and backpacks. The market was jammed with sound and movement, and she loved it.

"Thank you for bringing me," she said. "It's marvelous."

He smiled down at her, tweaked the sunglasses on her nose. "It's a risk, but I think no one will recognize you. You look very mysterious."

"And you stand out like a peacock," she grumbled as a woman turned her head to look back at Raj as she walked past them. The woman smiled. Veronica felt a stab of jealousy when Raj smiled back.

"The better to draw attention away from you," he said, leading her down another alleyway in the market.

Eventually, he stopped in a shadowed alcove and pulled her into his arms. She'd chosen to wear linen trousers and a big cotton shirt today. She'd belted the white shirt at her waist with a broad belt, and put on a straw hat that she'd found on a shelf in her bedroom. She'd been wearing ballet flats, but Raj had bought her a pair of beaded sandals as soon as they'd arrived in town.

Now, she braced her hands on his chest and gazed up at him through dark sunglasses. He was looking at her like as if was his favorite snack.

The thought made her shiver.

"I'm glad you're enjoying yourself today," he said. And then he bent and kissed her, as if he couldn't get enough of her. She felt the same, her arms going around his neck, her body arching into his. The alcove he'd pulled her into was private, but not that private.

He broke the kiss, though not before she felt the effect of it on his body.

"I can think of something else I'd enjoy even more," she purred.

"Me, too," he said. "But man cannot live on sex alone. We have to eat."

Veronica smiled. "I love to eat."

"Good, because I'm taking you somewhere special."

He led her from the market and down a wide street lined with wooden buildings painted in bright colors. People turned their heads as Raj and Veronica walked past, though she knew it was because they were looking at him and not her. Then Raj led her into a nondescript red building whose wooden facade had seen better days.

It was sun-bleached and dusty, with palms overhanging the entry. Inside, the building was clean, but Raj led her through the room and out the back to a plank deck overlooking the bright blue sea. Several tables were scattered on the deck, topped with grass umbrellas, and Raj took her to the farthest one and pulled out a rickety wooden chair for her.

The proprietor came bustling over, his chatter a mixture of English and Konkani. He seemed to know Raj, and they spent a few minutes conversing in both languages before the man clapped Raj on the shoulder and said the food would be out soon. Then he disappeared into the kitchen and started shouting orders.

"You're wondering why this place is special," Raj said.

Veronica shrugged a shoulder. The clank of metal and cacophony of voices in the kitchen had somehow blended together until it became white noise. "It seems like the kind of place that wouldn't get a second look from most tourists," she admitted.

"Exactly. That's part of it, since it's not overrun by tourists. The other part is that I was eating at this very table one afternoon when I decided to buy a house here."

She reached for his hand, knowing that he was sharing something important with her. Raj, who wasn't vulnerable or weak in the least, had experienced something profound and been moved into action by it. Her heart throbbed with love for him.

He squeezed her fingers. "It may not seem like a momentous step, but it was for me. This house here was the first I ever bought for myself. Until then, I'd lived in rented condos or hotel rooms." He turned to gaze out at the turquoise water. "Actually, it was the first real home I ever had."

Something in his voice carved out a hollow space inside her that ached for him. He was a little boy who'd never had Christmas, a man who'd waited—though he'd had money—to buy a home for himself.

"You never lived very long in one place, did you?" When he'd told her they'd moved a lot, she'd assumed he meant every few months or so. When you were a kid, any upheaval was traumatic. Now, she was beginning to think it had been something more.

He turned back to her, his golden gaze both hard and sad at once. "The one thing I wanted more than anything as a child was to be able to have a room of my own. My own bed, my own walls, my own toys. If I unpacked my suitcase—when I still had a suitcase—we moved again. So I stopped unpacking. Then one day it was gone and everything we owned could fill the backseat of the rusty car my mom somehow managed to keep."

"Raj," she said, her eyes filling with tears. She wanted to hold him, wanted to tell him she was sorry. She wanted to take his pain away.

He leaned forward and kissed her, swiftly and surely. "Don't feel sorry for me, Veronica. I didn't tell you so you would feel sorry for me."

She spread her palm over his jaw, caressed him. "I don't. I'm just grateful you felt you could tell me."

He turned and kissed her palm. "There's no one else I'd rather share it with."

The words were simple, but they choked her up. She dropped her gaze, stared at the bright tablecloth. If he knew the truth about her, he wouldn't think so highly of her, would he?

She had to tell him. "Raj…"

"Yes?"

But a waiter walked out with fresh *papadum* and sauces and she lost her nerve.

"Nothing," she said.

The rest of the meal came soon after. They talked and ate and enjoyed the view before Raj paid the bill and they walked back out to the street.

Soon, they were on their way to his house, the cars rolling through a beautiful tropical landscape. Goa was such a land of contrasts, she realized, as they passed a temple with a tall, conical bell tower, it's layers crowned with carvings and dotted with arched windows. A short distance away they passed a distinctly Portuguese church, its grounds scattered with tourists wielding cameras.

It was a beautiful place, and she could see why Raj loved it so much.

Though she'd intended to meet with her staff again this afternoon, all it took was one hot look from the man she loved to make her amend her plans. They spent the next couple of hours in bed, wrapped in each other, living off of kisses, whispered words and slow, deep thrusts that took them to heaven and back. It would be so easy to forget the world when nothing seemed more important than what took place when they were alone together.

But later, when the sun was sinking into the sea and they were dozing in each other's arms, there was a knock on the door.

"Yes," Raj managed to say, his voice husky with sleep.

"There is a call for the president," someone said.

Veronica looked up, met his gaze. She didn't want the outside world intruding, not yet. But she had no choice. They both knew it.

"Who is it?" Raj asked.

"Someone named Monsieur Brun."

CHAPTER TWELVE

VERONICA took the call on the terrace after hurriedly dragging on her clothes and wrapping an elastic band around her tangle of hair. Her chief of staff was in attendance, as well as her secretary.

Raj watched them all as Veronica sat like a queen—*a rumpled queen,* he thought with a surge of possessiveness—and spoke to the former president in French. Raj didn't understand French, but he could tell that Veronica was cool and professional.

The sun was a bright orange ball now, the sea beneath it purple and black. High above the setting sun, bright stars were winking into existence like sequins against the midnight-blue background of the night sky.

But Raj was focused on Veronica, and on the two people watching her so intently.

Martine glanced up at him, then quickly looked away. Her fingers hooked together in front of her body, her knuckles whitening. She was afraid.

But Veronica's eyes widened and Raj's attention snapped to her. Her chief of staff thrust a fist into the air in triumph as Veronica said something to the man on the phone, her voice laced with shock.

Martine seemed pale, her big brown eyes blinking in surprise. And then Veronica was speaking rapidly, smiling openly and nodding. Another few moments and she put the phone down again. Then she jumped up and hugged Georges and Martine before throwing herself into his arms.

"Brun has denounced the police chief," she said. "He is about to hold a press conference and publicly come out in support of me." Her eyes were shiny with tears. "He loves Aliz and wants the best for her, just like I do. Oh, Raj, this means I can continue working for my people. This is truly the best day ever."

He should be happy, and yet he felt as if she'd thrust a hot knife into his chest and twisted it. He'd begun to enjoy having her here, having her to himself. But when she returned to her life as president, he would return to his life, as well.

And it wasn't a life that included her.

"That's wonderful," he said, because he had to say something.

She squeezed him, pressing her cheek to his chest. "We can go to Aliz now," she told him. "It's not quite like here, but I think you'll like it. I want to show you everything, and I want you to have Christmas with me. It'll be wonderful."

He was numb. Absolutely numb. "Of course," he replied. Because now was not the time to say anything different. Now was not the time to hang a dark cloud over her happiness. There would be time later to talk, time to explain. Time to return to reality.

She hugged him again, then turned and started talking with her people. He watched her, watched the gestures of her long, slim fingers, the slide of her throat as she spoke, the way she talked so fast and excitedly that Martine could barely take the dictation.

For her sake, he tried to imagine it. Tried to imagine himself in Aliz, with her. She would live in the presidential palace, of course. He would visit her there whenever he had the time. It could work.

But it couldn't work. She deserved better. She deserved a man who could love her and give her the family she wanted. Without hesitation or reservation. He loved being with her, and he could happily spend the next several months—years, maybe—in her bed without ever wanting to leave.

But it wasn't fair to her. He knew what she wanted out of life because she'd told him.

He did not want the same thing, and it wasn't fair to let her believe he did. He'd known it wasn't going to last. He just hadn't thought it was going to end so soon.

It was late when Veronica wrapped up her meetings with her staff. There were more phone calls to be made, plans to discuss and Monsieur Brun's speech on CNN to watch. The chief of police hadn't surrendered yet, but he would soon. He had no support, and his last lifeline—the hope that Brun would be reinstated—was gone.

Veronica had done a set of interviews by phone, speaking with several news reporters live on various television and radio programs, and now she was exhausted. The situation in Aliz had exploded onto the international scene in greater force with Brun's speech.

Everyone wanted to know where she was, but she'd kept that information private. She just couldn't bear to have the press show up at Raj's door after everything they'd shared here together.

She found Raj on the terrace, a laptop computer open and glowing as he studied the information there. He looked up when she arrived, his eyes flickering over her before settling on her face again.

The hunger she usually saw in his gaze was missing.

Her stomach did a somersault. Resolutely, she walked over to his side and touched him, stroked her fingers along his jaw. He caught her hand in his, then removed it from his skin with a quick kiss to her palm. He stood and moved away before she could reach for him again.

She stood there, stinging with the ache of rejection, hoping she was reading the situation wrong.

Knowing she was not.

"So this is how it ends," she said, her throat aching.

He looked up, as if he was surprised she'd said it instead of pretending. And then he pushed his fingers through his hair. "I think it's best, don't you?"

"Why is it best? What rulebook says there is a specific way we have to do this? We—" she swallowed, knowing she couldn't say the word she really wanted to say, especially since she only knew it was true on her part "—enjoy each other."

"We hardly know each other, Veronica." He looked away, his jaw firming. "We've had sex, nothing more."

Sex, nothing more.

Oh, God.

"*I* thought there was more."

He swore. "This is why I tried not to be so weak, why I tried to deny myself when I wanted you. Because it won't work, Veronica. We both know it."

She clenched her fists at her sides, her eyes blurring. Angrily, she dashed the tears away. She was not about to cry. Not now, not when she'd just gotten a second chance in Aliz. She should feel happy, triumphant—instead, she felt desolate, ruined, as if nothing mattered.

It was too similar to the way she'd felt a few months ago. And that angered her far more than anything else ever could.

"I didn't realize you were a coward, Raj."

His eyes flashed as he glared at her. "I know what you're trying to do. It won't work." He closed the distance between them, gripped her shoulders in his strong hands. "Didn't you listen to a damn thing I told you earlier? I don't know *how* to have a home, a family. I don't want those things. You do, and I won't give you false hope just because I'm addicted to you."

A part of her—a tiny part—soared when he said he was addicted to her. But it wasn't enough, she knew that. Wasn't enough for him or for her. It hurt to think that it was only sex between them. But for him, it was.

"You won't even try," she said.

"No," he replied, letting her go again. "I won't. Because I know who I am, Veronica. I've had a lot of years to learn. And I won't hurt you by trying to be something I'm not."

She wrapped her arms around her body, trying to stave off the sudden chill that threatened to make her teeth chatter. It wasn't cold in the least, but she felt as if he'd turned into a block of ice—and she was freezing simply from being too close. "God forbid you challenge your own assumptions."

"Veronica—"

"No," she snapped, taking a step closer to him again, jabbing her finger into his chest. "If you're so damn smart, and know so much, then why didn't you just tell me no in the first place? No matter how much I wanted you, you could have said no. You could have spared us both."

He raised his hands as if to surrender. "You're right. I could have. I didn't because I'm human. Because I can be a selfish bastard. Because I still want the things I know I can't have."

"After everything I told you," she said, sucking in a harsh breath. She couldn't complete the sentence without screaming.

"Yes, after everything. Because I'm a man, and you're a damn sexy woman who was hot for me. It'd take a saint to say no to you."

Fury swelled inside her until she thought she would burst if she didn't act. She wanted to slap him, wanted to smack the arrogance right off his face. But she couldn't hit him, couldn't hit anyone.

It was so, so wrong.

And it was her fault, too. She wasn't blameless in this. It was her fault that she'd told herself whatever he could give her was enough.

It wasn't.

"I trusted you, Raj. Losing my baby was the most devastating thing that ever happened to me. I didn't think I could feel again, didn't think I—"

She pressed a fist to her chest, throat aching. She couldn't say another word. If she did, she would scream. He was looking at her, his expression stark.

Well, that's how she felt, too. Stark. Empty.

"You don't need me, Veronica," he said. "You're strong enough and brave enough on your own. And you'll find what you're looking for. Someday."

"I'm not so sure," she said, half to herself. "I knew this was inevitable." She tossed her hair defiantly. "Hell, maybe you *are* right. Maybe it's better this way. Because you wouldn't have wanted me once you knew the truth."

His gaze sharpened, his body stilling. As if he were a hunter scenting prey.

"The truth?" He sounded so dangerous.

She didn't care. What did it matter? She looked him in the eye. "It's my fault my baby died. So you see, even if you wanted a family, I'm not the sort of woman you'd want to take that chance with."

He swore, a rude word she'd never heard him use before. "I've spent enough time with you to know that's not true. You aren't responsible for your miscarriage, no matter what kind of crazy idea you've got into your head about it."

Anguish ate her from the inside out. "Don't tell me I'm not responsible! You weren't there. I didn't know I was pregnant, Raj. I kept drinking, kept staying out late and having a good time—by the time I knew I was pregnant, the damage had been done."

He put his hands on her shoulders—firmly—and forced her to look at him. "Women don't lose babies because they drink alcohol, Veronica. Haven't you ever seen a drug addict have a child? The baby is usually born with devastating health problems, but the baby is *born*. A few drinks didn't kill your child."

Her stomach was a solid ball of pain. "You don't know that."

His jaw clenched, his eyes glittering with some emotion she couldn't identify. "I do know. I've seen it. My mother was a drug addict. Not when I was young, but as I grew older. And I saw the kind of people she did drugs with. Believe me, if they didn't lose the children they were carrying because of what they did, you definitely didn't."

She sucked in a breath, refused to let it become a sob. She wanted to believe him. She'd always wanted to believe, but she'd never been able to. The doctors had told her it wasn't her fault, that the miscarriage would have happened regardless. She'd just never believed them.

Raj pulled her into his embrace, held her tight for a long time. She closed her eyes, breathed in his scent, her heart hurting so much she wanted to fall asleep and not wake up for a hundred years.

Because she knew, before he said it, that he was still saying goodbye.

"You deserve happiness, Veronica. That's why I'm letting you go."

Early the next morning, they left for the ten-hour flight to Aliz. Raj purposely kept himself away from Veronica for the duration. She never once looked at him, so he had plenty of opportunity to watch her. She was pale. Her hair was pulled back into a loose knot on her head, and she wore a black dress with a jacket and heels. There were circles under her eyes, and the tip of her nose was red, as if she'd been crying recently.

It gutted him to think she had.

Still, she was beautiful. Remote and regal, more like the Veronica he'd met the first night in London. The one who would never deign to lower herself to sleep with a bastard like him. Better for them both if she hadn't.

He'd lain awake last night, his body aching for her. His heart aching for her. That was a new sensation, but he'd shoved it down deep and slapped a lid on it. He had no room for sentimentality, not with her, not with anyone. If he let himself care, even the tiniest bit, tomorrow something would happen and it'd be time to move on again. He couldn't unpack the suitcase, no matter how much he wanted to do so.

Except that he did care, damn it. When she'd stood there, her eyes shining with pain, and told him she was to blame for what had happened to her, he'd thought he would have to punch something. Preferably Andre Girard.

She'd been living with so much pain and guilt. She'd needed someone to stand beside her during that time, and there'd been no one.

A little voice told him he could stand with her now, but

he shoved it away. He'd made the decision that was best for them both, and he couldn't go back on it simply because his heart felt as if it were being ground to powder.

Now, he was taking her back to Aliz and leaving one of his best teams there to protect her. They would also train the presidential guard on proper procedures before they left Aliz permanently.

He never wanted to worry about her safety again. He'd gotten the reports on the people she'd had with her in London; nothing stood out. No one had any reason to want to harm her, which brought him back to square one. The security guard who'd been dismissed had to have been in the employ of someone in Aliz.

It wasn't the former president, but it could have certainly been the police chief. He could have found out about the baby and decided to use that to frighten her. Perhaps he'd reasoned that if Veronica didn't want to return to Aliz, his power grab stood a better chance of being successful.

When they landed in Aliz, the television cameras were waiting. The tarmac was packed with supporters bearing signs with Veronica's name, with slogans, with the name of her hit song. They chanted and laughed and sang as she exited the plane and descended the stairs like a queen.

Veronica was so poised as she waved and smiled. His heart flipped. He was so proud of her, though he had no right to be. She wasn't his.

She stepped up to the microphone then and delivered a stirring speech about freedom and democracy and the rule of law. Monsieur Brun had wisely stayed away in order to prove that he really did want the torch to pass to his successor. The media pelted her with questions, all of which she answered expertly. She took a last question, and then thanked them all before turning away.

"Is it true that you and the CEO of Vala Security

International are dating, Madam President?" a tabloid reporter shouted.

He watched Veronica's shoulders stiffen, watched her turn back to the microphone. Her cheeks were full of color, but she looked so lovely that no one would think it was anything other than her natural beauty shining through.

"That was a cover," she said. "So Mr. Vala and his team could get close to me without alerting those who might wish me harm."

"But you've just spent three days in Goa, at his home. Why there?"

Veronica's smile didn't waver. "Because we believed I might be in danger. It was prudent not to broadcast my whereabouts to the world at large."

"Did you sleep with him?"

A collective gasp went up from the crowd, and then a buzz of anger began in the ranks of the loyal people who'd come out to welcome home their president.

Veronica laughed that bright, tinkling laugh of hers. For some reason, it pierced him to the bone.

And then she turned and pointed at him. "Look at that man," she said. "Is he not gorgeous? Tall and exotic, beautiful like a tiger." She paused for a long moment, her eyes locked on him—angry, accusatory, hurt—before she turned back to the microphone. "But I assure you, there is nothing between us. Mr. Vala is all business. He does not know the meaning of fun."

A ripple of laughter went through the crowd as she waved and turned away. He had to give it to her—she knew how to work the media. He had no doubt that everything she'd ever done had been carefully orchestrated for the fullest effect. Veronica was no idiot. She'd effectively marginalized him with that brief show.

It had been a brilliant maneuver.

They made their way to the waiting limos and on to the presidential palace—which was actually quite small by palatial standards, though definitely ornate.

Raj spent the morning with his team and Veronica's security staff, going over plans and procedures for her safety during appearances and travel.

Afterward, he found her at an antique French desk in a spacious and bright office. Beyond the windows, the Mediterranean sparkled in the sunshine. Not as wild and untamable as Goa, but pretty nevertheless.

She looked up, her pen poised over a document, Georges hovering with his hand on the paper, ready to take it away as soon as she finished. She scrawled her signature and smiled at the man. He took the paper, glancing up at Raj with a disapproving look as he passed.

Veronica sat back and folded her arms over her chest. He tried not to think of her breasts, of how perfect they were. How her dusky nipples had grown so tight and sensitive when he'd gazed on her naked body.

How they tasted in his mouth, how every glorious inch of her felt beneath his hands.

Goddamn it.

"I'm leaving," he said tightly. "My people will stay as long as you need them, and I'll only be a phone call away if necessary."

"Thank you for…" She cleared her throat and looked away. The sunlight was behind her, limning her pale golden hair like a halo. He'd never felt so rotten in his life. "Thank you for making sure I was safe."

"My pleasure." As soon as he said it, he knew they were the wrong words.

Her eyes narrowed. "And thank you for the sex," she said. "I don't know how I'd have survived without you to scratch my itch."

"Veronica, you don't have to do this."

"Do what?" she asked. "Make you feel like a bastard? I really think I do. It makes me feel better, for a short time anyway. If it's any comfort, I'll feel like hell ten minutes after you've walked out the door."

"It isn't a comfort," he said. "I never wanted to hurt you."

She shrugged. "Maybe I'm not hurt. Maybe I'm just a bit angry that I'm not the one calling it off."

"You'll thank me later," he said.

"I seem to remember you said that to me once before. And I told you then that I would decide what was best for me. That hasn't changed."

"You're truly an amazing woman, Veronica."

"Not amazing enough."

"Don't play the wounded martyr," he snapped.

Her eyes flashed. "Look who's talking about being a martyr. The man who would sacrifice even the prospect of happiness for a stale idea about himself that he refuses to let go."

Her words had the power to slice deep.

But she was a hypocrite, and he wouldn't let her get away with it. Not because he was angry, but because he wanted her to finally allow herself to heal.

"Have you decided to stop blaming yourself for your miscarriage?"

Her head dropped, her throat sliding as she swallowed heavily. "You're right about that," she said softly. "And unless I'm willing to let go of my guilt, I can hardly ask you to do the same, can I?"

She looked up again, speared him with that determined look he'd grown to love.

"I've been thinking hard since yesterday, Raj. And I'm done with guilt. As much as I can be. I don't think I'll ever completely forgive myself, but I'm going to learn to accept that things happen for a reason."

"I'm glad to hear it."

Her phone buzzed. They looked at each other over the blinking light for several moments. She seemed to be waiting for him to say something.

"Goodbye, Veronica."

Veronica finished the call with the Moroccan ambassador and hung up the phone. Raj was gone, no doubt on his way back to the airport and then on to wherever he had decided to call home for the moment. She wanted to scream. He'd left her, and she felt so bare and raw inside.

The room was quiet. Empty. She could hear the noise outside the window, of gulls and boats, of tradesmen yelling to each other across the way, of cars and horns and everyday noise.

But she was still empty. Desolate.

He'd gone away. The man she loved had been unable to love her back. It hurt so much she thought she might die of it.

She wouldn't, of course.

She thought of the lonely man who'd told her about living in a car, about being afraid to unpack a suitcase, about buying his first home, and her heart ached for everything that he'd suffered. They were a damaged pair, the two of them.

Veronica shoved back from her desk and strode through the office. Martine slapped the phone down, as if she felt guilty being caught talking, but Veronica could care less. In fact, she was getting tired of Martine's hangdog looks. The last thing she needed was someone who made her feel even worse.

"I'm going to my apartment," she said. "I need to change."

Martine nodded and Veronica swept out of the office and down the hallway toward the private wing that held the president's apartment. Madame Brun had decorated the private rooms of the old French Baroque palace in her own taste, and Veronica hated it. It was Marie Antoinette all the way, with fluffy ruffled things, mirrors and delicate furniture upon which one was afraid to sit for fear of collapsing the spindly legs.

One of these days, she would redecorate. But right now, it was hardly important compared to everything else that was required of her.

Damn it, she *would* do a good job. For Aliz, for everyone who'd believed in her. Just as soon as she had some time alone, as soon as she collected herself and felt more normal, she was calling Signor Zarella. It was time to press him for a commitment, and she wasn't taking no for an answer. She had to accomplish something positive or she would go mad.

She went into her bedroom and stripped out of her clothes. A shower and a fresh outfit would do her good. When she finished, she stepped from the shower and dried herself vigorously. Then she wrapped the towel around her body and went back into her bedroom to find a different outfit.

She came up short, her heart rocketing as she realized she wasn't alone. But then she saw who it was. She put a hand over her chest, felt the pounding of her heart. "Martine. You scared me."

"I'm sorry, Miss St. Germaine." Tears flowed down Martine's cheeks.

"What's the matter, Martine?" Veronica said, taking a step toward her secretary.

Veronica stopped when Martine shook her head. "I'm

sorry," she said again, her hand lifting, her arm stiff and straight.

It took Veronica only a split second to realize what was wrong.

Martine had a gun.

CHAPTER THIRTEEN

RAJ had just climbed into the car that would take him back to the airport when his phone buzzed. Dread settled in his stomach like a lead ball as he listened to the man on the other end.

Then he was yelling at the driver to stop and shoving open the car door at the same time.

If something happened to Veronica, he would never forgive himself.

His staff was already making their way to her office, he knew, but he broke into a run anyway. When he reached the ornate office, it was empty. Worse, the outer office where her secretary sat was also empty.

He made a hard dash to her private residence. Two of his men were already there, knocking on the door.

Raj pushed past them and into the interior of Veronica's apartment. The gaudy living area was quiet. Just then, a muffled thump and a cry came from the direction of the bedroom. Raj sprinted, drawing the concealed weapon he carried, and kicked open the double doors.

Veronica was naked in the center of the room, a gun hanging limply from her hand. She swayed on her feet, her eyes wide. Another woman lay on the floor, curled in a ball, sobbing. Veronica looked up at him with glassy eyes.

He went and wrapped his arms tightly around her. She was trembling. He took the gun from her fingers and unloaded it with one hand before tossing it onto the bed. Belatedly, he remembered her state of undress. He retrieved the towel lying on the floor, draped it around her. It was damp and cool, but it was all he had.

His men came to lift up Martine and take her away.

"Don't hurt her," Veronica said as Martine screamed.

"They won't, I promise you."

The room was quiet once Martine and the bodyguards were gone. Veronica lifted her head. Her eyes were red-rimmed. It tore him apart. She reached out as if to touch his face, let her hand drop when she thought better of it.

Despair tore into his gut. He'd done that to her. He'd made her wary of him, and he hated it.

"I'm sorry, Veronica," he said.

She sucked in a shaky breath. Clung to him.

As much as he knew he should set her away, should put distance between them, he couldn't do it. He loved the feel of her in his arms. He wanted to hold her for as long as he could.

His arms tightened around her. He'd almost lost her.

"Martine's mother…" she said.

"I know. I just found out."

"Madame Brun was behind it all," she said. "She probably talked the police chief into doing what he did."

"Some people don't deal well with the loss of power." In this case, it was the wife rather than the husband, who, though disappointed in the outcome of the election, was a true politician.

"She threatened to take away Martine's mother's pension if Martine didn't do what she wanted. Martine spied on me, Raj. She told Madame Brun about the baby, and she pasted together the letter and put the doll in my bed."

"I know. I just got the report. Her mother worked for the Bruns for many years, and lives in an old-age home paid for by the pension she earned from them. If it were taken away, she'd be homeless. Or worse, with the economic situation in Aliz."

Veronica looked fierce for a moment. "I wouldn't have allowed that to happen if she'd only come to me! I'd have taken her mother in, paid the pension, whatever it took. Martine was my secretary for two years! I thought she knew me better than that."

"I imagine she was just scared. And I doubt she ever believed Madame Brun would ask her to…" He looked at the gun lying on the bed, so dark and deadly and gleaming blue in the light. He couldn't speak the words he was thinking. *To kill you.* "How did you get the gun?"

"All I had was the towel," Veronica said. "I reacted without thinking. I threw it at her."

Ice formed in his veins. She'd thrown a towel at an armed woman.

"You were lucky."

She nodded, her arms tightening around his waist. "I couldn't let it end like this. Not after everything."

My God, she was brave. And incredible. In another life, he'd have probably hired her to work for him. With training, she'd have made a hell of a security professional. Except that he couldn't bear the thought of her in danger.

Raj tipped her head back so he could see into her eyes. She was frightened, but not to the point of shock. Not yet anyway.

Her gaze dropped to his mouth. And, damn, but he couldn't stop himself from kissing her. Softly, sweetly. He needed to know she was real, that she was still here and still capable of responding. That he wasn't imagining it. That he hadn't actually walked in on something much worse and started to hallucinate that she was unharmed.

Her mouth opened, her tongue tangling with his as she moaned softly. And then she was arching her body into his and he was pulling her closer, pressing her against the evidence of his need for her.

She broke the kiss first, her body stiffening in his embrace. He could tell the moment everything changed, and he let her go. His heart, his body, cried out in protest, but he loosened his grip and she stepped out of it.

Brave, brave Veronica.

She held the edges of her damp towel, her dignity not damaged in the least, and gazed up at him. "It's no good, Raj," she said. "We could fall into bed together now, but you'd still walk out in the end. I'm not putting myself through that again."

"I do want you," he said in despair. "I want to be with you." He shoved a hand through his hair, blew out a harsh breath. He felt tight inside, coiled, as if he had to do something or explode. Maybe they could work it out. He could try. For her, he would try.

"I'll come to Aliz when I can. You'll be traveling, too—we'll meet in different places, take it a day at a time."

She shook her head sadly. Her hair was starting to dry, curling over her shoulders and down her back. She was as wild and untamed as Goa, as beautiful as the sea. He wanted to possess her, ached to possess her.

Frustration arced through him. He knew she wasn't going to accept what he was trying to offer. What was he offering, really?

"It's not enough, Raj," she said. "I want more. I'm not going to settle for half a life with you."

"It's all I can give you," he said, aching for her. He wanted to give her exactly what she desired. But he was afraid he would fail if he tried to take it that far. He had to start small.

She smiled sadly. "I know. But it's not enough for me. Some women might accept whatever sort of life they could get with the man they love, but I won't. I can't. I've already lost something precious to me, and survived the experience. I'll survive you, too."

Love? She loved him?

He was stunned into silence. He couldn't think of a thing to say. He didn't need to.

She did it for him.

"Goodbye, Raj."

The days turned into a week, and then two weeks, three weeks, and still the pain of losing Raj was as raw as it had been that day in her bedroom when he'd held her close and tried to give her what he thought she wanted.

It still made her angry. And so very frustrated.

Veronica steepled her hands on her desk and rested her chin on the point. She'd been busy these past weeks. She'd worked hard to see her vision for Aliz come to fruition. There'd been endless meetings, phone calls, interviews and a speech to the nation.

Aliz wasn't out of the woods yet, but things were looking better. The economy was stabilizing, and foreign investment was beginning to trickle in again. People were getting fed and things were getting built.

She couldn't ask for more.

Her gaze strayed to the evergreen garland decked with red and gold ribbon that draped over the fireplace in her office. It was almost Christmas, but she hadn't taken time to do anything to prepare. There was no one to shop for, no one to bake cookies for, no one to sit before the tree and enjoy the lights with. She wouldn't even have a tree if it weren't for the fact she had a housekeeping staff who had put one up for her because they'd always put one up for the Bruns.

It stood in her residence, decorated with silver and red and gold, the white lights always on whenever she walked in at the end of the day. There were no presents beneath it. She thought of her baby with a pang. He would have been almost eight months old. He wouldn't have understood what the glitter and presents were about, but he would have likely relished the bright colors and enjoyed tearing the paper.

Veronica didn't bother trying to sniff back the tears that happened whenever she thought of moments like this. It hurt, but she no longer felt as if she was solely responsible for her loss.

She had Raj to thank for that.

Her private cell phone rang and she jumped. It was not Raj's name on the display. She hadn't expected it would be, yet she always seemed to hope it might. But why? There was nothing but heartache in going down that road.

And she'd had enough heartache to last a lifetime.

"Hello, Brady," she said as she answered the call.

"Angel," he replied. "How are you? It's been a few days and I wanted to check."

"I'm fine," she said, resting her forehead in one hand. "How about you? Any celebrity gossip for me?"

Brady chuckled. "I've heard some juicy things about a certain new heartthrob and a Hollywood icon," he said. Then he spent the next fifteen minutes giving her every salacious detail of a May-December affair currently delighting the Rodeo Drive set.

"So what are you doing for Christmas?" he asked when he'd finished the tale.

"Nothing much. I have a country to run, in case you hadn't noticed."

"Surely you can spare a few hours for fun. Come to the Hotel Lefevre tomorrow night. I'm throwing a party."

Veronica blinked. "The Hotel Lefevre? In Aliz City?" It was the oldest and best hotel on the island. Understated and elegant, it had suffered through the economic crisis like everywhere else. That it was still open was a miracle, though the owners had had to sell off many of the treasured paintings that had once adorned the walls, including one that van Gogh had painted for the original owners when he'd spent time on the island before going to France.

"Yes. I've decided I want to go somewhere nice, and I want my friends to come, too. Aliz is a charming island. I hear it's making a comeback."

Her heart swelled with gratitude and love for her friend. "Brady, I…" She didn't know what to say. "Are you here now?"

"We just arrived this morning."

"We?"

"Me and Susan. I really want you to meet her."

"Susan?" She was beginning to feel like a parrot.

Brady sighed. "The woman I plan to spend the rest of my life with."

Veronica's mouth dropped open. "Brady, when I saw you in London, there was no one in your life. What happened? And why didn't you tell me this first? It's the most important thing you've said so far!"

"It's crazy," he said, his voice filled with laughter. "I know that. But sometimes you just know when you've found that special person."

A twinge of pain throbbed in her heart, but she listened delightedly as Brady talked about Susan—who wasn't an actress or a celebrity or a gold-digging wannabe who worked as a cocktail waitress while waiting for her big break. No, Susan was a veterinarian he'd met when they'd both stopped to help an injured dog on the freeway.

"So will you come?" he finally said.

"Of course I'll come! I wouldn't miss this for anything."

She got off the phone feeling happier than she had in weeks. So her own life was a mess, but her friend was happy and he'd come all this way to show his support for her and her country. On Christmas.

Her eyes filled with tears again, but they were happy tears. Though seeing Brady would make her think of Raj, she would survive it. Besides, how could she be upset about being loved and wanted by her friends?

The next day was Christmas Eve. Veronica didn't have to work, but she went into her office and made some calls anyway. She'd already given her staff the day off, so the administrative wing was mostly silent. Afterward, she spent most of the day watching Christmas movies on television, then prepared for Brady's party. He'd sent over a formal invitation, and she knew there would be television cameras when she arrived.

It was part of the process, something that would delight people, and she dressed with care for the appearance. She donned a long red dress, strapless, that shimmered as she walked. The fabric was iridescent, gathered at the waist, and fell into a full skirt that was given shape by a tulle slip beneath. She wrapped a silver shawl around her shoulders and carried a small silver clutch. Silver-jeweled strappy high heels rounded out the look.

A bodyguard in a tuxedo opened the limo door for her as she emerged from her private entrance. He was Alizean, tall and handsome, but there was no spark of desire as she gazed at him in his black coat and tie. He climbed in beside her and they were on their way.

The media was camped out in front of the Hotel Lefrevre, and Veronica did her best to look glamorous and happy. She waved as the cameras flashed, then turned and posed—an old habit—before entering the hotel. Brady was waiting for her, a petite, smiling woman at his side. Veronica hugged them both as Brady introduced Susan. She was truly happy for them, and yet she was jealous, too.

If only her own love life had gone so smoothly. But Susan was a delightful woman, and Veronica found that she really liked talking with Brady's new love. Susan was down-to-earth, no-nonsense. She was pretty, but not gorgeous in that fake way that Hollywood encouraged.

They moved toward the old ballroom, and Veronica stopped in the entry, her head tilting back as she took it all in. The grand room was decorated beautifully, with candles, greenery and shiny lights and bows reflecting from the mirrored surfaces along the walls. The plaster was chipped in places, the paint faded, but it wouldn't remain that way for long if they had many more parties like this one. The room was filled with food and people, and Veronica's heart felt full.

"Thank you, Brady," she said, squeezing his arm when he came over and handed her a glass of champagne.

"For what?"

"For this. For doing this here. It means so much."

He smiled back, his gaze flickering to a point over her shoulder before coming to rest on her face again. "You might not thank me when you see what I've brought along with me."

She looked at her friend for a full moment—and then the hairs on her neck prickled as if an electrical current had zapped through the air. She knew who she would see the moment she turned.

He was, as always, achingly handsome. Her heart twisted in her chest. Looking at him hurt. And it made her happy, too.

"Damn it, Brady," she said to the man at her side. "You're always interfering."

He shrugged. "It's my nature." Then he kissed her on the cheek. "Don't say I never gave you anything."

She started to tell him he was an ass, but he'd disappeared. Raj smiled at her, and her insides melted. She had to work hard to keep the frown on her face.

"Hello, Veronica."

"Why are you here?"

His laugh was so rich, so beautiful to her ears. God, she'd missed him. And she didn't want to do this. Because she would have to miss him again when it was over.

"I've missed that directness of yours," he said. "You have no idea how refreshing it can be."

Her heart was thundering. "If you're about to tell me how other women are just not a challenge after me, save your breath. I don't want to hear it."

He looked puzzled. "I wasn't planning to say anything of the sort."

Looking at him made her ache. It brought all the loneliness of her life crashing down on her. "I really don't want to stand here and talk to you like everything is normal, Raj, so you'll have to excuse me."

She had to escape, right now, before she fell apart in front of everyone. Before she ranted and railed and told him what a miserable bastard he was for not loving her back. Before she revealed how pitiful she was because she still loved him, and a part of her was almost willing to take whatever crumbs he might bestow if only she could have another night, another day, another moment in time where they laughed and talked and made love as if they cared about each other.

Blindly, she turned and fled. When she reached the hall, she hesitated only a moment before she headed for the ladies' room, shoving open the door and going over to the small sink to press her hands on either side and breathe. Her face in the mirror looked perfectly normal, but she didn't feel normal.

The door swung open again and then Raj was there, looming in the mirror behind her. She heard the twist of the lock in the door and she spun to face him.

"Get out."

"It's like déjà vu," he said, his sensual mouth curving into a smile. "You, me, a ladies' room."

It was a much smaller ladies' room, with only this sink and mirror, the delicately papered walls and another door that led into the single toilet. There was no space, and she couldn't breathe with him so close. He filled her senses, made her ache with longing.

"It's a nightmare," she said. "I had no idea you hated me so much."

His brows drew together, two hard slashes over his golden eyes. "Hate you? My God, Veronica, I'm here because I can't forget you. Because I need you. Hate is the furthest thing from my mind."

She swallowed, shook her head, prayed the tears wouldn't fall. Because it was Christmas Eve and she was feeling vulnerable. Because she missed her baby, missed him. Because she was alone in this world and feeling very, very sorry for herself right now.

"Need isn't enough, is it? I need food to live, but I don't need chocolate cake. You need sex, but it doesn't have to be me."

He was beginning to look angry. "Sex? You think I'm here for sex?"

"What else? You've already told me it can be nothing more."

He blew out a breath. "I was wrong." Because he'd tried to move on with his life, tried to forget about the few days he'd shared with Veronica, the days where he'd felt more alive than he ever had before. He'd gone back to London, and then on to New York. When New York didn't work, when he still felt so restless he wanted to howl, he'd gone to Los Angeles.

In the past, when he wanted to escape, when he wanted peace, he'd gone to the house in Goa. But he couldn't go there anymore. Because he couldn't imagine himself there without her.

"You've ruined it for me," he said, watching the way her lip trembled so slightly, the way she was determined not to break in front of him.

She was so strong, so beautiful. She took his breath away. And he'd realized during the long, lonely few weeks without her that he didn't want to live like that anymore. He'd been denying himself because he'd thought he was doing the best thing for her. But the truth was that he'd been cheating them both.

"Ruined what?" she asked.

"Being alone."

She sucked in a breath, hugged her arms around herself. Bit her lip. An arrow of pure lust shot through him. That was *his* lip to bite.

"I'm the President of Aliz," she said softly. "I have a two-year term. This is my home. I can't go with you to

Goa, or to London, just to keep you from being lonely. Nor do I want to."

"Do you still love me?" he said, his heart careening in his chest. He didn't think she'd stopped in three weeks time, but he wouldn't put anything past Veronica St. Germaine. The woman was a force to be reckoned with. If she wanted to stop loving him, she could. She was a woman who didn't shrink from challenges.

She turned her head away, but he could still see her face in the mirror. Two red spots bloomed on her cheeks. Her nostrils flared. Her mouth was a flat line as she compressed her lips. "Does it matter?" she finally said.

"It matters to me."

Her head snapped around, her eyes flashing angrily. "Why? So you can congratulate yourself yet again on your amazing skills?"

"Skills?"

"Those in which you deny yourself any chance at happiness simply to prove what a strong man you are."

He'd hurt her deeply, more deeply than he'd realized. And he wasn't proud of himself for it. "I have no wish to deny anything." He clenched his fists as his side, frustration hammering through him. "I'm here because I can't deny it."

She lifted her chin. "I need more from you, Raj. Telling me you want me isn't enough."

He swore. "I know." And then he resolved to lay it all out there. If she rejected him, it was nothing less than he deserved. But he had to take the chance. "I love you, Veronica. I can't live without you. I don't want to."

She slumped against the sink, her red dress shimmering in the low light of the small room. "Did you just say…?"

He closed the distance between them, gripped her shoulders and put a finger under her chin. Lifted it so she had to look at him. Her eyes were liquid, beautiful blue pools in which he wanted to drown.

"I've spent my life running away, because it's all I knew. Because my mother was a drug addict and we were homeless more than we weren't. Because my father let us go and never bothered to find us again. Running is what I know, Veronica. Staying is much harder." He sucked in a breath. It felt like razor blades in his throat. "I'm afraid of unpacking the suitcase. Afraid that I'll have to move again tomorrow. Much easier to stay in motion. But you're in Aliz, and my heart is with you. You're the strongest, bravest person I know. I can't imagine my life without you in it. *You* are my home."

She gripped his sleeves then, her fingers twisting into the fabric. "I'm mad at you," she said, though her eyes were shining. "I really should make you sweat it out. I should make you wonder if you've ruined this irreparably."

"Have I?"

She gave her head a tiny shake, and then he was kissing her with all the pent-up passion and love that he could no longer deny. That he no longer wanted to deny. Her arms slipped around his neck, her body melding to his as if it had been made to do so.

"I love you, Raj," she said when he finally let her breathe again. "But I'm still mad at you."

He laughed against her throat, his lips nuzzling the sweet skin of her neck. "I'll look forward to letting you take your revenge against me. I'll even let you tie me up if it pleases you."

"Don't tempt me."

Veronica awoke sleepily, the church bells in the Aliz City cathedral chiming 4:00 a.m. on Christmas Day. It was still dark out, and her body was languid, lazy. She stretched, a pleasurable ache between her thighs. The bed was empty except for her. She sat up, smiling at the long length of her robe sash that was still knotted to one bedpost. She'd tied him up all right. Tied him up and tortured him until he'd begged her to put him out of his misery.

Until she'd taken him in her mouth and sent him to heaven.

Oh, yes, she'd gotten her revenge. A very pleasurable revenge indeed.

She slipped from the bed and found her robe. It took her a minute to untie the sash, but she did, slipping it around her waist and knotting it loosely. Then she went in search of Raj, knowing instinctively that he hadn't left her in the night.

She found him in the living room, sitting on the couch in the glow of the tree. He looked up when she approached, smiled that sexy smile she loved so much.

"I don't think I've ever sat and just watched the lights before," he said.

She knew he'd never really had an opportunity to do so in the past, and her heart hurt for the little boy he'd been. Moving from shelter to shelter and home to home. She sank beside him and curled up against his warm body. He slipped an arm around her.

"I'm sorry I didn't get you anything," she said, mesmerized by the twinkling lights. "But I didn't know you'd be here."

He laughed softly. "You gave me all I wanted," he said. Then he kissed the top of her head. A small package appeared in front of her nose.

"What's this?"

"I came prepared."

"Now I really feel bad," she said.

"Don't."

She sighed and untied the gold ribbon. Inside the red box was another box, nestled in tissue paper. A velvet box.

Her gaze flew to his. "Earrings," she said. "You've bought me earrings. I'll always treasure them."

He laughed. "Open it, Veronica. Stop guessing."

She did, her heart in her throat. It wasn't a pair of earrings. Her eyes filled until the large, emerald-cut diamond surrounded by smaller diamonds was nothing more than a blur.

"You can say no," he said. "I'd understand. Or you can say yes, and we'll have a long engagement."

She arched an eyebrow, sniffling. "Is the long engagement a condition?"

"No. I'm simply trying to give you a way out."

She shook her head. "I knew you were far too pretty to be smart. Men can't be gorgeous and brainy at the same time, you know."

She felt the tension coiling in his body. "Are you saying yes?"

A single tear spilled down her cheek. "Is this what you really want?"

"Do you think I'd ask if it weren't?"

"You didn't ask," she pointed out.

He smiled, and her heart squeezed with love. Then he slipped from the couch and got onto one knee. "I'm doing this right," he said, "because I don't ever want you to believe I didn't want this. Veronica, will you marry me?"

Her heart filled to bursting. Home. This was home—this moment, this feeling. This man. "Yes," she said simply.

Raj slipped the ring onto her finger. And then he made love to her on the Persian carpet in front of the Christmas tree.

There would never be, with the exception of their

third child born on December 25 a few years hence, a more perfect gift than the one they shared on this particular Christmas.

* * * * *

MILLS & BOON

THE HEART OF ROMANCE

A ROMANCE FOR EVERY KIND OF READER

MODERN

Prepare to be swept off your feet by sophisticated, sexy and seductive heroes, in some of the world's most glamourous and romantic locations, where power and passion collide.
8 stories per month.

HISTORICAL

Escape with historical heroes from time gone by. Whether your passion is for wicked Regency Rakes, muscled Vikings or rugged Highlanders, awaken the romance of the past.
6 stories per month.

MEDICAL

Set your pulse racing with dedicated, delectable doctors in the high-pressure world of medicine, where emotions run high and passion, comfort and love are the best medicine.
6 stories per month.

True Love

Celebrate true love with tender stories of heartfelt romance, from the rush of falling in love to the joy a new baby can bring, and focus on the emotional heart of a relationship.
8 stories per month.

Desire

Indulge in secrets and scandal, intense drama and plenty of sizzling hot action with powerful and passionate heroes who have it all: wealth, status, good looks…everything but the right woman.
6 stories per month.

HEROES

Experience all the excitement of a gripping thriller, with an intense romance at its heart. Resourceful, true-to-life women and strong, fearless men face danger and desire - a killer combination!
8 stories per month.

DARE

Sensual love stories featuring smart, sassy heroines you'd want as a best friend, and compelling intense heroes who are worthy of them.
4 stories per month.

To see which titles are coming soon, please visit

millsandboon.co.uk/nextmonth

JOIN US ON SOCIAL MEDIA!

Stay up to date with our latest releases, author
news and gossip, special offers and discounts, and
all the behind-the-scenes action
from Mills & Boon...

 millsandboon

 millsandboonuk

 millsandboon

might just be true love...

MILLS & BOON

HEROES

At Your Service

Experience all the excitement of a gripping thriller, with an intense romance at its heart. Resourceful, true-to-life women and strong, fearless men face danger and desire - a killer combination!

MILLS & BOON
MEDICAL
Pulse-Racing Passion

Set your pulse racing with dedicated, delectable doctors in the high-pressure world of medicine, where emotions run high and passion, comfort and love are the best medicine.